mrlg

HELL'S JAW PASS

Center Point
Large Print

Also by Max O'Hara and available from
Center Point Large Print:

Wolf Stockburn, Railroad Detective

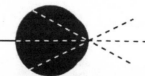

HELL'S JAW PASS

A
Wolf Stockburn,
Railroad Detective
WESTERN

MAX O'HARA

CENTER POINT LARGE PRINT
THORNDIKE, MAINE

HELL'S JAW PASS

CHAPTER 1

Spotting trouble, Wolf Stockburn reached across his belly with his right hand and unsnapped the keeper thong from over the hammer of the .45 Colt Peacemaker holstered for the cross-draw on his left hip.

He loosened the big popper in the oiled scabbard.

Just as casually, riding along in the Union Pacific passenger coach at maybe twenty miles an hour through the desert scrub of central Wyoming, he unsnapped the thong from over the hammer of the Colt residing in the holster tied down on his right thigh. He glanced again at the source of his alarm—a man riding four rows ahead of him, facing the front of the car, on the right side of the aisle.

He was in the aisle seat. An old couple in their late sixties, early seventies, sat beside him, the old man against the wall and idly reading a newspaper. The old woman, wearing a red scarf over her gray head, appeared to be knitting. Occasionally, Stockburn could see the tips of the needles as she tiredly toiled, sucking her dentures.

Most folks would have seen nothing out of kilter about the man in the aisle seat. He was

7

young and dressed in a cheap suit—maybe attire he'd purchased second-hand from a mercantile. The left shoulder seam was a little frayed and both shoulders were coppered from sunlight.

The young man wore round, steel-framed spectacles and a soot-smudge mustache. Stockburn had gotten a good look at him when the kid had boarded at the last water stop, roughly fifteen minutes ago. Something had seemed a little off about the lad as soon as Stockburn had seen him. Wolf wasn't sure exactly what that had been, but his seasoned rail detective's suspicions had been activated.

Maybe it was the pasty, nervous look in the kid's eyes, the moistness of his pale forehead beneath the brim of his shabby bowler hat. He'd been nervous. Downright apprehensive. Scared.

Now, the iron horse was still new to the frontier West. So the kid's fear could be attributed to the mere fact that this was his first time riding on a big iron contraption powered by burning coal and boiling steam, and moving along two slender iron rails at an unheard-of clip—sometimes getting up to thirty, thirty-five miles an hour. Forty on a steep downgrade!

That could have been what had the kid, who was somewhere in his early twenties, streaking his drawers. On the other hand, Stockburn had spotted a telltale bulge in the cracked leather valise the kid was carrying, pressed up taut against his chest, like a new mother holding her baby.

Adding to Stockburn's caution, a minute ago the young man had leaned forward over the valise he'd been riding with on his lap. The kid had reached a hand into the valise. At least, Stockburn thought he had, though of course he didn't have a full-frontal view of the kid, since he was sitting behind him. But he had a modest view over the kid's left shoulder, and he was sure the kid had shoved his hand into the grip.

As the kid had done so, he'd turned his head to peer suspiciously over his left shoulder, his long, unattractive face pale, his eyes wide and moist. He'd looked like a kid who'd walked into a mercantile on a dare from his schoolyard pals to steal a pocketful of rock candy.

He'd run his gaze across the dozen or so passengers riding in the car, the train's sole passenger car for this stretch of rail, between the town of Buffalo Gap and Wild Horse. His eyes appeared so opaque with furtive anxiety that Stockburn doubted the lad would have noticed if he, Stockburn—a big man—had been standing in the aisle aiming both of his big Colts at the boy. Wolf didn't think the kid even noticed him now, sitting four rows back, in an aisle seat, staring right at him.

Stockburn's imposing size wasn't the only thing distinctive about him. He also had a distinct shock

9

of prematurely gray hair, which he wore roached, like a horse's mane. It stood out in sharp contrast to the deep bronze of his ruggedly chiseled face. He wore a carefully trimmed mustache of the same color. He wasn't currently wearing his black sombrero; it sat to his left, atop his canvas war bag, which the barrel of his leaning .44-caliber Winchester Yellowboy repeating rifle rested against. His head was bare.

When the kid's quick survey of the coach was complete, he turned back around to face the front of the car, his shoulders a little too square, his back too straight, the back of his neck too red.

He was up to something.

Stockburn started to look away from the back of the kid's head then slid his gaze forward and across the aisle to his more immediate right, frowning curiously. A pretty young woman was staring at him, smiling. She sat two rows up from Wolf, in a seat against the other side of the car. The two plush-covered seats beside her were empty.

She was maybe nineteen or twenty, wearing a burnt-orange traveling frock with a ruffled shirtwaist and burnt-orange waist coat and a matching felt hat, a little larger than Wolf's open hand, pinned to the top of her piled, chestnut hair. Jade stones encased in gold dangled from her small, porcelain pale ears.

She was as lovely as a Victorian maiden

10

cameo pin carved in ivory. Her deep brown eyes glittered in the bright, lens-clear western light angling through the passenger coach's soot-streaked windows.

Stockburn smiled and looked away, the way you do when you first notice someone staring at you. It makes you at first uncomfortable, self-conscious, wondering if you're really the one being stared at so frankly. Certainly, you're mistaken. Wolf's gaze compelled him to look the girl's way again.

Her gaze did not waver. She remained staring at him, arousing his curiosity even further.

Did she know, or think she knew, him?

Or, possibly, she did know him but he didn't recognize her . . . ?

He smiled more broadly, holding her gaze now with a frank one of his own, one that was tempered ever so slightly with an incredulous wrinkle of the skin above his long, broad nose. That made her blush as she turned timid. Cheeks coloring slightly, she looked down and then turned her head back forward.

But the smile remained on her rich, full lips, which were the color of ripe peaches . . . and probably just as cool and soft, Stockburn couldn't help imagining. They probably tasted like peaches, as well.

He chuckled ironically to himself. Get your mind out of the gutter, you old dog, he admonished himself. This girl probably still wears her hair in pigtails at home, and you're old enough to be her father—a disquieting notion despite its being more and more true of late.

Stockburn returned his attention to the back of the shabby-suited lad's head. He looked around the car—a quick, furtive glance. He thought he probably saw more in that second and a half gander than the suited lad had in his prolonged one.

Wolf counted fifteen other passengers. Five were women, all older than the chestnut-haired cameo pin gal. A young woman, likely a farmer's wife, sat directly in front of Wolf, rocking a baby he guessed wasn't more than a few months old. She and the child were likely enroute to their young husband and father who'd maybe staked a mining or homesteading claim somewhere farther west.

A couple of men dressed like cow punchers sat nearly directly behind Stockburn, three rows back, at the very rear of the car. An old gent with a gray bib beard was nodding off on the other side of the aisle to his right. The rest of the men included a preacher and several men dressed in the checked suits of drummers.

One could have been a card sharp, because he was dressed a little more nattily than the drummers, but he probably wasn't much good with the pasteboards. You could tell the good ones by the way they carried themselves—straight and proud, usually smiling like they knew a secret about you and wouldn't you just love to know what it was?

This fellow, around Stockburn's age, with some gray in his sideburns, was turned sideways and laying out a game of cards, furling his brow and moving his lips, counseling himself, as though he were still learning the trade. Like his suit, his pinky ring had likely come from a Montgomery Ward wish book.

He wasn't a train robber. Stockburn knew his own trade, and he could usually pick a train robber out of a crowd. At least, seven times out of ten he could.

The two men behind him might be in with the lad near the front. He couldn't tell about the others, including the old couple. Just being an old, harmless-looking married pair didn't disqualify them from holding up a train. Stockburn had arrested Jed and Ella Parker, married fifty-three years, who'd preyed on passenger coaches for two and a half years before Wolf had finally run them down.

They'd enlisted the help of their forty-three-year-old son, Kenny. Kenny had been soft in his thinker box, as the saying went, but he, Ma, and Pa had gotten the job done, stealing time pieces and jewelry and gold pokes as well as pocket jingle from innocent pilgrims.

The Parkers had lost their Kansas farm to a railroad and had decided to exact revenge while entrepreneuring an alternative family business. Jed and Kenny had been as polite as church deacons. Ella, on the other hand, had cursed a blue streak, jumping up and down and hissing like a devil, as Stockburn had locked the bracelets around her wrists.

If the detective business did one thing for you, it taught you that you never really knew about people. Even when you thought you did.

Hell, the cameo pin gal might even be in cahoots with the lad with the lumpy valise. Maybe she'd smiled at Wolf earlier because she suspected what line of work he was in, and she'd been trying to disarm him, so to speak. Stockburn didn't think she was a train robber, but he'd been surprised before, and it had nearly gotten him a bullet for his carelessness. He wasn't going to turn his back on this pretty little gal, which wouldn't be hard, as easy on the eyes as she was.

When the train slowed suddenly—so suddenly that Stockburn and everybody else in the passenger coach became human jackknives, collapsing forward—Stockburn was not surprised. His heart didn't even start beating much faster than it had been when he'd just been riding along, staring out at the sage and prickly pear, going over the assignment he had ahead of him—running down the killers who'd massacred a crew of track layers working for a spur line near the Wind River Mountains.

Wolf could tell by the violent abruptness of the stop that the engineer must have locked up the brakes. That meant there was trouble ahead. Maybe blown rails or an obstacle of some kind—a tree or a telegraph pole felled across the tracks.

The brakes kicked up a shrill shrieking that caused Stockburn to grind his teeth against it. Gravity pushed him up hard against the forward seat in which the young mother had slipped out of her own seat and fallen to the floor.

The baby was red-faced, wailing, and the mother was sobbing, staring up at Wolf with holy terror in her eyes.

The train continued slowing, bucking, shuddering, squealing, throwing Wolf forward and partway over the seat before him. He felt as though a big man were pressing down hard against him from behind, one arm rammed down taut against his shoulders, the other clamped across the back of his neck. He wanted like hell to reach for one of his Colts in preparation for what he knew was coming, but at the moment gravity overwhelmed him.

"Oh, my God—what's happening?" the young mother screamed.

The young mother and the child were a nettling distraction. Stockburn's attention was torn between them and the young lad near the front of the train. That danger was bored home a moment later as the train finally stopped, and the big bully, gravity, finally released its iron-like grip on Wolf's back and shoulders. While Wolf stepped into the aisle, moving around the seat before him to help the young mother and the baby, the lad whom Wolf suspected of chicanery bounded up out of his own seat.

He, too, stepped into the aisle but without chivalrous intent.

He raised an old Schofield revolver and tossed away the valise he'd carried it in. He fired a round into the ceiling and bellowed in a high, reedy voice, "This is a holdup! Do what you're told and you won't be sent to hell in a hail of hot lead!"

At the same time his words reverberated around the car, evoking screams from the ladies and curses from the male passengers, another man— this one sitting at the front of the coach and on the same side of the aisle as Wolf—leaped to his feet and swung around, giving a coyote yell as he pumped a round into his old-model Winchester rifle. He was a scrawny coyote of a kid with a pinched-up face and devilishly slitted eyes.

Stockburn hadn't seen him before because he was so short that Wolf hadn't been able to see him over the other passengers. He doubted the kid was much taller than your average ten-year-old. He wore a badger coat and a bowler hat, and between his thin, stretched-back lips shone one nearly black, badly crooked front tooth.

"Do what he says and shut that baby up back there!" the human coyote caterwauled at Stockburn. He couldn't see the baby nor the mother, but the baby's screams no doubt assailed the ears of everyone on the coach, because they sure were assailing Stockburn's. "Shut that kid up or I'll blow its head off!"

Instantly, Stockburn's twin Colts were in his hands. He aimed one at the coyote-faced younker and one at the taller, bespectacled youth with the Schofield. "Drop those guns, you devils! Wolf Stockburn, Wells Fargo!"

Both youths flinched and shuffled backward a bit. They hadn't been expecting such brash resistance.

"S-Stockburn?" said the bespectacled younker in the shabby suit. He was aiming the Schofield at the rail detective but Wolf saw the hesitation in the kid's eyes. That same hesitation was in the coyote-faced kid's eyes, as well. They might have leveled their sights on him, but he had the upper hand.

For now . . .

"Wells . . . Wells Fargo . . . ?" continued the bespectacled youth, incredulous, crest-fallen. One of his clear blue eyes twitched behind his glasses, and his long, pale face was mottled red.

The coyote-faced youth swallowed down his own apprehension and glowered down the barrel of his cocked carbine at the big rail detective. "I don't give a good two cents who you are, Mister Stockburn, sir. If you don't drop them two purty hoglegs of your'n, we're gonna kill you and ever'body else aboard this consarned train— includin' the screamin' sprout!"

CHAPTER 2

The passengers had settled down. Most had, anyway.

A few women sobbed, and the baby, still on the floor with the mother to Stockburn's left, was still wailing. The other passengers were in their seats and merely casting frightened glances between the two gunmen at the front of the coach and Stockburn standing near the feet of the mother with the crying baby, in roughly the center of the car.

Stockburn kept his two silver-chased Colts aimed at the two firebrands bearing down on him with a rifle and a hogleg, respectively.

"Children," Stockburn said tightly but loudly enough to be heard above the baby's wails, "you got three seconds to live . . . less'n you lower those guns and raise your hands shoulder-high, palms out."

Sliding his gaze between the two would-be train robbers, on the scout for a deadly change in their eyes, knowing these two were too green-behind-the-ears not to telegraph when they were about to squeeze their triggers, Wolf stretched his mustached lips back from his large, white teeth and barked, "One . . . !"

Both younkers flinched. Fear passed over their

features. Their hands holding their guns on Wolf shook slightly.

"Two . . . !" Stockburn barked.

Again, they flinched. Both men's faces were pale, their eyes wide. No, they hadn't expected this. They hadn't expected this at all. They'd expected to come in here and fleece these defenseless passengers as easily as sheering sheep, then they'd be on their way to the nearest town to stomp with their tails up. "Apron, set down a bottle of your best labeled stuff and send in your purtiest doxie!"

Stockburn shaped his lips to form the word "Three" but did not get the word out before the coyote-faced lad slid his enervated gaze past Stockburn toward the rear of the car, shouting, "Willie! Roy! Take him!"

A black worm flipflopped in Stockburn's belly when he saw the two men dressed as drovers behind him lurch up out of their seats, cocking the hammers of their hoglegs.

Ah, hell . . .

Like any experienced predator, human or otherwise, when the chips were down, all bets placed, Wolf let his instincts take over. What he had here was a bad situation, and all he could do was play the odds and hope none of the passengers took a bullet.

He squeezed the triggers of both his Peacemakers, watching in satisfaction as the bespectacled youth, who triggered his Schofield at nearly the same time, screamed as he flew back against the coach's front wall. The coyote-faced lad screamed, as well, but merely fired his rifle into the ceiling before dropping it like a hot potato and falling back against the front wall, shielding his face with his arms, screaming, "Kill him! Kill him!"

As the guns behind Wolf roared loudly, he dropped to a knee in the aisle, wheeling hard to his right, facing the rear of the train now as the two "cow punchers" triggered lead through the air where his head had been a heartbeat before. All the passengers were yelling and screaming again, and the baby was wailing even louder, if that were possible.

Stockburn intended to take the two men at the rear of the car down as fast as possible, before a passenger took a bullet. He shot one of them with the second round out of his right-hand Colt. The man jerked back, acquiring a startled expression on his thinly bearded, red-pimpled face, as he triggered one more round in the air over Wolf's head before collapsing, Wolf's bullet instantly turning the bib front of the shooter's poplin shirt red.

Wolf shot the second "puncher" with the third round out of his left-hand gun, for that kid—they were all wet-behind-the-ears, snot-nosed brats, it appeared—ducked and ran for the back door, triggering his own gun wildly. Fortunately, that bullet only hammered the cold wood stove in the middle of the car before ricocheting harmlessly through a window on the car's north side, evoking a scream from the girl with the cameo-pin face but otherwise leaving her unharmed—so far.

Straightening, Stockburn aimed both Colts at the kid running out the rear door as the kid twisted back toward him, raising one of his own two hoglegs again. Wolf hurled two more rounds at the kid, his Peacemakers bucking and roaring fiercely, smoke and flames lapping from the barrels.

The kid yowled and cursed as, dropping to his butt on the coach's rear vestibule, he swung to his left and leaped to the ground, out of sight. A gun barked in the direction from which he'd disappeared. The bullet punched a hole through the back of the car and pinged through a window to Stockburn's right.

Cursing, Wolf ran out onto the vestibule. Swinging right, he saw the kid running, hunched over as though he'd taken a bullet, toward where three other men sat three horses about fifty feet out from the rail bed. Those men were holding the reins of four saddled horses.

Apparently, those were the men who'd blown the rails. They were trailing the horses of the four robbers in the coach. Or the four *who'd been in* the coach.

Three still were though they were likely dead or headed that way. These three out here didn't look any older or brighter than the four Wolf had swapped lead with. They appeared startled by the dustup they'd been hearing in the passenger car, and their horses were skitter-stepping nervously. One man was having trouble getting his mount settled down and was whipping the horse's wither with a quirt.

They were all yelling and so was the kid who was run-limping toward them, tripping over the toes of his boots.

"What in the bloody tarnation happened?" one of the horseback riders yelled at the wounded kid running toward him.

"Wells . . . *Fargo!*" the run-limping younker screeched.

Another horseback rider pointed toward Wolf. "Look!"

The run-limping kid stopped and glanced warily back over his shoulder toward Stockburn standing on the rear corner of the vestibule, aiming his right-hand Colt toward the bunch while holding the other pretty hogleg straight down in his left hand. Stockburn shaped a cold grin and was about to finish the limping varmint when a girl screamed shrilly from inside the coach.

Stockburn's heart leaped.

He'd forgotten that he'd left that sandy-haired

23

little devil with that dead front tooth still alive.

He lowered his right-hand Peacemaker and ran back into the car, stepping to his right so the open door wouldn't backlight him. Good thing old habits die hard or Wolf would have been the one dying hard.

A gun thundered near the front of the coach. The bullet screeched a cat's whisker's width away from Stockburn's right cheek before thumping into the front of the freight car trailing the passenger coach.

Stockburn raised his Colt but held fire.

The nasty little sandy-haired devil with the dead front tooth held the pretty cameo pin girl before him, his left arm wrapped around her pale neck. He held his carbine in his right hand. Just then he jacked it one-handed and aimed it at Stockburn, spitting as he bellowed, "I'm takin' the girl, big man! You come after me, she's gonna be wolf bait!"

The kid backed up, pulling the girl along with him toward the coach's front door, keeping her in front of him. She stared in wide-eyed horror at Stockburn standing at the other end of the car.

Her hat was drooping down the side of her head, clinging to her mussed hair, which had partway fallen from its bun, by a single pin. A red welt rose on her left cheek. The sandy-haired devil had slapped her. Her mouth was open, but she didn't say anything. She was too scared for words.

Rage burned through Stockburn.

As the kid pulled the girl out the coach's front door and then dragged her down off the vestibule, Wolf hurried forward, yelling, "Everybody stay down!"

He holstered both Colts and grabbed his Winchester rifle from where it now lay on the floor in front of the seat he'd been sitting in. He was glad to see that the young woman with the baby appeared relatively unharmed. She sat crouched back against the coach's left wall, against the window, rocking the still-crying baby in her arms, singing softly to the terrified infant while tears dribbled down her cheeks.

Stockburn pumped a cartridge into the brass-breeched Winchester Yellowboy's action, strode down the central aisle. The passengers were muttering darkly among themselves while another child cried and the old lady with the old man wept, the old man patting her shoulder consolingly.

Once they were all out of the carriage, the sandy-haired little devil started running toward the three men on horseback, pulling the pretty gal along behind him. The young robber Stockburn had drilled was toeing a stirrup and hopping on his opposite foot, trying unsuccessfully to gain his saddle and sobbing with the effort, demanding help from the others.

"Look out, Riley!" one of the men on horseback shouted, pointing at Wolf.

Riley stopped and swung back around. He pulled the girl violently up against him and narrowed his mean little eyes at Stockburn, showing that dead front tooth as he spat out, "I told you I'd kill her, an' I will if you don't—*owww!*" the kid howled.

The girl had spun to face him and stomped one of her high-heeled, black half-boots down on the toe of his own right boot. The kid squeezed his eyes shut and hopped up and down on his good foot before snapping his eyes open once more and then smashing the back of his right hand against the girl's left cheek.

There was the sharp smack of hand to flesh.

The girl screamed, spun, and fell with a violent swirl of her burnt-orange gown.

"I'll kill you for that," Riley bellowed, raising his Winchester, his face wild-fire red with fury. "I'll fill you so full of holes your rich old daddy won't even recognize you, you McCrae whore!"

"Don't do it, you little son of Satan!" Wolf narrowed one eye as he aimed down the Yellowboy at the kid. In his indignation at having been assaulted by the girl he'd been trying to kidnap, the little devil seemed to have forgotten his more formidable opponent with the Winchester. "Raise that carbine one eyelash higher, and I'll send you back to the devil that spawned you!"

Riley snapped his gaze back to Stockburn,

eyes narrowed to slits. A slow, malevolent smile spread his lips. "My father is Kreg Hennessey. Yeah, Hennessey. Get it? Understand now?"

The kid bobbed his head twice as though Stockburn should recognize the name. "If you shoot me, you're gonna have holy hell come down on you, Mister. Like a whole herd of wild hosses!" He turned his slitted demon's eyes back to the girl, who stared up at him fearfully. "This little witch just struck me. Thinks she's so much 'cause she's a McCrae! You just struck a Hennessey, and you're about to see what happens when even an uppity McCrae strikes a—"

Stockburn squeezed the Yellowboy's trigger. He had no choice. There was no way in hell the kid was not going to kill the girl. The little snake was not only cow-stupid, he was poison mean. And out of control.

The Yellowboy bucked and roared.

The bullet tore through the kid's shoulder and whipped him around to face Stockburn directly. The kid triggered his carbine wide of the girl, the bullet pluming dust beyond her. She gasped and lowered her head, clamping her hands over her ears.

The kid held the rifle out to one side, angled down. He held his other arm out to the other side as though for balance. The kid glanced at the blood bubbling up from his shoulder as he

27

stumbled backward, rocks and little puffs of dust kicked up by his badly worn boots.

A look of total shock swept over his face, his lower jaw sagging, mouth forming a wide, nearly perfect "O."

Still on one knee, Stockburn ejected the spent cartridge from the Yellowboy's breech. Wolf pumped a fresh round into the breech and lined up the sights on the kid's chest as gray smoke curled from the barrel.

"Drop it," he ordered. "Or the next one's for keeps."

Riley stared back at him. The kid glanced at his shoulder once more, then looked at Stockburn again. The shock on his face gradually faded, replaced by his previous expression of malevolent rage. Jaws hard, he gave a dark laugh as he said, "You're a dead man, mister!"

He cocked the carbine one-handed then took it in both hands, crouching over it, aiming the barrel at Wolf, who pumped two more .44 rounds into the kid's chest. The rounds picked the scrawny kid up and threw him two feet back through the air to land on his back.

The girl screamed.

The kid writhed like a bug on a pin, arching his back, grinding his boot heels into the dirt and gravel. He hissed like a dying viper. He snapped his jaws like a trapped coyote. He lifted his head to look at Wolf, and he cursed shrilly, his oaths growing less and less violent as the blood leaked out of him to pool on the rocks and sage beneath him.

Finally, his head sagged back against the ground.

"Dead man," he rasped, chest rising and falling sharply. "Oh . . . you're a . . . dead man . . ."

His bloody chest fell still.

His head turned slowly to one side.

His body relaxed against the gravel and sage.

CHAPTER 3

Stockburn straightened, holding the smoking Yellowboy in both hands across his chest.

He looked from the dead kid who lay in a pool of his own blood, to the girl, who sat a few feet away from him, one leg tucked under the other one. She looked from the dead kid to Wolf, and her eyes brightened. Her lips rose slightly upward at the corners.

Stockburn lifted his gaze behind and beyond her. The surviving four would-be train robbers had cut and run. They rode straight away from the train at a hard gallop. At least, three were galloping hard. The fourth one, who'd taken a Stockburn bullet in his side, lagged behind a little, crouched low in his saddle, casting cautious glances back over his shoulder toward the train.

A figure appeared in the door of the passenger coach, to Stockburn's right. It was the old man who'd been sitting with the old woman. His gray hair was cropped so close it was nearly nonexistent. A thin stubble of a beard carpeted his doughy, craggy cheeks. The top of his head came up to Stockburn's shoulder.

He gazed off toward the dead kid, toward where the four others were fleeing, then turned to

Stockburn and smiled, blue eyes twinkling. "That was some good shootin'. You Wyatt Earp?"

"Nope."

"Buffalo Bill Cody?"

"Nope, not Cody, neither, old-timer." Stockburn glanced into the coach behind the old man. The other passengers looked shaken but otherwise fine. Several were peering out the open windows at the dead kid. A loud conversational hum had risen as they relived the shooting, some chuckling and shaking their heads in relief and amazement, others glancing toward the vestibule where Stockburn stood with the old man.

"How 'bout Kid Curry?" asked the old man. He poked Wolf's shoulder with his finger. "Say, that's you, ain't it?"

"Nope, not Curry, neither. Stockburn. Wolf Stockburn." Wolf grinned.

The old man frowned, scratched his chin. "Hmm. Never heard of the jake."

Stockburn glowered at the oldster. He shouldered the rifle and moved off down the vestibule steps. He walked over toward where the girl still sat with one leg curled beneath the other one, both palms on the ground. She smiled more broadly and narrowed her eye shrewdly. "The graybeard might not, but I know who you are."

"You do?"

"You're the Wolf of the Rails himself—Wolf Stockburn. Formerly known, when you were

31

town marshal of Wichita, Kansas, as the Wolf of Wichita!"

Stockburn extended his hand to the girl and helped her to her feet. "Young lady, thank you for rescuing my tender ego."

She extended her hand to him. "Lorelei McCrae at your service, Mister Stockburn."

"Call me Wolf, Miss McCrae. You're far too pretty for such formalities."

"Only if you call me Lori."

"Lori you are."

"Thanks for saving my life, Wolf."

"Ah, hell. Since I was in the area . . ."

"Stockburn!" a man's voice thundered from up the train a piece.

Stockburn turned to see a big, swarthy man in blue pinstriped overalls and matching watch cap come ambling toward him from the direction of the engine in front of the tender car. Another man stood behind the man approaching Stockburn, similarly dressed. The second man was sort of slumped back against the tender car, clamping his gloved right hand over his upper left arm.

"Wolf Stockburn!" yelled the approaching man. "Wolf Stockburn—gotta be you!"

Lori McCrae smiled up at Stockburn and winked. "See how famous you are?"

"Some might say *in*famous," Stockburn told her, switching his gaze back to the approaching big man, who smiled broadly. "I'm at a disadvantage," Wolf said.

"Wally Frye, engineer. Pilot of this heap." Frye hooked a thumb to indicate the big, black locomotive behind him, wheezing like a sleeping dinosaur plagued by bad dreams. He pulled off his glove and extended his hand. "We've never met, but I've heard a lot about you. Most fellas who work for the railroads have."

"You don't have to work for the railroad to know who this big, tall drink of water is," corrected Lori McCrae, gazing admiringly up at the big railroad detective again. "All you have to do is read the newspapers."

As he and Stockburn shook hands, Frye chuckled and said, "Well, I never got around to learning my letters, but I've heard the stories, all right." He turned to Lori and frowned with concern, looking her up and down. "Say, are you all right, Miss McCrae? That devil slapped you mighty hard!"

"I'm fine, Mr. Frye." Again, she smiled gratefully at Stockburn.

"You two know each other?" Stockburn asked.

"This is a small country," said Frye. "Everybody knows the McCrae family. I've had the pleasure of trundling young Miss McCrae here a time or two to the main station in Cheyenne . . . during her frequent trips between Wild Horse and her school in the East, that is."

"I attend Miss Lydia Hastings Academy for Young Women in Poughkeepsie, New York," Lori told Wolf. "At least, I did. I, uh . . . well, never mind." She'd said these last words with a note of chagrin in her voice, flushing.

"You *quit?*" Frye asked, incredulous. "My, my, my, how does your family feel about that? Not that it's any of my business."

"Well, they, uh . . ." Lori bunched her lips, wincing. "They don't know yet. I'm sure it's going to be quite the surprise," she added with a fateful sigh.

Frye studied her for a second. When she looked off, obviously wanting to speak no more on the subject, the engineer turned to Wolf and tossed his head to indicate the passenger coach. "Everybody in the coach all right?"

"I believe so," Stockburn said. "They got off lucky. Those curly wolves were a might free with their ammo."

"How many were on the train?" the engineer asked.

"Four. Three still are."

"You took them down in fine fashion, Wolf!" Lori said, beaming up at him again. "I gotta admit I read those newspaper stories with a grain of salt. I shouldn't have. The scribblers got you right—you have uncompromising resolve, a razor focus, and a deadly aim. Those who go against you do so at their own peril!" She made a shooting motion with her right hand, blew on the "barrel," and gave him a wink.

Wolf fell instantly in love with the lovely child. He had a feeling he was in good company. She was about as ravishing and intoxicating a figure as he'd ever encountered—aside from his female express guard pal, Hank, that was. And, like the lovely Henrietta Holloway—Lori McCrae was obviously no hot-house flower. After what she'd just endured, most young ladies her age would need smelling salts to remain in charge of their faculties.

The engineer walked over and stared down at the dead kid, Riley Hennessey.

He called the kid by name and shook his head. "Oh, boy . . . this ain't good."

"Rotten to the core," Wolf said.

"Oh, he was at that. You'll get no argument from me or anyone else in the territory, but still . . ." Frye arched a grim eye at Stockburn. "He's got him a powerful father."

"Too bad he wasn't powerful enough to get this little devil in hand."

"You got a point there, Stockburn, but, still, Kreg Hennessey—"

"Is an evil man," Lori chimed in. "He owns the Wind River Saloon and Gambling Hall in Wild Horse. He's a vicious pimp and miser and does everything he can to discourage competition. Oh, he lets a few other saloons do business in town,

35

but only because the men who patronize those saloons couldn't afford his liquor, anyway . . . or a place at his gambling tables or upstairs with his girls.

"A man named Rumley tried to establish an opera house in Wild Horse, but Kreg Hennessey blocked him from doing so. He was afraid it would bleed off some of his own business. When sending his thugs out to threaten Rumley with physical harm didn't work, Hennessey bribed the city council into passing an ordinance outlawing singing after ten P.M. within the Wild Horse town limits. Can you imagine? Hennessey claimed singing was disturbing the peace. Hah! When my father and other fair-minded men got the ordinance thrown out, and Rumley started to build his opera house, Rumley and his wife died in a mysterious house fire."

Lori wrinkled her nose distastefully. "There you have Kreg Hennessey, Wolf. That is the demon that spawned this little devil here." She glared down at the bloody corpse of Riley Hennessey then turned to Wolf with a warning in her eyes. "Best watch your back."

"Don't worry, I always sleep with one eye open." Wolf turned to the engineer. "Any rail damage?"

"Nah, they just felled a telegraph pole. You and I can probably move it ourselves. My fireman, Melvin Blankenship"—he glanced at the man holding his arm over by the tender car—"took a bullet across his arm from one o' them horseback little devils when Melvin snapped a shot at 'em to try to change their minds about robbin' the train. Oh, he'll live, but he'll need a doc to take a look at him. The only crew is just him, me, and the brakeman back in the caboose. Since this is an irregular run with a small combination and only a dozen passengers, we don't have a regular conductor."

Stockburn had learned that when he'd boarded the train in Cheyenne, and the brakeman had collected the tickets. He'd seen the brakeman a minute ago, hustling up from the caboose to check on the passengers.

"Let's do 'er, then," Stockburn said. "I'll throw that little Hennessey devil aboard and we'll continue on into Wild Horse."

"Sure you don't wanna just bury him out here? Shovel a little dirt over him and call it done? No one will give one hoot except his father. I won't tell Hennessey if you won't." Frye winked and smiled.

"I sure won't tell," Lori said, wrinkling her nose at the dead little coyote again. "Good riddance, Riley Hennessey!"

Stockburn chuckled. "Thanks for the offer, but I can handle Hennessey."

The engineer and Lori shared a wary look. Turning back to Wolf, Frye said, "With Kreg

37

Hennessey, even you might need some help. The entire U.S. cavalry, say."

When Stockburn and the engineer had back-and-bellied the telegraph pole to the side of the rails, Wolf hauled Riley Hennessey's body into the stock car, which also carried his prized smoky gray stallion, which he had aptly if unimaginatively named Smoke.

He and the brakeman laid out the other three dead would-be train robbers in the stock car, as well, and covered them with burlap feed sacks. No point in further pestering the passengers with the bloody carcasses. They still had an hour's ride to Wild Horse, and it was smelly enough in the coach, with the fetor of sour wool, sweaty bodies, and the coal smoke slithering in through the open windows, without adding the stench of fresh blood to the mix.

After the engineer and the fireman had powered the locomotive back up, Frye blew the whistle three times sharply. The wheels spun, caught, and as the familiar *chugga-chugga-chugga* came roaring back from the engine, and steam clouds billowed out from the pressure release valves to sweep back against the passenger coach like morning fog, the couplings thundered, and the train rocked forward.

It shuddered, squealed, shuddered some more,

squealed louder, and slid forward . . . forward . . . forward . . . gradually increasing speed.

The rail seams clacked, the clacks coming faster . . . faster . . . faster . . .

Stockburn finished up in the stock car and leaped onto the passenger car's rear vestibule as the train was moving forward. Coal smoke billowed back over the coach's roof and down over the vestibule to burn his eyes and pepper his nose.

He opened the coach's rear door and stepped inside. Grateful smiles flashed at him now. Word of his legendary identity had spread. His fellow travelers were not only feeling fortunate and indebted to have been spared armed robbery and likely worse—who knows what those brigands would have done to the women?—but they also felt a little of the luster one feels when one finds oneself in the company of the rich or the famous.

Should have known that was him. Look at that thick thatch of gray hair . . . that golden tan . . . faded blue cat eyes . . . that height . . . those shoulders . . . the black suit . . . those big pretty pistols. Of course! *A gunfighter detective straight out of Deadeye Dick—only this one was real and he was* here!

One man rose to shake Stockburn's hand. The old lady pressed her leathery lips to his cheek and thanked him for sparing her and her old husband's life savings, which they were carrying in their carpet bags as they traveled west from Kansas to live with their minister son and his lovely wife in Oregon.

Stockburn patted the old woman's hand, then paused when he saw that he was no longer sitting alone. Lori McCrae had changed positions; the pretty young lady now occupied the seat to the left of his former seat on the left side of the aisle. Stockburn's Yellowboy rifle leaned against his seat as though saving it for him. His war bag and saddlebags and bedroll were in the overhead luggage rack.

As he approached, Lori looked up with a vaguely sheepish smile that made her cheeks dimple beautifully. "I hope you don't mind."

"Mind having a lovely young traveling companion? Surely you jest." Wolf smiled as he picked up the rifle and folded his long body into the soot-stained green plush beside the pretty girl, his shoulder brushing hers. "Not even a little bit."

CHAPTER 4

"To what do we owe the pleasure of having such a legendary railroad detective visit western Wyoming, Mr. Stockbu—I mean, Wolf? I have to admit, it feels a little funny to call one so famous by his first name."

"Don't be silly, Lori. And if you keep gushing over me so, you're going to run the risk of my believing all that ink that's been spilled over me. Liable to get a big head."

"If you don't have one by now, you never will," Lori said, canting her head and lifting her face toward his, gazing up at him with her faintly saucy smile in place. "Back to my question. If you can tell me, that is. I don't doubt that you often have to travel in secret."

"Oh, no. There's rarely anything so secretive about my work. This one's right out in the open for everyone to see—at least, everyone up around Wild Horse and Hell's Jaw Pass."

"That's my home territory."

"So you said."

"Hmmm. I grow curiouser and curiouser . . ."

Stockburn pulled a three-cent Indian Kid cheroot out of his shirt pocket along with a lucifer match. He showed her the short cigar. "Mind?"

41

"Not at all. My father smokes cigars, and I've missed the aroma."

Stockburn scraped a match to life on his thumbnail, lit the cigar, waved out the match, and tossed it out the half-open window to Lori's left. He blew a long plume of smoke toward the window, as well, and watched the wind suck it out and away.

He said, "It seems someone is running cross-ways to a spur line of rails being laid up north of Wild Horse. The Hell's Jaw Railroad Company intends to connect Wild Horse with the mining camp of Hell's Jaw, to bring the gold being mined out of that neck of the Wind River Mountains more easily and safely than via mule train down to Wild Horse and then off on the Union Pacific and Southern Pacific to the U.S. Mint in Frisco."

"Oh, the ol' Hell's Jaw Company, again, eh?" Lori said with a deep glower furling her brow.

"I take it you have a history with the company, Lori?" While he'd been talking, Stockburn had clamped the cheroot between his teeth and dug a manila file out of his war bag. Having reviewed the file recently, which had been provided by his Wells Fargo home office based in Kansas City, the file lay on top of a fresh change of clothes and other possibles, including toiletries, a flask of good Kentucky bourbon, and spare ammunition for his guns.

Now he flipped open the file, lifted a couple of pages, then frowned down at the typewritten page before him. "Yes, yes . . . I see why the McCrae name struck me as familiar."

"Yes," Lori said. "The owners of the Hell's Jaw Company, Jamerson Stewart and his equally money-hungry son, Jamerson Jr., purchased a strip of land from my father—several of his original homestead claims—on which to lay their rails."

The cheroot unfurling a gray ribbon of smoke in front of his face, Stockburn arched a brow at her. "You didn't approve? Wasn't your father adequately compensated?"

"Oh, he was more than adequately compensated. Believe me, my father made sure he was getting top dollar for his land. My father would never settle for anything less."

"Then I'm not sure I . . ."

"Oh, don't mind me. It's just that the whole rail line stirred up trouble on the range, that's all."

"Really? Can you tell me more about that, Lori?"

"Oh, I'll let my father tell it. Honestly, Wolf, the whole miserable affair tends to bite a little too deep. I can't tell you why. It's . . . well, it's a personal matter. Deeply personal." She looked up at him with beseeching in her pretty eyes. "Matters of the heart, if you get my drift."

"Ahhh." Stockburn did not get her drift but

43

decided to probe the obviously tender area no further.

Lori stared straight ahead in deep thought for well over a minute. Then she turned to frown up at Stockburn, curious and troubled. "Wolf, you said someone was running crossways against the Hell's Jaw line?"

"That's right."

"What did you mean by 'crossways,' exactly?"

"A party of horseback assassins raided the rail crew. Killed them all—every man jack of them—and tore up a couple hundred yards of freshly laid track." Stockburn flicked his thumb against the now-closed file on his lap before him. "Apparently, one survived long enough to tell the tale. They rode in hard and fast at night—on a full-moon night, just like the Comanche did down in Texas. And, according to the file, they were every bit as brutal as the Comanche, as well."

Lori stared up at him, her eyes stricken. For a moment, Wolf thought she was going to cry. "Oh, my God . . ."

Guiltily, Stockburn placed his hand on her forearm. "I'm sorry, Lori. Me an' my big mouth. I should've been more delicate." He would have been, too, but the stalwart way she'd handled Riley Hennessey had led him to believe she could handle almost anything. She looked more upset after hearing Stockburn's tale of murder than after she'd lived through actual killings herself.

"It's all right, Wolf. Never mind me. Like my father says, sometimes I can be a might high-strung."

"Certainly not about train holdups! You weathered that better than a drunk Irishman."

She feigned a smile at his attempt to lighten the mood, then glanced out at the sage-covered hills rolling past the window.

"Say," Stockburn said, "why don't you tell me where you went to school and why you quit? Homesick?"

His attempt to change the subject worked about as well as her attempt at levity. "I guess you could say that," she said with a long, droll sigh, keeping her eyes glued to the window. After another minute, she turned back to him, her eyes grave. "You see . . . you see . . . there's a young man, and, well . . ." She let her voice trail off as she looked down at the fingers she pressed together before her.

"Ah. A young man, eh?"

She looked up at him again. Emotion made her eyes glisten. "I'm sorry, Wolf. It's too hard to talk about."

"Totally understand. Love can be complicated."

"What about you?" she said, her eyes brightening once more. "Is there a woman in your life, Wolf?"

"Me? Ah, hell, no! Uh . . . pardon my French." Stockburn winked at her. "Oh, I reckon you

45

could say there might be one little ol' gal. But it's nothin' permanent, you know. We get together now and then when I'm in her neck of the woods. Or prairie would be more like it."

"And what would her 'neck of the prairie' be?"

"Dakota Territory."

"Hmm. And her name . . . ?"

"Comanche."

"You mean like the Indians?"

"Exactly. Only, her real, Comanche name is Denomi. She was orphaned very young and raised by white parents. It was only many years later that she acquired the nickname Comanche given to her by some of the rough white men she ran with. Has only one eye, Comanche does," Wolf added, pointing to his left eye. "Somehow, she's all the lovelier for the patch."

"Wow!" Lori said, thrilling to the tale. "She sounds every bit as romantic as a poem by Mr. Longfellow."

"Well . . ."

"How did she lose the eye? A whip wielded by a jealous lover?"

"Uh, well . . . something like that," Stockburn allowed with a pained expression.

He did not tell the romantic Lori the somewhat unromantic story about how his friend Comanche, as wild a woman who ever lived, had been caught by her first husband, a white deputy sheriff, sleeping with that husband's friend in an Abilene

46

hotel. The husband shot the friend then put Comanche's eye out with a red-hot fireplace poker.

Not to take such an assault lying down, Comanche, fueled by liquor as well as a wicked temper, wrestled the poker out of her husband's hand and beat him to death with it before stealing a horse and riding hell for leather out of town and into the tall and uncut beyond.

She hadn't been back to Texas since.

"Yeah, somethin' like that," Wolf repeated. "Let's just leave it at that, shall we?"

"Are you in love with Comanche, Wolf?"

"I guess as much as it is in me to love any woman, you could say I love Comanche."

"And how does Comanche feel about you?"

"I guess as much as it is in Comanche to love any man, you could say she loves this old, untethered Wolf of the Rails."

"How come you're not together?"

"Ah, heck," Stockburn said with a droll chuckle. "Why'd we want to ruin a good time?"

"You don't believe in marriage, I take it?" Lori laughed.

"Not for me, no. Comanche, she's been married several times. It never did work out. She's happy enough now, living alone out in the lonely wilds of Dakota. We get together now an' then, drink a little Kentucky bourbon, play some cards, cook some steaks, curl each other's toes." Again, Wolf winked at the girl.

47

She smiled up at him, blushing.

"I swear, Lori, you have the prettiest blush going." Stockburn caressed her smooth cheek with his thumb.

The girl's blush deepened, and her eyes grew dreamy. "I swear, Wolf, you are one charming man."

"Pshaw!"

The engineer blew the whistle. The screeching wail caromed around on the wind blowing past the window. Outside, shacks and shanties slid up close to the rails, half-buried in brush.

"Oh, darn," Lori said, peering out the window. "I think we're in Wild Horse, and just when the conversation was starting to get interesting!"

Stockburn laughed.

Lori placed her hand on his forearm and leaned toward him, giving one brow a coquettish arch. "It's nearly supper time, Wolf. I'd be happy to introduce you to the only palatable restaurant in Wild Horse. That would be the Cosmopolitan. Unfortunately, however, it's right next door to Hennessey's saloon." She gave a nostril a revolted flare.

Wolf frowned curiously. "Surely, you must have someone waiting for you at the station to take you on home. Your father and mother, perhaps?"

"No." Lori gave another grim sigh and stretched her lips back from her perfect teeth in one of her signature fateful winces. "They don't know I'm coming . . . just as they don't know that I've quit school."

"Ah. I thought it strange that you're not traveling with a chaperone—a pretty young lady such as yourself."

"Oh, I'm sure they would, too. My older brother, Lawton, has accompanied me on previous trips. This one, however, is a complete surprise. I'm going to spend the night here in town, save the, uh, surprise for tomorrow. My father keeps a room in the Territorial Hotel. The owner, Mister Rose, will turn it over to me for the evening without argument."

As if to show why she would have no dispute with the hotel owner, she cocked her head and fluttered her eyelids—a ravishingly beautiful coquette in full charge of all her charms, which she employed with neither reluctance nor shame.

Again, Stockburn laughed, tumbling for the coquette all over again.

The train was now screeching to a halt in front of the depot station, and most of the passengers were rising from their seats, gripping their seat backs before them to keep their balance.

Stockburn gave the girl's hand an affectionate squeeze. "As much as I regret it, I'll take a rain check on dinner. I'd best tend to the grim chore of delivering the bodies of those four cutthroats to the local law."

He did not add that Lori best stay clear of him for a while, since his killing Riley Hennessey might have pasted a target on his back. However, he could tell by the level look she gave him that she understood the unspoken remonstration.

"How 'bout if we ride together out to the Triangle tomorrow?" she suggested. "Maybe you can help me cushion the surprise of my unexpected appearance . . . ?" Lori gave a wry smile. "You'll want to talk to my father sooner or later, I'm sure. Since the rail crew was attacked on what was once Triangle land . . ."

"Right you are, young lady. Sure. Why not?" Riding together in the country should be harmless enough as long as Wolf watched his back trail, which it was his second nature to do even when he hadn't killed a nasty little coyote with a truculent pa. "I'll have to have a palaver with the Stewarts over at the Hell's Jaw Rail office first, so why don't we plan to take that ride, oh, say late morning?"

"Wonderful. I do so like to sleep in." Lori gave him a winning smile then leaned over to press her soft lips against his cheek.

A few minutes later, Wolf stood on the station's brick platform, watching the pretty gal in the expensive traveling gown flounce off toward the heart of Wild Horse, a half-breed young porter with long, shaggy brown hair pushing a handcart loaded with her luggage along behind her. The half-breed walked with a slight hitch in his gait, so he had trouble keeping up with Lori. She seemed oblivious as she walked forthrightly straight ahead, chin in the air, twirling the orange parasol over her head.

"I'll be hanged if it ain't a curiosity," came a man's voice from Stockburn's left.

Wolf turned to the slender, middle-aged man walking toward him, holding a sheaf of lading papers in one hand, a pencil in the other. He must have been talking to the engineer and the fireman.

Now Frye helped the wounded fireman into the little clapboard depot building, and the slender man stepped up to Stockburn. The brass name plate pinned to his unbuttoned wool jacket read AVERY COLE, STATION AGENT.

"If what ain't a curiosity, Mister Cole?" Wolf asked.

Cole was staring after Lorelei McCrae, just now leaving the brick platform and flouncing off down the dusty main street of Wild Horse, heading toward the Territorial Hotel. "What that girl's doing home so soon. A curiosity. Why, I just shipped her back out to her fancy girl school only a month ago. Saw her and her brother off myself."

The station agent glanced up at Wolf, who stood a whole head taller. "Did she say?"

"Nope. Women have their secrets."

"I reckon." Cole extended his bony right hand. "I'm Avery Cole, Station Agent."

"I see that," Wolf said, shaking the man's hand. "I'm—"

"I know who you are, Mister Stockburn. I just talked to Mister Frye. Been expectin' you. I heard you was headed this way to investigate the Hell's Jaw trouble. I understand from Frye that you fended off a passel of train robbers, and somehow Miss McCrae got in the middle of it."

He gave an ominous sigh. "And Kreg Hennessey's little snot-nosed serpent child is lyin' dead in the stock car. That's all right. I like him better that way, but his old man sure won't!"

CHAPTER 5

"He's with three others," Stockburn said.

"I heard that, too," Cole said. "Frye recognized them as some of the other polecats young Hennessey regularly ran off his leash with."

"The kid's father couldn't control him? Or *wouldn't?*"

"The second one. Hennessey's a nasty man, Mister Stockburn. He may wear a Prince Albert coat and run a business and have his hands in several others as well as own a nice big house—the biggest, in fact, in Wild Horse—and strut around town like a respectable man of business."

The station agent glanced around secretively then turned back to Stockburn, raised his hand to his mouth, and whispered, "But he's a devil." Keeping his voice low, he added, "He was just like Riley back when he was Riley's age. The way he saw it, Riley was just cuttin' his teeth. Showin' some spunk. He usually covered up for the kid by payin' back the money he stole to keep him out of jail. Around here it worked, because the town marshal, who doubles as a deputy county sheriff, is in Hennessey's pocket. Or so I've heard. Makes sense. The kid's wanted for crimes outside of this county, however, and there've been a few federal men sniffin' around about him."

"Nothing came of it, I take it?"

"Nothin'. Wouldn't doubt it if Hennessey paid them off, or . . ."

"Or . . . ?"

"Killed them."

"Hmm."

"There you have it," Cole said grimly, nervously tapping the end of his pencil against the sheaf of shipping bills in his hand. "You killed the wrong man's son."

"Yeah, well, I rarely kill the right one's son. Why don't we get those bodies hauled over to the town marshal's office so I can get that damnable paperwork behind me and get started on what I was sent here to do."

Wolf had walked over to the stock car, Cole following closely. Several other passengers were leading their horses down the stock car's wooden ramp, shod hooves drumming hollowly on the worn wood, fresh apples dropping from beneath the arched tail of a dapple-gray and filling the air with that green-hay aroma that, unlike cow manure, was not particularly unpleasant.

At least, not to a man who loved everything about horses, even their smell.

"The town lawman's out of town," Cole said. "Same with his two deputies. I seen 'em ride out to the south a couple hours ago, and I haven't seen 'em ride back. All I had to do till the train arrived was sit and watch on that chair yonder.

That's mostly what a station agent in a town this size does—sit and watch—so I know they're still out dealing with rustlers or somesuch. Usually when they all go, it's a rustling matter, sure enough. Nothin' riles the ranchers around here like rustlin'."

Stockburn cursed as he walked up the ramp and into the car. Cole followed again as Wolf walked over to his smoky gray stallion, Smoke, and set down his war bag and leaned his Yellowboy rifle against the car's near wall. "I'll have Wally Skutter fetch the town undertaker for the bodies," Cole said, staring down at the four dead men lying belly up at the base of the car's front wall. "I'll let the marshal know what happened when he rides back to town."

"All right." With a grunt, Wolf threw his saddle blanket and saddle on the stallion's back. "I'm gonna fetch a good hot meal then look for a passable mattress sack. Any suggestions?"

"The Cosmopolitan Restaurant is the best grub around. It ain't purty, but it's the best. You'll find it on the corner of the main drag there—Wind River Avenue—and Second Street. Just beyond Hennessey's place. You'll find the Territorial Hotel directly across the street from the restaurant—all conveniently located for you, Mister Stockburn."

Stockburn led the stallion down the ramp then mounted up, easing his weight into the leather.

"Thanks, Mister Cole. How 'bout a livery barn?"

"I recommend the Federated. Half a block beyond the restaurant. It's run by a Mexican but, unlike most Mexicans, Señor Ortiz keeps a clean place and runs a tight ship. Has a wonderful touch with a curry brush. Really knows how to bring out a shine!"

Stockburn smiled and pinched his hat brim to the station agent. "Obliged."

"Enjoy the meal, Mister Stockburn."

"Thank you—I intend to," Stockburn said as he booted Smoke out onto the main drag, Wind River Avenue, which sat directly north of the depot building, and ran perpendicular to the railroad tracks. He glanced over his shoulder at Cole.

The man was looking at him as though he'd just wished him an enjoyable last supper.

Avery Cole had been right about the Cosmopolitan. It wasn't a pretty place, but it served up a juicy T-bone and a savory pile of potatoes with two sunny-side-up eggs on top, just the way Wolf had ordered them. A side dish of green beans cooked in ham lent a little roughage to the array.

It was a large, dark, low-ceilinged place with a lunch counter running along the rear of the room, fronting the kitchen that lay beyond a half-wall over which Stockburn could see a big, fat man with a bushy gray mustache, a loosely rolled cigarette dangling from his lips, ambling around amidst rising steam and the din of frying and boiling food.

The man yelled orders in German to the two stout women—one young and one the cook's age, late forties, early fifties—who seemed to be dancing around back there with him in some loosely choreographed hoe-down while a slender Chinese gentleman who could just barely speak English poured coffee and took orders.

The slender Chinese gentleman had his hands full, for it had been a quarter after six when Wolf had entered, and a good three-quarters of the dozen or so tables were occupied. There were two long eating tables, also, each able to serve maybe ten men on each side. Only one end of one of the long tables was occupied—by three burly, trail-hardened characters whom Stockburn knew, because he'd eavesdropped on part of their conversation, to be a stagecoach driver and two shotgun messengers.

His table was relatively close to these three sun- and windburned toughnuts, and he eavesdropped because, as a detective, he made it a habit of eavesdropping on other people's conversations— you never knew when you were going to run into useful information—though if he were to be honest, it was also because he was just plain snoopy. He supposed it was because he lived alone and didn't socialize enough.

He learned nothing of interest from the men, however, aside from the gruesome fact that the old father of one of the shotgun messengers, whom he lived with, had had "a leaky bowel" corrected by a particularly gruesome surgical process that the man seemed to insist on going into detail about despite the protestations of his fellow diners. The squeamish reactions of his listeners delighted the story-telling messenger no end. Stockburn swabbed his plate clean with a chunk of bread, picked up his coffee cup, and turned his attention to Wild Horse's main street, which he could see out the window to his left.

Just as he did, three men stomped with grim purpose past the window, on the boardwalk fronting the restaurant. Stockburn knew even before he glimpsed the shimmer of late-day light off tin that this would be the town marshal and his two deputies. A few seconds after they'd passed the window, they reappeared at the front door straight ahead of Stockburn, on the other side of the room.

Stockburn leaned back in his chair, dug a lucifer match out of his shirt pocket, produced his Barlow knife from a pocket of his whipcord trousers, and opened the blade. As he began to shave the lucifer, he looked at the three newcomers—a large, older man and two younger ones. They all wore dust-streaked dusters and high-topped boots with jingling spurs. The spurs jingled and jangled as they walked around the room, scrutinizing the diners and casting each other puzzling, silently conferring glances.

Stockburn smiled as, leaning forward, his elbows on the edge of his table, he continued to file the match.

Finally, the sheriff, whose big gut bowed out the front of his hickory shirt, behind a black vest revealed by the open duster, stopped between two tables to Wolf's right. He cast his gaze about the shadowy, smoky room until his eyes landed on Stockburn.

The rail detective had removed his hat. It sat on the table ahead and to his left. The light of recognition shown in the lawman's eyes beneath the broad brim of his own hat as he saw the thick thatch of roached gray hair.

Locking eyes with Stockburn, he acquired a sour expression, and he gave his nose a disapproving wrinkle. He gestured broadly, angrily at his two deputies, each at opposite sides of the room, then walked toward Stockburn's table, cursing when he stumbled on a chair leg and nearly fell.

The two deputies moved through the crowd, as well, hurrying to catch up with the marshal. They did so as the big-gutted marshal stopped off the right front corner of Wolf's table and slid both flaps of his duster back and planted his bare fists on his square hips. An old-model Colt with worn walnut grips sagged low on his left hip, positioned for the cross-draw. The cartridge belt was well hidden beneath the man's sagging gut.

"Well, well, well, if it ain't the great man himself," he said through a sneer. His voice was deep and gravelly, a little nasal, as well. His long hair was streaked with gray, his eyes were a washed-out jade, his broad nose badly pitted.

"That him?" asked the deputy standing off Wolf's right shoulder. He was of average height and chunky, and he held a double-barrel shotgun in both hands. The other deputy, tall and thin and wearing a bowler hat and dragoon-style mustache, stood straight out ahead of Wolf's table.

He held a Winchester carbine, the barrel resting on his right shoulder.

"That's him, all right."

Stockburn set the match and the knife on the table, slid his chair back, tossed his napkin onto the table, and rose. He smiled and extended his hand to the marshal. "If you mean Wolf Stockburn, Wells Fargo, you've got your man, all right, Marshal . . ."

"Watt Russell, Town Marshal of Wild Horse," the man said, not shaking Wolf's hand but merely scowling at him as though at fresh dog dung on a boardwalk.

"Pleased to make your acquaintance."

"Well, the feelin' ain't mutual!"

The chunky deputy snickered at that. Watt Russell said, "Shut up, Sonny!"

Sonny winced and looked down at the floor. The deputy with the Winchester and dragoon-style mustache bedeviled Sonny with a sneer.

"I'm sorry you feel that way, Marshal," Stockburn said.

"Why'd ya have to come, huh?" Russell said, his raspy voice now plaintive, whiny. "Why'd ya have to come and make things complicated. Me an' my deputies here are hot on the trail of them owlhoots that shot up the rail crew. I done told the Stewarts that, dammit. But still they go and send for you and here you come and kill the son of a very important man in these parts, Stockburn!"

"Had a feelin' you might've heard about that," Wolf said with irony in his voice.

"Hell, the whole town knows!" said the taller deputy with the bowler hat and mustache.

"Shut up, Diggs!" Watt Russell admonished him.

It was Sonny's turn to snicker.

By now, most of the nearby diners had overheard the raised voices around Stockburn's table. They themselves had fallen quiet and had turned to stare at the scene of the commotion. Alarm was spreading, the room going more and more quiet as more and more conversations died and more faces turned to stare toward this side of the room.

Russell turned his anxious, angry gaze back to Stockburn. "Well, what do you have to say for yourself?"

"You want me to spill it right here?" Wolf asked. "I sort of thought you'd want to bring in the coroner, seat a jury for an inquest. There were plenty of witnesses, including the girl that little devil was going to kill before I trimmed his wick—Lori McCrae."

"Lori McCrae?" Russell asked, incredulous. "Pshaw! You got the name wrong. Lori McCrae's off to a girl's school back East somewheres."

"Not anymore she's not."

"You sure?"

"Sure, I'm sure."

"Of course, he's sure," said Sonny, gazing sidelong up at Wolf and curling his upper lip with bald disdain and open mockery. "He's the Wolf of the Rails!"

"Shut up, Sonny," Stockburn said.

"You can't tell me to shut up!"

"I can," Russell said, glaring at the thick-set deputy. "Sew them lips!"

Again, Sonny flinched and looked at the floor. Diggs squealed a short laugh.

Russell turned to Stockburn again. "What's Miss McCrae doin' back home so soon?"

"Your guess is as good as mine, Marshal."

"Hmmm." Russell rubbed his jaw thoughtfully, briefly lowering his gaze to the floor. Returning to the topic at hand, he returned his angry gaze to Wolf and slid his jaws from side to side, like a cow chewing its cud. "We don't trouble ourselves with no coroner's inquests or judges 'n' juries nor any such nonsense as that in these parts, Stockburn."

"I had a feelin' you were going to say that," Wolf said.

"Nah, nah, none o' that. Especially when it comes to the killing of the sons of important men, we usually just send a wire to the hangman."

A snicker lifted from one of the many onlookers in the now silent dining room.

"I'm surprised you go to that much trouble," Wolf said.

Another onlooker laughed.

"You can joke all you want, Stockburn," Russell said, ignoring the onlookers. "But this here is serious business. I suggest you go back to where you came from an' let me and my deputies look into the Hell's Jaw business on our own—since it's our jurisdiction, after all, an' there's no reason for Wells Fargo to mess with it!"

"Wells Fargo already signed a contract with the Hell's Jaw line, Russell. In anticipation of the rails being finished before the snow flies and the first gold loads being shipped down—via Wells Fargo strongboxes with Wells Fargo messenger guards—by Christmas. That's what makes it my business. Those contracts can't be honored until that line is finished. I am here to see that those rails get laid all the way to Hell's Jaw Pass."

"Ain't he just so high 'n' mighty!"

"Shut up, Diggs!" both Stockburn and Watt Russell said at the same time.

Diggs glowered. Sonny chuckled.

Russell looked at Wolf again and said, "Well, you got off on the wrong foot before you even got here, Stockburn. Now, you'd best take my advice and head back to Kansas City before—"

"Holy cow!" a man shouted from the eatery's front door. "It's Kreg Hennessey. Him an' three of his big hardtails are headed this way!"

CHAPTER 6

"Ah, hell." Marshal Watt Russell turned back to Stockburn, his eyes wide and dark. "Now you done it!"

The restaurant got even quieter than before. An elderly couple eating together near the counter, shuffled up out of their seats then hurried out the back door. The others sat in hushed silence, muttering quietly among themselves, squirming in their seats. They were like church parishioners knowing the preacher was on his way and he had a holy mad on.

From out in the street came the heavy thudding of boots—several pairs, the thuds out of step with each other. Gradually, the raucous sounds grew louder.

Watt Russell took one step back from Stockburn's table and turned slowly to face the front of the restaurant, hands hanging straight down his sides. Diggs, who'd been standing directly in front of Stockburn's table, now stepped to the right, flanking the big-gutted town marshal. Sonny, standing just off Stockburn's right shoulder, took a couple more steps in that direction.

Stockburn stood rolling his sharpened matchstick around between his teeth. He felt right unpopular, all of a sudden, as though he were one of those parishioners whom the angry preacher had singled out for a particularly strident dressing down. He slid his right hand across his belly, reaching under his black frock coat to unsnap the keeper thong from over the hammer of his cross-draw Peacemaker.

The boot thuds grew louder until a big man stepped into the restaurant. He was so large that for a moment he filled the doorway, nearly blotting out all of the outside light. He wore a three-piece suit that was one or two sizes too small; he was all muscular bulges. He stepped to the left of the door and stood like a sentry, high-topped boots spread a little farther than shoulder width apart.

He held a double-barrel, sawed-off shotgun in both his meaty hands.

Another man stepped into the doorway, filling it momentarily before stepping to the right, taking his own sentry-like position on the opposite side of the door from the first man. This fellow wielded no shotgun, but there was a tell-tale bulge under his coat where a gun in a shoulder holster would be.

Another man came in, similarly clad and built. He took three or four steps straight into the restaurant then swung around to half-face the doorway. He held what appeared to be a hide-wrapped bung starter in his right hand. He tapped it absently against the palm of his left hand.

A fourth man stepped through the door and into the restaurant.

He was tall but leaner than the three obvious bouncers who'd preceded him. He was also older by a good twenty years. He wore a checked, rust-color suit over a white silk shirt and black foulard tie. He wore no hat. His hair was black and coarsely curled and sitting close against his head. He wore long side whiskers that bowed up from his jaws to form a heavy mustache over his mouth.

He walked about six feet into the restaurant then stopped and looked around. His face was doughy and pale, and it sagged on his broad cheekbones. His gaze landed on Marshal Watt Russell and then slid from Russell to Stockburn and held for several seconds.

Stockburn saw that the man had been crying. That's why his face looked so ravaged, his eyes severely red-rimmed.

Kreg Hennessey lifted his chin slightly, drew a deep breath through his nose, then walked heavily forward, turning toward Stockburn, his shoulders slumped forward and down, as though he were carrying a heavy but invisible burden. He walked so uncertainly, shuffling his feet, that at times he appeared to nearly fall before catching himself.

He staggered up in front of Stockburn and

stopped three feet away. He was breathing through his mouth. His breath smelled like a warm wind blowing over something dead. It almost made Stockburn wince; he fought the urge to take a step back away from the man.

"Are you Stockburn?" Kreg Hennessey finally asked. His voice was a wheezy rasp, as though he were out of breath.

"That's right."

"I understand you murdered my son."

"You're wrong. I killed your son to keep him from killing an innocent young lady he'd pulled off the train that he and his friends were trying to rob."

"Liar!"

"It's not a lie," Stockburn said.

"Liar!" Hennessey glanced at Watt Russell who stood behind him, looking stricken, as did everyone else in the place. "Lock him up for the murder of my boy, Russell!"

Stockburn kept his voice even as he said, "I won't be arrested, Hennessey. The way I see it I was doing everyone in this town and probably the entire county—except you but maybe *even* you—a big favor."

"Why, you—" Hennessey stepped forward, bringing a roundhouse punch up from his knees. Stockburn caught the man's right wrist in his own left hand then hardened his jaws as he rammed his right fist against Hennessey's mustached mouth—three quick jabs that he thrust straight out from his shoulder.

The three smacking sounds came swift and certain. Hennessey grunted with each one as he staggered backward and dropped to a knee, holding both hands across his mouth.

There was a collective gasp as everyone in the restaurant filled their lungs and held their breath.

The three bouncers took three or four steps toward Stockburn then stopped, looking from Stockburn to their boss, eyes wide and round with shock.

Hennessey lifted his eyes to Stockburn. He removed his hands from his smashed lips. His hands were bloody. Rage fairly glowed in his eyes.

His face turned from flour white to sunset red as he jerked a look to the three men behind him and bellowed, "Don't just stand there with your thumbs up your bums—*kill him!*"

"Ah, hell!" Stockburn heard Watt Russell complain, taking another step back away from Wolf's table.

Stockburn saw the marshal of Wild Horse in the periphery of his vision. He kept his eyes locked on the three bouncers. The one with the shotgun gritted his teeth as he raised the double-barreled gut-shredder and swung it toward Wolf but not before Stockburn slid his cross-draw Peacemaker from his holster, clicked the hammer back, and fired.

The .45 round punched through the bouncer's thick black necktie, flipping it up off his chest while throwing the man himself backward. The bouncer triggered both barrels of his shotgun into the ceiling just before he flew out the front door and onto the boardwalk.

A roar of fear rose from the diners, who literally fell over themselves and each other as they scrambled from their chairs to the floor.

The second bouncer who'd been standing at the door fished a pearl-gripped revolver from his shoulder holster and was hardening his jaws as he ran forward then crouched and raised the hogleg, clicking the hammer back.

He, too, fired his weapon into the ceiling as Stockburn's second Peacemaker bullet drilled through his heart and hurled him onto a table behind which two drummers cowered, one of them muttering a prayer.

The third bouncer, nearer to Wolf by eight feet, bellowed an angry curse then hurled the bungstarter end over end toward the rail detective. The hide-wrapped mallet gave a wicked whorl as Wolf ducked, and it flew over his head to break the window flanking him before thudding onto the boardwalk fronting the restaurant.

Straightening, Stockburn extended his Colt at the big man who'd thrown the mallet. The man froze with one hand inside his black silk jacket, his broad face red with anxiety.

He smiled as he slowly pulled the hand out of the jacket, showed the empty palm to Stockburn, then let it drop low against his side.

"Good decision," Stockburn said.

A shadow moved on his right—a man coming in fast and close.

Wolf wheeled too late. He saw the grinning face of Sonny half a blink before the chunky kid thrust the butt of his shotgun against Wolf's right temple. Stockburn grunted, stumbled backward against his chair, hearing the kid give a victorious whoop and howl, *"There—take that Mister Wolf of the Rails!"*

Wolf clawed at the table but his fingers brushed the end without finding purchase, and then he fell over the chair, taking the chair with him to the floor with a heavy crashing thud. His head smacked the wall beneath the window and then a cave-like darkness wrapped itself around him.

"Wakey." The voice came from far away but also from close by.

Strange.

"Wakey-wakey." There it was again, both from far away and near. A girl's voice.

"Wake-wakey, Wolf. Rise an' shine."

Someone pulled up Stockburn's left eyelid. Light assaulted it. He wanted to close it, but the finger held it open.

Finally, he wrestled it closed but then the girl's voice came again. "Can you wake up, Wolf? Hey, Wolf, it's Lori McCrae. I can get you out of here. I rather think it's a good idea if you come now. If you wait till morning . . . well . . . there might not be a morning, if you get my drift . . ."

She slid her face down close to Stockburn's. One of her pretty, shimmering brown eyes looked into the one of his that she was holding open with her thumb.

Stockburn groaned, pulled his head back. He opened both eyes though the lids felt as though they weighed as much as a blacksmith's anvils. He looked around briefly.

He was in a jail cell. The cell door was open and two men, silhouetted against a lantern burning on a square post, stood in the hall. Lori McCrae was squatting on her haunches beside the cot on which Stockburn lay, wincing and gritting his teeth against the large, tender heart throbbing in his head.

Stockburn cleared his throat. "What . . . what're you doing here, Lori?"

"Busting you out of here, Wolf. What's it look like?"

"How, uh . . . ? How, uh . . . ?" Stockburn's brain was foggy, thoughts as turgid as ice floes.

"I got you a lawyer. A good one. In fact, Mr. Powderhorn represents my father."

"Can you stand, Mister Stockburn?" asked

one of the men in the hall. It was the voice of a cultivated man.

"That's George Powderhorn," Lori said. "Can you stand, Wolf?"

"Yeah." Stockburn pushed up on a hand, dropped his feet to the floor. "Yeah . . . I can . . . stand."

He wasn't sure yet if he could but he was willing to try if the alternative was to spend the night in Watt Russell's jail. He couldn't remember how he'd got here, or why, but he could sense the answer skulking around in the back of his head, like a coyote sniffing around the perimeter of a fire over which a tasty spit of meat was sizzling.

He rose with Lori's help, and as soon as he was standing, the answer came to him. He remembered Sonny's broad, dull-eyed, grinning face, and the butt of the shotgun hurling toward Wolf's head.

Lori handed Wolf his hat. Holding it, he frowned at her curiously. "How did you manage this?" He also remembered smashing Kreg Hennessey's mouth and killing two of his bodyguards or bouncers or whatever the hell they were.

"Ridiculous," came the reply from the cellblock hall. One of the two men out there had spoken again. He was the smaller of the two, and he stood to the left of the other man, the man who was holding open the door and who, judging by the man's big gut and long, greasy hair, was Watt Russell.

"Lori told me the whole story," George Powderhorn said.

"I went to George's house after I heard about Hennessey"—she cast a cold glare at the other man in the cell block hall—"and Marshal Russell locking you up."

Russell was a blocky shadow who didn't say anything. His face was a grim, black oval beneath the brim of his black Stetson.

Powderhorn said, "Lori signed an affidavit testifying to your killing Riley Hennessey because he was about to shoot Lori. I talked to the engineer and the brakeman, who was wounded by one of the gang's bullets. They corroborated your story and have agreed to write out their own testimonies. Russell has no right to hold you here."

"Them two bodyguards of Hennessey's are another matter," said Watt Russell for the first time, his angry voice raspy. Stockburn could hear the heavy man breathing through his nose. "Same with the big fella's assault of Mister Hennessey himself. Them smashed lips will go a long way to gettin' you run out of town on a greased rail, Stockburn."

"One of the diners, a respected man in town, told me it was all in self-defense," Lori threw in forthrightly.

Powderhorn, who held a crisp derby in his hands, over his chest, turned to Russell. "We'll deal with the doings in the Metropolitan later— before a judge, if Hennessey thinks it wise for him, a known outlaw, to be heard by a judge and jury. In the meantime, Marshal, I'll be filing a complaint against you with the county sheriff in Rawlins and with Judge Orville McDermott in Cheyenne. The complaints against you for unlawful arrest are stacking up. Eventually, they will bring you down whether you have Kreg Hennessey behind you or not!"

Russell glared at him but said nothing. The look was threatening enough.

CHAPTER 7

"Come on, Wolf," Lori said, placing her hand against the small of Stockburn's back. "Let's get you over to the doctor's office. He should have a look at you."

"He'll just see a goose egg on my forehead," Stockburn said, stepping out into the hall. "I just need a couple shots of decent whiskey and I'll be finer than frog hair split four ways." He glanced at Russell. "No thanks to that yellow-livered little deputy of yours, Russell."

"Yeah, well, Sonny did all right by Mister Hennessey." Russell closed the cell door with a purposefully loud clang that made Stockburn's head kick like a mule. "He'll likely get a bouncin' job over to Hennessey's Wind River Saloon, seein' as ol' Kreg suddenly has a couple of holes to fill on his payroll!"

Stockburn gave a caustic snort as Lori led him down the hall to the mouth of a stairs that apparently dropped to the building's first story. George Powderhorn followed, still holding his hat. Russell tramped along heavily, breathing loudly and hacking phlegm from his throat and spitting it on the floor, behind the lawyer.

Stockburn and Lori descended the stairs to a wooden door with three bars across the small window in the top of it. The door stood partway open.

Stockburn followed Lori through the door and into the jailhouse's lamplit office, where Sonny sat in a chair beside a cluttered rolltop desk. A pretty, blond-haired girl dressed like a boy sat in the swivel chair behind the desk. The tall deputy with the stylish but worn suit and dragoon mustache, which needed a trim, stood against the room's back, brick wall and a large framed map of the Wind River Mountains and the town of Wild Horse sitting on the range's south end.

Sonny and Diggs could barely contain devilish grins.

"When I heard there was trouble over at the Cosmopolitan, I didn't know you were part of it, Miss Lori," the blonde said, studying Miss McCrae with an insinuating sneer.

Lori merely smiled at the girl, tolerantly.

"Ivy, what're you doin' here, dammit," Russell complained. "I told you to stay home after dark!"

"Well, gee, Pa, when I heard there was a shootin' over at the Cosmopolitan and it involved the Wolf of Wichita his own big, handsome self"— she raked her eyes up and down Stockburn's rumpled frame several times, her baby blue eyes fairly glowing—"you know I couldn't just sit in the parlor, practicing the piano. Besides, I knew Diggs needed pestering."

Diggs flushed, glanced warily at Russell, then

77

averted his gaze, kneading his hat brim as though it was dough he was pressing into the lip of a pie pan.

"Dammit, Ivy, I told you to stay away from Seth. He's my deputy and that's all he is to you and all he'll ever *be* to you. He makes less money than I do, and you by God are going to marry a man of wealth if I have to lock you in our cellar till the right man of wealth comes along!" The big-gutted lawman looked at Diggs and said, "Dammit, boy, eyes off my daughter!"

"Ah, hell!" Diggs dropped his gaze to the floor. "I didn't invite her here, but now that she's here, you can't expect me to not look at her, Marshal Russell!"

Stockburn had to admit that the blonde was a heartbreaker if in a rough-hewn way. There was something particularly fetching in the way she carried herself, even sitting down. And in the way she wore her checked shirt, with her suspenders pulled taut against her ample bosoms.

Stockburn felt Lori's eyes on him. He looked down at her. Sure enough, she was scowling up at him with cold, jealous chagrin. She hugged his arm and started for the jailhouse door. "Come along, Wolf of Wichita. Let's get you out of this snake pit and over to the hotel."

"Hold on." Wolf stopped and turned to Russell, aware of the blonde's eyes still on him. "My guns."

"How do I know if I give 'em to you, you won't shoot Sonny?"

"You don't."

Sonny glared at Wolf and said in a low, throaty voice that was meant to be menacing but sounded more like the empty threat of a chicken-livered schoolboy bully: "I was just doin' my job, Mister Wells Fargo!"

"You're a coward," Stockburn told him. "You stay away from me, Sonny. If I spy you within hollerin' distance of me again, you'll get a Peacemaker enema free of charge."

"Hah!" Ivy laughed and, eyes glowing up at Stockburn, she slapped her hands jubilantly down on the arms of her chair. "I bet he would, too, sure enough!"

Sonny's face turned sunset red.

"You be quiet, daughter!" Russell had pulled Stockburn's gunbelt and Peacemakers out of a padlocked footlocker near his desk. Now he shoved them at the big rail detective and said, "Go on home, Stockburn. If you don't, I won't give you the courtesy of locking you up next time you get in trouble. And all the Miss McCraes and Mister Powderhorns won't be able to put you back together again, despite the law reader's threats!"

Russell stood over the diminutive Powderhorn, clenching his fists threateningly.

Stockburn buckled his six-shooters around his

waist, tied the thong of the right-hand holster to that thigh, and said, "I'm not going anywhere till my job here is done and the men who massacred the Hell's Jaw rail crew—and whoever hired them to do so—are either behind bars or six feet under." He walked up to the big-gutted lawman and gave him the same look Russell had given Powderhorn. "Despite your threats, you fat old tin star!"

"Damn!" intoned Ivy, slapping her hands on the chair arms again.

Stockburn wheeled toward Lori, gestured at the door, then followed her out. Powderhorn came up behind them and drew the door closed with a click of the latching bolt.

"Thanks, Lori . . . Mr. Powderhorn." Wolf extended his hand to the attorney, who shook it. His hand was small and a little moist, but his grip was firm. "How much do I owe you for your services?"

"Not a dime. Lori's father keeps me on retainer for just such shenanigans, and to get his men out of jail on weekends when they've stomped a little too high and hard with their tails up." He glanced at Lori with an ironic smile. "Besides, I'm very glad to hear that you took down two of Hennessey's very worst attack dogs. Phil Bergson and Miles Miller were pariahs."

"If only you'd taken down Keith McCafferty, as well," Lori said, crossing her arms on her chest.

McCafferty must have been the attack dog with the bungstarter.

"Maybe next time," Stockburn said. "In the meantime, I believe I'll have a shot of whiskey and sleep off this, um, hangover courtesy of Sonny." He touched two fingers to the lump on his temple, and winced.

"Good-night, Mister Stockburn," Powderhorn said, giving his chin a cordial dip. "Sleep well and . . . oh, watch your back. Hennessey will no doubt replace those two deceased attack dogs with fresh ones right soon."

"Thanks again, Powderhorn."

The attorney pinched the brim of his crisp derby to Lori then turned and ambled off along the boardwalks, darker under the awnings where the light of a waxing moon couldn't find them. It being late in the year, the sun set early.

Stockburn thought it was probably around ten or ten-thirty, but it was good dark. The only lights were from a few sundry watering holes he could see up the street in both directions, where clumps of horses tied to hitchrails stood in silhouette against lamplight washing out from windows.

He and Lori were on a side street he didn't recognize.

"Where in blazes are we?" he asked his lovely companion.

"We're taking a short cut. Have you checked into the hotel, Wolf?"

81

"I have." Securing a room and stowing his gear in it was the first thing he'd done after leaving the train station.

Lori hugged his arm again, intimately, as though she and he were old lovers, and began leading him west along the boardwalk, walking very close to him so that he could feel her curves and the heat of her body against his own.

At least, he thought they were heading west, but he wasn't sure. Wild Horse seemed bigger at night, darker. It being a weeknight, it was also relatively quiet. The only sounds were night birds and the tinny, faraway patter of a saloon piano, the distant barking of a dog.

"Right this way," Lori said.

Stockburn walked along beside her. "Thanks again for your help."

"My pleasure. Hennessey is an evil man. Vile. He gobbles up smaller businesses just because he can and because he wants full control of the town. My father hates him."

"I can see why. Seemed pretty broken up about his son, though."

"I'm sure he saw a lot of himself in Riley, and vice versa. Riley was like a mad dog his father had sicced on the county, just to remind everyone who Kreg himself really was . . . what he was capable of . . . and to keep them nervous."

"How long has Hennessey been here?"

"Most of his life. I think he came from back

East. Way early on, I mean, when he was very young. He was an outlaw. Rustler, mostly. Distilled and sold whiskey and rifles to the Indians. Punched cows for a few outfits, market hunter. Mostly, he rode the long coulees. Spent a few years in jail, got out, and made money through evil ways. Claim jumping in the mountains, I heard. Stagecoach holdups. He bought a saloon here in town, then another . . . and then he built the Wind River, Wild Horse's crown jewel. A black diamond is how I see it."

They'd turned the side street corner and were walking past the Wind River Saloon & Gambling Hall now. It occupied two corner lots. The entrance was on the corner, behind a dozen or so saddled horses tethered out front.

The big plate-glass windows on each side of the front door were painted umber by inside lamplight. Shadows swayed against it. There was the low roar of conversation and occasional bursts of raucous laughter.

Shadows moved intimately behind the drawn curtains of the second-story windows, beneath the garishly painted false façade looming over Wild Horse's main drag that could be seen, Stockburn knew, from a long way away. It was one of the first signs he'd seen upon leaving the train station.

Gold lettering set against a dark green background backed by cobalt sky. At least, earlier it had been backed by that deep blue Wyoming sky. Now that blue had been replaced by a broad wash of flickering stars.

Lori didn't say anything more until they'd entered the Territorial, nodded at the desk clerk, and climbed the broad carpeted stairs to the second floor. Stockburn stopped at his door, gave the girl's chin an affectionate nudge, and said, "Good-night, Lori. Thanks again."

Lori glanced at the door, then arched a brow as she looked up at him with a strange beseeching in her gaze. "Let me in . . . ?"

"Uh . . ." Wolf glanced up and down the hall lit by a couple of bracket lamps. Allowing a young woman into his room without benefit of chaperone was nowhere even close to proper.

"Don't worry, the hotel's almost empty. No one will know."

"All right." Stockburn really just wanted a few shots of whiskey and to go to bed, but the girl seemed sad, out of sorts.

He dug the key out of his pocket, unlocked and opened the door. He followed her inside, closed the door, and pegged his hat on the wall.

He walked over to the big, canopied bed and sat down on it, leaning forward, probing the goose egg with his fingers while brushing his other hand through the thick thatch of gray hair.

"Where's your whiskey?"

"In the war bag there." Wolf gestured to the

canvas bag on the room's small table, near the door and a mirrored chest of drawers.

Lori retrieved the bottle from the bag. There were two water glasses overturned on the table. She splashed two fingers of whiskey into each.

"A drinkin' gal, eh?"

"I'm my father's daughter."

Smiling coyly, Lori walked over to the bed to give Stockburn his drink. She returned to the table for her own glass and the flask. Stockburn threw back both fingers of his whiskey, put his head down, and held his glass out for more.

"That helps," he said with a ragged sigh.

Her smile in place, Lori poured more whiskey into his glass and sat down beside him. Very close. So that their legs were snugged up against each other. Stockburn frowned at her speculatively.

"I just need a friend, Wolf," Lori said, taking a healthy pull from her own glass. "You're a friend, aren't you? After all, you saved my life. Don't the Indians think that when you save someone's life you become as close to that person as a relative . . . and that person is beholden to you forever?"

"Some do. But you're not beholden to me in any way, Lori."

"I know. At least, I don't mean like that." She leaned her head against his shoulder. "I just don't know what I'm doing back here, Wolf."

"I thought you did know."

"I don't. Maybe I was too impulsive. Nothing good has come of my return so far. You had to risk your life to save mine and got a target painted on your back for your trouble."

She glanced up at him regretfully. "I'm afraid Hennessey won't let this go. He'll kill you. And it will be my fault."

CHAPTER 8

"No one's gonna kill the old Wolf of the Rails," Wolf quipped. "Don't you know I got eyes in the back of my head?"

"Really? Then how did that idiot deputy of Russell's sneak up on you to give you that nasty tattoo?"

"Ah." Wolf warmed with embarrassment and hardened his jaws as he probed the goose egg on his temple again. "That."

"Yes, that." Lori looked up at him askance, concern in her eyes. "Does it hurt miserably?"

"I've endured worse."

"I'm so sorry!" She rose from the bed. "I'm being selfish. Here you are in terrible pain, and you'd just like to be left to your whiskey and a good-night's sleep. I'll leave now and see you in the—"

Despite his wanting to do just what she'd intuited, Stockburn grabbed her hand and pulled her back down beside him. "Hold on, there, little gal. Suppose you tell me what's got you so sad."

She slid up against him once more and looked up at him from over his shoulder again. "Do I seem sad?"

Wolf wrapped his arm around her, gave her an affectionate squeeze. "Very. And I got a feelin' it's about more than that little hydrophobic rat, Riley Hennessey."

Lori stretched her lips back from her teeth then lowered her gaze to the floor. She seemed to ponder for a time, then said, "Have you ever wanted something more than anything but felt the whole world was in cahoots against you, to make sure that object of your desire never becomes yours?"

"Why, yes. Yes, I have."

That seemed to surprise the girl. "Really?"

"When I was a boy, the Cheyenne raided my family's farm in western Kansas. They murdered my parents and kidnapped my eight-year-old sister, Emily. I got knocked on the head, left for dead. I knew the Cheyenne had taken Emily, because I'd seen a brave pull her up, kicking and screaming, over his horse, just before I took a club to the head. When I came to my senses, and as I buried my poor dead murdered parents, I vowed not to rest until I found Emily."

Stockburn sipped his whiskey, thought back to that miserable, haunted time. "Years passed. I mean, many, many years during which I felt just like you do now. That the stars had lined up against me to keep me from ever seeing my little sister again."

"Did you find her, Wolf?"

"Yes, I did. Just last year. She's a beautiful woman, almost thirty now, with a young half-

Sioux boy named Pete. They live together on a ranch in Dakota. Emily changed her name to Melissa Ann.

"She gained her freedom from the band of Sioux that had taken her in trade from the Cheyenne who'd first captured her, when her warrior husband was killed in battle. She took her boy to Bismarck and worked in a hotel, and mended clothes at night. In Bismarck, she caught the eye of a prominent rancher, Thornburg, her senior by a good twenty years. He was a good man, good to her son despite his being a half-breed. He set them both up well, on a very nice spread up there in Dakota. She runs it herself now with a sure hand, Emily does."

Wolf stopped, smiled. "I should say, Melissa Ann does."

"That's a heckuva story, Wolf."

"Isn't it?"

"Do you see her often, Melissa Ann?"

"I haven't seen her since last summer, but we exchange letters regularly. I plan to pay her and Pete a visit again, though, real soon." Stockburn gave Lori another reassuring squeeze. "See? Things work out sometimes. Even when the odds seemed stacked unbelievably high against us. Till last year, I hadn't seen my sister in twenty-one years."

Lori smiled up at him. She brushed a tear from her cheek then sat up straighter and pressed her lips to his jaw. "Thank you for that. I feel encouraged."

She rose. "With that, I will bid you adieu, sir." She set her empty glass on the table then flounced to the door, opened it with a flourish, turned back to him, smiled again winningly, and said, "Sweet dreams, Mister Wolf of the Rails."

"Good-night, Lori."

She gave a parting curtsy and left.

"Ravishing creature," Stockburn said, and tossed back the last of his whiskey. But he had to admit he was relieved she was gone. His head was splitting, and the pillow beckoned. He had a lot to do tomorrow, and he needed a few hours' sleep.

Still, he couldn't help wondering what it was that had called the girl back home after she'd left for school only a month ago. Whatever it was, it certainly had her considerably troubled. Apparently, there was something she wanted but couldn't have.

Hmm.

Oh, well—no concern of Stockburn's. He had enough on his plate dealing with the massacre of the rail-laying crew.

Wolf sat on the bed to kick out of his boots. He rose and removed his six-guns and looped them around the bed's upper right post in case he needed to make a quick grab during the night. A situation not unheard of in his past, more's the pity.

He skinned out of his shirt, hung it over a chair back, then went to the marble-topped washstand. He opened his longhandle top and peeled it down his arms to his lean waist, laying his upper torso bare.

He splashed tepid water from the washbowl onto his face and used a cake of soft soap to lather his face and torso. He scrubbed the soap and grit from his body with a wet cloth and had just finished drying with a towel when a knock sounded on his door—two quick playful taps followed by a third.

He frowned at the door.

"Lori?"

"Guess again." It was a girl's voice. He couldn't place it.

Could be a trap laid by Hennessey.

He walked over to the front of the bed, slid a Peacemaker from its holster, and held it straight down against his side. His thumb caressed the hammer as he made his way back to the door. With his left hand, he turned the key in the lock, turned the knob, and pulled the door open quickly, clicking the Peacemaker's hammer back.

The girl gasped, eyes widening. The blonde from the jailhouse. The marshal's daughter, Ivy. She was the only one in the hall.

She splayed her fingers across her chest, over where her unbuttoned shirt formed an inviting V, the nose of the V showing the dark mouth of her cleavage. "Scared me! I'll be hanged if that ain't a big gun!"

Wolf depressed the hammer and raised the barrel. "What're you doing here?"

The blonde's eyes roamed across his bare chest, the nubs of her cheeks flushing. "I thought we should have a little chat before you get all entangled with Miss Fancy Britches McCrae and she goes filling your head with a bunch of nonsense."

"What kind of nonsense?"

"Let me in and I'll tell you."

"Can't it wait for tomorrow, Ivy? I have one whale of a headache, and I was just getting ready for bed."

She smiled as her eyes strayed to his exposed chest again. "I see that. I won't be long. I promise. Besides." She grimaced and glanced down at her right foot on which she wore a boy's sized stockman's boot. "I hurt my foot on the stairs. Twisted my ankle. I need to get off it for a spell."

"Oh, sure, sure," Stockburn said, not sure if the irony was plain in his voice. "I guess you'd best come in and take a load off."

"Thank you," she said, as Wolf stepped back and she limped through the door, smiling.

Stockburn closed the door and shoved his hands through the sleeves of his longhandle top, raising it up over his chest and covering himself. Now he knew how women felt about being ogled. "Take a seat."

"How 'bout here?" Ivy limped over to the bed and sat on the edge of it, where Stockburn and Lori had been sitting a few moments ago.

Stockburn gave a wry chuff as he walked over to the table and splashed more whiskey into his glass. "Does your father know you're here?"

"What do you think? Can I have some of that?" She glanced at the flask and then at the second glass on the table. "I can use Miss Fancy Britches' glass. I'm sure she doesn't have any germs. No, not a McCrae."

Stockburn sighed and poured a finger of whiskey into the second glass. "How'd you know she was here?"

"If she wasn't here, whose glass is that?"

"You're a shrewd one, Miss Ivy," Stockburn said, walking over to the bed and handing the girl the glass.

She was pretty in a tomboyish way, but in a dress, with her hair done up, maybe a little paint on her lips, she would have caused a riot in any male crowd. Her face was tan, her eyes lilac blue. Her straight hair, hanging well past her shoulders, was the gold of late-summer wheat.

"A girl has to be shrewd around here or she gets taken advantage of. It's called survival."

"You live with your father?"

"He lives with me!" She laughed. It was a husky laugh. Then she winced and looked down at her right foot. "Mind if I take my boot off? I should take a peek at my foot. Might need to pay a call on the sawbones though he's likely upstairs with one of Hennessey's whores."

"Be my guest," Wolf said with another weary sigh as he slacked into one of the two chairs at the table.

She took a sip of the whiskey and swallowed like it was nothing stronger than lemonade. She set the glass on the table by the bed then leaned back on her hands and used the toe of her left boot to maneuver out of the right one. She grimaced, cheeks coloring, and gave Stockburn a plaintive look.

"A little help . . . ?"

Wolf chuckled.

He set his glass down, rose from his chair, then dropped to a knee in front of Ivy. He felt like her man in waiting. But, then, he had a feeling that's how every man in Miss Ivy's orbit felt. She was like Lori McCrae in that way, but in only that one way.

He took the sole of the boot in his left hand, wrapped his other hand around the heel, and tugged.

Ivy sucked air through gritted teeth.

"Hurt?"

"A little gentler, please, big fella . . . ?"

"Sorry." Stockburn tried again.

The girl groaned as the boot slipped over her heel. Wolf removed it from her foot. The white sock had slipped halfway off her foot, exposing her ankle and half of her foot, which was as comely as the rest of her.

"Thanks," Ivy said, sitting up and raising her foot with the sock hanging off. "If a lady's bare foot arouses you, you can look away." She grinned, brashly flirtatious. "Or . . . not . . ."

Stockburn pulled the sock off the foot and dropped it to the floor. A pretty foot, indeed. He took it in both hands and inspected it thoroughly. "Where's it hurt? Here?" He pressed his thumb and index finger around the ankle near the heal.

"Ahh . . . yep!"

"Hurts, eh?"

"Yeah. Think I might've sprained it. I'm gonna sue that Rose for not properly maintaining his premises!"

"I don't know," Wolf said, continuing to probe the pretty appendage gently. "Doesn't look so bad to me." There was no sign of swelling or discoloration.

"Hurts worse than it looks."

"Must."

"I reckon I can wait to see the sawbones tomorrow," Ivy said, "since he's likely drunk and cavortin'. I'll just sit here for a minute, keep some weight off it, rest it . . . have another

95

drink." She reached for her glass but the way she was sitting, she couldn't quite fetch it.

She smiled at Stockburn.

He suppressed the urge to chuckle again and gave her the glass.

"Thanks kindly."

"Don't mention it."

As she tucked her upper lip over the rim of the glass, looking up at him, Wolf rose, backed up, and sank back down in his chair. Ivy lowered her glass, swallowed, and said, "You're as big as they say, Mister Stockburn."

"Wolf."

"A big man with two big guns." The girl's eyes strayed to the Winchester leaning against the wall. "And a big Yellowboy rifle."

"A fella in my line of work has to be ready."

"I bet you do." She smirked at that and took another sip of her whiskey.

"If you just came over here to bedevil me, young lady, you're doing a right good job of it."

"Oh." She raised her wrist to her mouth, snickering. "Thank you."

"But, then, I got a feeling you've had a lot of practice."

"Well, I filled out early. Realized I could take my ability to turn a man's head to my advantage."

"And what advantage is that?"

"Oh, I don't know. Relief from boredom, I reckon. Wild Horse is growing, but it's still a small town. Not much for a girl to do in these parts except pester the menfolk."

"Well, I have more to do than be pestered by pretty girls with feigned injuries, Miss Ivy." Stockburn rose to his full six-feet-four inches and glowered down at the shameless coquette. "Now, if you'll excuse—"

"Oh, sit down! Sit down! Don't get your neck in a hump! I just came here—call it a courtesy visit—to warn you that Miss Fancy Britches ain't the Goody Two Shoes she's got everyone believin' she is. You'd best watch out for her!"

CHAPTER 9

Stockburn frowned at the pretty blonde sitting on the edge of his bed, one boot off and one boot on. He sat back down in his chair and leaned forward, one elbow on the table to his left, the other hand on his thigh. "What're you talking about?"

"I know things. About The Princess herself. Everybody thinks she's so pure that butter wouldn't melt in her mouth."

"But you're saying it would."

Ivy studied Stockburn. She was obviously angry. And jealous. Wolf could tell she was thinking through her next words very thoroughly. "Like I said—I know some things. A girl who gets around as much as I do, while my pa is workin' or drinkin' when he's not workin' . . . learns things about a town. And about the people outside of the town, too."

"Chew it up and spit it out, Ivy. What do you know?"

Ivy studied him again, her eyes narrow, hesitant. Coyly, she shook her hair back from her pretty, oval-shaped face, then glanced around the room as though she were suddenly interested in the furnishings. "That's all I'm gonna say on that subject. I wouldn't want you to think I was a shameless gossip."

"No, no!"

"I do have some other information for you, though."

Stockburn gazed back at her, one brow arched, waiting.

Ivy sank back on her elbows, crossed her bare foot over her other knee, and gave the "injured" foot an absent shake. "I know who murdered that railroad crew." She looked down at her foot, which she was still shaking. "I have it from a good source."

"Well, that's what I'm here to find out, so . . . pray tell."

She gave a glib smile, tucked her chin low, and gazed at him from beneath her brows. "What's in it for me?"

"What do you want to be in it for you?"

She continued to smile at him, insinuatingly. "You got a woman?"

Stockburn chuckled. "I don't want one."

"Why not?"

"I travel too much."

She tossed her hair back again. "You like women though, don't you? I mean, you're not one of those fellas . . ."

Again, Wolf laughed. "I like them well enough. When they're a little closer to my age and their father doesn't wear a badge."

"My pa would like to see me married off to the right man. Age doesn't really matter to him. Only money."

"I doubt that he'd approve of a Wells Fargo detective's income."

Ivy tipped her head to one side and studied him while shaking her bare foot, which hadn't swollen anymore since he'd first removed her boot. She was making Stockburn uncomfortable, the way she sat back against her elbows with her shirt and suspenders drawn taut against her chest, shaking her bare foot.

Some of her hair hung down close to her eyes. He had a feeling she knew the affect she was having on him, though he tried not to let on. He was sure he was not the first man who'd tried and failed in that department.

"Rufus Stoleberg," she said finally, quietly, but with a coyote grin tugging at her mouth corners.

"Stoleberg . . .?"

"The other big rancher north of town, in the foothills of the Wind Rivers."

"I remember the name from the file," Stockburn said. "The Stolebergs are in competition with Norman McCrae for the open range. They crowd each other."

"Brand each other's cattle," Ivy said.

"I was also told that they'd been in competition for the sale of the right-of-way to the Hell's Jaw Rail Line. Stoleberg lost out."

"That ain't the half of it."

"I'm waiting."

"McCrae hanged one of Stoleberg's sons. Years back. When they both moved up here from Texas. Stoleberg came from south Texas. McCrae from the Panhandle. The story goes they got crossways with each other when they were both trailing their herds to Montana. The feud continues to this day. Bad blood. I mean, *really* bad blood!"

Stockburn pondered that. Little about the feud, aside from the two ranchers' having competed for the sale of their land to the rail line—had been in the file. Interesting, though he warned himself to take anything this little coquette told him with a big grain of salt.

He sipped his whiskey then leaned forward, resting his elbows on his knees, holding his glass in both hands. "Why did Norman McCrae hang Rufus Stoleberg's son?"

"Caught him rustling Triangle beef with three of his outlaw pards."

"That seems like pretty severe punishment."

"Not for rustling."

"No, but to hang the son of a neighboring rancher."

"That's how deep the hatred was. Is. Stoleberg was angry because McCrae claimed the better part of the graze up there. McCrae has some nice green meadows, with water in the ravines where the cows can shelter in the winter and during spring storms. Stoleberg's land, farther east, is flatter and drier. And McCrae has closed off access to some of the water with barbed wire. He has armed sentries guarding that wire religiously."

"Why would Stoleberg massacre a rail crew? They were innocent men only doing their jobs."

"Like I said, that's how deep the hate runs. Lots of innocent folk have gotten caught up in the McCrae/Stoleberg feud."

"Still . . ."

"McCrae's lawyer, Powderhorn, worked the deal so that both him, Powderhorn and McCrae, get a percentage of the rail line's profits. Since the geologists who surveyed this side of the Wind Rivers said there's a whole El Dorado of gold up there—gold that's relatively inexpensive to haul out of the rocks—there's a nice-sized fortune to be made. That gravels Rufus Stoleberg somethin' awful."

"Awful enough to massacre an entire rail crew? In a mere attempt to stymie a railroad line to nettle a competing rancher?"

"The way I see it, that's just the beginning of Stoleberg's war against McCrae. I mean, it started long ago, before the two men even reached Wyoming. But the attack on the rail crew was the start of Stoleberg's final push. I think there's other stuff he's got up his sleeve. That was just a start."

"What other stuff?"

Ivy made a big display of yawning and tapped fingers across her open mouth. "I'll be hanged if I ain't sleepy all of a sudden!"

"What does Lori have to do with any of this?"

"Like I said . . ." Ivy was still yawning.

"Who did you get your information from, Miss Ivy? About Stoleberg. And Lori McCrae."

"I wouldn't want to get my source or sources in trouble. Besides, a big famous detective like yourself should be able to find it out easy enough, if I can." She grinned.

"It would probably help if I wore a shirt as nicely as you do."

"You noticed! Here I thought my charms were wasted on you, Wolf!"

"Not hardly." Stockburn rose, yawning now himself—authentically. "Put your boot on and get out of here. I have to get at least a couple hours of sleep."

"What if I told you more?" she asked, kicking that bare foot again and showing her teeth through another enticing grin.

"You won't."

"How do you know?"

"A girl like you doesn't blow all her ammunition in the first skirmish."

"You know me too well!"

"I don't think you know as much as you think you do."

103

"I do so! I mean, mostly."

"Skedaddle!"

"All right, all right. But I'll have it all put together soon—mark my words!"

When he was alone at last, Stockburn poured himself another drink. A bigger one. He skinned out of his duds, used the chamber pot, crawled into bed, and finished the whiskey.

A second after he'd turned down his lamp, he was asleep.

It was a deep sleep in spite of the pain in his head, which the whiskey had dulled. When he woke at dawn, the pain was still there, but it didn't go as deep as it had before. Now it was mainly on the surface of his head.

Still, it was an excuse, whether a good one or not, to begin the day with a bracer.

He dressed and sat in a chair at the table and sipped the whiskey and smoked an Indian Kid, thinking through his day's agenda. First, he'd pay a visit to the people who'd called him out here in the first place—Jamerson Stewart and his son, Jimmy Jr, owners of the Hell's Jaw Rail Line. Then, since he was heading north toward the McCrae Triangle Ranch, he'd ride that way with Lori then take a little side trip to investigate the scene of the massacre.

Thinking of Lori, he also considered what the little blond succubus, Ivy Russell, had hinted about her. That she wasn't all that she appeared to be on the surface.

But, then, who was?

Stockburn knew to take Ivy with a big grain of salt. She was likely more than a little jealous of Lori McCrae's moneyed station in life, which was understandable. Ivy was also more than a little devilish. Stockburn had found that out firsthand. Twisted ankle, his foot!

He chuckled at the wounded fawn routine, the mocking glitter in the shameless coquette's lilac eyes. Still, he'd keep in mind what she'd told him. He'd be a fool not to chase down every lead, even every hint of a lead, including uncorroborated, probably fabricated innuendo.

He was well off the beaten path out here, a total stranger. It would take him a while to get his land legs, to be able to sift the wheat from the chaff with confidence. Right now, he was getting the unadulterated grain.

He finished the whiskey, stubbed out the Indian Kid, and headed back to the Cosmopolitan for breakfast. As could be expected, he was met with more than a few incredulous stares upon entering the place, for the blood stains on the floor were still fresh. As were memories of last night.

The window through which Kreg Hennessey's bouncer had thrown the bungstarter had not yet been repaired. A cool morning breeze blew through the jagged break in the glass, along with the high strains of birdsong.

He swabbed the last of his ham, fried potatoes, and four fried eggs with the last of his grainy wheat toast, finished his coffee, stubbed out his second cheroot of the day, set his hat on his head, and grabbed the rifle from where he'd placed it across a corner of his table.

He headed outside. He'd fetched Smoke from the feed barn and tied the smoky gray stallion to the hitchrack fronting the restaurant.

Now he glanced around at the lightening street, which was a little busier than before he'd entered the restaurant though not by much, it still being before eight, then slid the rifle into its scabbard and pulled himself into the leather. As he did, he noticed a man standing back against the side of the Cosmopolitan's front wall, near the broken window.

The man wore a shabby suit coat over gold-and-brown checked vest and baggy broadcloth trousers. He wore a high-crowned black Stetson that had apparently weathered the abuse of many high-country storms and possibly crows pecking on its brim.

He himself looked a little like a crow, with narrow eyes, long nose, and sharp, upturned chin. Three days' worth of beard stubble darkened his pale features.

He wore two pistols on his hips. They were

easy to see, for the man had tucked the flaps of his coat back behind the handles.

He stood leaning back against the wall, the sole of one boot planted against the wall as well, arms crossed on his chest, staring blankly but insinuatingly at Stockburn, a weed stem drooping from between his thin lips.

Stockburn had been about to turn Smoke out into the street but he rendered the maneuver stillborn and frowned at the man eyeing him darkly from beneath the ragged brim of his black hat. "Can I help you?"

The man said, "Nah. Just got a message from Mister Hennessey's all."

"All right."

"He said to tell you good morning."

"Good morning?"

"Yep. Said to tell you good morning." The man grinned, the weed stem slipping out from between his lips to flutter to and fro on the breeze as it fell to the manure-crusted boardwalk beneath the crow-faced man's boots. "Said to tell you good morning and to have a nice day."

He held his mocking smile on Stockburn.

"He did, did he?"

"Yessir, he sure did."

"Hmm." Stockburn considered the message, nodding. He swung down from the saddle and dropped Smoke's reins. As he stepped around the hitchrail and mounted the boardwalk fronting the

Cosmopolitan, the stranger's smile faded slowly from his lips and a look of incredulity entered his small, dark eyes.

Stockburn stood before the man, staring into the man's eyes. He gave a phony smile as he said, "Wasn't that nice of him?"

The man smiled again, but this time it wasn't as confident and jeering as it was before. It seemed a little nervous, tentative. "Why . . . it sure was." He chuckled.

"What's your name, son?"

The man frowned. "Huh?"

"What's your name?"

"Why?"

"What's your name?" Stockburn asked, louder.

"Cove. Stanley Cove."

"I tell you what, Stanley Cove. Let's go over to the Wind River so I can return the friendly gesture."

Again, the man frowned. "Huh?"

"Get moving!" Stockburn gave the man a hard shove to the left, toward the Wind River, which sat on the opposite side of the side street from the Cosmopolitan.

"Hey, get your damn hands off'n me!"

As Cove tried to swing toward him, Stockburn gave him another hard shove. Cove went stumbling into the street, nearly falling.

"Damn you—what the hell you think you're doin'?" Cove said, getting his boots beneath him once more and trying to swing toward Stockburn again, raising his right fist.

Stockburn stepped into the man, gave him another hard shove. As Cove went stumbling toward the big, ornate, clapboard building on the other side of the street, Stockburn kicked him in the ass.

Cove gave an indignant cry and went flying, arms and legs pinwheeling, up onto the boardwalk, tripping over the edge of the walk then falling on top of it and sliding up against the Wind River's two stout, brass-handled doors.

"Damn you to hell!" Cove cried, slapping leather and whipping out one of his walnut-gripped six-shooters.

As he angled the gun up toward Stockburn, Wolf stepped onto the boardwalk and drove the toe of his right boot against Cove's wrist. Cove screamed as the six-shooter flew up out of his hand to bounce off the doors then tumble back onto the boardwalk with a heavy thud, spinning off the boardwalk and into the street.

Cove gritted his teeth and clutched his injured wrist with his other hand. "Oh, you black-hearted cuss—you broke my *wrist!*"

Stockburn crouched to jerk the man up by his arms. He reached his hand around the man to pull open one of the two heavy doors then kicked the man inside. Cove gave another scream as he flew down the four shallow steps to the floor of the big main casino and saloon.

"What the hell's goin' on?" yelled a big man behind the large, ornate, horseshoe bar to the right. He'd looked up from reading the newspaper spread on the polished oak bar before him.

"The boss in?" Stockburn asked.

"He's upstairs with his son!"

"Tell him Wolf Stockburn just wanted to stop in and say good-morning, will ya?" Stockburn crouched again, jerked Cove to his feet then tossed him forward, onto a big baize-covered craps table sitting in the middle of the room.

Again, Cove screamed and clutched his wrist. He turned onto his side and bellowed, "Black-hearted son of Satan!"

"Are you crazy?" bellowed the barman.

There were maybe a half-dozen men in the place—four standing at the bar, half-turned toward Stockburn and Stanley Cove, and two men in business suits sitting at a table against the front wall, to Wolf's right. They were eating ham and eggs and drinking beer.

A door opened on the balcony running along the rear of the room. Kreg Hennessey stepped onto the balcony. He moved across the balcony to stand with his hand on the rail, staring down into the main drinking and gambling hall.

He looked blankly down at Stockburn and at Cove lying atop the craps table, grimacing and groaning and clutching his wrist, which hung at an odd angle from his arm.

Hennessey closed both his hands around the balcony rail, tightening his grip until his knuckles turned white.

Stockburn glared up at the saloon owner and said, "If you have any messages for me in the future, Hennessey—good-morning or otherwise—be man enough to deliver them yourself."

Stockburn wheeled, climbed the steps to the front door, then pushed through the door to step out onto the boardwalk. He turned left and started across the side street, slowing his pace when he saw Ivy Russell standing against the hitchrack near where Smoke stood, the horse's reins dangling.

Ivy leaned back against the rail, arms crossed on her chest. She wore the same clothes as last night—wool shirt and suspenders and faded denims and boots—but she'd brushed her hair and washed her face.

She grinned at Stockburn walking toward her. "Up early making new friends?"

Stockburn stepped past the girl and grabbed his reins. "You can't have too many friends, Ivy—you know that."

CHAPTER 10

Stockburn followed the spur line rails north to where the Hell's Jaw Company's office sat, on the east side of the recently laid tracks and about a hundred yards from the northeast end of Wild Horse. The building was a long, story-and-a-half wood frame structure without frills—purely utilitarian by design. It wasn't even painted.

The company office appeared to be on the structure's left side, behind a door and two sashed windows, one on each side of the door. A simple shingle over the door identified the place as Hell's Jaw Railroad, Jamerson Stewart— Jamerson Stewart, Jr., Props.

To the right side of the building appeared a warehouse or supply shed, several hundred feet square. It had a pair of closed double doors, not unlike the main doors of a livery barn. Behind the building were a stable and corral and several heavy wagons, tongues drooping, as well as piles of new rails and railroad ties that filled the air around the place with the smell of pine tar. In fact, Stockburn had first detected the odor of the pine tar, used to weatherproof the ties, even before he had left the town proper.

Smoke rose from a stove pipe poking out of the building's slightly pitched, shake-shingled roof, on the office side. The elevation here was high, and though it was early September, the mornings and evenings were cool. Loud voices sounded from inside the place, too muffled for Wolf to hear.

He dismounted, tied Smoke at the hitchrail, and mounted the awning-covered porch. As he did, he could hear the voices more clearly now, one man saying, ". . . just yesterday evening and he's already left a path of death behind him!"

Another man said, "He was jailed for several hours and then Wally Stigen saw him enter the Territorial Hotel with Lori McCrae clinging to him like they were newly married man and wife!"

"What kind of man did Wells Fargo send me, anyway?"

Wolf decided not to knock. Instead, he tripped the latch, shoved open the door, and poked his head into the office with a wolfish grin. "A busy one, I'll tell you that!"

The three men in the cluttered, smoky office jerked startled looks toward the door. Two were dressed in suits. These were obviously father and son Stewart.

They were not only physically the spitting image of each other despite an age difference of twenty-five or so years, they were dressed almost identically, as well. They even wore the same round, steel-framed spectacles on identically shaped noses above identical mustaches, though

113

the father's 'stache had some traces of gray in it.

The third man, sitting casually in a Windsor chair with his back to the building's left wall, was dressed less formally in a cream shirt, string tie, corduroy jacket, and denim trousers. A cream Stetson hung from a knee of a crossed leg. A brown paper quirley sent a curl of smoke into the shadows above his right hand, which was draped casually over a chair arm.

The three men flushed with surprise and sheepishness. The flush in the more plainly dressed man was closely followed by a smile.

"Stockburn?" the elder Stewart said. He sat behind a large desk, his back to the rear wall. An angry scowl furled his brow. He had a pen in his hand and several open account books before him.

Wolf stepped into the room, doffing his hat and closing the door behind him. "I'd have knocked but I figured you were expecting me. Apparently, you knew I was in town."

"Indeed, we did, Mister Stockburn!" This from the young Jamerson, who sat at a desk, slightly smaller than his father's desk, facing the wall to Stockburn's right. A long, slender black cheroot burned in an ashtray near his own pile of account books and ledger.

He slid his chair back, rose, and turned to face the detective. "Good Lord—you certainly know how to make an entrance, don't you?"

"Sorry. Should've knocked."

The elder Jamerson rose from his own desk, showing Wolf that the father was several inches shorter than his otherwise nearly identical offspring. "He meant your entrance into Wild Horse. Good Lord, what do you do—travel the country seeing how many new notches you can add to your pistol grips?"

"Well, I—"

The other man rose from the Windsor chair to Stockburn's left, smiling, holding his hat in his hands. "Did you really kill that little snake, Riley Hennessey?"

Jamerson Jr. scowled at the man, "Paul, it's no laughing matter."

"It's not a laughing matter," Stockburn said. "But it would have been a lot less funny to the McCrae family if I hadn't snuffed that little polecat's wick. As for Kreg Hennessey—he's the one who started the dance last night in the Cosmopolitan. I finished the hoe-down to keep from being fitted for a wooden overcoat this morning instead of heading over here to get started after the men who killed your rail crew."

He fingered the goose egg on his temple. "Albeit with a bit of a headache."

"And Lori McCrae?" the man called Paul asked with another delighted smile on his rugged-featured face. He was not a tall man, but, even slightly pot-bellied, he had the look of a working

115

man, not a pencil-pusher and bean counter like the Stewarts.

The older Stewart said from behind his large, messy desk, "If you've gotten us crossways with the McCrae family, too . . ."

"Ah, there's nothing for them to get crossways with you about. One, I'm a big boy. I can stand for myself. Two, Lori McCrae and I got to be friends. Just sort of happened after that jasper Hennessey pulled her off the train and I had to put him down like the rabid dog he was."

"Was it she who bailed you out of jail?" Paul asked with that smile again that said he wasn't nearly as bothered by the whole affair as father and son Stewart were. In fact, he appeared well entertained.

"No one bailed me out of jail. Her lawyer, Powderhorn, threatened to drag Russell in front of a judge."

"Oh, right," Paul said. "No, no—Watt Russell wouldn't want to answer to no judge." Smiling down at his hat, he chuckled and shook his head.

The elder Stewart drew a deep, tolerant breath, filling up his chest and throwing his shoulders back, chin up. "Mister Stockburn, it's very important that you give our matter your full attention. You can't afford to be distracted by Kreg Hennessey or Watt Russell or, or . . ."

"Lori McCrae," Paul said, jostling the hat in his hands.

"Or Lori McCrae," scolded the younger Stewart.

Or Ivy Russell, Stockburn silently opined, then covered the grin threatening to spread his lips by brushing his fist across his chin and clearing his throat. If they didn't know about Ivy's visit to his room last night, on the heels of Lori's visit, all the better, since the Stewarts seemed to have their drawers in a twist.

"I always give business matters my full attention, Mister Stewart."

The elder Stewart drew his mouth corners down, nodded, then came out from around the desk to extend his right hand. "Proper introductions are in order. I'm Jamerson Stewart."

"How do you do? Wolf Stockburn at your service."

Junior stepped forward to shake Stockburn's hand, as well. "Jamerson, Jr. Call me James. My father goes by Jamerson."

"Pleased to meet you," Stockburn said, shaking the young man's hand. He judged the younger Stewart to be in his late twenties.

The older Stewart, somewhere in his late fifties, gestured toward the other man in the room. "This is Paul Reynolds. He's the ramrod of our rail crew. At least, he was when we still had a crew."

"Pleased to meet you, Reynolds," Stockburn said as the ramrod walked up to shake hands.

"Pleasure's mine. I've heard a lot about you. Sounds like you're the man for the job."

"I reckon the proof will be in the pudding."

"Mister Stockburn," said the elder Stewart, "would you like to sit down, perhaps enjoy a cup of coffee with us? I was just brewing a fresh pot."

He glanced at the potbelly stove in the room's corner on which a black pot ticked and thumped as coffee started to boil.

"I had plenty for breakfast. I'd just as soon get headed up to where the massacre happened as soon as possible. I've gone over the file the company provided several times on my journey from Kansas." Stockburn looked at the elder Stewart. "I just have a couple of questions. Were those men that were killed the only men you had on your payroll?"

Stewart nodded. "I'm afraid so. There were fourteen including a cook and a horse wrangler. All dead. Paul was spared because he'd returned to town for a meeting with James and myself. We like to keep up to date on the progress up there, and as yet there is no telegraph operating between Wild Horse and the end-of-track. There won't be one until the rail line is finished all the way to Hell's Jaw Pass."

"You got lucky, Reynolds," Stockburn said.

"Lucky, I guess. I sure wish I'd been there to help. Some of those dead men were close friends of mine."

"You couldn't have helped, Paul, and you know it," the elder Stewart assured the man. Returning

118

his gaze to Stockburn, he said, "The raiders came at night when all of the men were asleep in their tents. They were wiped out likely within minutes."

"I found them when I rode back up there the next day," Reynolds said. His previous humor had vanished, and it was a grave-faced, angry man speaking to Stockburn now. "Some of them lay dead on their cots. A few had grabbed guns and ran outside in their longhandles only to be cut down close to their tents. I doubt if more than a couple managed to snap off any return fire at all. Those men that lay wounded were finished off"—the foreman placed two fingers to his forehead—"with a bullet to the head. Fired at close range. I was in the Indian Wars. I know what close-range bullets look like."

The foreman sighed, shook his head. "Whoever pulled that lowdown dirty trick were about as lowdown dirty mean as men can get."

"Professional killers, most likely," James Stewart said.

"Hired by who?" Stockburn glanced at each man in turn.

The men looked at each other, hesitant, vaguely sheepish.

"What?" Stockburn said with a wry chuckle. "You want me to guess?"

The elder and younger Stewarts shared another silently conferring look, then the older man

119

settled his brown-eyed gaze on Wolf. "We think it's someone from the McCrae Triangle Ranch."

Wolf was nudged by genuine surprise. "Why's that?"

"The raiders did a pretty good job of covering their tracks, but I managed to follow some sign onto Triangle graze."

"It could be they merely crossed the Triangle, or circled back, hoping to confuse trackers," Stockburn said. "I thought Norman McCrae owned a percentage of the company."

"He does," said Jamerson Stewart. "But his oldest boy, Lawton, was dead-set against the rail line. He'll inherit the Triangle one day—probably not too long down the road, in fact—and he's always hated the fact that gold was discovered above the Triangle. He thinks our spur line will encourage more prospecting, more mining . . . more rustling."

"Some of the independent prospectors," said the younger Stewart, "are poor men living remotely. Some right on Triangle graze. Or on what Lawton calls Triangle graze even though up there it's all officially government land. Norman doesn't mind feeding a hungry prospector or two, but Law, as he's called, sees the problem as an existential threat to Triangle. If more and more outsiders move onto so-called Triangle land . . ."

"He's a bit of a hothead, Law," put in Reynolds. "Nothing like the Hennessey boy, but

. . . he's bullheaded. Scrappy when pushed. Even scrappier when he's been drinking. He's also greedy."

The older Steward said, "Just like his old man used to be, when he was younger. He's settled down some now in his later years, Norman has."

"Maybe a little." The younger man seemed reluctant to agree.

Stockburn raked a thumbnail down his cheek, pondering.

Finally, he turned to the elder Stewart. "What about McRae's rival rancher?"

"Rufus Stoleberg?" The older Stewart shook his head. "Nah. I wouldn't think so."

"Why not?"

"He don't have a dog in the fight."

"He hates McCrae, doesn't he? Because he lost the sale of the right-of-way?"

"Sure, but he wouldn't try to ruin us just because of his age-old feud with Triangle. McCrae has a percentage in the Hell's Jaw Line, but it's not enough to do Norman any real damage if we went under. He doesn't really need that kickback. He's rich in beef."

"Besides," Reynolds added, "Rufus Stoleberg is way more, shall we say, *direct?* If he killed men, they wouldn't be our men. They'd be McCrae's men, sure enough." He gave a dark chuckle. "Nah, he's too busy just surviving on second-rate graze," the ramrod added, "to go to war with us."

"I agree," said the younger Stewart. "Rufus Stoleberg would save his lead for McCrae."

"All right, then." Stockburn turned and walked to the window right of the door, and peered out, thoughtful. After a time, he turned back to the three men facing him expectantly. He glanced at the stove. "You're coffee's boiling, gentlemen. I'll be on my way."

"Would you like me to ride up to the sight of the massacre with you, Stockburn?" Reynolds asked.

"Thanks, but that won't be necessary. I'd like to check it out on my own. Besides, I already have a guide."

Stockburn grinned as he hooked a thumb to indicate Lori McCrae looking fresh as a spring daisy and straddling a fine sorrel filly just beyond the office window.

"Good morning, young lady," Wolf said as he stepped out of the Hell's Jaw Railroad office. "You look every bit as ravishing as this late summer morning!"

"Oh, stop it, you charmer. I know about you." Lori glowered down at him, pooching her red lips out in mock anger. She was dressed in a tailored riding outfit with a split skirt and wasp-waisted blouse open at the neck and a black silk choker trimmed with a fat, glistening pearl. Gold-buckled, black patent riding boots climbed nearly to her knees. Besides the choker around her neck, she also wore a red silk kerchief whose long tapering ends blew in the breeze.

She wore her thick, lovely chestnut hair down about her shoulders, a few strands braided and tied behind her head. A felt hat, the same color as the skirt of her riding dress, shaded her face with its broad brim.

Stockburn stopped. "What do you know about me?"

"I know who paid a visit to your room last night—not fifteen minutes after I left. Ivy Russell."

Stockburn grinned as he untied his reins from the hitchrail. "Well, darlin', I never let on I was a one-woman man. Say, where's all those steam trunks and portmanteaus I saw the porter killing himself to haul over to the hotel yesterday?"

"I'm having it delivered by wagon later. But the subject was Ivy Russell. Steer clear of her, Wolf. She is as ugly on the inside as she is pretty—albeit in a rather crude and rough way—on the outside."

"Oh?"

"She's a conniver. She's always working both ends against the middle. Everybody knows that about Ivy. Smart men steer clear."

"And dumber men?"

Lori arched a brow with meaning.

"Hmmm." Stockburn swung up into the leather, absently marveling at the similarities in the girls' warnings to him about each other. "It's not serious, I assure you. We just had a little whiskey and . . . well, she did show me her ankle but only because she was feigning injury."

"That harlot!"

"I gotta admit it was a pretty ankle but obviously uninjured." Stockburn chuckled as he reined Smoke out away from the railroad office and booted him northeast along the trail paralleling the newly laid spur rails.

"You're a shameless cad!" Lori accused as she trotted up beside him, her hair bouncing on her shoulders, the crisp golden sunshine dancing in the tumbling tresses.

Laughing again, Wolf said, "I've been called far worse than that by some much less easy on the eyes than you."

"I have a feeling you have." She tossed him a saucy smile and a wink.

"Say, what ends against what middle do you think Ivy is working on me?"

"I don't know," Lori said. "But you can bet she is." She narrowed a warning eye. "Just watch your back."

"Oh, believe me, darlin'—I was born with eyes in the back of my head." Wolf had a feeling that second set of eyes was going to come into particularly good use here around Wild Horse.

"Beautiful, isn't it?" Lori asked an hour later as she and Stockburn followed the rails northeast of Wild Horse and into the rocky dikes and cedar-stippled canyons of the southwestern flank of the Wind River Mountains.

"Certainly is."

"This is Big Sandy Creek," she said, glancing at the wide, dark, sun-dappled creek that tumbled through the wolf willows and purple mountain sage to their right, on the opposite side of the newly laid and still intact spur line rails. "That peak ahead and left is Desolation."

"Good name for it." The gray, cone-shaped crag looked like a massive, spade-shaped rock tipped with the dirty white of last winter's snow.

"Straight ahead is Philsmith Peak." Lori threw up a glove hand, pointing, gradually sliding her arm from left to right. "That one is Gannett Peak. Henderson is over there, Klondike Peak that way, and way over there, nearly out of sight to the south, is Jackson."

"Breathtaking."

The surroundings really were.

As Wolf and the girl followed the rails into the mouth of a canyon through which Big Sandy Creek tumbled toward the lowland on which Wild Horse lay below and behind them, the crisp air grew winey with the smell of cold rock, snowmelt rivers, pine resin, cottonwoods, and aspens. The deep green grass that turned shorter, browner, and yellower as they climbed higher and deeper into the mountains, rippled like a rug on a clothes line, and was swept with cloud shadows.

As the riders followed a curve in the rails as well as the canyon floor and the creek on their right, Stockburn spied a black-tailed doe and a fawn tugging on wild berry branches on the creek's opposite side. The deer were partly shaded by the high, pine-covered slope behind them to the northeast, but the morning sun laid a glistening gold stripe across their sleek, fawn-colored front quarters.

Their dark-brown eyes regarded the two passing riders with mute interest; they twitched their big ears as they chewed the berry leaves, moving their mouths nearly in unison with each other, from side to side.

Eyeing the strangers warily, the little fawn, a third of its mother's size, stepped up close to the doe for protection and reassurance then lifted its left hind leg suddenly and angled its head back to snatch a bug from its spotted-furred flank.

As it lowered its leg, Wolf could hear beneath the creek's quiet rippling the soft thud of the hoof set down on the grassy turf. Black flies glinted like dust motes in the red-hued sunshine, contrasted against the dark shadow of the mountain behind.

Crows cawed from the high tip of a fire-blackened spruce to the left of the rails.

"It's hard to leave a place this beautiful," Lori said, looking around with a pensive expression, her voice pitched with a curious sadness. "No matter how much you need to leave . . . know you should leave . . . know that you should follow your family's wishes . . ."

The girl shook her head, her eyes following the three crows lighting from the top of the spruce and flapping their large, black wings out over the creek. "Still . . . it's hard." She glanced at Wolf riding on her left. "It's like leaving heaven."

"Is that why you came back?" Stockburn asked, unable to resist the urge to pry—a professional habit that he could forgive himself for.

"I don't know. No." Again, she shook her head, her thoughts and emotions obviously in conflict with one another. "I don't know," she repeated. "I suppose, partly." She looked at him again across her slender left shoulder. "There are other things. Other reasons I can't go into."

She turned her head forward again, leaving it at that.

They followed the rails into a broad open valley hemmed in on both sides by steep stone walls tufted with hardy-looking conifers and occasional pockets of aspens to which dark-gold leaves flashed like new pennies in the lens-clear light.

Stockburn had been noticing cow plop along the trail they'd been following—some of it old and flaky, some relatively fresh. Now as they passed a copse of aspens mixed with white-stemmed birches and a few cottonwoods, he spied several cows, two dark-brown ones and their calves born earlier in the spring, one heifer, and a large brindle cow with two big-shouldered, curly-headed bull calves. One of the young bulls was just then trying to mount the other.

"Boys will be boys," Lori quipped.

"Are those your father's?"

"I think so. I can't see the brands from here. This is open range, though, so the herds get mixed. They'll be gathered soon if they aren't already, and driven down to the lower pastures for the winter." Lori pointed again, this time to the left side of the rails. "Do you see that break there?"

Stockburn followed her gaze to a gap in the canyon wall, roughly a hundred feet wide.

"That's the trail to my father's Triangle headquarters." Lori slid her arm to the right, pointing with her gloved finger now to another, larger break in the wall to the east of the rails and beyond a broad, sunlit meadow that appeared to have been shorn recently of its grass by cattle. "That gap there leads down to Rufus Stoleberg's Tin Cup spread."

"Drier over there on that side, I take it?" Wolf asked.

Lori nodded, drawing her mouth corners down as though with sadness. "Most of the moisture falls on our side of the mountains. Stoleberg's spread is on the southeastern flank. By the time the clouds roll over his place, they've already spent most of their moisture on us."

"That doesn't appear to make you all that happy, if you don't mind me saying so, Lori."

Lori glanced at him, one brow arched. "Why should it? That lack of moisture has meant the difference between my father's relative wealth and Stoleberg's poverty. Well, not poverty, but close to it, anyway. No man's misfortune makes me happy. Besides, the difference has made both men truculent and sour in their relations with each other.

"Stoleberg makes an adequate living for a cattleman—especially now with the markets so fickle—but the nasty twist of fate in him happening to build his ranch on the wrong side of Desolation Peak, and my father's happening to build his on the right side, drove a wedge between the two men. Between our families. It made my father happy and wealthy. It made Stoleberg surly and bitter." She added, after a brief, brooding pause, "His family has suffered."

"Oh?" Stockburn asked. "How so?"

Lori rode along, thinking, then turned to Wolf and said with a forlorn air, "They just have—that's all, Wolf."

"All right, then." The girl was a puzzle, Stockburn reflected. A puzzle with secrets. He couldn't help remembering Ivy's warning about Lori. But, then, Lori had issued her own warning about Ivy.

Damned right confounding . . .

Lori turned her head forward again, then said, "Whoah!" and drew back on her horse's reins. As the horse stopped, blowing and shaking its head, switching its tail at black flies, Lori dipped her chin to indicate the railbed ahead of them. "Looks like we've come to the end of the line, Wolf."

Stockburn halted Smoke and then followed the girl's gaze along the fresh rails to where the two, arrow-straight lines of steel became badly twisted and separated, angling off to each side of the bed like a peeled banana.

"We must be approaching the sight of the massacre," Lori said, rising up in her stirrups to gaze farther ahead along the ruined rails.

"I'll take it from here, young lady," Stockburn said. "I might be awhile, sniffing around. Why don't you ride on to the Triangle and announce yourself to your family?"

The girl turned to Stockburn, frowning. "I'm not in any hurry to do that, Wolf. I can wait for you."

"I don't want to delay you. Besides, your homecoming is a personal matter." Wolf smiled.

Lori studied him, scowling. She pooched out her lips and nodded. "I suppose you're right. All right—into the breech, I reckon. You'll be along shortly? I can't wait to show off the famous rail detective who saved my life . . . and killed that hydrophobic dog, Riley Hennessey," she added with a curled nostril.

"Indeed, I will."

"All right, then. Good luck, Wolf. I hope you find some clues."

"I do, too."

When the girl had galloped off to the left side of the canyon, heading toward the gap in the cliff wall showing where the trail to the Triangle branched away to the west, Stockburn slowly slid his Yellowboy from its scabbard jutting up from under his right thigh. He cocked the Winchester one-handed.

Setting the hammer to half-cocked with his gloved right thumb, he rested the barrel on his saddle pommel and shuttled his narrowed gaze to the right side of the canyon where, two minutes before, he'd spied a rider moving furtively amongst the forest beyond the creek.

At least, he thought he had. Now, gazing in that direction, he wasn't so sure that what he'd seen hadn't been a trick of the wind, light, and shadows. He saw nothing now but the trees with their boughs and branches dancing in the wind, the wood making occasional, eerie creaking sounds.

If he had seen a rider, it might only have been a rider from one of the nearby outfits keeping an eye on the herd though he'd been doing so with a mighty furtive air about him.

Stockburn perused the forest on the canyon's south end carefully one more time. Not spying the rider—if *there had been a rider*—he nudged Smoke forward along the trail. He kept the Yellowboy in his right hand, index finger curled through the guard, drawn up taut against the trigger.

He'd keep those two eyes in the back of his head wide open. Hennessey might have sent a man to put a bullet in his back.

He booted the horse into a trot, perusing the

bent and twisted rails as he rode. Whoever had vandalized the rails had put some effort into it. The rail bed showed the craters of where dynamite had been detonated, blowing the rails up out of the ground and throwing them wide.

In some places, the rails appeared iron jackstraws lying in various angles along the bed and down its sides. The tracks had been vandalized to the point they couldn't merely be reset upon the ties but would have to be replaced. There were a lot of them, too, which meant the need for many replacements at great expense.

The modesty of the small office and grounds had told Wolf the Hell's Jaw line was not a wealthy company. At least, he didn't think it had money to spare. Destruction like this could hamstring the Stewarts, which is most likely what the man or men who'd sent the killers had intended.

Finding out the reason to affect such an atrocity might very well lead Stockburn to the culprits.

A hundred yards beyond the first of the destroyed rails, he rode up on more destruction. The work train that had supplied the workers at the end of the tracks had been blasted off the rails.

There was a locomotive, a tender car, a flatbed that had transported the rails and ties, and an equipment car, which would have hauled the sledgehammers, tongs, shovels, bars, and kegs of spikes and bolts and the plates for fastening the rail ends together.

The last car, which lay a burned-out hulk on its side beside the rail bed, was a bunk car though apparently the workers had opted to sleep outside this time of year. Bunk cars were notoriously cramped and uncomfortable.

The white canvas tents—or what was left of them—lay off to the right side of the rails, maybe a hundred yards away, near the creek that curved between the tents and the pine-stippled ridge. That was where the workers had been killed, some while still asleep, others while scrambling to their feet and grabbing pistols and rifles to combat the attackers.

Continuing to keep a wary eye skinned on the forest beyond the creek, in case he had an ill-intentioned shadow, Wolf rode through the wreckage of rails and blasted cars. He scoured the ground for clues.

What those clues might entail, he had no idea. He'd likely know if and when he found something. The problem was that the massacre had occurred three weeks ago, so the weather had likely scoured away any sign of hoof or boot prints the killers might have left behind.

When he found nothing around the work train and the strewn rails, he turned Smoke toward the tents, most of which had been leveled, the soiled pale canvas and the ropes flapping in the wind.

He'd just ridden up to some brown-stained sage—the brown being old blood shed by one of the murdered workers—when the eerie whine of what could only be a heavy-caliber bullet preceded the heavy *thunk!* of that bullet slamming into the ground jarringly close to Smoke's right front hoof.

The stallion gave a screeching cry of deep indignation, and reared. Since he still had his right hand wrapped around the Yellowboy's neck, Wolf had a hard time reaching for the horn.

Too hard a time. He missed it.

He gave a bellowing yell of shock and fury as he went flying ass over teakettle over the smoky gray stallion's arched tail.

CHAPTER 12

Stockburn struck the ground hard on his chest and belly. The air was punched from his lungs. His head spun. His ears rang.

"Damn!"

He rose to his hands and knees, spat grit from his lips. He shook his head to clear the cobwebs. He heard the thuds of his fleeing horse.

"Thanks, Smoke. Appreciate that."

Again, came that eerie whine. Stockburn's heart turned a somersault half a wink before the heavy-caliber round slammed into the ground four inches to the right of his right hand. It blew up dirt, gravel, and a chunk of sod, throwing it over his hand. The sulfur smell of hot lead assaulted his nose.

The thundering roar of the big rifle vaulted around the valley, fading and swirling as it climbed skyward.

Stockburn saw his Winchester lying a few feet away on his right. He rolled toward it, grabbed it, and looked around for cover.

Damned little.

The ground within a good two hundred square feet was nearly pancake flat. His heart raced. He knew the bushwhacker was drawing a bead on him. He could feel it like a hot dime pressed to his forehead.

He sucked a breath and threw himself to the right again, rolling.

Good thing he had. Again came that consarned whine. It was like the ghost of a moaning old whore, growing louder as she approached the crest of her pleasure. The bullet slammed into the turf just behind where Wolf had been before he'd rolled.

That one would have taken his head off.

"You son of a bitch!"

Stockburn took a quick look toward the southeastern ridge. That's where the bullets were coming from. He spied movement atop a cluster of rocks on the ridge wall about thirty feet down from the crest. He didn't risk getting his head shot off for a second look. That was the shooter, all right.

He took another breath then cursed sharply as he rolled to his left. He rolled again, hearing that whore's ghost give another tooth-gnashing moan that grew louder . . . and louder . . . until—WHAM!!

The bullet plowed into the ground where he'd been a second before, uprooting a sage tuft, tossing it along with a handful of gravel high in the air and back toward the ruined rails.

The thundering crash of the big-caliber rifle followed a second later, echoing like thunder around the canyon.

Stockburn fired another look toward the ridge.

White smoke rose from that cluster of rocks, just above where a rifle barrel rested on a rock, pointing toward him. Above the rifle was the low crown of a black hat topping the dark oval of a man's face silhouetted against the rocks behind it.

"You son of a bitch!"

Again, Wolf rolled, this time back to the right.

Another whine . . . another bullet plowing up rocks, dirt, and bits of sage where he'd just been.

Wolf, having recovered somewhat from his fall from his horse, heaved himself to his feet. The only cover was the forest on the other side of the stream, where the trees formed a tongue shape as they pushed out from the base of the ridge wall, to the right of where the bushwhacker was shooting from. He had to cross the stream and get into those trees. Using the cover of the trees, he could work his way to the ridge wall and get within range of his Yellowboy and return fire on the cowardly bushwhacker and his large-caliber gun—a Sharps Big Fifty or some similar-caliber sporting rifle, Wolf figured.

A bullet the size of those being fired at him could cut a man nearly in two.

He took off running as hard and as fast as he could, leaving his hat behind him on the ground. He held the Yellowboy in his right hand.

The bastard on the ridge had reloaded the single-shot rifle by now. He was fast, might have been a buffalo hunter back when there were still buffalo. Most likely, he'd slid another long cartridge into the rifle's breech. He'd clicked the rifle's heavy hammer back. He was squinting down the long, octagonal barrel, taking aim again.

Trying to draw a bead on his target.

"Here we go!" Wolf said to himself, swerving sharply to the right.

He'd hoped the next shot would come then, just when he'd swerved to avoid it. No dice. The bastard was still tracking him, trying to line up the sights on him.

Gritting his teeth against the cold fear of knowing the next bullet could come at any time and shred his heart or blow the back of his head onto the ground behind him, Stockburn swerved again.

The shot came—the eerie whine growing louder until it was replaced by a sharp *spang* as the big bullet ricocheted off a rock just over Wolf's left shoulder.

"Missed, you coward!" Wolf shouted, shaking his left fist in the air.

He continued running.

"I have three seconds," he told himself. "It takes him three, four seconds to seat a fresh round. Three seconds to reload, another couple of seconds for that black-hearted cuss to line up the sights. That means . . ." He swerved sharply to his right, ducking. "He's shooting now!"

He'd no sooner spat the "now" from his lips than the moan came again, growing louder.

Thump-PEWWW!!! went the bullet hammering into the ground behind Wolf but not before warming and curling the air the breadth of a cat's whisker off his right ear.

"Close one!" Wolf leaped off the creek's low bank and into the water. "That's all right," he mused, breathless. "Save the barber from having to cut the hair out of that ear next time I go in for a trim!"

He ran hard, throwing his rifle and left arm out for balance, negotiating the slippery rocks polished by the shallow stream. He counted to five then stopped suddenly and ducked.

The bullet didn't come.

"Damn!"

Wolf took off running again. The water was maybe six to eight inches deep through this broad stretch of stream. It splashed up around his hips as he ran.

Glancing to his left, he saw smoke puff above the barrel of the rifle on the ridge. He swerved sharply and ducked. As he did, his left boot slipped on a rock and he fell forward, dropping his left hand to the bed of the stream, catching himself.

Again, he was lucky. The shooter must have anticipated Stockburn's sudden swerve and duck, because the bullet sang through the air only inches above Wolf's head—where his head *would have been* had he not slipped on the rock and fallen forward.

"The fella means business!" Wolf heaved himself to his feet and continued running.

He reached the stream's far side just as another bullet caromed toward him and kissed the nap of his coat collar on the left side of his neck.

He ran.

One more stride. Two more strides . . .

Another bullet moaned.

Stockburn's third stride carried him into the forest beyond the stream.

The bullet thudded sharply into a tree just as Wolf ran past it and into the forest. Bits of bark and slivers of wood rained through the air around him, pattering onto the spongy forest floor. He dropped to his hands and knees, drawing air in and out of his lungs, trying to catch his breath.

"I smoke too damn much, methinks."

More bullets caromed toward him, thumping into trees. The trees offered good cover. Glancing around an aspen, he could see the ridge from which the shooter was continuing to fire at him even though he was no longer a good target.

The man was madder than an old wet hen. He was firing out of frustration. He should have cored his target before Wolf had made it to the stream, but he hadn't.

"Not as good as you think you are, you fork-tailed devil!"

Stockburn rose and trotted forward. His wet boots squawked on the soft ground, crunching fallen leaves. His wet pants hung on him. They were cold, but he was too hot from the fury and the hard run to be chilled.

Trotting, meandering around trees and leaping over blowdowns, he quartered to his left, approaching the base of the ridge. He came to where the forest ended, and dropped down behind an uprooted cottonwood, the giant ball of roots and dirt mounding up to his right.

He stayed low but inched a look over the top of the cottonwood, casting his gaze up the ridge.

The nest of rocks was fifty feet up from the base of the ridge. He could see the barrel of the big rifle resting on a rock. He could also see the crown of the shooter's black hat. The man was cheeked up against the rifle's rear stock, probably aiming through a sliding rear sight ladder.

The son of a bitch was aiming into the trees on Wolf's left.

Looking for his quarry.

Stockburn stretched his mustached upper lip back from his upper teeth in a cold grin and said under his breath, "You're my prey now, you black-hearted coward!"

He raised the Yellowboy, rested the barrel on the top of the cottonwood's trunk. He lined up the sights a little above the barrel of the bushwhacker's rifle and squeezed the trigger.

Smoke, flames, and lead lapped from the barrel. Stockburn blinked against the wafting powder smoke as he stared up toward his target. The man's hat disappeared. The rifle barrel rose sharply then it, too, disappeared in the rocks as the man either dropped it or pulled it back into his nest.

Wolf ejected the spent cartridge and pumped a fresh one into the action.

He waited, staring up at the shooter's nest of rocks. Nothing moved for nearly a minute, then the man appeared. He was no more than a shadow from this distance and against the gray rock behind him. The shadow moved to the right side of the stone nest.

Stockburn triggered three quick rounds toward the man, who disappeared right after the second shot had blasted rock dust out of the ridge above the nest. The man had jerked down and to the right, and then he was gone.

Wolf pumped a fresh round into the Yellowboy's breech. He spied movement against the ridge, above the nest. He couldn't see much because the shooter was partially hidden from his view. There must have been a perpendicular niche in the ridge. The shooter had stepped back into that niche and was climbing toward the top.

"You bastard," Wolf muttered, and hurled several more rounds at the man.

143

It was his own turn to fire in frustration. He did so until the hammer dropped with an annoyingly benign ping, the last round having been spent.

He stared at the ridge. He couldn't tell if he'd hit his target. The man was gone.

Wolf cursed. He sat back against a tree bole, laid his rifle across his thighs, and began reloading from his cartridge belt.

"Stockburn!"

Wolf whipped his head back around to stare up the ridge. The man stood on the crest. A lean, dark figure wearing that low-crowned, black hat. Long hair fell straight down to his shoulders. The man turned full around, dropped his pants, leaned forward, and reached around with both hands to open the rear fly of his longhandles, exposing his bare behind.

"Black-hearted, chicken-livered coward!" Stockburn shoved another round through the Winchester's loading gate then raised the rifle, slamming a live round into the action.

By the time he'd leveled the gun over the fallen cottonwood, the man was gone.

Wolf gritted his teeth in anger. He wanted so much to drill a round through the bushwhacker's bare ass. Despite himself, he chuckled. He sat back against the tree and had a good, hearty laugh over the ridiculousness of the man's last gesture.

Finally, his laughter dwindling, he raked a hand

down his face and shook his head. "Till we meet again, you devil." He stared up the ridge again, and the humor faded from his eyes, replaced by a stony resolution. "Till we meet again."

CHAPTER 13

As Lori McCrae rode up and over the last hill and saw the Triangle headquarters spread out in the broad valley before her, at the foot of the fir-clad Crow Mountain, she choked back a lump of deep consternation and churning sadness.

God, how she loved her home. She'd missed it and these mountains so much when she'd been away at school. She'd yearned to come back here, had virtually cried herself to sleep every night out of loneliness and a deep, almost morbid longing for the hauntingly beautiful valley in which she'd been born and raised.

But seeing it now, the Triangle and the lush valley it sprawled in, surrounded by the black dots of lowing cattle, had lost its luster, the sweet feeling they had once filled her with. Not all of that luster and sweetness was gone, of course. She still felt better being here than in that bland old school back East, in that wretched city with its smell of offal everywhere. But the Triangle did not look nearly as fairy-tale idyllic and wonderful and welcoming as it had before, back when Lori had been a younger, more innocent girl.

Now, it even appeared a little forbidding—due in no small part to the fact that she was no longer wanted here.

She'd been ordered away from here, from her home, sent away by her parents, *escorted* away, *like a prisoner,* by her oldest brother, Lawton. She'd attended Miss Lydia Hastings Academy for Young Women last year. She'd spent the summer back here on the Triangle though her parents had wanted her to live with her mother's brother's family in Philadelphia until school resumed in the fall. But Lori had resisted.

Her parents had relented and allowed her to return to the Wind Rivers for the summer. One last summer. The Triangle was no longer her home, they'd explained. Now, as a beautiful, intelligent, and precocious young lady—one with money behind her, no less—"she must prepare for a life in the more civilized world of the East."

Those words, she knew, had merely been short-hand for marrying an appropriate suitor—one with even more money than the McCrae's—and raising a family. Back East. Far away from the Triangle and the trouble she'd gotten herself into here in these beautiful mountains that, because of that former trouble, would no longer be the fairy-tale mountains she'd known when she'd still worn her hair in pigtails.

Still, even with a dark patina of danger, grief, and sorrow that obscured them now, like a perplexing fog that refused to burn off with the sun, these mountains, this valley and ranch were her home. She wouldn't . . . *couldn't* . . . leave them again.

She was here to stay.

How would she explain that to her father and mother? How would they take it? Would they sternly forbid it, or would they . . . eventually, after much argument, no doubt . . . see that she'd made up her mind and that there would be no point in refusing lest their head-strong daughter take to the streets of Wild Horse and live a life most unbecoming of a McCrae.

Yes, that's exactly how she would put it, if she had to, she silently opined as her horse's hooves clomped across the bridge spanning Crow Creek. She trotted smartly through the wooden portal at the edge of the yard, glancing up at the two triangle brands burned into the cross timber, one to each side of the name MCCRAE blazed deeply and darkly—proudly—into the weathered wood.

As she entered the yard, she saw a dozen or so cowboys gathered in and around the breaking corral, most sitting on the rail. Oh, what a sweet sight! The men were watching one of the horse-breakers working with a horse tied to the snubbing post. They had their backs to her.

That was good. Lori didn't want to be seen just yet. As soon as she was seen, there would be so much surprise . . . so many questions. She wasn't ready to explain herself just yet to the men. She wasn't even ready to explain herself to her parents, but that was not a matter she could delay any longer.

While she felt a little giddy about being home and being surrounded by so much that was warm and familiar—even the smell of the horse manure finely ground into the dust of the yard was a sweet perfume in her nostrils—she felt sick with dread, as well.

As she turned the horse toward the stables on her left, a boyish man's voice yelled, "Lori! Hey, Lori! What're you doing back so soon, sis?"

Lori winced and tightened her shoulders with dismay.

She glanced over her shoulder. All of the men on the corral fence had their heads turned to regard her dubiously. Lori's brother, Hy, short for Hiram, stood inside the corral, holding the halter rope of the horse he was working with.

Three years her senior but with the guilelessness of a much younger man, he grinned at her innocently, and waved, rising up on the toes of his worn boots to peer over the corral fence, between a couple of the incredulous riders.

"Hey, Lori!" He called again. Hy had always been her best friend and advocate here at the Triangle while her oldest brother Lawton had been more of a father figure.

Lori waved, feigned a smile. "Brother, you just saddle that jackrabbit and hang on. I'll tell you about it later!"

As Lori handed her horse's reins to one of the stable boys who'd been helping the taciturn blacksmith put new shoes on a wild-eyed peg pony, Lori caught sight of her oldest brother, Lawton.

Tall, rangy, and curly-haired, and with a tough and formal way about him, the oldest of the three McCrae sons sat atop the corral. Lawton stared at her darkly from over his shoulder, brows severely furled as he took a drag off a cigarette and blew the smoke out forcefully, angrily.

As Lori met his gaze, he turned his head abruptly forward, dismissing his younger sister in bitter disgust.

"All right, Law," Lori said, "have it your way." Turning to the stable boy who was leading away her horse, she said, "Billy?"

"Yes, miss?"

"A man from the hotel will be bringing my luggage along in a few hours. Bring the bags to my room, please. He'll be returning the filly along with its saddle and bridle to the Federated Livery back in Wild Horse. Make sure she's fed and groomed."

"You got it, miss."

"Thank you," she said, ignoring the incredulous look in the stable boy's eyes. He was the black-smith's son. Now she noticed the blacksmith, lightly hammering a smoking horseshoe on his anvil, regarding her the same way. Not staring but darting his eyes at her, speculatively. Wondering what the little princess was doing home so soon. Maybe knowing the row it would cause . . .

Lori swung around and started for the house, feeling as though she were walking the proverbial plank. The ship housing that plank—the McCrae ranch house—stood before her, set back and at an angle to the yard where the unseemly but necessary toil happened.

It was a sprawling, white clapboard structure with a wide, wraparound porch outfitted with wicker chairs and ashtrays that had to be emptied regularly, for Lori's mother forbade her husband to smoke his cigars indoors. Even in the winter, he'd bundle up in his long, wolf fur coat and floppy-brimmed hide hat and long, mule-eared elk hide boots and baggy corduroy breeches, and slump down in one of the scattered wicker chairs, smoking and scowling off across his holdings—a grumpy king with undisputed reign save the ability to smoke inside his own house.

A low brick wall ringed the house as well as the small, irrigated yard with its transplanted trees freighted in from the East and Midwest and immaculate vegetable and herb gardens. Lori opened the gate, passed through the wall, and stopped suddenly.

Her mother, clad in the rugged clothes she wore when tending her trees and gardens, stood atop the porch steps, regarding her only daughter gravely but with a building sadness, as well.

Lori glanced down and drew a breath to steel herself. *Here we go . . .*

She walked the plank of the long brick path between an ornamental ash and a small poplar and an apple tree and stopped at the foot of the steps. She smiled up at the tall, once-beautiful woman standing customarily erect on the porch above her. Elizabeth McCrae held a mum flower, its roots ensconced in a ragged ball of black dirt, in one hand, a garden trowel in the other.

"Hello, Mother."

"Lori . . ."

Lori smiled painfully. "I'm back . . . to stay." She tightened her voice on that last word.

Elizabeth McCrae just stared at her, her eyes as black as her hair once had been. She was a tall, reedy woman, her silver-streaked black hair pulled up into a bun beneath her canvas gardening hat.

Her hands were skeletal, liver-spotted, untrimmed by rings, not even a wedding ring. She'd birthed Lori when she was forty-two—"an unexpected surprise." Her current expression was no surprise to Lori. She'd always regarded her youngest child with a vague curiosity, as though everything Lori did touched her with a mix of weariness, incredulity, and wry amusement.

Now she shook her head slowly and quirked her thin, lightly mustached mouth up at the corners.

"Oh, *God!*" came a man's raspy voice behind her.

It was only then that Lori realized her father had been standing several feet back from the open doorway. She could see only the lumpy shadow of his slump-shouldered, potbelly figure. He must have been sitting in the large parlor to the right of the door. Hearing Lori's voice, he'd stepped into the foyer, likely with a great deal of dread and exasperation.

Now he swung around and disappeared into the house's deep shadows.

Elizabeth glanced behind her then returned her gaze to her daughter. She smiled gently. "Go to him, dear."

Lori nodded and climbed the steps. She stepped up in front of her mother and gazed directly into her eyes, not something she'd always been able to do in the past. Elizabeth McCrae was a formidable, often frightening woman for whom motherly tenderness came hard.

Suddenly, Lori wrapped her arms around her mother's slender shoulders, hugging her gently, feeling the fragile bones in her body that belied the toughness of her spirit. But, then, it had taken a tough young woman, recently from Scotland, to marry the tough Texan that was Norman McCrae and then to follow him with his first two babies up here from the Red River country, fighting Indians, outlaws, sickness, dust, pounding wagon wheels, and dangerous rivers. And then to take and hold this land they'd fought from the Arapaho and Shoshone who'd called it home for hundreds of years and who'd fought desperately to keep it.

Then, of course, there was the feud—an ongoing one—with Rufus Stoleberg, which turned out to be nearly as savage as the war with the Indians.

Yes, a tough woman was Elizabeth McCrae. And a skinflint when it came to paying out affection, even to her only daughter. She did, however, after a few seconds, raise her arms slowly and returned Lori's hug, albeit a bit stiffly. Lori warmed at the feel of her mother's slender arms pressing against her, drawing her however briefly taut to her mother's bony chest.

Lori pulled her head away. "I'm staying, Mama. You won't send me away again. Do you know why?"

Elizabeth regarded the girl with a curious furl of the skin between her thin brows.

"Because I'm as tough as you are."

"Dear . . ." Elizabeth slid a lock of stray hair from her daughter's cheek with one cold, leathery finger. "You're not telling me anything I haven't known since you were three years old."

That made Lori smile though she wasn't sure that her mother had meant the remark as a compliment. Still, she took it as one. There were worse things than being as tough as Elizabeth

McCrae, though Lori hadn't realized she owned such strength until just a few days ago, when she'd made the firm, final decision to defy her parents and return home.

Elizabeth placed her hands on Lori's shoulders and held the girl back away from her, gazing at her gravely. "The question is, though"—she canted her head to indicate her husband, Lori's father who'd stomped away in a huff—"are you as tough as he is?"

Lori looked into the house, then returned her gaze to her mother and pulled her mouth corners down. "I guess we're about to find out."

She kissed her mother's cheek, then strode across the threshold.

CHAPTER 14

As his calico gelding splashed across Dutch Joe Creek, Slim Sherman brushed his hand across his right cheek. He looked at the blood smeared across his palm and cursed.

Sherman, a tall man in his early forties, crouched low in the saddle, grunting against the burn of the bullet wound. The slug had ricocheted off the barrel of Sherman's rifle and cut across his face.

A little higher and it would have taken out Sherman's right eye. That would have meant Taps for Sherman. A regulator wasn't much good without his shooting eye. He'd tried to shoot left-handed before, but it just hadn't felt right and, though he'd practiced long and hard, he'd never got the hang of it. If he lost the use of his right arm or right eye, he'd have to go into another line of business, though that wouldn't be easy for a man who knew only how to kill other men.

Usually from behind.

"Damn that big gray-haired son of Satan!" Sherman said sharply, gritting his teeth against the burn. "What a lucky damn shot! *Hell!*"

He crossed a small tributary of Dutch Joe then rode through some pines and cedars, the tall, blond grass brushing against his stirrups, and saw the old line shack he was currently calling home. No one had used the shack in years, so he'd had to fight it back from the brush and tree saplings not to mention the mice, the skunks that had lived under the floor, and even a coyote that had come and gone through a hole in one of the shutters.

It was a good, tight place, though, when all was said and done, and he'd hammered some corrugated tin over a hole in the shake-shingled roof. A nice place for a single man, a loner who didn't mix well with others—who hated most people, in fact—and valued his solitude.

It was good he valued solitude. A man in Sherman's line of work had to spend a lot of time alone. You show your mug around too much, you're likely going to be recognized by a friend or family member of a man or men—maybe even one of the four women—you'd sent to their reward.

You were liable to get a bullet for your tomfoolery.

Sherman reined the calico up in front of the sun-bathed shack. Despite the burn in his cheek—it felt like a blacksmith had lain a glowing hot andiron against his face—he found himself smiling. Of course, he hadn't been able to see his own naked backside, but he could see it in his mind's eye the way Stockburn had likely seen it—his butt cheeks glowing in the sunshine atop that ridge, grinning mockingly down at the famed rail detective.

There was no insult quite like the insult of a man flashing another man his naked behind. Just nothing else like it. What could you say to that? There was no response equal to such an insult.

Stockburn had probably been as mad as a stick-teased rattlesnake, being exposed to Sherman's behind like that. He might have sent a bullet across Sherman's cheek—*damn, it hurt like hell!*—but he didn't know that. The detective wouldn't have been able to see Sherman's face from that distance and position.

No, no—Stockburn didn't know anything about the pain he'd inflicted. But he sure as hell had seen Sherman's lewdly taunting gesture.

Hah!

He'd remember that for a long time, Stockburn would.

"What's so funny?"

The voice so startled the regulator that he nearly tumbled from his saddle. He looked around quickly, automatically wrapping his right hand around the grips of his .44 Colt in the holster on his right hip.

He didn't see anything until a hand rose from behind the half-rotted rail of the equally rotted front stoop of the cabin. A small, pale hand at the end of a slender arm clad in checked wool. A girl's hand and arm. The voice had belonged to a girl, too, though that hadn't taken any of the start out of Sherman's reaction.

He did, however, leave the pistol in its holster while keeping his hand wrapped around the stag horn grips. "Who's there?"

"Ivy."

The pretty blonde rose from the fainting couch resting back against the line shack's front wall. Don't ask Sherman how anyone had hauled a fainting couch out here—and a fancy one, at that, if now badly worn and mouse-chewed—to this remote line cabin, which had likely been used on fall roundups by crews from various spreads in this neck of the mountains.

A pair of drunken cow punchers had probably stolen it out of a whorehouse.

"Russell," she added, standing now, with a grin. She frowned suddenly. "What happened to your face?"

Suddenly self-conscious, Sherman frowned. "Never mind. What're you doin' out here? Your old man know you stray this far from the herd?"

"There's a lot my old man doesn't know about me. Not because I keep it from him, necessarily, but because he doesn't want to know, because he knows there's nothin' he can do about it."

She'd moved down off the porch and walked now to Sherman's horse, staring up at him from over his right stirrup. "Come on in. We'd better get that cut cleaned up."

"Who's we?"

"You an' me." Ivy smiled. "What's wrong? Don't tell me you're not happy to see me." She gave him a leering, vulgar smile.

"I ain't happy to see you. Not out here, girl. This is my secret haunt. I didn't want no one to know about this place. Hell, I don't want no one to know I'm even in the area. My reputation precedes me. What'd you say your name was—Ivy?"

"You don't even remember my name?"

"Did you tell me? I forget. All I remember is you said you was Russell's daughter."

"Well, you weren't all that unhappy to see me the other night." Ivy Russell smiled again and reached up to place her pale hand on his thigh. "In Wild Horse."

Sherman looked at the girl's hand on his thigh. It was a pretty hand. Warm. It went with the pretty rest of her. He couldn't feel much at the moment, however, except the galling burn in his cheek.

"Forget that. I was drunk. Shouldn't have done it. I'm on a job, but even a professional's gotta let his hair down from time to time."

"Yeah, well, we let it down together—didn't we?" She shot him that lewd smile again. "In grand fashion."

Sherman should have known she was trouble. Ladies that aren't trouble don't frequent saloons. Especially not the little hole-in-the-wall whiskey trough and whores' crib he'd patronized three nights ago, on a supply run to Wild Horse.

The pretty blonde in boy's garb had been playing the piano and drinking whiskey from the bottle before she'd wandered over to his table. He'd been sitting most happily alone in a dark corner, playing a game of solitaire and nursing a bottle of cheap whiskey.

Sherman didn't mind cheap whiskey. In fact, having been raised on busthead back in the hills of Tennessee back before the little dust-up between the states, he preferred it. His father and uncles had brewed it. Just as he was a man who got by very well on his own, Sherman was not a man of frivolous tastes.

Frivolous tastes led to trouble. Just as women led to trouble. He knew that.

Still, when this pretty daughter of the town marshal had beat him at poker and lured him upstairs to an empty room in that squalid hole at the edge of town—he'd had the impression he wasn't the first man she'd led up there, either—he'd gone ready and willing.

What man wouldn't? She filled out her blouse in comely style and put the right curves in her tight denims. Besides, there was added alluring danger in the fact she was the town marshal's daughter.

What man—even a practical loner, a professional man, a killing machine—could resist something like that?

He hadn't.

Now, here she was again. But he was sober now. And hurting. And he didn't want her here.

Clutching his cheek, Sherman swung down from his saddle. "How'd you find this place?"

"Followed you back the next morning," Ivy said, tauntingly.

He scowled at her. "You did?"

"Yep."

Sherman stared at her aghast, horrified by his own negligence. He couldn't go around letting folks follow him. At least, not without his knowing about it. Embarrassing.

Downright humiliating.

His chagrin must have shone in his face, because, as she grabbed his arm and led him to the cabin, Ivy said, "Oh, don't feel so bad about it. I'm good at following folks. Hell, I follow everyone who passes through town and is one bit interesting. I'd live such a dull life otherwise!"

They mounted the rotting two steps together. "I've never been caught yet, so don't go beating yourself up about it. That looks bad. You're lucky you didn't lose that eye."

"Tell me about it," Sherman said as she ushered him into the cabin.

He tossed his hat onto a chair then reached for a whiskey bottle.

"No, no, no," the girl said, slapping his

shoulder. "You just take a seat. I'll tend that cut. I'm good at that, too."

"You're good at a lot of things, aren't you?"

"Indeed, I am!"

Sherman kicked a hide-bottom chair out from the small eating table cluttered with leavings from his previous meal, and sat down. "What're you doing out here, anyways?"

"I wanted to find out how it went."

Sherman scowled at her again. "How what went?"

"Mister Wolf of the Rails himself," Ivy said, taking a tin pot out onto the porch for water from the rain barrel. Coming back in, she looked at him with eager expectance. "Did you get him?"

Sherman could only gaze at her, even more amazed and horrified than he was before, when he'd learned he'd let her shadow him out from town. Her—a girl only a few years out of pigtails!

Ivy set the pan on the table then picked up the unlabeled whiskey bottle. "Well—did you?"

"How did . . . how did . . . ?"

"Oh, never mind! I learn everything interesting that's going on about Wild Horse sooner or later," she added with gold flecks sparkling in her crystal blue eyes. "You needn't feel bad about that, neither."

She pulled a handkerchief from the back pocket of her denims and poured a little whiskey onto it. She sopped a little water from the pot onto it, as well, then drew a chair up to the right side of Sherman and leaned toward him to begin cleaning his cheek.

"Hold on." Sherman waved her off then grabbed the bottle and took three big pulls. Between pulls, he swallowed, drew a deep breath, then pulled again.

Finally, he set the bottle down and turned to her, exasperated but trying to keep his nerves on a short leash. Fear was not good for a man in his line of work. You couldn't think straight when you were fearful.

A little fear was all right, but the kind of fear this girl evoked in his otherwise steely nerves—a heart-thumping, palm-sweating anxiousness—was off-putting.

If she knew, who else knew? Maybe a trap was being set.

Maybe Stockburn himself had known and that's why he'd been so damned hard to perforate! Hell, maybe Stockburn had followed him here!

Sherman jerked a paranoid look at the open door. Nothing out there but his horse standing with his head lowered, sunlight, and breeze-brushed weeds. Birds flitted here and there about the pine boughs.

"What is it?" Ivy asked, following his gaze to the door.

"Close it."

"Why? It's kinda stinky in here. Let's just—"

Sherman palmed his Colt and cocked it, aiming at the open door. "Close it!"

"All right, all right." Ivy walked around the table to the door. She poked her head out, looked around cautiously, then closed the door and turned her curious gaze to Sherman. "You didn't get him, didja?"

She smiled with subtle jeering.

Sherman depressed the Colt's hammer and set the gun on the table. He felt blood rise in his face. "The Son of Satan must have nine lives. I never miss from that distance. Not with the Big Fifty. I never miss!" He took a pull from the bottle then slammed his fist down on the table.

"Maybe you were just nervous—him bein' a big, capable fellow and all. The Wolf of the Rails himself! Maybe you were worried what would happen if you missed, and—well, you missed!"

Ivy laughed as she sank back down into her chair beside the regulator.

"I'm never nervous," Sherman said, suddenly indignant. But had he been? "I never miss! And I'm not afraid of Wolf Stockburn!"

"Well, I would be, but all right, all right. Hold still now and let me clean that wound. Wow—it looks nasty. You might need a few stitches."

"No stitches. Just clean the damn thing."

"Hold still."

"I am!"

"No, you're not—you're fidgeting around like a cat with a dog in the room!"

Was he? Yeah, he guessed he was. My God—he was nervous.

He forced himself to hold still and let the girl tend his wound. The water and whiskey burned. He took several pulls from the bottle. It did a good job of quelling the pain in his cheek that fired up with renewed energy every time the girl poked around at it with the damp cloth.

As she worked, Sherman kept his gaze skinned on the windows to each side of the door. The shutters were closed, but sunlight streamed through the cracks between the shutters' planks. If a man moved around out there, Sherman should be able to see him.

The girl's words echoed around inside Sherman's head:

"Maybe you were just nervous—him bein' a big, capable fellow and all. The Wolf of the Rails himself! Maybe you were worried what would happen if you missed, and—well, you missed!"

Could she be right?

Sherman looked at her. She caught his eye as she dabbed at the wound. She smiled bashfully though there wasn't a bashful bone in her body.

She looked into his eyes like she could see right through him. Like she could see the fear devils scuttling around inside his soul.

"Don't look at me like that."

"Like how?"

"Like you're lookin' at me."

"All right, all right." She chuckled then set the cloth into the basin again then wrung it out.

"Don't laugh, neither. I don't like being laughed at."

"I'm sorry," Ivy said, sounding like she really meant it. She dabbed at the wound again, carefully, gently, tucking her lower lip under her two front teeth. "I didn't mean to laugh. I just think you might be over-reacting a bit, is all."

"Oh, you do, do you? Do you know how many men I've killed?"

"I've heard anywhere from between twenty and thirty."

"You have? From who?"

"Pa."

"How would he know?"

"You were involved in that land war down in Colorado, weren't you? The one between the cattlemen and sheepmen down around Estes Park? Two, three years ago now?"

Sherman reached up and wrapped his hand around her hand holding the cloth. "How'd you know that?"

"Pa was down there at the time. He was a deputy town marshal in Camp Collins. Ran a saloon down there, too. I slung drinks for him even though I wasn't more'n about thirteen. I wore a tight little dress right well even then, on account of how I filled out early, and Pa said I could wear it because it brought business in. I could do anything . . . as long as it brought business in."

Sherman released her hand. "I bet you did. I bet you brought in the business." He let his eyes roam down the front of her shirt.

Suddenly, he liked her being here. He liked her sitting so close to him that he could feel the little puffs of her breath on his cheek, soothing the wound. He could feel the warmth of her body, sitting so close to him.

Suddenly, he was aware of her right leg pressed up against his left one.

He took another pull from the rotgut as she continued cleaning the wound, a faint little grin playing across her lips.

Yeah, he didn't mind her being here so much now. Women were a distraction, but maybe a man needed a distraction now and then. A distraction besides whiskey, that was. Now he didn't feel so worried about Stockburn. He felt some of his old pluck returning. He could handle Stockburn. His having missed the man with that fifty-caliber round had been a fluke.

Flukes happened. He'd get him next time.

So what if Stockburn did come after him?

He'd be ready. Good, good. Let him come. Then Slim Sherman would drill the legendary Wolf of the Rails through his heart. End the legend right

168

then and there. Not like it was anything personal. He'd been paid to do a job, so he'd do it.

End the legend.

Sherman would be the legend then, wouldn't he?

"Hey, you're feelin' better—ain't ya?" Ivy said, smiling precociously as she stared into his eyes.

Sherman drank more whiskey. He wiped his mouth with his hand, smiled, and nodded. "Yeah."

"I can tell." She narrowed one eye in mock recrimination as she glanced at the bottle. "Is it me . . . or the who-hit-John?"

Sherman slid the bottle aside. Still smiling, feeling his blood warm with desire, he turned toward the girl, took the rag out of her hand, and dropped it into the basin. He wrapped his arms around her shoulders and slid his face up close to hers. "I think it's you."

"Really?" she asked as though not believing it.

"Sure, sure, it's you, honey." Sherman smiled again, drew her a little closer, until he could feel her bosoms pressed again his chest.

She did not resist the way most women usually did at first. Most women, even the bought kind, were usually hesitant to be with him, his being a killer and all. That fact seemed to repel them.

That was all right. He didn't mind. It wasn't like he'd wanted to marry any of them.

His being a killer didn't seem to repel this girl at all. In fact, she seemed attracted by it.

"You ain't in any hurry to get home, now, are you?" Sherman asked.

"What're you asking?" She was being coy now. She pressed her right index finger to the cleft in his chin. "Are you asking me to . . ."

"To stay awhile," Sherman said, and closed his mouth over hers.

Her lips parted for him. Her body relaxed in his arms.

"I'm my own boss," Ivy said.

CHAPTER 15

Stockburn rode Smoke up a long hill between slopes of conifers mixed with changing aspens.

He'd started smelling wood smoke a few hundred yards back along the trail he'd followed out of the canyon in which he'd been ambushed by the bastard with the big rifle. That's why he wasn't surprised to see, as he halted Smoke on the hill's bullet-shaped crest, the Triangle Ranch headquarters sprawled across the broad valley below.

Smoke lifted from several chimneys. It was around one-thirty in the afternoon, so the stoves in the bunkhouse and main house had been recently stoked to cook the mid-day meal and had yet to cool down. The fires had probably been kept burning to ward off the early-autumn chill that was always a little more intense in the mountains. Making it feel even colder to Stockburn was the fact that his pants and one shirt sleeve were still damp from his fall in the stream.

Wolf figured, judging by the way his heart was pumping faster than before, and by the pressure in his ears, that he was probably somewhere around ten thousand feet above sea level. Smoke was breathing a little harder, as well. The long ride out from Wild Horse and into the thin mountain air had tired the mount enough that he hadn't been hard to run down after Stockburn's skirmish—if you could call it that—with the man who'd tried to turn him toe down with the hunting rifle.

The detective sat and surveyed the Triangle headquarters—an impressive layout with the big, frame house set back and at an angle from the barns, stables, and corrals. It also had a low, brick wall, partly concealed by a tangle of green vines, encircling it. Smoke curled from the house's big fieldstone chimney jutting up from its right end.

On the yard's left end, cowboys were working in a corral with a couple of horses; other hands perched on the corral fence to watch the proceedings. Wolf could hear them joking and laughing and occasionally yelling instructions to the men working with the horses.

Some were smoking cigarettes; others spat chaw in the dirt.

Three more punchers, clad in batwing chaps, were just then riding down toward the headquarters from the northeast, on the opposite side of the compound from where Wolf sat. A blacksmith was hammering an anvil. Stockburn couldn't see the smithy, but the sharp rings of the hammer echoed up from the yard.

Two boys in their early teenaged years were

shoeing a mouse-brown horse in front of the small, square building with two big open doors that Stockburn assumed was the blacksmith shop. It lay on the right side of the yard, near one of the several stables.

The dun just then lurched forward, trying to kick the boy trying to hammer a shoe to its hoof, while the other boy jerked back on the reins he was holding, getting dragged several feet forward.

"Dammit, hold him, Billy!" the boy holding the hammer screeched.

The boy with the reins got his boots set, dust licking up around him, and the horse stopped. The other boy, slightly older, continued to scold him though Stockburn could only hear his tone, not the words.

Near the blacksmith shop, the blades of a windmill turned lazily, the tin blades glinting in the crisp sunshine. Water murmured from a pipe into the corrugated tin tank at the windmill's base. Stockburn could hear even that. That was how thin the air was. Sounds carried a long way at this altitude.

Just then a scream rose. A girl's scream. Wolf thought it had come from the house. The punchers must have thought so, too, because they all turned their heads quickly in the house's direction.

A thick-furred, brown dog ran into the yard,

barking and looking around as though searching for the source of the commotion.

The girl yelled again though Wolf couldn't make out the words, as she was inside the house. A man yelled then, as well—a deep, raspy voice pitched with scolding.

Smoke heard it, too. Wolf felt the muscles tensing warily beneath his saddle.

"Easy, boy," Stockburn said, reaching forward to give the mount's left wither a reassuring pat. Gazing toward the house, he said, "But I'm with you—wonder what that's all about."

He booted the mount on down the hill.

Smoke clomped across the wooden bridge spanning a creek then passed under the ranch portal in which the McCrae name and brand had been burned. Two men ran toward him from the group clustered around the corral. Only one wore a six-shooter, and he closed a hand around it now as he and the other man approached.

Stockburn halted Smoke and raised his right hand to show he wasn't a threat. "Easy, pards. The name's Stockburn. I'm a railroad detective here to talk to Mister McCrae."

"Rail detective?"

"That's right. Wells Fargo." Slowly, Wolf reached into his black frock coat and pulled out his bonafides.

The two punchers eyed him cautiously. They might not have been in open war with another spread at the moment but apparently they had been recently enough that a strange man riding into the Triangle compound would draw ire if not fire.

He held up his shield and identification card.

As he did, the shouting inside the house grew louder, as did the stomping of angry feet. A girl strode angrily out of the house's front door and onto the porch.

Lori McCrae stopped on the porch and, holding her arms straight down at her sides, fists clenched into red balls against her legs, she swung back around and yelled, "You can't send me away against my will! You can't! If you try it again, I'll go to the Tin Cup! If not the Tin Cup, then I'll go to town . . . and the shame will be on you!"

She wheeled around and, holding her skirts above her ankles, hurried down the porch steps, heading through the yard toward the gate in the low brick wall.

A short, old bulldog of a man in a white shirt and light tan vest and bolo tie stomped through the house's door and onto the porch, pointing a commanding finger at the obviously enraged Lori. "Get back here, young lady!"

"No!" she screamed, keeping her back to the old man.

He strode forward, stopped at the top of the porch steps, and bellowed, "Did he answer even one of your letters? Even one?"

Lori had just opened the gate. Stockburn had stopped Smoke near one of the hitchracks near the gate. The old man's words had stopped Lori halfway into the yard.

She stood as though frozen for several seconds then, her face slackening and turning pale, she turned back around and strode a few steps toward the porch and stopped to face the old man facing her, his own craggy features swollen with anger.

"How, pray tell, Papa, did you know about my letters?" Lori asked. She'd spoken quietly but with barely restrained exasperation and outrage.

The old man stared back at her, unable to answer the question.

"Norman!" came a woman's scolding voice behind him.

The woman followed her voice out onto the porch. She was a slender, leathery figure clad in men's rough work garb, with her silver-streaked hair pulled up into a bun. Somehow elegant and queenly despite the humbleness of her attire, she clenched her hands in front of her iron-flat belly.

"You intercepted them," Lori said, breathless. Her shoulders swayed from side to side. Stockburn was afraid she was going to faint and prepared to dismount and go to her to catch her if she should fall but waylaid the action when she swung around again and strode angrily out through the gate.

Her eyes swept across him as he sat there on his tall smoky gray stallion. She stopped.

"Oh," she said with mock surprise. "Here he is now, Papa. The man who saved my life on the train. Wolf Stockburn, rail detective. The great Wolf of the Rails."

Her voice was breathless, shrill, her red cheeks mottled white, her eyes glazed with a dangerous anger. "Damn you!" she cried suddenly, bending forward at the waist and firing her rage at Wolf. "Damn you for saving me! Why didn't you let that scurvy little devil Hennessey blow my head off? Why didn't you? You'd have done me the biggest favor anyone has ever done me in my whole, damned, wretched, miserable life!"

She turned and strode away from Stockburn, angling across the yard toward the stable near the blacksmith shop. The blacksmith and the two boys working with him stood in front of the shop's open doors, regarding the girl in wide-eyed fascination.

The dog now sat near one of the boys, also staring at Lori with hushed incredulity, tongue sagging down over its lower jaws.

As she passed the blacksmith shop, Lori yelled, "Billy, saddle Miss Abigail!"

The boy jerked to life then stopped when the old woman said, "No, Billy!"

The old woman, who Stockburn assumed was the girl's mother, had followed Lori out through the gate. She turned now toward where two of the cowboys had been walking toward the house from the corral, their faces taut with tension and worry. "Law, Hy!" the woman said, then jerked her chin toward where Lori was approaching the stable, back ramrod straight, fists still clenched at her sides.

Both men broke into jogs.

"Lori," the oldest one said. "Lori, for god-sakes!"

Stockburn swung down from Smoke's back and stood helplessly holding Smoke's reins and watching the two young men, at the direction of the old woman, run up to Lori. Stockburn felt an urge to intervene on the girl's behalf—they'd gotten to be friends, after all—but this was a family affair.

"Let me go!" Lori yelled, jerking her hand out of the older of the two young men's grip. She whipped around toward the two young boys and the blacksmith and the dog. "Billy, I told you to—no, Hy, let me go! Law, let me go—damn you both!"

Both young men—her brothers, it seemed—grabbed Lori between them and half-carried, half-dragged her back toward where the old woman and now the old man stood to each side of the gate in the brick wall.

"Let me go!" the girl raged, writhing, trying to pull herself free of the young men's grips. "I'm going to town! I'll live as a whore and then won't you *really* be ashamed!"

"Lori, please!" the old man said.

As her brothers dragged her past where Wolf stood holding Smoke's reins, looking on and feeling as helpless as he'd ever felt in his life, Lori locked pleading eyes on him and said, "Wolf, don't let them do this to me! They think I'm crazy! I'm not! Please, Wolf, if you're any friend at all—*stop them!*"

Stockburn stepped forward. "Lori, I'm sorry . . . I . . ."

"Never mind," the old woman told him. "She gets this way." To the young men carrying Lori through the open gate, she said, "Take her up to her room. I'll bring a sedative."

"Is that really necessary?" Wolf asked.

The old woman turned back to him, looking annoyed. "Yes. She . . . gets like this." Her annoyed frown turned to a scowl. "Just who are you, sir?"

"Stockburn, Lori said," said the old man, stepping up to Wolf. "I'll handle it, Elizabeth. You'd best tend to the girl." When the woman had gone back into the house, the old man extended his small but thick and severely work-calloused hand. "Hello, Stockburn. I'm Norman McCrae."

He was short and rugged-faced, his body going to seed. His thick hair was entirely gray. His deeply sun- and wind-burned face was a mask of small dark freckles. His eyes were the same light brown of his daughter's. Stockburn figured him to be in his late sixties though the hard western years had made him look a good twenty years older.

Wolf shook, giving the man an affable nod but furtively gnashing his teeth at the sounds of Lori's struggle echoing around inside the house. "I guess I could have chosen a more opportune time to come calling."

"Yes, well . . ." McCrae winced as he glanced toward the house. The sounds of struggle were dwindling. The girl's brothers had probably gotten her into her room and closed the door. Now, for the sedative. "Lori's not a well girl and, well . . . her return was unexpected."

"I gathered as much. A rather harsh way of treating homesickness, though, wouldn't you say?" Wolf couldn't help asking, unable to keep an accusing tone out of his voice.

"Suppose you leave my family's concerns to me and my wife, Mister Stockburn."

"All right, fair enough. It's just that I got to know the girl. We came in on the same train, and I wouldn't want to see her hurt."

"She won't be hurt, I assure you. My wife and myself and Lori's brothers want nothing but the

180

best for her." McCrae paused, frowned up at the detective who had several inches on him. "What was that she said about 'that devil Hennessey'?"

"Riley Hennessey stopped the train. He tried to take your daughter. I prevented him from doing so."

"He tried to rob another train, eh?" McCrae scowled, his jowls swelling, and slowly shook his head. He glanced at Wolf darkly and said, "You stopped him?"

"Yes."

"Did he hurt Lori?"

"Roughed her up a little but nothing serious."

McCrae asked the next question silently as he continued to frown up at the rail detective.

"He's dead," Stockburn responded.

Wolf didn't think Norman McCrae was a man who customarily betrayed his emotions, but the detective's answer had plainly shocked him. McCrae's eyes widened, silver brows crawling up into his freckled, brick-red forehead, and his chin rose slowly until he was almost looking up at the sunlit sky for a second. "I see. Does his father know?"

"Oh, yeah." Stockburn took note of the painful goose egg on his temple, hidden by his hat.

"Come on in, Stockburn," McCrae said, his mood having improved.

He ran his hands down the front of his doe hide vest that had bright patterns stitched into it, in red and green thread, and considered the ground. He turned toward the house, beckoned over his shoulder with a small, tough hand and said, "You deserve a drink."

CHAPTER 16

A tall, brown-skinned woman in her thirties, obviously Indian—probably Shoshone or Arapaho—brought a silver tray with a liquor decanter and two matching, diamond-cut goblets into McCrae's study.

Silent as a church mouse, her broad, black-eyed face devoid of expression, she set the tray on the low table between the two overstuffed leather armchairs in which Stockburn and the rancher had seated themselves.

Also on the tray were a wooden plate of thickly sliced sausage, several hard-boiled eggs cut in two, a wheel of sliced cheese, and small crackers with nuts and berries baked into them.

"My favorite afternoon snack," McCrae said, huffing and puffing as he maneuvered around in the deep chair to lean forward over his knees. Glancing up at the servant, he said, "That will be all, Yellow Feather. Thank you." The rancher popped half an egg into his mouth and chewed.

Yellow Feather left the room as silently as she'd entered it.

McCrae removed the glass stopper from the decanter and splashed two fingers of what appeared to be whiskey into each glass. He set down the decanter and slid one of the heavy glasses toward Stockburn's side of the table.

"Go ahead," he said, picking up the other goblet and sniffing the lip. "Good stuff. I have it shipped here directly from the Scottish Highlands. Just the right balance of peat and smoke." He swirled the whiskey, took a quick sniff, and sipped. "Ah, yes."

Stockburn picked up his own glass, sniffed, then took a deep sip, rolling the liquor, which tasted the way a campfire smells on a cold winter night, across his tongue to savor it before swallowing.

When it hit his belly, it sent a soothing warmth throughout his body and into his head, tempering the pain of the goose egg. "Just what the doctor ordered. Thank you. I have to be careful not to get spoiled. I couldn't afford anything even close to this on my Wells Fargo salary."

"What part of Scotland are you from?" McCrae asked.

"I was born in Kansas, but my father and mother both came from Speyside. Poor fishing families. They didn't do much better in Kansas— especially when the Cheyenne came calling."

"I'm sorry."

"It's life in the West. *My* life in the West, anyway." Stockburn took another sip of the Scotch, held it on his tongue, and swallowed as he glanced around the well-appointed study boasting a large, hide-covered desk on the opposite end of the room, near two large bay windows. There were several sturdy gleaming bookcases, varnished tables supporting a globe and an intricate model of a clipper ship.

A gunrack displayed a good dozen handsome sporting rifles behind its glass door. Game trophies including a huge, snarling grizzly peered dubiously down from the walls. The wooden floors were deep carpeted, and a small, aromatic cedar fire crackled in the hearth near where the two men sat across from each other. The smells of the Scotch and old leather mixed with the perfume of the cedar smoke.

"You obviously did better," Wolf remarked with a wry smile.

"Not necessarily better," McCrae said, legs crossed, tapping one finger against the rim of his Scotch glass. "I just made more money. Long ago I learned the difference between living well and making a lot of money. The two don't always walk hand-in-hand."

"I'm sure acquiring all this wasn't easy. Not out here."

"Did you really kill Riley Hennessey?"

"I didn't know he was Riley Hennessey at the time. Or what the name meant. But, yes, I did." Stockburn raised and dropped his right hand onto the arm of his chair in capitulation to the fates. "Don't bother warning me about his father. We've already locked horns."

"You haven't killed Kreg, too?"

"Not yet."

That made McCrae laugh. He'd just taken a sip of his Scotch and now he leaned forward, red-faced, coughing. He sat back, pounding his chest with the end of his fist, and said, "Let me know when you do, and I'll kill a steer and host a barbecue!"

He laughed some more.

"You're not a fan, either, I take it?"

"You met the man. What do you think? He's a brigand. A common thug. A thug from New York. Doesn't belong here. He let that wretched son run off his leash for way too many years. The law was afraid to arrest him, and no one was willing to kill him and suffer the consequences, but"—McCrae snorted another laugh, regarding Stockburn with a jubilant smile—"here you, an outsider, kill him before you even hit Wild Horse!"

He threw his head back and laughed. "I'd give anything to have seen the look on Kreg's face when he found out. Letting that little rabid coyote run wild all these years . . . molesting young women . . . girls . . . mocking the law . . . common human decency."

The old rancher laughed again, shook his head. He arched a cautious brow at his guest. "I hope you got eyes in the back of your head."

"You're not the first person who's said as much."

"You'll need 'em."

186

"So I've seen."

"Please, don't judge me too harshly. I wouldn't normally laugh at the death of any man. But Riley Hennessey was not just any man. He was like a slippery wildcat preying on a beef herd."

"That's what I heard. I'm honestly sorry I had to be the one to do it. But he would have killed your daughter if I hadn't."

"I'm glad you did it. Especially since he was playing rough with Lori. I thought that kid and his father knew to keep their hands off my family. I was the one man in this part of Wyoming the Hennesseys never ran afoul after an earlier conflict involving a proposed opera house in town and an ordinance he tried to pass against it."

"I heard about that."

"I'm sure he's harbored his grievances against me, but he's never acted on them. For good reason. One, I'm a better man than Kreg Hennessey. A law-abiding citizen. And I have the men to stand against him."

McCrae took another sip of his Scotch. "When someone messes with my family, my crew, my stock, or my land—there's hell to pay. The Indians and a good many rustlers found that out the hard way."

"I guess the Stolebergs have, too."

McCrae jerked a surprised look at him, beetling his gray brows. "Who told you that?"

"I have my sources."

"Already? You just got here last night."

"I learned a lot from your daughter . . . among others I met after the dustup with Hennessey."

"So you really did become fast friends, you and Lori. I should warn you to take everything she told you, especially regarding me and the Stolebergs, with a big grain of salt."

"Advice noted."

Studying Stockburn, the old man smiled. "I like a man who works fast. At first, I wasn't sure it was good for the Stewarts to bring an outsider in on this matter. Even a Wells Fargo man. Even a man with your reputation."

"You mean in on the rail crew's massacre."

"Exactly." McCrae leaned forward, reaching for the decanter. "More?"

"Why not? I'll probably never taste the like again."

Wolf held his empty glass over the table, and McCrae filled it liberally. The rancher splashed more into his own glass, then grabbed some meat and cheese. "Take some of this. The sausage is from an elk one of my sons shot last fall. Yellow Feather made the cheese. I have a small but good dairy herd."

Wolf took some of the meat and cheese and sampled each. McCrae had been right. The rich, spicy flavors of the smoked meat and the cheese were a nice complement to the peaty Scotch. "Damn, that's good," Stockburn said, chewing.

Also chewing, McCrae sank back in his chair again. It was a large, leather chair, and it appeared to half swallow his lumpy, aged body. "Let's not discuss the Stolebergs. They're a sore point for me. Now more than ever."

Stockburn frowned. "Oh?"

"Never mind." McCrae wagged his head, brushed cheese crumbs from his trouser leg. "Let's get down to brass tacks. How do you think I can help you, Stockburn? That's obviously why you rode out here."

"The answer to that question is very simple." Stockburn finished his meat and cheese then gave the rancher a pointed look. "Who do you think might have wanted those men killed, those rails blown, and why?"

"Stoleberg." McCrae frowned down at his glass again. He was running his right index finger quickly around the rim. His red face had turned a darker red from a sudden flare-up of a deep-burning anger.

He took a quick sip of the Scotch, smacked his lips, and looked at Stockburn. "Stoleberg," he repeated, flaring his nostrils and narrowing his eyes.

Suddenly, he was deadly serious. Grave. His head swelled until it looked as though it might explode.

When he said nothing more but just sat casting that glassy, ancient-warrior's blood-thirsty gaze at Stockburn, Wolf said, "Would you, uh . . . like to tell me why you suspect your neighbor, Mister McCrae?"

"Surely Lori told you about our, uh . . . trouble?"

"Your daughter was fairly tight-lipped on the topic."

"Ah."

"But a few others told me about the old trouble. Is that why you think the Stolebergs are responsible for the carnage?"

"Yes." McCrae took some more cheese and an egg and looked across the table at Stockburn. "I haven't seen or heard from Rufus in a while. I usually see him on the range a few times a year. Mostly from a distance or when we've hoisted the truce flag to cut our beef from the mixed herd during the fall gather.

"We've started the roundup now, just taking a break today to rest the men and horses, but I haven't seen old Rufus. He's hanging low. Likely keeping his head down." The rancher popped the meat and cheese into his mouth. Chewing, he said, "He always stays low when he's up to something."

He popped the egg into his mouth.

Pondering, Stockburn leaned forward and plucked a couple of the egg halves off the plate. He ate one and said, "And his motive for killing those men and sabotaging the rails and the work train is simply he's peeved that the Hell's Jaw Company didn't buy the right-of-way from him."

"Sure." McCrae brushed his hands on the legs of his corduroy trousers. "That's reason enough for that old devil. I made good money off that deal, and I'll make more when they start contracting with the mines up at the pass. There's a lot of gold in that mountain up yonder. More than I ever thought. It's all gonna come down . . . across Triangle." He grinned in devilish delight. "And three percent of what the rail line makes will line my pockets. Not Stoleberg's. Mine. And it gravels that old son of a bitch more than you could ever know!"

"You take delight in that," Wolf observed, chewing the second half of his egg, picking up his glass again, and leaning back in his chair.

"We hate each other, Stockburn. As only two rival landowners can. He hates me because I got the better graze and the better water. He tried to take my land by underhanded ways, wicked schemes, by force. When he couldn't get it that way, he tried to steal my cattle."

"You hanged one of his sons for just that, I hear."

Here came that keen anger again—the fuming dark fury of an old Scottish warrior as he sharpens his broadsword on the eve of battle, anticipating the spilling of buckets of English blood. "Yes, I did. And I'd do it again. Riley Hennessey didn't have anything on Sandy Stoleberg."

"How do your sons feel about the spur line?"

"What do you mean?"

"Are they both in agreement that it's a good thing for you?"

McCrae cast the detective a knowing smile. "Boy, you do work fast. Someone told you Law isn't on board with it."

Stockburn waited, holding the man's amused gaze.

McCrae chuckled. "It's true that my son doesn't agree with the mining. He thinks it's going to somehow impinge on Triangle graze, and that the spur line is going to bring more unwanted settlement. He might have a point, but I disagree. That disagreement, however, is certainly not motive enough for Law to commit murder. Besides, my oldest son would never, ever cross his old man."

He cast Stockburn a grave, direct look, smiling certainly. "That might sound naïve, Stockburn, but it's true."

Stockburn drank the last of his Scotch, set the glass on the table.

McCrea reached for the decanter. "More? There's plenty."

"No, no." Stockburn laughed. "The day is still young, and I have a few miles to ride."

"You goin' over to Stoleberg's?"

"I aim to venture that way, yes. Can you give me directions?"

"Might be trouble. I know your reputation, Stockburn, but you're only one man. Ol' Rufus doesn't really employ cow punchers anymore. Most of his men are gunnies. Leastways, that's what I've heard and what my sons and other men have seen. He's working himself up into something.

"I don't know what. Maybe his move against the Hell's Jaw Rail Line was only the beginning. I can send men over there with you. Be happy to, in fact."

He arched his brows, letting Wolf know it wasn't an idle offer.

Stockburn smiled. "Thanks, Mister McCrae." He rose, snatching another chunk of meat off the plate and popping it into his mouth. He plucked his hat off the chair's left arm. "I think it might be best if I mosey over minus the war paint."

"Are you sure?" McCrae rose with a grunt. "If he's going to make a move on me directly, I'd just as soon he made it, and we got it over with."

"I'm sure." Stockburn shook the man's hand. "Nice talking to you. And, uh"—he glanced at the food and the whiskey decanter—"and the repast. I'll remember it fondly."

"The pleasure was mine, Stockburn. I'd hoped I'd meet you one day. Thank you for snatching my daughter from the claws of that savage Hennessey boy."

"I'm glad I was there. I like Lori, and I hope she's feeling better soon. Please give her my regards."

"I will. Good luck to you. Mind your top knot, as they say in Indian . . . and Stoleberg . . . country." McCrae laughed dryly then turned to the study door. "I'll draw you a rough map to the Tin Cup and send you on your way."

Stockburn followed the man back through the house. He paused at the base of a staircase and stared up toward the dark mouth of a second-floor hall.

Lori.

He set his hat on his head and followed McCrae to the front door.

CHAPTER 17

It took Stockburn an hour to ride back into the canyon of the Big Sandy River, where the scene of the massacre lay and where he'd narrowly escaped his own untimely demise at the hands of the bastard with the big rifle.

He'd made a mental note to keep an eye out for that fella. He hadn't gotten a good look at him. All Wolf knew was that the man had long hair, a low-crowned black hat, and a Big Fifty or something similar. A long range, single-shot rifle of some kind.

The kind of rifle that would stick out in a crowd. If the man was ever in a crowd. Probably a loner.

Probably a regulator. Most regulators were loners.

Who had hired this one?

Stockburn had a feeling that when he found that out, he'd have the man who'd sent the killers out to massacre the Hell's Jaw rail crew.

As he crossed the canyon, passing the work-train wreckage, he checked his time piece. It was pushing on toward four in the afternoon. He didn't have much light left. Only an hour or two. He wouldn't make it to the Tin Cup headquarters before dark. He'd look for a good camping sight and then throw down his gear, tend to his horse, and build a fire.

He needed a night out under the stars, alone, to think over what he'd learned so far. And what he was going to do with what he'd learned. He had trouble thinking in town. Too much noise, too many people. Stockburn didn't like distractions.

The thing about him was, and he'd always known this to be true, was that he was a loner. He'd probably have made a good regulator.

Enjoyed his solitude. Had a sharp aim. Good power of concentration. Picked up after himself. Always kept an eye skinned on his back trail.

The trouble was, he was severely allergic to hemp.

He chuckled to himself as he trotted Smoke through the gap in the canyon's southeast wall. Stoleberg's graze started just beyond the wall.

As he entered that land now, the rock walls pulling back behind him, another valley opened before him. He was at the high end of it. He rode straight ahead and down into the valley, which instantly appeared drier than the terrain behind him.

He could see far ahead, because there were few trees, only short brown, ochre, and yellow grasses spiked here and there with prickly pear cactus. The lower land ahead was gently rolling, peppered with sparse cedars and aspens. There were bare patches where cattle had been allowed to overgraze.

Fingerling hills cropped out into the valley from steep ridges on both sides. Those ridges, too, had a dry look about them. If there were trees on them, they were sparse and stunted, mostly consisting of willows and small cottonwoods growing in shallow troughs running down the sides of the slopes.

Cattle grazed here and there, obviously a shorthorn hybrid, with very few white faces. From what Stockburn could see as he loped down the center of the gently dropping valley floor, Stoleberg's cattle didn't look as healthy as those he'd seen of McCrae's herd. They appeared smaller, scrubbier, some with ribs showing, hips pushed up like saddletrees beneath the lusterless hides.

To Stockburn's left, beyond the lower ridges and quartering behind him as he continued east along the valley, loomed the gray, snow-tipped peak of Gannett Mountain. It was near the base of that formidable-looking formation that Hell's Jaw Pass lay, and all the gold being ripped out of it and needing transportation down the slopes to Wild Horse.

If what Stockburn learned here on Tin Cup range didn't satisfy him, he'd head up toward the pass tomorrow. Mining camps were usually good places to sniff out secrets.

Stockburn stopped and set up his night camp forty-five minutes after beginning his trek down the dry valley toward the Tin Cup headquarters. The sun had dropped suddenly behind the peaks to his right, and deep, cool shadows bled across the range. Stars flickered to life in the soft velvet sky, and coyotes yammered from the surrounding knobs.

Cattle lowed and owls hooted mournfully.

The detective tended his horse, gathered wood, built a fire in a stone ring, and set his coffee pot to boil on a flat rock in the crackling flames. He'd packed fatback and beans in his war bag, and he cooked the meal now in a tin pot over the flames.

He ate the simple meal sitting close to the fire, his back to it so's not to compromise his night vision. A knife-edged cold had tumbled down from the higher reaches, rife with the smell of pine and cold rock, and even wearing his buckskin coat, which he'd carried wrapped around his bedroll and rainslicker, Stockburn shivered against the penetrating chill.

For a time after he'd turned into his bedroll, he lay sleepless against the wooly underside of his saddle. He thought about Lori McCrae. Maybe he should have intervened on her behalf. Her family's actions against her simply wanting to stay home instead of returning to school in the East seemed insensibly, damn near savagely, harsh.

He remembered her father mentioning letters and wondered what that had been about. Lori's letters to whom? Who hadn't answered them? The letters had really set her off, poor girl.

Finally, Wolf let it go. It was a family affair. It had nothing to do with what he was here to investigate.

He turned his thoughts to the business at hand—to what Norman McCrae had told him about Rufus Stoleberg and about how McCrae so firmly believed that his competing rancher was responsible for the massacre and the attempt to ruin the rail line.

McCrae couldn't be considered a disinterested party. Nor an objective one. Obviously, McCrae would like nothing better than to see Stoleberg run out of the country.

It sounded like both ranchers had been trying to destroy the other one for years. McCrae had even hanged a Stoleberg son. Stockburn took what McCrae had told him with a grain of salt. The same grain of salt with what Lori had told him.

But she hadn't told him that much. Not about the Stolebergs.

Finally, Wolf let that matter go, as well, for now. Tomorrow was another day.

He slept deeply, rose early, built up the fire to rewarm the leftovers of the previous night's supper, including the coffee, and ate watching a spectacular sunrise straight ahead of him to the east and slightly south. It was an explosion of light—bayonets of golds, salmons, coppers, and yellows stabbing across the high-arching sky belted with flat clouds and sending shadows scampering like a vast pack of frightened coyotes.

He took his time smoking an Indian Kid, lounging a little longer than usual to further enjoy the show. He had not lived so long, nor become so jaded by all that he'd experienced, that he did not still enjoy the simple, magical spectacle of a western sunrise.

As the air warmed, Wolf wrapped his coat around his bedroll and strapped the roll to Smoke's back, behind the cantle of his saddle. He kicked dirt on his fire, mounted up, and continued his journey down the long, broad valley.

He headed toward a craggy stone formation, shaped roughly like a giant clipper ship run aground and humping up out of the valley floor a few hundred yards ahead. According to Norman McCrae's hastily sketched map, the Stoleberg headquarters lay another five miles beyond that formation, identified as "Ship Rock" on the map.

He was two hundred yards from the rock when four riders appeared, moving into view from the other side of the ship-like formation, angling around its left side in single file and then spreading out across the valley as they continued trotting toward Stockburn.

"Well, well—what have we here? Welcoming party?"

Wolf slowed Smoke to a fast walk, scowling curiously beneath the brim of his black sombrero. One of the riders riding toward him turned his head toward the others, issuing orders.

"Let's get around him," he said, probably thinking Wolf couldn't hear. But it was a quiet morning, the air was light, and the man who'd spoken was only a hundred yards away.

Two peeled off the right side of the man who'd spoken, putting their mounts into hard gallops and approaching Wolf now from ahead and left. The other man peeled his own mount, a blue roan, off the left side of the man who'd issued the order. He galloped hard, elbows raised, leaning slightly forward in his saddle, toward Wolf on the detective's right.

"Hmmm," Stockburn said, pulling back on Smoke's reins, stopping the horse. "Trying to surround a man doesn't seem all that welcoming if you ask me."

He looked at the man who'd issued the order. That man was trotting his horse straight toward Stockburn. The others were riding up on him hard but swinging wide to get around him. The scissoring hooves of their galloping horses thudded against the hard, dry ground.

When the two riders on his left were roughly fifty yards away, and the single rider on his right was about the same distance but closing fast, Stockburn reined Smoke around sharply and rammed his heels against the stallion's flanks.

"Let's go, boy!"

Not about to let himself get caught in a whipsaw, Stockburn rode straight back the way he'd come.

"Get him!" one of the men shouted behind him. "Get that son of a bitch!"

Crouched low over his saddle horn, his hat brim pulled low, Smoke stretching his legs out in a ground-burning stride, Wolf said, "Now, how would those fellas know if I was a son of a bitch or not? I wouldn't know any of them from Adam's off-ox!"

Behind him, one of the riders whooped.

Another triggered a pistol, the crackling report rising through the hard thuds of the several sets of galloping horses and through the rush of the breeze brushing past Wolf's ears.

Ahead and to the right was a low ridge sloping down into the valley from another, higher ridge on that side. Wolf swung Smoke toward the ridge.

As he did, more whoops and shouts rose behind him. A pistol cracked two more times. Stockburn heard one of the bullets sing through the air to his left. The other thudded into the ground off to his right and behind him.

Smoke gained the lesser ridge and shot up the side at a northwesterly angle.

Stockburn glanced over his left shoulder. The riders had closed together again, strung out side by side, roughly twenty feet apart. They were galloping hard and fast, crouched low, the man who'd issued the orders to get around Wolf holding a pistol barrel up in his right hand.

As Smoke reached the top of the secondary ridge, Stockburn swung him right, following the upward tilting crest toward the larger, higher primary ridge dead ahead now. As horse and rider gained the pass where the two ridges intersected, Stockburn shot one more glance behind him.

His four shadowers were keeping pace, maybe even closing a bit.

Wolf reined Smoke on down the other side of the pass. A narrow canyon opened between two stone walls just ahead and on the right. Wolf swung Smoke into the mouth, knowing it could be a box canyon.

On the other hand, he might be able to lose his pursuers in the rugged terrain. After another fifty yards the canyon forked. Stockburn reined Smoke into the left fork, which joined the right fork again soon after.

The canyon swerved to the left, then right, then back left, the ground dampened by a runout spring. As Stockburn and Smoke swerved right again, a loud whoop sounded nearby. Too late, Wolf saw a man sitting a steel-dust horse atop the canyon's right wall, which was only ten feet high at that point.

The man grinned beneath the brim of his bullet-crowned cream sombrero. He wore a sack coat over a checked shirt, and leather chaps. Two pistols bristled on his hips.

He was swinging a loop out from the lariat coiled in his left hand.

Wolf tried to duck but not before the loop settled over his head and drew taut around his shoulders. The man dallied the lariat around his horn, and the braided leather drew suddenly taut, jerking Wolf out of his saddle.

He kicked free of his stirrups so he wouldn't break an ankle.

Suddenly, Smoke was gone from beneath him. He turned a backward somersault and hit the ground hard about his head and shoulders— the second time in twenty-four hours he'd tried that painful maneuver, though it had not been voluntary either time.

"Dutch ride!" screeched the man holding the other end of the lariat. His long face was a mask of predatory glee.

Vaguely, Wolf was aware of other riders galloping toward him as he lay facing up canyon on his chest and belly, again trying to clear the fog from his brain. The man with the lariat spurred his own mount off the canyon's low wall to Wolf's right, shouting louder, "Dutch ride, fellas! Let give Wells Fargo the time of his life. Yee-HAH!"

Wolf swung around to face the man spurring his horse past him, heading up canyon and intending to drag Wolf along behind him. At the moment, the lariat around Wolf's arms was slack. It would not be in a few seconds, when his tormentor had gained some distance and pulled it taut.

Wolf grabbed the Colt holstered on his right thigh and slid it out of the leather. Cocking it, he rolled up onto his left shoulder, aiming the Peacemaker from just above his right hip, angling the barrel up and hardening his jaws as he fired.

The first shot missed the whooping rider galloping past him, but Wolf's second shot took the man through the back of his left shoulder.

The man screamed. So did his horse, which reared suddenly, clawing at the air with its front hooves and arching its tail. The rider flew over the tail to hit the ground and roll.

Wolf whipped the lariat loop from over his head, and the fleeing horse dragged it off behind it, past its rider who was still rolling in the brush along the canyon's right wall.

Stockburn rose. The fallen rider rolled up on his left shoulder, showing his face, gritting his teeth, glaring at Stockburn.

He had a pistol in his hand.

As he cursed and clicked the hammer back, Stockburn extended his own Colt and shot the man twice in the chest. The man grunted as he fell back against the canyon wall, smashing his gun against the wall, as well, before dropping to a shoulder in deep brush, jerking.

Still hearing riders galloping toward him, Stockburn ran to Smoke standing to his left, looking around warily, sidestepping and whickering. Wolf holstered his Colt and shucked his Winchester from its saddle sheath. He slapped Wolf on the butt, and the horse galloped back down the canyon the way they'd come.

Guns crackled. Bullets sliced the air around him.

Stockburn cocked the Winchester and dropped to a knee. "You want to dance," he said, "we'll dance." He pumped a cartridge into the action.

CHAPTER 18

The other three riders were galloping down the forested slope on Stockburn's right. Somehow, the man Wolf had just sent back to his maker had come down ahead of them. These men knew the terrain out here. Wolf did not. They had the advantage.

The three riders galloped through the forest, meandering around pines and cedars, all three firing six-shooters as they rode, their horses hurling deadfalls and blowdowns, kicking up dead leaves and forest duff behind them.

Stockburn lined up his sights on the man riding to the left of the other two and fired.

The man screamed as the bullet punched him back over his horse's rear end.

That caused the other two to rein up suddenly and leap from their saddles.

One paused to slide a carbine from his saddle sheath, eyeing Stockburn warily as Wolf ejected the spent casing, seated a fresh one in the chamber, and aimed at the man who'd been riding in the middle of the pack. That man was running toward a tree roughly thirty feet up the slope from Wolf. The man wore a red-checked shirt with a red neckerchief and a wool-lined deerskin vest; he held two pistols in his hands.

Wolf fired.

"Ach!" the man cried, wincing and grabbing his left thigh.

He paused, glared toward Wolf, then hopped on his good leg to the tree he'd been heading for. He spat angrily then slid a look around the tree's right side.

Just as his hatted head came into view, Stockburn fired. A quarter-sized, black hole appeared in the man's left cheek, just beneath his eye.

Stockburn didn't watch the man fall. He didn't need to. The man was dead. Hearing only the satisfying thud as the man hit the ground, Wolf threw himself to his left. He'd sensed the third rider lining up the sights of his carbine on him. His senses had not failed him.

As he hit the ground on his left shoulder, the carbine belched. In the periphery of his vision, Stockburn saw the orange flames and smoke stab from the carbine's barrel as it poked around the left side of a birch tree straight up the slope from Stockburn's position.

Keeping his head down beneath the canyon's low, rocky wall, Wolf crabbed to his left. As he did, the man with the carbine sent three bullets hammering toward him fast.

Angrily.

The bullets zinged off the rocks and plunked into a cedar on the opposite side of the narrow canyon.

They were followed by one more that spanged loudly off a boulder to Wolf's left.

Crows cawed loudly.

Stockburn stopped, rose to a knee, and raised the Yellowboy to his shoulder. The barrel of the carbine poked out from behind an aspen tree, the aspen leaves making a bright golden carpet around the tree's base.

Wolf aimed at the carbine's barrel. He chewed his lip and narrowed his right eye, watching the barrel extend farther and farther out from the tree until it was followed by the upper half of a brown-hatted head.

The eye of the carbine-wielding pursuer appeared, staring toward Wolf. The eye was partly shaded by the brim of the man's hat. As that eye found Stockburn, and the man saw the rifle aimed at him, the eye widened.

Stockburn fired.

The eye disappeared as the bullet pulverized it on its way through the socket and back through the man's head, exiting the skull and thumping into the upslope behind the man, kicking up dirt and leaves. The back of the man's head turned the yellow leaves red.

He gave a soft grunt then fell straight back and lay on the gold-leaved carpet, thrashing his arms and legs for a moment, as though trying to make a leaf angel. Then he fell still. He broke wind— the last sound he'd ever make on earth.

Stockburn pumped a fresh round into the Yellowboy's chamber then lowered the hammer. He stared through his own wafting powder smoke, surveying the three dead men sprawled on the upslope before him.

"Nice to meet you fellas, too."

Stockburn reloaded the Yellowboy in case others like these four had similar intentions.

What those intentions had been, exactly, Wolf didn't know. Probably the same ones as the bastard with the Big Fifty. Whatever their intentions had been—to kill him or rough him up—a Dutch ride, which was frontier parlance for dragging someone behind a galloping horse until every stich of clothing had been ripped off, was no joke.

The punishment Wolf had dished up had been severe but appropriate to the offense. Frontier justice, maybe, but justice, by God.

He gathered the three bodies from the slope until all four dead men were lying shoulder to shoulder at the bottom of the shallow canyon. He inspected them closely. He recognized one, the man with the red shirt and neckerchief, as Lester Bohannon, a killer from Oklahoma.

Wolf had once played cards with Bohannon in the Eldridge Hotel in Kansas City. Bohannon had walked freely in public because, while it was widely known that he'd killed a good dozen men—even he himself had bragged about it, flaunting the information as though on an unwritten public résumé for more of the same kind of work—the law had never been able to gather enough evidence to issue an arrest warrant.

So, he'd drifted around, his cunning having made him modestly famous—or infamous, as the case may be, to those and the families of those he'd killed. He'd hired out his guns mostly to wealthy cattlemen in the southern Midwest with problems with nesters or rustlers or Indians but who wanted no blood on their own hands.

Wolf toed Bohannon's body. "You got careless, Lester." Riding with other men will make a man careless for some reason when, riding alone, he would never let his guard down. Wolf thought it probably had something to do with believing others would back you. Or distract your opponent.

Relying on others could get a man's clock cleaned.

Lester Bohannon stared up at Wolf Stockburn through heavy-lidded eyes. Beneath the left eye was the quarter-sized, puckered blue hole bored by Stockburn's .44 rifle. A little blood had oozed out of it while Bohannon's heart had pumped its last; that blood was now a half-inch, crusted, dark-red streak to the left of the hole, where it had started to run down the side of the dead man's face.

Stockburn studied the other three dead men. One looked vaguely familiar, but he couldn't place him. He'd probably run into the man—possibly even the other two at one time or another. While the West was vast, there still weren't that many people in it. You could run into the same stranger over and over again quite by accident.

After rummaging around in all four men's pockets, including Bohannon's, he found nothing to identify them or to give him any clue to who they'd been riding for. He had to assume, however, that they'd been riding for Rufus Stoleberg, since that was whose graze he was on.

"What do you say, fellas?" Wolf asked, hooking his thumbs behind his cartridge belt as he scowled down at the four sad-faced, dull-eyed dead men. "Let's go pay a call on the Stoleberg bunch and see what they got to say for themselves."

As Wolf gathered the three men's horses then tied the bodies over the horses' backs, a warning voice told him: "Could be riding into one hell of a hot bailiwick, Wolf. You gotta figure you might be going up against a whole lot more men similar to these. With the exact same intentions, which is more than likely to turn you toe down and kick you out with a cold shovel."

"Could be," Stockburn responded to the warning voice of his more conscious and possibly more intelligent alter ego. "But I don't have an army at my disposal, and I'm not gonna learn a damn thing dancing around the edges of this thing, so . . ."

Having tied three horses together and holding the reins of the first horse in the string, Stockburn swung up onto Smoke's back and booted the horse back in the direction he'd been heading before he'd been so rudely interrupted. The other four horses followed, whickering edgily at the blood and death stench.

Smoke wasn't overly keen on the smell himself. He occasionally glanced back at his rider, giving his copper-colored eyes a dubious roll, as if to say, "What kind of trouble have you gotten us into this time, you gray-headed devil?"

Stockburn loped the five horses back down the valley and around Ship Rock. He picked up a well-worn trail curving into the valley from the west, and continued riding through rugged canyon and low mesa country peppered with widely scattered cattle. Now Gannett Peak was back behind him as he traversed the Wind Rivers' southeastern slopes.

As he rode, he spied a half-dozen cowboys moving a herd of cows on a distant slope to his right, just below dark volcanic caprock and a fringe of cedars. He couldn't tell if the men spotted him. If they did, they gave no indication but continued to work their herd down toward the valley floor that Wolf and his grisly cargo were passing through.

Though the punchers were a good half a mile away, Stockburn could hear them whistling and calling, "Come bossy! Come boss, come boss!" Occasionally, they tossed a loop at a herd-quitting calf or a calf and its mother.

Ahead, the Tin Cup headquarters grew from a distant brown splotch in a shallow, fawn-colored bowl in the valley, abutted on its left by a distant but steep, rocky mountain ridge capped with snow, into separate buildings and corrals. A hitch-and-rail fence of unpeeled pine rails surrounded the entire compound, both ends connecting at the obligatory wooden portal straddling the trail with a high wooden crossbar bearing the Stoleberg name and brand.

The house sat up front and right with the barns, stables, and other outbuildings flanking it. There were two windmills, one before the house, the other to the rear, supplying water to the stock and the bunkhouse.

Just as the McCrae range's verdant health was reflected in the relative grandeur of its headquarters, the drab ill-health of the Stoleberg range shone in its own weathered gray buildings and the lack of greenery of even a single tree. The yard was entirely brown, minus any grass save a little dun-colored needle grass growing up around the foundations of the buildings.

Tumbleweeds had been allowed to collect against the surrounding fence until they'd made a formidable bastion.

The meek look of the place extended to the Tin Cup house, a humble log, barrack-like affair weathered to the color of the sky on a cloudy day. It appeared that the original cabin, consisting of only one or two rooms, had been added onto once or twice, when money had allowed, so that now there was an extended rear in the shape of a log rectangle, and part of a second floor.

The chinking between the cabin's logs appeared brittle and in need of patching. A single, sashed and dusty window looked down on the yard from the house's front gable, beneath the steeply pitched, shake-shingled roof. The window frame had been painted white, but little white remained. Many of the shakes on the roof were missing or had been replaced by tin long since gone to rust.

The large front porch sat listing to one side, adding to the house's resemblance to a derelict ship.

In front of that porch now, ten or so horseback riders sat facing the lodge.

"Hmm," Stockburn said to himself. "That's quite a few fellas there. Maybe I should've listened to my smarter self and run in the other direction."

Too late now.

He was within thirty yards of the portal and several of the riders, having heard the hoof thuds of his approach, had turned their heads to study the visitor. One by one and two by two, more heads turned to Stockburn as he passed beneath the portal and came on into the yard. He stopped about halfway between the portal and the house.

All of the horseback riders had turned toward him now. A few had turned their horses so they could face him full on, hands sliding toward holstered pistols.

A hasty count of the men told Wolf there were twelve. They'd all been facing a man on the ground. Now that man had turned toward Stockburn, as well. They all regarded the newcomer warily, some even pugnaciously, but none appeared ready to grab a riata and play cat's cradle with his head. Or even to take him for a Dutch ride over rough rocks.

That, Wolf figured, was a plus in his column.

He kept his hands away from his own holstered Peacemakers as he gigged Smoke forward, the other horses following in rough single file, whickering, one shaking its head and rattling the bridle bit in its teeth.

"Halloo the ranch," Stockburn called.

All of the men sitting horses before Stockburn had turned their mounts to face him now. The man on the ground shoved one horse aside with both hands—no, with only *one* hand, Wolf quickly amended, seeing that the man had only one hand and one arm. His left arm was missing.

The horseback riders seemed to defer to this man, who was maybe thirty, possibly a few years older, as he stepped away from the close-clumped horsebackers and walked a little unsteadily toward Wolf. He appeared to have a problem with his legs, which moved stiffly, apparently not wanting to bend at the knee.

He was a good-looking man with a thick mane of dark-brown hair parted on one side and hanging over his collar in back. Clean-shaven, suntanned, he was slender, of average height, and clad in a red silk shirt with Mexican embroidering on the breast, collar, and sleeves.

The cuffs of his black denim trousers were shoved down into high-topped black boots. He wore no gun, only a wide, black leather belt with a hammered silver concho for a buckle.

He held a notebook and pencil in his lone hand. He wore a scowl as he scrutinized the horses over which the dead men rode.

"Can I . . . help you?" he asked, glancing skeptically between Stockburn and the dead men.

Stockburn dropped the lead horse's reins and canted his head toward it. "These your men?"

The one-armed, handsome man studied Stockburn, frowning. He glanced behind him as two of the riders peeled away from the pack and rode up near the one-armed man, flanking him and regarding Stockburn truculently.

One was big and rawboned, with a blond

soup-strainer mustache and a brooding bulldog face with heavy-lidded eyes. His face was shaded by a big cream sombrero. "What do we have here, brother?"

"Not sure yet, Carlton," said the one-armed man, Daniel. "Not sure what we have here."

He looked at Stockburn again then stepped forward in his painful way though his face did not betray any such pain. He walked over to the ground-reined horse and crouched to study the face of its dead rider, who was Lester Bohannon.

Daniel walked around to the other dead men. After inspecting the fourth man he limped back up and stopped near Stockburn. His face betrayed no emotion.

"Nope," he said. "Can't say as they are. Good thing, too, since all four are looking a little worse for the wear. If they were Tin Cup riders, you'd be in a whole heap of trouble, mister."

The big, rawboned rider named Carlton cursed and gigged his horse forward. Dust lifted from his horse's hooves to churn thickly in the sunlit air as he rode around the horses carrying the dead men, leaning out from his saddle to inspect each dead man in turn.

When he'd given them each a cursory appraisal, he galloped back up and stopped near Daniel, scowling balefully at Stockburn and saying in his thick, throaty voice that was half snarl, "What the hell is the meaning of this—ridin' in here like you're king for the day, toting dead men?"

"Did you kill these men?" Daniel asked.

"Yes," Wolf said.

"Why?" asked both Daniel and Carlton at the same time.

"They tried to kill me." Stockburn looked from Carlton to Daniel. "Did you send 'em?"

He'd always believed in getting to the point, even when he might possibly be in enemy territory. It was just his way.

The second near horseback rider rode his own mount up beside Carlton. He was tall and lean with a broad face with a few old acne scars and wide-set blue eyes. Stockburn could see a family resemblance in him and Carlton and the one-armed man, Daniel, who was maybe a few years younger than the lean one who'd ridden up, a smile on his lips but challenge in his eyes.

"What kinda trouble we got now, brothers?" he asked, his fiery gaze on Stockburn. "What kinda fool rides onto the Tin Cup toting dead men and sits there like he's cock of the walk, spewing accusations? If you're from Triangle . . ."

He let his words trail off as he leaned forward in his saddle and closed his hand around the butt of the old Schofield revolver jutting up from the holster on his right hip.

"Keep it holstered, Reed," Daniel said. He hadn't looked at the man, but he obviously knew him well enough to know he was ready to slap leather. Keeping his eyes on Stockburn, he said, "Who are you?" He frowned and canted his head to one side, curious. "Law?"

"Wells Fargo. Stockburn. Wolf Stockburn. I'm investigating the massacre of the Hell's Jaw Railroad Line's rail crew."

"You think *we* did it?" Carlton asked. Snapped, rather. Glaring coldly and with no little threat at Stockburn. It had been more of an accusation than a question.

Angry mutters rose from the other men sitting their horses a good ways behind the nearest three. By twos and threes, those men closed hands over their own holstered six-shooters, angry scowls on their faces, and came forward.

Here we go, Stockburn thought, feeling the devil's cold fingers reach up from hell's bowels to tickle his toes.

CHAPTER 19

"Stand down, fellas," Daniel said, holding up his lone hand in which he held the notebook and pencil. "Easy, now. Easy, now. I think there's just been a little misunderstanding, is all."

"You know how I don't like bein' misunderstood, Daniel," growled Carlton.

"Me neither!" added Reed, still leaning forward in his worn stockman's saddle, his gloved right hand still on his holstered Schofield. He was grinning, but his grin nowhere nearly reached his eyes.

"I tell you what," Daniel said, smiling amicably up at his two brothers, one on each side of him. "Why don't you two go ahead with the day's work? Head on up to Table Rock, bring the herd on down to the South Fork of Dutch Joe, and cut out the two-year-olds. Stop by the Borger place, and make sure old Ephraim and his boys will start hauling hay down here tomorrow, as planned. Long, cold winter ahead. I'll see you back here for supper."

"I don't know, Daniel." Carlton kept his truculent gaze on Stockburn. "I think we need to stretch some hemp."

"Nah, nah," Daniel said, good-naturedly. "I don't think that'll be necessary. We don't need trouble with Wells Fargo. Go on, now, brothers. Take the men and get to it. Days keep getting shorter all the damn time, which means we got to pack more work into each and every one. Go on, now. Off with ya. Git!"

Chuckling, he hazed them all off with his notebook and pencil.

Grudgingly, Carlton and Reed and the other ten men rode across the yard and out through the portal, each and every one casting belligerent gazes back behind him, one glaring at Stockburn as he leaned out from his saddle to spit distastefully into the dirt.

As their dust sifted and their hoof thuds dwindled, Stockburn looked at Daniel, impressed. "You're in good command here, I see. Daniel Stoleberg, I take it?"

Young Stoleberg nodded then narrowed one eye and crooked a mouth corner. "Someone's gotta be in command. Out in the field, leastways." He swatted his empty left sleeve with his notebook. "Not much else I can do but spew orders."

Stockburn nodded grimly.

"Snakebite," Stoleberg said. "Horse threw me on my twentieth birthday. A half-wild mustang my father gave me. I took ol' Lightning out for a wild ride and he threw me into a rattlesnake nest along Dutch Joe. A neighbor who'd been an army surgeon, and still good with a bone saw, cut my arm off or I would have died of gangrene."

While the young rancher had been talking, he'd been limping around the horses carrying the dead men, giving them each another brief, casual study. "I still wasn't expected to pull through. The pain was so bad I howled and howled for days . . . till my old man and brothers wanted to shoot me to give 'em some peace and quiet!"

He chuckled, swatted his right leg with the notebook, and grinned wryly up at Stockburn. "Nerve damage gave me this limp. Keeps me off the cutting horses. Oh, I can ride, but mostly I just limp around here . . . giving orders. That's what I do now. I limp around and give orders. Or relay orders from Pa, I should say. He's still ramrod—officially, leastways."

Young Stoleberg continued to smile ironically up at Stockburn, squinting an eye against the sun, as though the misfortune that had befallen him was a favorite joke of his.

"Like you said," Wolf said, "someone's gotta do it."

"That's right."

Stockburn turned to the dead men again. "These aren't your men, then? Your father didn't hire them?"

"No, sir, he did not. Sorry to disappoint you, Mister Stockburn. Where'd you run into 'em?"

"On your range maybe six, seven miles back up the valley."

"Back up the valley, eh?" Daniel stared in that

223

direction, rubbing his jaw. "Triangle range up that way." He glanced at Stockburn. "Could be McCrae's men. He might be rustling our beef again. He does that every once in a while. Just to needle us."

"That's what he told me you do—to him."

Daniel Stoleberg smiled. "He would say that. It's hard for the old fellas to bury their hatchets." He paused a moment then frowned and said, "Pardon my manners. For Heaven's sake—you've had a long ride. No matter where you came from, it's a long ride to the Tin Cup. Light and stay a spell, Mister Stockburn. I was about to head in for a cup of coffee."

"I'll take you up on that." Stockburn swung down from Smoke's back.

"What shall we do with the fresh beef, Stockburn? These men don't belong here."

Wolf grinned at the young man. "I shot 'em, Daniel. You can't expect me to bury 'em, too." He was not, however, convinced the four dead men had not come from the Tin Cup. It would take the word of more than one interested and likely prejudiced party, even if young Stoleberg's word had been backed by his brothers.

Stockburn wanted to hear what the elder Stoleberg had to say on the topic.

Daniel sighed and rubbed his jaw again, thoughtful. "Well . . . I reckon I can have the stable boys bury 'em out on the range. I'll have them lay them out in the icehouse for a few days, in case someone comes around for 'em."

"That might be a good idea. No telling who they belong to. I know one is Lester Bohannon, a regulator for cattlemen back in Oklahoma. I have no idea about the other three. Probably of the same ilk."

As Stockburn and Daniel began walking toward the house, Stockburn leading Smoke by his reins, Daniel said, "I assure you, Mister Stockburn, my father did not hire those men."

"I'd like to believe that, Daniel. Perhaps I could have a word with him?"

"Sure, sure, for all the good it'll do."

"How's that?"

"You'll see."

As they approached the house, Stockburn glanced at Daniel and said, "What about the younger fellas?"

"What?"

"Have the younger fellas buried their hatchets? In regard to the old trouble between you folks and the McCraes, I mean."

Daniel shrugged. "I've buried mine. I've convinced my brothers to do the same. Clinging to the past is no way to move ahead. We have a dry range here, Mister Stockburn. Most of the moisture gets dropped on the other side of the divide.

"That means we have to move our herds

around often. It also means we have to work extra hard for water. That means digging wells. Deep ones. We have two more to dig before next summer. We're going to get started right after roundup."

"That is a lot of work."

"A helluva lot of work. It leaves little time for fighting outdated wars." Daniel stopped as Stockburn tied Smoke to one of the two hitchracks fronting the house. "Old men's wars."

"All right," Stockburn said, with a non-committal nod.

Just then a guttural cry rose from behind the house's heavy oak door, which was propped open with a rock. The cry was so loud and startling that Stockburn found himself automatically reaching for the Peacemaker holstered on his left hip.

He removed his hand from the big piece when a young boy, just a toddler of maybe three, scampered out of the house's inner shadows and onto the porch.

Clad in knickers and a black jacket, he was trailing a frayed, pale blue blanket and pressing an index finger to the corner of his wet mouth, yelling and chortling incoherently. The boy's big grin and large, sparkling brown eyes accompanied his impassioned cries.

The boy stopped just outside the door, saw Stockburn then pointed his finger straight out from his shoulder, rose up onto the toes of his black patent shoes, and wailed, "Dodo-hoh! Dodo-hoh! Kweeh! *Kweeh!*"

"Say, there young man," Wolf said, planting one boot on a porch step then leaning forward on his knee. "I've been called a might worse by taller gents than you!"

That seemed to delight the boy no end. He stomped both feet, a maneuver that nearly sent him sprawling, then bent his knees and rose up, straightening them quickly, and howling skyward.

"Estella! Estella!" Daniel called, limping up the porch steps and intercepting the toddler before he could gain the edge.

"Coming!" came a woman's breathless voice from inside the house. Footsteps followed and then a round Mexican woman in a black maid's dress, gray hair betraying her middle age, appeared in the doorway.

"Please, Estella—take the kid back inside. I have a guest here, and the kid's liable to fall down the porch steps. What on earth is the door doing open, anyway?"

"For Grace," the maid said, glancing at Stockburn. She appeared flushed from work. "She said she needed fresh air. For her headaches." She waved her hand in the air beside her head.

"Another headache?"

"Si, si." The maid threw up both hands then crouched to pick up the boy, who was chortling more quietly now, as though realizing his presence here was not approved of. He absently fingered the lace on the maid's dress collar but kept his interested eyes on Stockburn.

Wolf grinned at the boy then reached out to give the small, doughy nose a squeeze between his thumb and index finger.

The boy jerked back to life, laughing hysterically.

"Please, take the boy away," Daniel urged the woman. "Keep an eye on him until Grace can manage him."

"I am not as young as I used to be, Daniel," the maid crisply retorted, giving young Stoleberg a piqued look before carrying the child inside.

"Oh, and please have Oscar fetch the horses yonder—oh, there he is." As a Mexican man roughly Estella's age appeared in the shadowy hall—a trim, balding man wearing a white shirt and broadcloth trousers—Daniel said, "Oscar, please lead the four horses in the yard to the stables. Have the stable boys lay the bodies tied to the saddles in the icehouse until further notice."

"Bodies?" Oscar said, glancing from Daniel to Stockburn then, brushing between the two men as he stepped up to the door, he peered into the yard.

He glanced back at Daniel, then crossed himself, and went out.

Daniel looked at Stockburn and gave a wry smile. "Superstitious Mexicano. Good folks, though, Estella and Oscar Ramirez. They've worked for my father since my mother died."

"I see," Stockburn said, holding his hat in his hands. "And the toddler?"

He could no longer see the boy, but he could hear him yammering away while the maid spoke to him in Spanish.

Daniel's handsome face acquired a funny look, one that Stockburn couldn't define. He covered it with another of his boyish smiles and said, "That's Buster. My brother and sister-in-law's boy. Carlton's the father. Buster came as quite a surprise because the doctor in Wild Horse said she couldn't have children. Oh, well."

Daniel threw his hands out and sighed and grinned once more. "Oh, well—we'll make do until Carlton and Grace can get their own place."

He turned, brushing the wall for support, then headed down the short hall to a narrow staircase, the treads and risers constructed from split pine logs, the rail merely a single, long pine pole, bowed and warped in places but otherwise solid. "Follow me. I'll introduce you to Pa. He doesn't get many visitors. He'll enjoy the company . . . if he's in the right frame of mind."

"Right frame of mind?"

"You'll see."

Daniel placed his right hand on the rail and

229

mounted the stairs. He rose slowly, clumsily, neither foot, it seemed, really wanting to make the climb.

Stockburn had heard about rattlesnake bites leaving nerve damage though he'd never witnessed the actual thing himself until now. He found himself feeling deeply sorry for the young man. An accident had taken his youth right at the crest of his virility, just when most young men were thinking about settling down with a young lady and raising a family.

Daniel grunted, breathing heavily, as he climbed. Obviously frustrated.

"I'm sorry, Mister Stockburn," he said when he stopped halfway up the stairs for a breather. "This is why I sleep on the first story. I rarely come up here, though Pa's office is up here. We usually discuss business at the kitchen table, over breakfast and supper."

"Not a problem, Daniel. Take your time."

"You're too kind," Daniel said, staring straight ahead and laughing.

It was a weird laugh. Sorrow mixed with rage and humiliation.

Stockburn wanted to place his hand on the young man's shoulder, to show some sympathy and affection for Daniel's travails, but he sensed the gesture would only further embarrass him. He wanted to suggest that he make the trip to Rufus Stoleberg's upstairs office alone.

But, again, he thought the suggestion might offend the young man.

"Here we go," Daniel said, drawing a breath, hardening his jaws, and resuming the climb.

His boots clomped loudly on the stairs—one loud clomp at a time, spaced about two seconds apart. Wolf followed patiently, running his own left hand lightly along the rail. He found himself prepared to catch the young man if he fell.

When they'd gained the top of the stairs, Daniel took another short breather, sucking deep breaths, blowing the air out, sucking it back in again, all the while smiling, laughing, his thick, mussed, dark-brown hair hanging over his eyes.

"All right," he said, brushing his hair back out of his face with one hand. "To the end of the hall. I'll be damned if I won't make it!"

Stockburn strode beside him, going slow.

The hall was paneled in simple, unadorned, vertical pine planks. Only one picture hung on the wall—an old tintype of a young couple in wedding attire, the man sitting, the white-clad young lady standing beside him holding flowers in a photographer's faux parlor getup. As per the times, neither smiled.

"Your folks?" Stockburn asked as he and Daniel passed the picture on their right.

Breathless, Daniel merely nodded.

As he and Stockburn continued, a door in the hall's left side opened, hinges whining.

A young woman with lusterless blond hair and ashen features leaned her head into the hall, frowning. Her eyes found Stockburn's host, and she said wearily, "Daniel? What's all the commotion?"

Daniel laughed and poked Stockburn in the ribs. "This is my lovely sister-in-law. Appropriately named Grace. Ain't she sweet?" To Grace, Daniel said in a razor-edged tone, "The commotion dear, sis, was me climbing the stairs. I'm sorry if I awoke you from your slumbers, but it is well past noon. We missed you for the midday meal."

"I have a headache," she snapped.

"Yes, well, the boy is running around like a mad dog downstairs. Why don't you fetch him and keep him up here with you before he kills himself in a tumble outside?"

"Oh, go to hell, Daniel!" Scowling, her face growing even paler, Grace slammed the door. She'd given Wolf a single, passing glance, dismissing his presence out of hand.

Daniel smiled. "Told you she was sweet."

"Uh-huh."

Stockburn followed young Stoleberg to the closed door at the end of the hall.

CHAPTER 20

Daniel Stoleberg knocked on the closed door lightly with the back of his hand. "Pa? Can I come in?"

Stockburn heard only muttering on the other side of the door.

Frowning, Daniel twisted the knob and opened the door. "You have a visitor, Pa."

Stockburn waited in the hall, hat in his hands, while Daniel limped into the room, which was no larger than the average bedroom. Beyond Daniel, Wolf saw a cluttered rolltop desk and some simple pine shelves bowing under the weight of many books and papers. A clock on a wall showed the wrong time.

Young Stoleberg turned his head to his left and said, "I have a visitor for you, Pa. Isn't that nice? We don't get many visitors."

"Oh?" came a low, phlegmy voice. It sounded like someone waking up from a nap. "Who is it?"

Daniel glanced at Stockburn.

Wolf stepped into the room, shuttling his gaze to the left. Rufus Stoleberg sat on one end of a battered sofa partly covered by an old Indian trade blanket. The man looked ancient and lumpy and unshaven in his longhandle red underwear and frayed plaid robe loosely tied about his bulbous waist. He wore thick wool socks; his big toe with a thick yellow nail protruded from a hole in the right one.

The room was badly cluttered with disarranged chairs and a couple of low tables on which sat glasses, bottles, playing cards, and overfilled ash-trays. There were plates with old food scraps. A small plate bearing an uneaten sandwich sat on a pile of yellowed papers on a low table to the old man's left, accompanied by a half-full glass of milk with a faint vertical steak on one side, where the man had recently taken a sip maybe a half hour ago.

The room was foul with old-man odors and stale cigar smoke.

Rufus Stoleberg looked at Stockburn, squinting each eye in turn, his heavy gray brows moving out of sinc with each other, like two hovering moths above eyes as blue as the autumn sky over the Wind Rivers.

"Hello, Mister Stoleberg," Wolf said. "I'm Wolf Stockburn. I'm a rail detective from Wells Fargo. I'm here to investigate the murder of the Hell's Jaw Rail crew."

Stoleberg appeared not to have heard the question. He stared at Stockburn with a strange expression, the moths of his brows still fluttering above his eyes. His face looked like an ancient hide water flask only half-full, creased where it fell in around itself. It was carpeted with several days of steel-filing beard stubble.

Stoleberg sat slumped back in the sofa, his neck bulging out and forming a thick, fleshy pedestal for his bullet-shaped head.

"Did you hear me, Mister Stoleberg?" Wolf asked. "You let me know if I need to speak loud—"

"Sandy?" the old man said, his blue eyes slowly widening and glinting with a strange recognition. He jerked to life, squirming around, twisting his shoulders, struggling to sit up. "Sandy-boy?"

Stockburn glanced from the old man to Daniel, who returned the look then turned to his father. "No, Pa. This isn't—"

"Sandy!" Stoleberg squirmed around, leaning forward, getting his weight settled over his knees. With a fierce grunt, he heaved himself to his feet.

He stood staring at Stockburn, eyes wide now, a delighted smile slowly shaping itself on his broad ruin of a face. "Sandy!"

"No, Pa," Daniel said, shaking his head. He cast Stockburn a nervous smile then said again, "No, Pa. This isn't—"

"Sure, it is." Stoleberg began walking toward Stockburn, slipping on scattered papers and old account books.

He knocked a plate of food scraps and a half-eaten apple off a table. Ignoring it, he continued toward Stockburn until he stood four feet away from the rail detective, staring up at him, appearing almost giddy with joy.

He was short—as short or shorter than Norman McCrae—but he was as broad as Stockburn. While old and obviously soft in his thinker box, the old rancher's body gave the impression of still-great power.

His arms were thick as were his short, stubby legs. He'd probably dug a lot of wells on his dry land in his day, back before he had sons or could afford other men to help. He retained the thickly muscled body to prove it.

He smiled, showing his small, square, discolored teeth between his thick, pink, badly chapped lips.

"Sandy, you've grown up on me, boy!"

Stoleberg reached up to place his hands on Stockburn's square shoulders. "A big strappin' lad!" He frowned, curious. "Where've you been all these years, Sandy? So many years. Didn't you know your mother and I have been waiting for you? You had us worried sick. We were *heartsick!* We thought McCrae hung—"

The old man's puzzled frown deepened.

Stockburn and Daniel shared a glance. Neither man said anything. What was there to say? Obviously, the old man was out of his head. Now, Stockburn knew what Daniel had meant when he'd said that his father would enjoy company if he was "in the right frame of mind."

Stoleberg stared up at Wolf now with a mix of rage and sorrow brewing in his eyes. His cheeks rose as the muscles tightened. "That black-hearted devil hung you, Sandy! Leastways, we thought so. All those years ago . . . *he hanged you!*"

A sheen of tears dropped down over the old man's eyes, and he shook his head in grief and misery. "We done found you on that hill in a thunderstorm. Just hangin' there—you and three others. You . . . my son. *Hangin' there* . . . I can see you now . . . turning in the wind . . . *dead!*"

Daniel placed his hand on Stoleberg's shoulder. "Easy, Pa."

"Who are you?" Old Stoleberg dug his fingers into Wolf's upper arms, raging, "Who are you? You're not my son! My son's dead! What are you tryin' to pull on me, you devil?"

"Pa!" Daniel reached up with his one hand to pry his father's hand off Wolf's arm. "You're mixed up, Pa—let him go!"

"What trick are you tryin' to pull on me . . . makin' me believe my son is still alive?"

Daniel was shoving his father back away from Stockburn but the old man looked around his son to continue raging at the rail detective: "He murdered my son! My firstborn! Hung him from a cedar tree! Took him from me forever, my firstborn, *Sanderson Rufus Stoleberg!* Why are you tryin' to trick me? You want my land? That it? You tryin' to weezle my land away from me—so he can have it all?" He raised his small,

237

clenched fist. "I been waitin' for this! I'm still here! I'm ready!"

"Come on, Pa. Let's go sit down. Let's go sit down, Pa!" Daniel glanced over his shoulder at Wolf and jerked his chin to indicate the door.

Stockburn stepped back, glancing once more at the raging old man, then stepped into the hall and drew the door closed behind him.

As he did, Stoleberg shouted, "First we take that devil child in! That demon spawn! *His* spawn! And now he sends some son of a bitch over to make me believe he's my son? Why, Daniel?"

"No, Pa!"

"Why, Daniel? Why? Why have you thrown in with McCrae against me? For that *girl?*"

"Pa!"

"You can't have her, I tell you! And we should kill the child! Kill the boy, I say, or there'll be hell to pay—you mark my words!"

"Sit, Pa. Sit, now, or you're going to give yourself a stroke. There you go—easy does it!"

Stockburn heard footsteps on the stairs, two people coming fast. He peered down the shadowy hall. Grace had opened her door and was staring toward him with concern in her wide, round eyes that looked more than a little drugged. Slowly, she shook her head and said to Stockburn, "He goes out of his head, but . . . never this bad." She smiled faintly as though she'd found something amusing in the situation.

The Mexican couple hurried toward Stockburn, the woman, Estella, on the heels of her husband, Oscar. Stockburn stepped aside as Oscar, casting Wolf a dark glance, brushed past him and moved into the room.

Estella followed. She was holding a flat, blue bottle that Stockburn took to be a narcotic of some kind.

Estella closed the door. The old man was still raging but not as loudly as before. He was crying now, as well, and the emotion garbled his words.

Stockburn felt rattled. It must have shone on his face.

"Need a bracer?" Grace had pushed a bottle, not unlike the one that Estella had taken into Stoleberg's office, out toward Stockburn. "Go ahead. Around here, you can't do without a bracer."

Stockburn read the fancy lettering on the bottle: Laudanum.

He smiled, shook his head. He could hear Daniel and the Mexican couple talking behind the door behind them, but he could no longer hear Rufus Stoleberg. They must have gotten him settled down. "No, thanks," he said. "The old man—how long has he . . . ?"

He let his voice trail off when he spied movement on the stairs. The little boy, Buster, just then crawled over the top step and into the hall. He gained his feet with a grunt and ran toward Grace's half-open door, yelling, "Ma-Ma! Ma-Ma! Ma-Ma—*yohhhhahhhh!*"

"Oh, Buster," Grace said with a pained look. "All right, all right." She took the boy by the hand and led him into her room. She glanced once more at Stockburn—a decidedly dark, ominous look. She closed the door with a click.

Stockburn studied the door. What had that look meant? It had almost seemed like a warning.

Other questions needled the rail detective.

Was Buster the boy Stoleberg had been raging about, calling him "that devil child"? Was Buster the boy Stoleberg, in his mania, wanted to *kill?*

What about "the girl" the old man had mentioned?

The questions continued to roll through the detective's mind until the door to Stoleberg's office opened behind him. Daniel limped out and drew the door closed softly, quietly.

Turning his hat in his hands, Wolf said, "I apologize if I was the cause of that."

Daniel shook his head. "It wasn't your fault, Mister Stockburn. He goes out of his head sometimes. He'll be in a happy dream state for days. Those are the good days. Other days, not so good days, he believes that I and my brothers have thrown in with the McCraes, and we're out to take his land away from him, send him packing. It makes no sense. All that you heard in there—put it out of your mind. Pure nonsense."

240

"The girl?"

Daniel laughed, shook his head. "Utter nonsense."

"Hmm."

Daniel threw his hand forward to indicate the stairs then began limping that way, unsteadily, brushing his hand against the wall for support.

"How long has he been like this?"

"We started to see changes in him over a year ago. Sometimes he'd be sitting downstairs with a glassy stare and a dreamy smile. Seemed happy enough. But he was confused. He'd get we boys mixed up. He'd lose track of the seasons. Sometimes, when he was riding alone on the range, he'd get lost, and I or someone else would have to ride out and fetch him."

Now Daniel and Stockburn were starting the slow descent of the stairs.

"After he took a fall from his horse early this spring—he simply hadn't cinched the belly strap—he got worse. He cracked a couple of ribs and had a helluva back ache for a few days, so he took to bed. That's when he started imagining things and speaking nonsense. He's grown steadily worse. Carlton fetched the doctor out from Wild Horse, and the doc looked at him and just said he was getting old-timer's disease. Some get it, some don't. Forgetfulness, confusion, hallucinations, that sort of thing."

Daniel winced and shook his head. "Poor Pa. It's hard to see him like this."

As they reached the bottom of the stairs, Daniel turned to Wolf. "He really did think you were my older brother, Sandy. He was just talkin' about Sandy the other day, Pa was. Talked about how he had a dream that Sandy came back and he was a big, tall, square-shouldered man. A man to be proud of.

"Poor old fella just broke down in tears. Cried almost as hard as he did the day they buried Sandy. I remember it well though I was only eight years old at the time. Long time ago now, but I don't think a day goes by Pa doesn't think about him. He was his oldest. For that reason, his favorite." Daniel shrugged. "I don't begrudge him that."

"He has a pretty good reason to hate the McCraes, doesn't he, Daniel?"

"Are we back on that again, Stockburn? You've seen my father. Does he look like he's in any condition to reignite our war with the Triangle?"

Stockburn pondered it briefly.

"I reckon you're right," he admitted. Again, he looked at Daniel. "Who do you think might have attacked those track layers?"

"I have no idea, Mister Stockburn. All I can tell you is it wasn't us." He and Wolf walked toward the front door, Daniel adding, "There are a lot of men in these mountains who've gotten crossways with Norman McCrae. McCrae has hung a lot of squatters and nesters, calling them rustlers. That means there's a lot more men who'd like to see him ruined."

"Makes no sense," Stockburn said as he stepped out onto the porch.

"What doesn't?"

"You don't ruin a man as big as Norman McCrae just by ruining—or trying to ruin—a spur rail line crossing his property. That would be a thorn in his side, sure. But little else."

"What do you think the motive is, then, Mister Stockburn?"

"It's gotta be somebody with a bigger dog in the fight."

"Chew that up a little finer for me, will you?"

Stockburn looked at Daniel. "It has to be somebody with a reason beyond McCrae for not wanting that rail line completed to Hell's Jaw Pass. Usually, issues like this can be attributed to a competitor."

"So now you've come back to Tin Cup again." Daniel gave a sardonic chuckle and shook his head.

"I didn't mean that. It may not be an issue over the sale of the right-of-way. It might be an issue of someone wanting to ruin the Hell's Jaw outfit so they can move in and lay the rails themselves, for their own company."

"Ah." Daniel nodded. "Now, that makes sense."

Stockburn sighed and gazed off past the Tin Cup portal and into the scrubby rangeland beyond, where Stoleberg cattle peppered the fawn-colored slopes. "So now I reckon I gotta see if I can root out that competitor."

"If it is a competitor."

"Right, right. If it is a competitor."

"How are you going to do that?"

"I don't know. They're likely laying low. Wouldn't want to show themselves or betray their intentions until the Hell's Jaw Line is kaput. Then, after enough time passed so they wouldn't draw suspicion, they could make their own move on building a line."

"Boy," Daniel said, nodding, smiling at Stockburn admiringly, "you're good at this. Now I know why you're such a big name. If anyone can root those killers out, Mister Stockburn, I reckon it's you. Faster the better, to my way of thinking. I'd just as soon there be no doubt that my family has nothing to do with it."

"All right. I reckon I'm not getting any work done standing out here palavering." Wolf extended his hand to young Stoleberg. "I appreciate the hospitality, Daniel. I am truly sorry about the trouble with your father."

"The pleasure was all mine, Mister Stockburn. I mean that. It's been nice to meet you."

"Enough with the Mister Stockburn stuff." Wolf was walking down the porch steps, smiling over his shoulder. "The name's Wolf."

"The Wolf of the Rails!"

"Well, that's a big mouthful for casual conversation." Chuckling, Wolf untied Smoke's reins from the hitchrack.

Standing atop the porch steps, Daniel said, "Where you off to next, if you don't mind my asking?"

"I'm gonna ride on up to the pass." Stockburn swung into the leather. "I've already done a little sniffing around Wild Horse. Now I'll give Hell's Jaw a try. You never know what you'll turn up in a mountain mining town."

"Not much up there, but good luck."

Wolf touched two fingers to his hat brim, said, "Good-bye, Daniel," and booted Smoke into a gallop, heading toward the ranch portal.

Daniel watched the big rail detective gallop out of the Tin Cup headquarters, dust churning behind the big horse and the tall rider.

Footsteps sounded behind Daniel. He turned to see his sister-in-law, Grace, step out onto the porch, still wearing her duster over her nightgown, her pale blond hair hanging loose and unkempt about her shoulders. She was barefoot, as usual, and, just as usual, she was smoking a cigarette.

Now she stepped to the right side of the door, shook her hair from her eyes, and leaned back against the house's front wall. She lifted the cigarette to her lips and took a deep drag.

Blowing the smoke out in a long, slender plume, she said, "I put your son down for his nap, Daniel." That none too subtle mocking tone of hers.

Daniel snapped his head forward and gazed out toward where Stockburn's jostling figure grew smaller and smaller behind the screen of his wafting dust. "Shut your damn mouth, Grace, will you? Just shut your damn mouth!"

CHAPTER 21

Lori McCrae ate the last small bite of her steak.

She swabbed her plate with a slice of her mother's grainy bread, and ate that, too. She set her fork and knife down and waited for comment.

During the meal, she'd felt all eyes on her—her father's and mother's eyes from where they sat at their age-old stations at opposite ends of the long, cloth-covered eating table in the dining room of the Triangle ranch house; and the eyes of her brothers, Lawton and Hy, sitting across the table from Lori.

On the heels of one of her "spells," as her prolonged emotional eruptions had long been called, her parents and brothers always watched her closely, fawningly, skeptically—looking for signs of improvement or deterioration. Signs of improvement were always celebrated quite vocally, sort of like the whoops and hollers of the men hazing the cattle into the right chutes for shipping, voicing a buoyant hybrid of relief and commendation.

As Lori had known it would be, it was Lawton who spoke first, exclaiming, "Well, lookee there—look at the way she cleaned her plate! Cleaner'n a dog-licked bowl! Li'l sis must be getting her pluck back!"

"Gosh, Lori," said the sweetly simple Hy, five years her senior though because of his intellectual age she'd always seen him as younger. "You musta been hungry!"

"Nicely done, Lori. Nicely done," said their father, smiling at her from his end of the table as he finished his own steak.

Her mother, the soft-spoken but iron-hearted Elizabeth, didn't usually make a comment but usually only dipped her chin and blinked slowly in approval. Tonight, however, she must have felt relieved enough at spying evidence of her daughter's emotional mending to mutter, "Hmmm, yes . . . always best to feed an aching heart."

She looked at Lori, chewing and smiling though the expression never looked entirely natural on her craggy face.

Elizabeth swallowed and said, "Feeling more settled now, dear?"

"More . . . rational?" added her father, one eyebrow raised.

He studied her as though she were a prisoner under interrogation. If she answered correctly, certain restraints might be loosened, privileges bestowed. She might even be set free of the solitary confinement of her upstairs bedroom. If her recovery continued, she might soon be allowed to roam freely around the ranch yard.

Eventually, if no signs of backsliding were

exhibited, meaning if she had no more outbursts of "high" emotion and treated everyone, especially her mother and father, "respectfully," she would be given the freedom to ride her horse out on Triangle range as long as she stayed within view of the headquarters.

Lori managed to pull off a smile. She could see her reflection in the looking glass attached to the sideboard flanking her brothers and abutting the far wall; she was amazed by how authentic the expression looked. Affable, demure, even chagrined.

"Yes, all better now," she said.

"Whew!" said Hy, pretending to brush sweat from his brown with his shirtsleeve.

"I am rather tired, though." Lori shifted her gaze from her father on her right to her mother on her left. "May I be excused? I know it's only six o'clock, but I think I'd like to retire to my room and read. I'd like to turn in early."

"Yes, I understand you had quite a trip home," Elizabeth said. She said no more, but her meaning was clear: Her daughter had been extremely foolhardy in traveling alone, a fact proven by the attack on the train—and on Lori herself, no less—by Riley Hennessey's gang of notorious misfits.

Lori shaped another demure smile, wiped her mouth with her napkin, placed the napkin on her plate, and rose from her chair.

"Good-night, everybody," she said.

"Good-night, Lori!" said Hy. "Sure am glad to see you feelin' better. I was worried!"

"Good-night, darlin'," said her fatherly older brother, Lawton.

Her mother did not say good-night but merely stared down at her plate. Elizabeth was still angry, and her silence was her way of communicating that fact. No one defied Elizabeth McCrae without paying a very high price, most of which was tendered in the good old-fashioned but very effective currency of the cold shoulder.

Norman McCrae, however, bestowed upon his daughter a warm smile over the rim of the china coffee cup he held in both hands in front of his chin. "Good-night, honey."

"Good-night, Papa," Lori said, placing her hand on his arm and giving it an affectionate squeeze. She looked at his cheek, hesitating.

Should she kiss it? Might the gesture, so close on the heels of her "high emotion," betray the lie to her sudden display of equanimity?

Possibly. But she knew her father as well as she did her mother. She could pull it off.

She went ahead and pressed her soft lips to his rough cheek, prickly from beard stubble this late in the day.

Did it work?

McCrae smiled, removing one hand from his cup and patting Lori's hand with genuine approbation. "Sleep well, honey," he said as Lori strode toward the dining room door. She could feel her mother's cold eyes on her, but Lori didn't dare look back at her.

Her father's reaction was enough. It filled her with relief. It also emboldened her to go through with her plan . . .

Holding the skirts of her dress above her shoes, she climbed the house's broad staircase. She gained the second floor and strode toward her bedroom door.

As she did, she passed the door of her mother's room. Norman and Elizabeth McCrae hadn't slept in the same bed for years. Elizabeth had made the excuse that Norman snored and kicked all night, but Lori knew, from having overheard a clandestine argument late one night in her father's office, that Elizabeth had learned of an affair Lori's father had carried on for several years with a whorehouse madam in Laramie.

She stopped.

She turned to stare back at the varnished walnut door. Her heart quickened. Her palms grew warm.

When she'd been a little girl much younger than her brothers, she'd often found herself alone on the house's second floor. Her mother, a splendid rider, often helped Lori's father and brothers out on the range, especially when they were short-handed either late or early in the year, before the summer hirings. Yellow Feather was usually working downstairs or in the wash house flanking the main lodge.

At those times, Lori, being a curious and precocious child, would sometimes go on snooping missions through the bedrooms. Her parents' bedroom, especially, held a strong attraction for her.

Once, while going through her mother's closet, Lori had discovered an old steamer trunk her mother had hauled over here from Scotland. Lori had opened the trunk, finding her mother's wedding dress, which had been Elizabeth's mother's before her, as well as family photos and family jewelry. At the very bottom, Lori had found a small packet, secured with a silk ribbon, of love letters that had been written to Elizabeth McCrae from a former lover from the East.

The young man had obviously been very much in love with Lori's mother, and his long, flowery, and sometimes even sexually explicit letters had betrayed the young man's heartbreak at Elizabeth's decision to follow her family's wishes to marry a wealthy Texas rancher who'd been in business with Elizabeth's father.

Lori, a devout reader of romantic poetry and the plays and poetry of William Shakespeare, had not found the letters particularly jarring. Her mother had been a beautiful young woman; it wasn't surprising she'd known love before she'd married her father when she'd been nearly thirty.

Lori had found the letters as sad in places as Mr. Byron's poetry and Mr. Shakespeare's sonnets. At the same time, Lori had thrilled to the idea of her mother living a life of love and adventure before marrying her somewhat dowdy father, who was Elizabeth's senior by twelve years.

The point of the memory of Lori having discovered those letters so many years ago now was not the letters themselves but the hiding place. Lori could think of no better place in the house to hide something as possibly volatile as love letters. Especially letters expressing forbidden love.

Something told Lori that Elizabeth wouldn't have destroyed the letters. That would have been going too far. She'd confiscated them in a most duplicitous way. That would be as far as Elizbeth would dare go.

At least, Lori hoped so.

She was taking a big gamble, but, chewing her lip outside her mother's door, her right hand on the knob, her heart thudding in her chest, Lori looked up and down the hall. Finding herself alone, she turned the knob and stepped quickly into the proscribed chamber.

Chewing her lip again, wincing, she closed the door.

She turned and looked around.

Elizabeth had left a lamp burning, the wick turned low, casting thin, watery light and shadows around the large, immaculate room furnished with a canopied four-poster bed, a chest of drawers, an armoire, a dressing table, and a large porcelain bathing tub half-hidden by an Oriental room divider.

The closet lay behind the tub and the divider.

Lori turned up the lamp then strode to the door quickly. If she was caught in here, going through her mother's most private possessions, she'd likely be sent to a convent to live out the rest of her days in chaste captivity, whipped daily by evil nuns with wet ropes. Lori chuckled at the thought, but the laugh was evoked more by acute anxiety than from any humor in the notion, which she didn't think was all that far from what would actually happen to her.

She opened the closet door. She found the steamer trunk under several quilts. It had been a long time since she'd seen it. It was like finding a relic from her ancient past.

She pulled it into the light, tripped the double hasps, and opened it. Old, pent-up air wafted up. When she was a young girl, Lori had imagined it was the air of Scotland rising into her face. It smelled of ancient leather and of the cedar the trunk was lined with.

The contents hadn't appeared to have changed much over the years. It was possible that

Elizabeth hadn't opened it over the past decade. Lori rummaged beneath the wedding dress and the pasteboard boxes of old photographs, trinkets, jewelry, old Christmas decorations, and other heirlooms, until her hand reached the very bottom.

She felt around, closing her hand around the packet of old love letters.

She pulled the packet out of the trunk. She looked at it. It appeared the same as she remembered. She turned it over to inspect the bottom of the packet and frowned.

The envelopes on the bottom looked newer than the ones on top.

Quickly, her heart still thumping anxiously, Lori glanced over her shoulder, toward the bedroom door, then slipped the silk ribbon from around the envelopes. She peeled the last several envelopes off the bottom of the packet.

Now, her heart almost stopped. She was looking down at an address written in her own hand. She shuffled through the eight or nine envelopes under the first one. They were all addressed in her own hand, from the Miss Lydia Hastings Academy for Young Women in Poughkeepsie, New York.

She looked at the last envelope.

Again, her heart almost stopped. That envelope had been addressed to her, "Miss Lorelei McCrae in care of the Miss Lydia Hastings Academy for Young Women in Poughkeepsie, New York."

The handwriting was decidedly masculine, the letters uncertain, as though written by a slightly shaky, masculine hand. Lori had never seen this envelope. Someone, however, had opened it.

Of course, she knew who that someone was.

Lori's chest rose and fell sharply as she breathed. She took a deep breath, trying desperately to tamp down the rage flaming inside her.

"How dare she," she said tightly, through gritted teeth. "How dare she, how dare she, how dare—"

She stopped as her shaking fingers managed to pull the leaf of cream-colored paper from the envelope. In her haste to unfold it, she dropped it. She picked it back up, almost ripped it as she unfolded it and held it, turning her shoulders slightly, where the light settled over it.

Her eyes rushed over the words, which were as heart-breakingly honest, sad, and beseeching as they were inelegant. In fact, their inelegance made them all the more poignant.

Lori looked at the date on the letter.

"Last year," she whispered, dumbfounded. "That's why I didn't hear from him all summer. I'd sent him letters from school . . . one after the other . . . but received no response. He wrote me, wondering why *I* hadn't written *him!*"

Tears rolled down Lori's cheeks. "But I did . . . I did send letters. They were intercepted before they reached Daniel." She drew a deep breath, hardened her voice, had to try very hard not to scream her next words: *"Damn her! Damn that mean, nasty, cold-hearted woman straight to hell!"*

Breathing heavily, Lori climbed to her feet.

Clutching the letters—her nine notes and his one, the one he'd written Lori asking why she hadn't written to him (but she had!)—she strode stiffly to the door. She stopped before she reached it. She drew a heavy breath, held it for a few seconds, then let it out.

She felt a burning, almost overpowering need to confront her mother about the letters. Elizabeth had obviously used her influence to coerce the postmaster in Wild Horse to intercept any letters from or to her daughter in New York. Lori wanted to throw the letters in Elizabeth's face. She wanted to do far more than that. If she went downstairs right now, she would likely get herself into even more trouble than she was already in.

She had to calm down and think clearly, strategically.

Earlier in the day, she'd secretly sent a note to Daniel. She'd convinced Hy—poor, kind Hy, her hapless unwitting brother—to take a note to the one hand in the bunkhouse she knew she could trust, Randy MacDonald.

Randy had once vied for Lori's affections

himself but, knowing who her heart really belonged to, had settled for her friendship instead.

She trusted that Randy, using another intermediary—a young man who cut hay near Dutch Joe Creek for the Tin Cup ranch—would get her note to Daniel. And that Daniel would meet her tonight, at midnight, at their old meeting place.

Lori put the trunk back in order in her mother's closet, turned down the lamp, then returned to her own room to wait until everyone had gone to bed. Then she'd slip outside, saddle a horse, and ride out to meet her lover at long last.

CHAPTER 22

Stockburn took a deep drag off his Indian Kid cigar and blew a smoke plume into the cold, dark night.

He followed up the smoke with a couple sips of his strong, black coffee, first blowing ripples on the surface to cool it. Only a few minutes ago, he'd poured himself a fresh cup. Some gray ash from the fire snapping and crackling behind him had drifted into the coffee. He slurped it down with the hot liquid itself.

He didn't mind the flavor of wood ash in his coffee. In fact, he liked it. It gave the mud an extra toasty edge, sometimes even adding a little aspen or pine tang to the brew. He was at home out here in the big open. He liked the sight, sound, smell, and even taste of it.

He believed himself to be somewhere in the no-man's-land between the Triangle and Tin Cup ranges. He was likely on open range though he was well aware that both spreads contested the government graze, each having claimed it as their own.

After leaving the Stoleberg headquarters several hours ago, he'd quartered northwest, moving slowly, studying the ground for signs of a large group of horseback riders. A dozen or so men were believed to have attacked the rail crew. He'd counted twelve men leaving the Stoleberg yard earlier in the day. There was a good chance they were the same men who'd killed the track layers. There was a chance they were not, as well. If he could find the tracks of a large group of horses and riders, and track them to their source, he'd be ahead of the game.

Of course, Wolf couldn't be sure the killers were still in the area. Possibly, the men or men who'd hired them to kill the track layers had simply paid them off and bid them adieu.

On the other hand, maybe that hadn't been the only killing job the killers' boss or bosses had in mind for the hired guns. Whoever had ordered the massacre might have wanted to keep the killers in the area in case the Stewarts brought in a new work train and formed another crew to repair the ruined rails and to lay more. To continue with their plan to build the railroad all the way to Hell's Jaw Pass. The culprits likely had no way of knowing just how hard it would be to break the Stewarts and send them and their rail line packing.

It wasn't easy to gather a dozen killers. At least, not inconspicuously. Once you had them, you'd most likely want to hold onto them until you were sure you didn't need them anymore. And you'd likely want to keep them out of sight.

Off the beaten path.

You could usually pick killers like Lester Bohannon, whom Stockburn had killed earlier that day along with the three others in Bohannon's company, out of even a good-sized crowd. Whomever had hired the crew of gun wolves would probably have ordered them to hole up out in the mountains somewhere—possibly around an abandoned mine or a ranch headquarters. They'd demand a few creature comforts. They might even have demanded a woman or two.

Killers were usually restless.

Stockburn had discovered tracks just before sunset, but only a couple of sets—two riders riding separately though generally in the same direction. The tracks had been relatively fresh. Since he'd uncovered few other clues out here as to the identity of the killers, he'd decided to follow the tracks and see where they led.

They might belong only to drifters or range riders employed by either the Tin Cup or the Triangle. Wolf might find they only belonged to rustlers, even. There were likely plenty of those out here.

On the other hand, Bohannon and the three others had been out here. If Bohannon had belonged to the same group of killers who'd killed the track layers, then maybe the rest of the group was out here, as well.

Stockburn hoped to get lucky and find that the tracks he'd picked up would lead him to the killers' hideout. Probably a long shot, but sometimes that's all you had. And a long shot was about all that Wolf had so far.

He had the frustrating feeling that he'd uncovered clues in the two days he'd been here, but those clues remained too slippery to name. Which meant he had no way of knowing where those clues might lead.

The early mountain night had forced him to make camp before he'd been able to follow those fresh tracks more than a couple of miles. He would continue to follow them in the morning.

Until then, he'd keep the two eyes in the back of his head skinned. He may not be alone out here. Two riders had passed through this area relatively recently—possibly two killers having retrieved supplies from town and were riding back to their hideout separately, to avoid suspicion.

Also, the bastard with the large-caliber rifle might still be shadowing him, looking for another opportunity.

Stockburn stared into the night, all senses alert.

He'd set up camp on a piece of high ground between two valleys. From here, he had a good view of a broad stretch of terrain. He'd hoped that after good dark he'd spy a flickering campfire, which might indicate the killers' hideout.

So far, no luck.

While his own fire was small, it could probably be seen from a good distance away, and that was all right with him. If the killers were out here, why not lure them to him? He just had to stay alert and be ready if and when they came.

He also had to be ready for the bastard who'd almost greased him with the large-caliber rifle. He had to assume the assassin had been sicced on him particularly, to get him off the killers' trail, and that he'd try again.

Stockburn sat, waiting, watching, sipping the coffee, and smoking.

The stallion whickered softly.

Wolf looked toward where he'd tied the gray horse a couple dozen feet down the slope on his left. The moon was three-quarters full and kiting high, fading the stars and casting pearl light onto the gray's long back. Silhouetted by the moonlight, the mount was staring off behind him, to the west.

A horse trail threaded through the mountains from that direction. In fact, the man whose tracks Wolf had been following earlier had followed that trail, heading northeast.

Again, Smoke whickered—a little louder this time.

A few seconds later, the muffled thuds of a distant rider touched Wolf's ears. As the thuds grew louder, Wolf stretched his own gaze to the west.

Sure enough, a rider was coming hard and fast along the trail. The trail snaked around the base of the slope on which Stockburn was camped. That meant that if the rider was following the trail, which he must be, for it was the only trail Wolf had come upon, the man would be here soon— within a long stone's throw of where Wolf sat now.

Stockburn rose from the log he'd been sitting on. He set down his coffee cup, dropped the cheroot, and mashed it out with his boot toe. He hurried over to his fire, and kicked dirt on it, smothering it. Smoke wafted in the moonlit darkness, the still-glowing coals crackling.

He picked up his rifle, levered a round into the chamber, then lowered the hammer to half-cock. He looked down the slope toward his horse, and said, "Easy, boy. Keep quiet, now—hear?"

He knew the horse would. They'd been together a long time, and they understood each other.

Holding the rifle in one hand, he walked down the west side of the slope, meandering through tall pines, cedars, and large rocks. As he gained the base of the slope, he crouched behind a rock. The trail passed within ten feet of his position. From his left, the hoof thuds grew louder as the rider approached.

They grew still louder and were joined by the rattle of a bridle chain and the squawk of saddle leather until the jostling shadow of horse and rider appeared, following a curve in the trail then coming straight on toward where Stockburn crouched behind the rock.

The rider was pushing the horse too hard. There was plenty of moonlight, but not much of it reached the trail down here in this hollow. The horse was liable to trip over a fallen branch or a chuck hole and kill them both.

As horse and rider came to within fifty feet, they rode into a large pool of milky moonlight. The light shone on long, dark hair tumbling down from the hatted head and on a nicely filled cream blouse. Not a shirt.

A woman's blouse.

Stockburn rose from behind the rock, took the rifle in his left hand, and raised the right one palm out. "Lori?"

The girl gasped as she jerked back on the horse's reins, stopping the horse, which curveted, aiming its head at Stockburn. Sweat lather streaked its snout and withers, glistening like silver in the moonlight.

Lori McCrae jerked her own startled gaze toward the tall man standing beside the trail. Her face was shaded enough that he couldn't clearly make out her features.

"Lori McCrae, is that you? It's Wolf Stockburn!"

The horse, a long-legged buckskin, danced in place, tail arched, and shook its head, rattling the bit in its teeth. The girl stared toward Stockburn, her wide eyes reflecting the moonlight. Fear and anxiety fairly radiated off of her. *"Wolf?"*

"What are you doing out here, Lori?"

Stockburn heard her sob, shoulders jerking. She sniffed, tossed her head, shaking her hair back from her face. "Please, don't try to stop me, Wolf!"

She reined the horse around then rammed her heels against its flanks. The buckskin lunged off its rear feet and broke into another ground-consuming run, hooves thudding loudly.

Stockburn yelled, "Lori!"

Horse and rider continued around another bend in the trail, and the dark night consumed them.

Stockburn stood listening to the quickly dwindling thunder of the horse's hooves. He raked an anxious thumb down his jawline. "Where in holy blazes is she off to this time of night?"

The last time he checked his time piece, it had been nearly eleven-thirty. Owls were hooting, and coyotes were yammering.

She'd told him not to try to stop her. Something told him he should, that she was riding into trouble. At least, he had to find out where she was headed and what trouble she might be getting into.

The last time he'd seen her, she'd been in a bad way. It appeared she still was.

Stockburn hurried back up to his camp. He threw his saddle blanket and saddle on his horse and strapped the saddle into place. He tied his bedroll and war bag on, as well, and tossed his saddlebags over the bedroll. He swung up onto Smoke's back and eased the horse down the dark slope and onto the trail.

He booted the gray into a trot. That was all the faster he cared to travel over rugged mountain terrain.

He'd catch up to Lori when she stopped. Judging by how tired her horse had appeared, that would likely be soon. There was only one trail, and she was following it. Wolf would follow the trail to the girl.

The trail traced a crease between two forested ridges. It rose up and over a low pass, then curved sharply to the left. It followed a canyon, the canyon floor rising toward yet another pass.

Wolf stopped Smoke in a patch of moonlight and swung down to study the trail. Fresh hoof prints shone in water trickling over the trail from a runout spring in rocks to the right. Lori's tracks. She'd passed this way, all right.

It was too dark for him to see the tracks from the saddle. He'd wanted to make sure he wasn't on a wild goose chase.

Stockburn mounted up and continued on up the canyon. He'd ridden maybe a quarter mile before he jerked back sharply on Smoke's reins.

Maybe forty yards ahead, something had just leaped onto the trail from the left—a shadowy figure roughly shaped like a deer. The deer gave a horrified bleating sound as something else leaped onto the trail behind it, in close pursuit.

This figure was low and long and gave the impression of speed and sleekness.

Stockburn's pulse quickened.

Both figures were gone in an instant—fleeing deer and pursuing mountain lion—dashing up the steep ridge on the trail's right side. A loud snarl slashed across the night, exploding the relative silence. The snarl was followed by the deer's clipped scream.

Up the wooded slope to Stockburn's right rose violent thrashing sounds followed by more snarls and a few more screams, each scream softer and quieter and more plaintive than the last.

The thrashing dwindled, stopped.

Stockburn winced, shook his head. He could feel Smoke's heart beating quickly. He knew it wasn't merely from the exertion of the hard mountain run. The horse had smelled the mountain lion on the heels of the deer. The only thing a horse was more afraid of than a mountain lion was a grizzly bear.

"Relax, Smoke," Wolf said, patting the horse's left wither. "Just the call of the wild's all."

He booted the horse on ahead, eager to be a good long way from the puma, though the cat would likely be occupied till morning, feeding on its midnight meal of fresh venison.

He continued to the top of a saddle and reined

Smoke to a stop. A light appeared ahead and below and slightly left—a dull yellow glow. Too large for a campfire.

Likely a cabin.

Stockburn gigged Smoke on down the saddle and into another valley. At least, he thought it was a valley. It was dark down here, the moonlight blocked by the tall timber on both sides of the trail.

Down here, he could no longer see the cabin, for inky black slopes tufted with forest rose to either side of him, but he'd made note of the cabin's general position. He continued following the trail until it turned into what appeared a narrow side canyon.

Smoke hazed the air above him, where the moonlight shone on it, making it look like cobwebs. Stockburn could smell the pine tang.

The cabin wasn't far.

Stockburn reined Smoke into the brush off the trail's right side. He crossed a small, muddy stream then swung down from the mount's back, led him into the cover of some large rocks and brush, and tied him to a cedar branch.

Stockburn slid his Winchester from the saddle boot, patted the horse's neck, said, "Stay, boy," and began walking along the stream, heading deeper into the side canyon.

The ground rose.

After Wolf had taken several more strides, the

light appeared again, quartering on his right, maybe sixty yards away. He took a few more strides, crouching, trying not to be seen, keeping the rifle low so the moonlight wouldn't glint off the barrel of the engraved brass receiver.

The stream trickled very softly to his right. Occasionally, his boots came down in soft mud. He could smell the muddy, green odor of the stream and the tang of wood smoke from the cabin as well as the cold birches, pines, and aspens surrounding him.

The cabin took better shape as Stockburn kept walking, moving slowly, quietly, wincing when his boots crackled on the coarse grass. The cabin crouched on the other side of the narrow canyon, on the opposite side of the tiny stream. It was a simple log affair with a small front stoop.

Two windows, one on either side of the cabin's closed door, pushed the dull yellow light onto the stoop, revealing two figures silhouetted there as well as two horses standing before the cabin, heads down. One was tied.

The reins of the other one drooped to the ground. The untied horse was Lori's buckskin.

Wolf's heart beat with more urgency. He'd come to the end of the trail.

What in the hell was she doing out here? Well, at the moment, as he stopped walking now and stopped off the cabin's left front corner, maybe thirty yards away from it, he could see pretty well what she was doing. She was currently locked in an embrace with another silhouetted figure.

The night was so quiet that he could hear her softly sobbing. The two were talking in hushed, intimate tones. As quiet as the night was, Stockburn needed to get a little closer to hear what they were saying.

Did Lori have a lover? Apparently so. Who?

It might not be any of his damn business. But, then, that had never stopped him from sniffing around before. It sure as hell wasn't going to stop him now.

CHAPTER 23

Keeping to the shadows on his side of the little stream and staying behind the brush growing up along the stream's edge, Stockburn strode forward.

The two people on the cabin's stoop were still speaking in hushed tones. One was Lori, the other a male. They spoke too softly for Wolf to make out what they were saying.

Stockburn continued walking up canyon until he could no longer see the front of the cabin. As he turned to the stream, he faced the side of the cabin, roughly two thirds of the way down from the front wall. He crossed the stream in a single, short leap, wincing as his boots landed in mud and short, spongy grass, making wet sucking sounds.

Wolf froze, ears pricked.

If the two people on the stoop had heard him, they gave no indication. Wolf could still hear their soft, private voices.

He moved forward, pushing through the brush on the cabin side of the stream, trying to make as little noise as possible. He bit his tongue as the brush rustled against the sleeves of his buckskin coat and his boots crunched the cool, brittle grass.

There was roughly a twenty-foot gap between the brush and the cabin. No cover here, so Stockburn had to be especially quiet and hope there was no one else in the cabin, for a curtainless window looked out from the wall facing Stockburn.

Staying low, he moved slowly, holding the rifle straight down against his right leg, keeping one eye skinned on the window, the other on the cabin's front corner, on his right.

Lamplight flickered beyond the small window, pulsating and wavering inside the shadowy cabin, like light under water.

Stockburn approached the cabin to the left of the window. He turned his back to the cabin then sidestepped toward the window.

He removed his hat and edged a look around the frame and into the shack. He pulled his head back suddenly when his gaze found a person in there. He edged a look around the frame again, squinting through the warped, dusty glass that had a small crack in the bottom right corner.

He swept the entire one-room shack with a quick glance then returned his gaze to a man—the only person in the cabin—standing with his back pressed to the front wall, between the door and a window to the right of it. The man stood oddly, back straight, chin up.

Stockburn frowned.

What the hell was the fella doing in there?

As Wolf studied the man more closely, he realized the man was eavesdropping on Lori's conversation with the man on the stoop, only two or three feet from the eavesdropper. The man was grinning, showing his teeth. He held a cigarette down low in his right hand.

As he continued listening and eavesdropping, he raised the quirley to his mouth, took a shallow puff, briefly making the coal glow red, then lowered his hand and blew the smoke out through his mouth.

Wolf felt the scowl lines on his forehead cut deeper as he studied the eavesdropper. The man wore no hat. Long, thin, dark-brown hair hung straight down to his shoulders. The crown of the man's head was nearly bald. What piqued Wolf's interest even more was the bandage on the man's left cheek.

Stockburn remembered that one of the bullets he'd flung at the bastard with the large-caliber rifle had caused the man to jerk his head back sharply, as though the bullet had struck him or at least grazed him.

Wolf looked at the rifle leaning against the front wall, roughly four feet to the left of the eaves-dropper. It appeared to be a Sharps. Likely with a caliber somewhere in the fifties, large enough that the bastard wielding it could blow a man's head off from a distance of up to three hundred yards. Four hundred if he had an eagle eye.

Was Stockburn now staring at the bastard who'd nearly blown his head off?

If so, what was Lori doing here? And who was the man she was on the stoop with?

Only one way to find out.

Stockburn ducked under the window as he walked up to the front of the cabin. Near the corner, he pressed his shoulder up taut against the wall, feeling a little chagrined that he was eavesdropping on the pair now, just as the man inside the cabin was.

The two were still speaking quietly, but their tones were urgent. He still couldn't hear them clearly.

Oh, hell—enough messing around!

Stockburn stepped around the cabin's front corner and raised the rifle up high across his chest, not aiming it but ready to aim it if needed. "Lori."

The girl jumped. She'd had her back to Stockburn but she swung around now quickly, gasping.

"Who's there?" asked the man she was with, angrily.

Stockburn saw the man now standing to one side and a little behind Lori reach for a revolver on his right hip. "Keep it in the leather!" Wolf warned, aiming the rifle, clicking the hammer back.

"Wolf, no!" Lori cried.

Daniel Stoleberg had closed his lone hand around the grips of the revolver holstered on his right hip, but he did not slide the piece from the leather.

Stockburn eased the tension in his trigger finger. He lowered the Yellowboy's barrel slightly, scowling, deeply puzzled. "Lordy be," he said. "Don't tell me—Romeo and . . . Juliet?"

Neither one seemed to know what to say. They looked at each other in stunned silence. Lori wrung her hands together in front of her belly.

Stockburn walked around to the front of the stoop, mounted the single step, and leaned his right shoulder against a splintering support post that wasn't doing a very good job of holding the awning up anymore. The spindly roof sagged precariously to one side, threatening to fall to the ground.

The pair on the stoop had followed the detective with their gazes and now turned to face him. The light from the window to their left washed over them, covering them in fragmented light and shadows.

They looked as guilty as a pair of acolytes having been caught sampling the communion wine.

"Now I see why your family wasn't so happy to see you," Wolf said, lowering the Winchester's hammer, then lowering the rifle itself, letting it hang down against his right leg. "They aimed to make sure this forbidden love affair did not continue."

Again, Lori and Daniel shared an incredulous glance.

Turning to Stockburn, Lori said, "The problem is . . ."

"We love each other, Stockburn," Daniel finished for her. "I didn't realize it was mutual anymore." He turned to Lori. "When you didn't answer my letters, I thought they'd turned you against me."

To Stockburn, Lori said, "My mother—and maybe my father, too, but probably only my mother, the evil witch that she is—must have had the postmaster in Wild Horse intercept any correspondence between Daniel and me. Tonight, I went through a trunk in my mother's closet, and found them."

She patted the pocket of the coat she wore. "My parents insisted on sending me away to school and arranging for me to work for an attorney in Poughkeepsie once I'd graduated, as a law assistant, which would have been at the end of this year."

"They were bound and determined to keep you apart for good," Wolf observed.

"Exactly," Lori said. "They hoped that I'd find a life in the East . . . as well as a husband—probably one of the attorneys I would work for." She shook her head slowly, obstinately. "They just didn't see that it couldn't be. How could I start another life without Daniel, without . . . ?"

Lori glanced demurely up at her lover.

He cleared his throat, drew a breath, looked at Stockburn gravely. "We had a baby together."

"Buster?"

"How did you know?"

"I noticed a family resemblance. And Grace didn't seem too natural as a mother."

"Buster's ours," Lori said. "My parents were going to send him to an orphanage in Cheyenne, but the Stolebergs took him instead. They agreed to raise him . . . as long as I, their blood enemy's daughter, was not involved."

Daniel leaned against the cabin wall, near the window, and hooked his thumb in the pocket of his black denims. He wore a blanket coat and a low-crowned Stetson with a curled brim. "I think my pa sort of saw it as getting back the son Lori's father took from him when he hanged Sandy all those years ago."

Stockburn drew a breath. He was having trouble comprehending it all—all the misery, the heartbreak. The bittersweet love of two young people caught in a whipsaw between their families who were going at it like two wildcats locked in the same privy.

He removed his hat, scrubbed a hand down his face, then set his hat back on his head and asked, "How in blazes did you two meet?"

"In church," they both said at the same time, chuckling.

"Huh?"

Lori and Daniel shared a smile. "It was just a few months after my accident," Daniel said. "I was in a bad way. Lori saw it and wanted to help."

"You see, Wolf," Lori said, "on Sundays our families once called a truce to attend services at the Wrath of Jehovah Lutheran Church on the Big Sandy River, established equal distance between our two ranches, on open range. Miners, prospectors, small ranchers, and the Stolebergs and McCraes as well as several pious hands from both outfits attended every Sunday."

"Everyone associated with either ranch sat on separate sides of the aisle," Daniel said.

"You two obviously, uh . . . mingled," Wolf said with a smile.

"In secret," Daniel said. "Usually after church and during picnics. We'd steal away together, take a short walk along the river. We were like-minded. Whoever would have thought a McCrae and a Stoleberg would think alike? We both liked to read . . ."

"And write." Lori gave Daniel a playful nudge. "We used to write stories for each other and exchange them after church. In those stories, we said what we didn't have time to say to each other on those stolen moments on Sunday."

"Some Sundays, when it didn't seem safe, we didn't try to get together, no matter how bad we wanted to and had looked forward to it," Daniel said. "We didn't take any chances. The closer we grew, the more careful we got. We knew it would all be over if anyone from either family grew savvy to our secret."

"Finally, we skipped our Sunday meetings altogether and started meeting out on the range somewhere, or . . . well," Lori said, throwing up her hands and glancing at the cabin, "here. It was here that Daniel confessed his love for me . . . and I confessed mine for him."

Stockburn whistled his surprise and shook his head. He studied them both and said, "How did you arrange your meetings without either family finding out? Or . . . did they?" he added darkly, since both families obviously now knew.

"We found people we trusted . . . mostly, outside of either family," Daniel said, "to deliver notes. I had a friend in the bunkhouse at Tin Cup I swore to secrecy, and he knew . . . knows . . . a young man whose family cuts hay for us and sometimes wood for both the Tin Cup and the Triangle. They usually found a way to get my notes to Lori."

"I used a similar delivery system," Lori said. "But we also had our tree." She smiled at Daniel. "Our own special tree. Our 'love tree,' we called it."

Daniel flushed and chuckled. "A big cotton-wood between the two ranches. There's a hollow in it. We'd leave notes for each other there and check the tree regularly."

"Until we were found out," Lori said. "My getting careless . . . and pregnant . . . managed to be the nail in our coffin. I thought our fathers would kill us both."

"It came close a time or two," Daniel said with grave sincerity.

And if my father didn't kill me, I was sure my mother would. It's not that she hates the Stolebergs so much, it was the defiance and the impropriety of what we did. She saw it as a betrayal. She's a good Scot, my mother, and to her, betrayal is the eighth deadly sin."

Stockburn shook his head again. He was a tough man, not usually susceptible to sentiment. The story of these two young folks' obvious burning love for each other—a love that had produced a child in one of the most impossible situations he could imagine outside of slavery—had tied a knot in his throat.

He swallowed it down, drew a deep breath. "So . . . what now?"

Lori turned to Daniel and took his hand in both of hers. "We're going away together. The two of us. A long, long way. Daniel, me, and our child. Forever."

Daniel's face acquired a pained expression.

"Daniel, what is it?" Lori said. "Now you know about my letters. About my mother intercepting them . . ."

"Yes, I understand that, Lori. It's just that . . . well . . ."

"Well, what?"

"Lori, we . . ." Again, Daniel let his voice trail off. This time it wasn't because he couldn't find the words but because the thunder of galloping horses cut through the night's intimate silence.

Stockburn heard it, too. A good half-dozen riders, at least.

Coming fast.

CHAPTER 24

"Who do you suppose that is?" Daniel said, staring down the dark canyon.

The hooves thudded softly, sounding a good distance away. As they grew louder, it was obvious the riders were headed in this direction.

"They're coming from the direction of the Triangle," Wolf said.

Tightly but urgently, Lori said, "My mother probably checked my room and found me gone!"

"She doesn't know about the line shack, does she?" Daniel asked her.

"Yes. At least, my father does. He guessed that this was where you and I probably met. Where . . . Buster was conceived. He told me he was going to burn it down. Obviously, he didn't, but . . ."

"He knows where it is," Stockburn said. "And he's guessing he'll find you here."

Daniel drew the revolver from the holster on his hip and stepped stiffly up to the edge of the stoop. "I've had enough of this cat and mouse game." Holding the gun straight down against his side, he clicked the hammer back.

"Put it away," Wolf said. "Don't be a fool, kid. Get on your horse and hightail it back to Tin Cup.

I'll stay here with Lori and run interference for you."

Lori turned sharply to Stockburn. "I'm not going back there, Wolf!" Turning to her lover, she said, "Ride home, Daniel. Hurry. Wolf's right—it would be suicide to stand against them."

Daniel stood staring stubbornly in the direction of the loudening hoof thuds. It sounded like the riders had entered the side canyon in which the line shack lay. "I may be a one-armed gimp, but I can hold my own in a lead swap."

"Daniel!" Lori said, sobbing, grabbing his wrist. "Please! I won't watch you die! Don't make me do that if you still love me even a little! Buster needs a father, and I need a husband!"

Daniel turned toward her. "Yeah, well, I haven't been Buster's father since you left. I couldn't. He only reminded me of you. Carlton and Grace have been raising him."

"We'll be together soon, Daniel," she said, squeezing his wrist with both of her hands, leaning toward him, pleading, tears streaming down her cheeks. "But for now, *go!*"

Daniel stared toward the approaching riders. Wolf looked that way, as well. The riders were close. Too damn close. Wolf could feel the reverberations of the galloping mounts in the ground beneath his boots.

"All right!" Daniel kissed Lori then turned to

Stockburn. "Take her, will you? After tonight, I'm afraid what . . ."

He didn't finish the thought. He didn't need to. Both Stockburn and Lori knew exactly what he was worried about. Stockburn had seen how Lori's family had treated her only the day before. Still, he had no business involving himself in the rift between these two families.

At the moment, however, he didn't see as how he had much choice in the matter.

"Please, Wolf," Lori urged, staring up at him, tears glistening in her eyes. "I won't go back there. Not ever again!"

Wolf took her hand. "Let's go!" Leading her off the stoop and over to her horse, he turned to Daniel. "Head home, boy. Lori will be safe with me."

He swung up onto Smoke then took her hand and pulled her up behind him.

"I love you, Daniel," Lori said.

Daniel had stepped into his own saddle. He stared back at Lori, feigned a smile, dipped his chin. "What a damn mess we've gotten ourselves into." He snapped a look at Stockburn. "Get her out of here."

"You first." Wolf reached down with his right hand and slid his Winchester from the saddle boot. Cocking it one-handed, he said, "I'm going to buy us both some time."

Daniel glanced once more at Lori then reined

his horse away from the cabin. He crouched low and rammed his heels into the horse's flanks. *"Hee-yahh!"*

As Daniel's Appaloosa shot up the trail in the opposite direction from the one in which the riders were coming hot and hard, Stockburn turned to Lori. "I hope you know a back door to this canyon, or our goose is cooked!"

Lori was sobbing. In a pinched voice, she said, "Behind the shack. There's a game trail up the canyon wall."

The hoof thuds of the approaching riders had risen to near thunder. Stockburn turned to see the first of the riders gallop around a bend in the canyon wall and head toward him, one throwing an arm out and shouting, "There!"

Stockburn raised the Winchester, shouted, "It's Stockburn! I have Lori. She's safe. I'll bring her home when you and the Stolebergs have agreed to end the war. Now turn around and go home!"

He triggered three quick rounds into the dust several feet in front of the two lead riders. "Those were warning shots. The next ones won't be!"

Horses screamed as the riders jerked sharply back on their reins, checking the mounts down to skidding halts. The men barked at each other, cursing.

Stockburn reined Smoke around, yelled, "Hold on tight, girl!" and rammed his boots against the mount's ribs. The gray galloped around the side of the cabin and straight back behind it. Riding low in the saddle, feeling Lori's arms wrapped around him, her head snugged against his back, Stockburn glanced back at the cabin.

It was a dark box bleeding yellow light onto the ground around it from its two side windows. The back door was open, bleeding more light out through the rectangular opening.

Wolf had been so distracted by Daniel and Lori's story that he'd forgotten about the man in the cabin. That open door told him he'd likely cleared out.

Wolf regretted not asking Daniel about him.

Problems and mysteries swirling inside of the detective's brain, he gave Smoke his head. The horse knew the terrain out here better than he did. The horse found the trail, revealed by the pearl moonlight behind a small stable and a wood pile, and climbed it fleetly.

As the horse gained the top of the ridge, which was maybe a hundred feet high, Wolf glanced back into the canyon.

The cabin was a small black box set in the darkness of the canyon bottom, lamplit windows and open back door flickering, showing tiny trapezoids of wan light on the ground beside or before them. Stockburn heard the McCrae men shouting angrily, their voices echoing distantly. He couldn't see them on the other side of the cabin.

He didn't think they were coming after him; he didn't hear the din of pursuing horses or men.

He gigged the horse back away from the canyon rim, so the moonlit sky wouldn't silhouette him against it. He turned the horse to face back toward the canyon though he could no longer see into it.

The men's angry voices grew quiet. Then the night, too, became very quiet.

In the corner of his eye, Stockburn saw Lori look up at him from under his left shoulder. "I can't hear them anymore. Can you?"

"No."

He waited. He felt the warmth of Lori's body pressed against him. The cool night air shifted against his face as the breeze switched directions.

Small creatures rustled in the dead leaves and brush around him. The buckskin breathed heavily, a soft sawing sound, its ribs expanding and contracting, until it recovered from the fast, steep climb.

Hooves thudded distantly. Wolf could feel Lori's body stiffen a little behind him. But the thudding did not get louder; it got quieter.

Finally, the distant rataplan fell away to silence.

Stockburn stared out across the canyon, back in the direction he'd come from, following Lori. Presently, he spied movement on the canyon's far side. The movement appeared a small silver

288

worm climbing a black incline. That was the McCrae riders trotting their horses up a pass.

"They're going now," Wolf said.

"That's a relief."

"Hold on."

Stockburn nudged the buckskin ahead with his heels. He followed the rim of the canyon to the west, until he was on the west side of the cabin still marked by the flickering lamplit windows below. He found another game trail and eased the horse down off the rim and onto the wooded slope declining toward the canyon floor.

Lori didn't say anything. She rode with her arms around his waist, her head canted forward resting against his back.

Deep in thought, most likely. Tonight, everything had changed. She'd come to a watershed. Now she was wondering what was going to become of her, Daniel, and her child. He sensed the fear in her. But also the determination to live her life on her own terms, let all others go to hell.

He found himself admiring the girl. She was as tough as she was pretty. She'd sacrificed much for love. He just hoped she hadn't reignited the old land war. He knew Lori was hoping the same thing.

"Where will we go, Wolf?" Her voice was thin with anxiety. Maybe it was sinking in that she no longer had a home to go back to. Maybe she never would again. At least, not the Triangle.

Stockburn stared up at her. "I was hoping you might have an idea."

She looked off, pensive. Then she turned back to him and gave a brief nod. "I do."

Wolf handed her the buckskin's reins. "I'll follow you, then."

An hour after leaving the line shack, Stockburn and Lori reined up at the edge of a small meadow.

A stream trickled beyond a thin fringe of autumn-naked trees to the right. Stockburn was a little turned around, for the unfamiliar mountains were a maze at night, but he thought the stream was the Big Sandy River south of where the rail crew had been massacred.

Ahead, painted a ghostly pale by the angling moon, which cast as many shadows now as it did light, was a white-washed log church with a steeple poking out of the roof above the front door.

Stockburn turned to Lori, frowning, half-smiling incredulously. "Let me guess—Wrath of Jehovah Lutheran Church."

Lori smiled, shrugged. "I doubt anyone will look for me here. At least, not soon."

She nudged her horse forward. Wolf followed suit, casting his gaze about, customarily wary about riding into an ambush. "No one lives on the premises, I take it?"

Lori shook her head. "When it was still in operation, itinerant preachers took turns giving the sermons. Sometimes a lay minister from nearby. There's a small living area in the back of the building, where the preachers would stay overnight."

"What do you mean—when it was still in operation?"

"It's not used anymore." Lori shook her hair back from her eyes. "After the, uh . . . the *trouble* with my pregnancy, my father and Daniel's father nearly came to blows one Sunday. They had to be physically restrained. Guns were drawn on both sides. War was on the verge of breaking out. I was horrified that I and Daniel had caused it."

She drew a fateful breath, released it. "The McCraes didn't return to church after that, and I heard from Daniel that his family didn't, either. Since both ranching families and their hands made up the bulk of the congregation, the church was closed. That was three years ago now, and it's never reopened."

As they approached the simple structure, Stockburn saw that brush and weeds had grown long in the yard and around the stone foundation. The lilac shrubs standing to each side of the log steps rising to the small front porch were overgrown, their branches having wended their way onto the porch itself. The path that wound up to the church from the main trail had nearly gone back to sod.

"There's a stable around back," Lori said, urging her buckskin around the building's right side.

The stable stood to the right of a privy. A shed attached to the side of the stable, opposite a small barked rail corral, offered moldering firewood. A roofed well with a winch and a wooden bucket fronted the stable.

A small graveyard flanked the stable and privy—milky with moonlight and dappled with deep black shadows. It was peppered with stunt cedars and a few Ponderosa pines. Stone and wooden markers leaned here and there, nearly hidden by the knee-high grass.

Stockburn sent Lori to the living quarters at the rear of the church, for she wore only a light jacket. It was cold now at two-thirty A.M., the temperature likely at freezing, frost furring the grass. Lori said she'd get a fire going in the stove and heat water for coffee.

Meanwhile, Wolf unsaddled the horses, gave them each a handful of grain, and rubbed them down thoroughly with burlap. He drew water from the well and set the bucket in the corral in which he'd turned out the horses to graze the grass growing wild in there. He'd given Lori his war bag and his saddlebags, which contained his coffee pot and his pouch of Arbuckles.

Now, carrying just his rifle and bedroll, he walked out of the stable and stood just outside the stable's double doors, looking around carefully.

During the ride from the line shack, he'd sensed someone on his and Lori's back trail. It might just be his paranoia flaring. On the other hand, someone might really have followed them from the line shack. Possibly one of the Triangle men.

Possibly the bastard with the large-caliber rifle.

He stood for a time, looking around the moonlit meadow, listening. When five minutes had passed, and the only movement he spied was the breeze-nudged grass and branches, and the only sound he heard was the piercing cry of a rabbit likely being plucked off the ground by some raptor's sharp talons, he walked slowly to the small door at the rear of the church.

He turned to look around once more. He had more than only himself to worry about. He had to look out for Lori now, too. The last thing he wanted was for her to take a bullet meant for him.

Again, sensing nothing amiss, he turned to the door. As he placed his hand on the latch, sobs sounded from within. Frowning, he pushed open the door and stepped inside. Lori sat at the small table to his right. She leaned forward, resting her face in her hands, sobbing.

"Say, say." Stockburn set down his blanket roll and leaned his rifle against the wall. "What's all this about?"

What's all this about? an inner voice castigated him with a caustic chuff. *What do you think it's about, you simple fool?*

Lori looked up at Wolf with tears flooding her eyes, the tears glistening in the light of a lamp hanging over the table. "I don't think he loves me anymore!"

CHAPTER 25

"Now, now," Stockburn said, placing his hat on a wall peg near the door. He shrugged out of his coat, hung it over the back of a chair, then pulled the chair out from the table and sat down in it.

He leaned forward, placing his big right paw over Lori's left one, consuming it, and gave it a gentle squeeze. "Why do you say that, honey?"

"He's different now. Somehow . . . I'm not sure how, but . . . he's different now, Wolf. There was something in his eyes. Something . . . that I hadn't seen before. A coldness."

Lori shook her head, deeply troubled. "I can't put my finger on it, but . . ." Her voice broke. Quietly sobbing, she said, "I don't think he loves me anymore!"

She sobbed again, brushed tears from her eyes. She sniffed, trying to compose herself. "Not that I blame him. My mother intercepted our letters, so he probably thought I'd forgotten about him and Buster. I never did, though."

She stared down at the table, shaking her head. She'd stopped sobbing, but the tears still ran, dribbling down her cheeks and making little wet marks on the badly scarred table's rough wooden surface. "I never did. I wouldn't. All I've ever wanted was to be with Daniel and our son.

The three of us. Despite our fathers' so-called *arrangement*."

Lori had placed the pot on the little sheet-iron stove on the right side of the small room, the black tin chimney running up through the ceiling above. The pot was spewing steam from its snout.

Stockburn slid his chair back, rose, and walked over to remove the pot from the stove. He set it on a small counter, dumped in a couple of handfuls of ground Arbuckles from his coffee sack, then returned the pot to the fire.

When the coffee boiled again, he added a little water from a canteen to settle the grounds, then found two stone mugs on a shelf above the counter. He blew dust out of the mugs, filled them, and brought them over to the table.

He set one in front of Lori. "What you need is a nice hot cup of coffee. Good and strong. It'll make you feel better, give you a fresh perspective."

"Thanks, Wolf," Lori said, lifting the cup in both her small hands and blowing on the coal-black liquid. "But I don't think anything's going to make me feel good . . . ever again."

Stockburn's heart twisted for the poor gal. She was really up against it. She wanted to marry the father of her little boy, and she wanted them to all be together. She'd given up everything to achieve that goal, only to find . . . what?

That Daniel had changed. That he was no longer as committed to that goal as she was.

Stockburn sipped his own coffee then held the mug before him and frowned curiously. "Tell me, honey—in what way do you think Daniel has changed?"

She was still staring at the table, the very picture of bleakness and sorrow, her features pale and slack. Again, she slowly shook her head.

"Like I said, I can't put my finger on it, Wolf. But while he said the words that he still loved me . . . and assured me that we'd be together . . ." She frowned across the table. ". . . I didn't quite believe him. I'm not sure that even he believed it. I don't know—he just seemed to have something else on his mind. Maybe an even bigger complication."

"Do you have any idea what that complication might be?"

"No." Deep lines cut across the girl's pale forehead. "Do you?"

Stockburn let the question go because he wasn't sure how to answer it. He wasn't sure what he himself was thinking at the moment. Those mysterious, unnamable clues kept fluttering like butterflies around in his head. All he knew for certain was that his thoughts kept returning to the line shack.

He took another sip of his coffee and set the cup down. He frowned curiously at Lori again, who was studying him with her own befuddlement branded onto her face, as though trying to read his mind.

"Did you know there was someone else in the line shack?" he asked.

"Tonight?"

"Yes."

"No! What makes you think there was?"

"I saw him."

"You did?"

"Through a window." Stockburn nodded then took another sip of his coffee.

"Who was it, Wolf?" Lori asked, concern now creasing her brows.

"I don't know. I thought maybe you would. Lean fella with long, straight brown hair on the sides, nearly bald on top. Kind of craggy-faced, looks older, weathered beyond his years."

Stockburn did not tell her about the cut on his cheek. Nor that the man had been eavesdropping on her and Daniel's conversation. She was distraught and perplexed enough at the moment. She didn't need to know about Wolf's growing suspicions.

About the man in the line shack . . . the large-caliber rifle that may or may not have been used in the attempt to blow Wolf's head off . . . and Daniel Stoleberg.

Lori shook her head. "Doesn't ring any bells. Who do you think he was . . . is, Wolf?"

"I don't know."

"I wonder why Daniel didn't mention him to me." Lori studied Stockburn closely, suspicion growing in her eyes. "What are you thinking, Wolf?" She paused. The frown lines cut deeper across her forehead. "You don't suspect that—"

Stockburn reached across the table and closed his calming hand around hers. "I for one can no longer think clearly about anything. Time to stop trying. I think we could both use a couple hours of sleep. It's going to be light soon."

He glanced at the room's single bed on the far side of the narrow quarters. It was outfitted with several Indian blankets and a pillow. "You take the bed. I'm going to go out and sleep in the stable. I scoped out a nice pile of hay in there."

"Moldy hay, you mean," Lori said. "You take the bed. I won't be able to sleep, anyway."

"Please, darlin'," Wolf urged her, giving her hand another squeeze. "You have to try. You've had a long day. A long *couple* of days."

Lori looked at him, drew a breath, and pulled her mouth corners down in appeasement. "Oh, all right. If you insist. I'll try. I wish you'd stay in here, though. I feel safe with you around."

Stockburn didn't tell her that the opposite, in fact, was true. Under the current circumstances, anyway.

"You'd want to shoot me once I set to snoring." Wolf chuckled, finished his coffee, and rose from his chair, stretching and yawning. "That hay just started calling me loud, of a sudden." He set his hat on his head then grabbed his rifle and blanket roll and turned to the door. "Goodnight, gal."

"Wolf?" She sat staring up at him worriedly. "What's going to happen tomorrow?"

"What would you like to have happen tomorrow?" he asked her, gently. "If you decide to go home, I'd be happy to ride—"

"Never!" A flush rose in her otherwise pale cheeks.

"All right, all right. I just thought after you slept on it, you might have a change of heart, is all."

Her expression transformed into one of desperation. "I know I'm in a bad place. But I refuse to return to the Triangle with my tail between my legs. I need to get my son back. If not Daniel, then at least my boy. Somehow, Buster and I will build a life together despite everything."

Wolf smiled, nodded.

"Wolf?" she asked suddenly.

"Yes, honey?"

"My heart is so sore over what I did . . . about allowing my parents to take my baby away from me . . . to give Buster to the Stolebergs . . . that sometimes I think I just can't go on."

Tears returned to her eyes. "Do you know what I mean? Has your heart ever been so sore . . . for such a long time . . . that you often think it can't possibly keep beating, feeling as sore as it does?"

Tears trickled down her cheeks; her upper lip quivered. "Have you ever felt that way, Wolf?"

Stockburn returned her gaze with a grave one of his own. Just hearing her words conjured his own deep, bitter sadness, so that his heart began to thud heavily, achingly at the memory of his own grave mistake and what it had cost him.

He nodded. "I have. I know how you feel." He smiled. "Good-night, Lori."

"Good-night, Wolf."

CHAPTER 26

Stockburn drew the church's rear door closed and looked around.

The moon was almost down behind the western ridges, so it was darker now than it had been before. Long, dark shadows slanted across the ground before him, nearly hiding the corral, stable, and woodshed. It totally concealed the cemetery. Black as velvet over there.

Anyone could be hiding out here—in the cemetery or behind the stable, say, and Stockburn probably wouldn't know about it until the bullet from that big Sharps cored his skull like an apple. Which is to say, he'd probably never know about it. He'd be dead before the blasting report reached his ears.

He clamped his bedroll under his left arm and took his Yellowboy in both hands. Holding it out from his right side, he strode toward the stable.

He shifted his gaze from left to right and back again. He turned full around as he continued walking, in case a bushwhacker had sequestered himself to either side of the church building.

Something moved on his right.

Wolf stopped, swung the Yellowboy right, cocking it, drawing his finger back against the trigger. The bedroll fell from his side. He eased the tension in his trigger finger as the gray blur of a figure disappeared into the darkness of the cemetery, the beast's padded feet thumping softly, making the grass and brush rustle.

Wolf off-cocked the Winchester's hammer, exhaling. Only a coyote. Maybe a gray fox.

He looked around once more then stopped to pluck his bedroll off the ground.

He continued to the stable, opened one of the doors, then stepped back and to one side quickly, half-expecting the bright flash of a gun maw.

Nothing. Only silence. The smell of the moldy hay Lori had mentioned pushed out through the half-open door.

Wolf shifted his gaze to the corral off the left side of the stable. Both his horse and Lori's buckskin stood close together, watching Stockburn curiously, each twitching an ear. Neither looked nervous, like there was an interloper about. They were just wondering what had the tall man in the buckskin coat and black sombrero so on edge.

The horses' non-reaction was a good sign.

Still, Stockburn felt that someone was near, watching him, waiting for the right opportunity. It had to be the bastard with the big rifle. He hadn't finished the job he'd been sent out to do. His employer—whoever he was—wouldn't like that. Not one bit. The man or men who'd arranged the rail-crew massacre wanted Stockburn scoured from their trail.

The man with the big rifle would try again.

Stockburn stepped into the stable, looked around, then stared out through the half-open door. "You're out there," he said beneath his breath, sliding his gaze around the meadow to each side of the church building. "You're out there somewhere . . . aren't you? Biding your time. Wanting to get it right next time . . ."

He drew the right door toward him, leaving a one-foot gap between that one and the closed one. He backed up, sat down in a pile of musty hay, and leaned back against the stable wall.

He held the Winchester across his legs and stared out through the one-foot gap in the door. From this vantage point, he could see the entire back wall of the church, and a good chunk of the yard between the stable and the church building.

If anyone moved around out there, maybe made a play on the church, Stockburn would know about it. Maybe, just maybe, he could take the bastard with the big Sharps alive. If so, the man might very well be a font of valuable information. Stockburn knew how to extract such information from even the most unwilling of stubborn souls.

It wasn't pretty, but it was effective.

He settled himself back against the wall, squirmed around a little in the hay, getting comfortable—if it was possible to get comfortable in a small pile of moldy hay on a cold, high-mountain autumn night with a killer with a big rifle most likely on the lurk, intending to blow your head off.

No, it wouldn't be the most comfortable of nights. Morning, rather. Dawn soon.

But Stockburn had known such nights in his past. Plenty of them. They were all part and parcel of the life he had chosen. Most men his age, forty, were settled down, raising families. At such an ungodly hour, they were snuggled down in warm, soft beds with their warm, supple wives.

Not Stockburn. He had no wife, no family. He never would. He'd chosen to go it alone, to live the mostly itinerant and dangerous life of a Wells Fargo rail detective.

Why?

The single word and the image slipped into his brain, instantly making his shoulders tighten.

Mike.

The only close friend he'd ever had. For some damn reason, Stockburn had betrayed that friend. He'd slept with the woman Mike had been going to marry. Mike had found them together, in a hotel room when the three of them had taken a gambling trip to San Francisco.

Mike had been so distraught he'd walked into the busy street fronting the hotel, and into the path of a cable car, which had run over and killed him.

Stockburn had no idea why he'd gone to bed with Mike's girl, Fannie. He hadn't loved her. In fact, he'd found her only nominally attractive. Of course, he and Fannie had been drunk, and they'd found themselves alone when Mike had been called away on a family matter.

Neither was an excuse to betray a friend.

Why? The question had plagued him.

Wolf had decided there was a deep darkness in him. A black creature lolled at the bottom of the well of his being. That black creature corrupted the well. That's why he'd never married. Why he preferred to live alone.

He couldn't trust himself in friendships or in love. He could never know when that black creature was going to raise its ugly head again, and destroy someone else—another good friend, maybe even a wife . . . a family.

He kept to himself and he rode the outlaw trails. That was the only life for a man with such darkness in him.

He hated thinking about Mike. The guilt, the self-recrimination, the self-hatred bit him deep. He turned his thoughts now to his sister. That was the one bright spot in his personal life.

He'd found her at last, his dear Emily, kidnapped by the Cheyenne when she was only eight years old. She was a beautiful, dark-haired, dark-eyed, full-grown woman now, who went by the name of Melissa Ann Thornburg. She had a half-breed boy, born when she'd been in Sioux captivity, named Pete.

She and Pete had a good ranching life over in Dakota Territory, on land left to them by the man Melissa Ann had married after she'd left the Sioux she'd lived with for fifteen years.

Melissa Ann and Pete—the two bright spots in Stockburn's life.

He hadn't seen them again since he'd first discovered his sister at last, after nearly twenty years of searching. But he knew where she was. He would see her and his nephew again soon.

But only for a short time. He had to mind the black beast wallowing at the bottom of the well of his being.

He blinked away the disturbing image of the beast. As he did, he stared through the opening between the stable doors. The moonlight was gone. It had been replaced sometime during his musings by the faint light of the false dawn.

Since he'd spied no movement out there in the past two hours, maybe the killer would not show. Or maybe Stockburn had been wrong about him and Lori having been followed.

Maybe.

At any rate, he thought he could risk a few winks now. He'd need a little sleep behind him when he took to the trail again at sunrise. He had the nagging urge to revisit the sight of the rail-crew massacre.

His investigation of the sight had been interrupted by the ambusher. He wanted to go over the sight one more time, more slowly and thoroughly.

At that sight lay his only hope of gathering any solid clues as to the identity of the killers. He had several half-formed opinions on the matter, a few sketchy ideas of which direction to look in, but as yet he had no solid clues.

He hoped that would change after he'd scoured the sight of the massacre.

He closed his eyes and was almost instantly asleep. It was an intentionally shallow slumber, his senses still attuned to the world around him. If footsteps sounded, or if one of the horses so much as snorted uneasily, he'd be instantly awake.

He must have unconsciously sensed the sun's rise, because when he awoke and strode to the open door, the lemon orb was painting the eastern sky behind the toothy, darkly silhouetted peaks an amazing array of reds and yellows.

He led Smoke into the stable, gave him a handful of oats, and saddled him. He shoved the Yellowboy into the scabbard then led the horse outside and over to the back of the church.

He dropped Smoke's reins then opened the back door quietly, not wanting to wake Lori. He was glad to find her still asleep.

Moving quietly, he gathered his gear—his war bag and saddlebags. He left enough coffee for her to brew a pot for herself when she awoke. As he started back to the door, she stirred, opened her eyes, and stretched.

"Is it morning?"

"Still early," Stockburn said. "Go back to sleep, darlin'. I'm sorry I woke you."

She sat up a little, frowning. "Are you leaving?"

Wolf nodded. "Work to do."

"Detective work?"

"That's what I'm here for."

"Can I come with you?"

"No. Too dangerous, Lori."

Lori looked around the small quarters. "I don't want to stay here alone."

"You'd best go back to town. Get yourself a room in that fancy hotel. I'll pay for it."

Lori shook her head. "Word will get back to my family. They'll come for me."

Stockburn considered it. "All right. I'll head back here mid-afternoon. We'll ride into Wild Horse together."

Lori drew her mouth corners down and nodded. She lowered her gaze, frowning, troubled. She raised her sad eyes again to Stockburn and said, "And what then, Wolf?"

He moved to the bed, crouched down, and gave her arm a squeeze. "One day at a time, kid."

He winked and went out.

CHAPTER 27

As soon as he'd given the morning work instructions to his two brothers and the ranch hands, Daniel Stoleberg returned to the house and strapped a gun and holster around his waist, still an awkward maneuver with one hand despite his having had nearly ten years to practice it.

He cursed until he finally got the damn thing secure, then grabbed his hat off the tree by the door.

He'd just turned to the door when a voice sounded atop the stairs behind him. An all too familiar one. One with a grating tone to it. "Daniel, where are you going?"

He turned and winced when he saw Grace standing atop the stairs holding the kid, who was gooing and gawing and making all sorts of other nonsensical sounds and noises. He was staring with his wide brown eyes—his mother's—down the stairs at Daniel, pointing at his father with one wet, crooked finger.

To Daniel's mind, it was an accusing finger despite the broad, happy smile on the boy's red lips.

"I'm heading to town, Grace."

Grace's forehead creased. "What on earth for?"

"Business."

He reached for the doorknob but stopped again when Grace said, "I was hoping you could keep an eye on your child for an hour or so while I lie down . . ."

Your child.

She hadn't emphasized the words. Grace was too subtle for that. Just speaking them in a normal tone was enough for her. Just reminding him very subtly that the kid was his responsibility as much as her own despite her and Carlton having agreed to formally raise him, was enough castigation.

Daniel knew that his sister-in-law took some kind of devilish pleasure in shaming him for his past sins despite the rest of the family having forgiven him. He didn't know why she did. Maybe she was just bored. She'd been out here with Carlton for five years, but she'd never taken to the ranch.

You'd think that imagining she was dying from some mysterious illness all the time, one imagined ailment after another, would be enough to keep her busy. But, no—she had to harass her husband's younger brother—a cripple, no less.

A cripple with a dark past. A disloyal past.

"I'm sorry, Grace," Daniel said. "You'll have to tend your child. *Your child.* The one you agreed to raise, *remember?*"

Again, he turned to the door. He got it partway open this time before he again stopped on the heels of Grace's shrill voice plunging down the stairs at him, badgering. "You're up to no good, Daniel! I don't know what it is, but I know it's no good. You've been leaving on horseback much too often these past few weeks. And I saw you ride out late last night. I know because I couldn't sleep, and I was rocking by the window upstairs."

Daniel froze. Anger flared in him. It was probably good those snakes had killed half the nerves in his legs. Otherwise, he'd likely run up the stairs, grab his infuriating sister-in-law by her skinny neck, and wring the life out of her.

Then who would raise the kid?

He sucked back his fury, taking a long deep breath and blowing it out.

He turned to Grace, casting a frigid smile at once insolent and mocking. "*Business,* Grace. Just business. Enjoy the day. Why don't you take the kid outside? Might be one of the last nice ones we have for a while."

He winked at her, causing her pale cheeks to flush with fury, then jerked the door open and went out. He made his stiff, limping way to the stable and had one of the stable boys saddle his favorite horse, Two Dot, named for the two splashes of white paint on each side of the dun's otherwise brown hindquarters.

He mounted up, rode out through the wooden portal and a little over two hours later rode onto the main street of Wild Horse. It was a few minutes shy of one. The street was mostly deserted. Not that Wild Horse could ever be called bustling, but it was quieter than normal because most folks were settling in for their mid-day meal, which always began a little earlier and lasted a little longer in the generally sleepy town.

Daniel could smell the aromas of various foods wafting in the wood smoke billowing down over the roof tops, shoved low by downdrafts. Ordinarily, the smells would have made him hungry. Today, they did not.

He had too much on his mind.

Why had Lori had to show up out of the blue and throw a jackrabbit into the wheel spokes of everything?

While Lori weighed heavily on him, she was actually the least of his worries.

He rode along the brightly sunlit, nearly deserted Wind River Avenue, and reined up in front of Hennessey's Wind River Saloon & Gambling Hall, sitting on the south side of an east-to-west cross street from the Continental Restaurant. A dozen or so horses stood drooping their heads and tails at the two hitchracks fronting Hennessey's.

Daniel slipped his dun in between a mouse brown gelding and a calico mare, the gelding giving a sudden start and lurching to one side, brushing up against the horse on its left.

"Easy, easy," Daniel said, testily, and stepped stiffly down from the saddle.

Once on the ground, he paused, leaning forward against the stirrup, waiting for feeling to return to his legs. Riding always made them number than usual. He closed his eyes, drew a breath. He was a young man, only thirty, but the two-hour ride weighed heavy on his brittle body.

"Need any help?"

Daniel opened his eyes. The town marshal, Watt Russell—a fat, useless man—stood on the boardwalk near the three steps rising to the door of Hennessey's place. He scowled with concern at Daniel from beneath the brim of his battered black Stetson.

His tall, mustached deputy, Chet Diggs, was just then stepping out of Hennessey's, behind Russell. The deputy's eyes found Daniel standing between his horse and the mouse brown gelding, and Daniel saw the faint glint of mockery in the deputy's dull blue eyes.

Men were essentially wolves. You learned that when you were crippled. Other men looked at you like younger, stronger wolves eyeing one of the weaker ones in the pack, pleased by their own dominance. Some pitied you, but that was even worse.

Russell studied Daniel with pity in the old lawman's eyes hooded by wrinkled droopy gobs of sun-browned flesh. Chet Diggs, a former sodbuster and cattle rustler as useless as Russell, felt buoyed by Stoleberg's obvious weakness. He stepped up beside Russell and feigned a look of concern but could not quite wash the mockery from his gaze.

"I'm fine," Daniel said, reaching for Two Dot's belly strap and feigning a smile of his own. "Just loosening the latigo cinch is all, so my horse can take some water. Thank you for your concern, gentlemen."

Diggs turned to Russell and chuckled.

Russell did not look at his deputy nor respond to the insolent laugh. The marshal kept his concerned, curious gaze on Daniel. "You in town alone, Daniel?"

"Yes, I'm in town alone." Scowling, feeling the heat of anger in his ears, Daniel stepped up onto the boardwalk and set his lone hand on the hitchrack for support. "You got a problem with that, Marshal?"

"No, no," Russell said, wagging his head and holding his hands up, palms out, "no problem at all. I was just wondering if you're all right, is all. Looked like you might've been having a little trouble there."

"Thank you for your concern, Marshal," Daniel said crisply, shoving away from the hitchrack and maneuvering his feet to Hennessey's door. "I assure you I was having no trouble at all." He fashioned a taut smile. "I am just fine."

"Here to see Mister Hennessey, I see."

Daniel hadn't missed the subtle accusatory tone

in the marshal's voice. At least, he'd thought the tone had been accusing. Or was he just getting paranoid?

"There a law against that?" Daniel asked.

"Nope, nope." Russell held up both hands and shook his head. "No law against having a conversation with the man, I reckon." He chuckled softly but without mirth. He stared into Daniel's eyes until Daniel flushed and turned away, knowing right then and there that he had not imagined the castigation in the old lawman's voice.

"Go to hell, you fat fool," he felt like saying but did not.

Diggs looked at Russell again and laughed.

Casting a hard glare at the deputy over his right shoulder, Daniel climbed the three steps and limped through Hennessey's front door.

Wolves.

As soon as Daniel was out of earshot, Russell would have a good laugh with Diggs. Unlike Diggs, he wasn't stupid and ill-mannered enough to laugh in his face, for Daniel came from one of the two most powerful ranching families in the area.

But old Russell would mock him behind his back, all right. Everyone did. Why should Russell be any different?

That was why after the accident he rarely rode to town.

He stopped just inside Hennessey's door and looked around the saloon's sunken floor. A smoke haze obscured the crowd of men and a few of Hennessey's pleasure girls enjoying Hennessey's free lunch counter while nursing beers and/or whiskey shots.

A team of mule skinners must have pulled in on the train, for eight of the burly, bearded men in checked shirts, suspenders, and canvas pants sat at a large table in the middle of the room, near the big, ornate, horseshoe-shaped bar, eating pickled eggs and sandwiches of cheese and sausage slapped between thick slabs of grainy brown bread while swilling beer from buckets, playing cards, and generally loudly and good-naturedly cavorting around the table covered in red and white oilskin.

A doxie in a short, low-cut red dress sat on the lap of one of the mule skinners, her arms around his neck, talking and laughing into his right ear while he somehow managed to play poker, drink beer, and eat his sandwich while flirting with the girl—a plain-faced brunette named Clara.

Yes, Daniel knew her name. He'd been here before, mixing pleasure with business.

Clara glanced at him now and smiled.

Daniel looked away from her, his ears warming slightly.

Several men stood at the bar, one boot propped on the brass rail. Men occupied most of the tables to Daniel's left and right. Two bartenders toiled behind the mahogany. Two other girls were making the rounds, parrying butt swats and out-and-out fondling.

Daniel looked closely around the room, hoping to see Hennessey down here so he wouldn't have to climb the stairs. The saloon owner was usually down here this time of the day, milling with the crowd, laughing with his customers and keeping an eye on the chuck-a-luck and poker tables against the wall to the right, as well as on the roulette wheel and on the one-eyed fellow, Darl Murphy, who dealt faro on days he wasn't working as a brakeman for the Union Pacific.

Daniel saw two bouncers, one sitting in the overlook chair near the chuck-a-luck layout, and the other playing a game of solitaire near the bottom of the stairs running up the rear wall, on the bar's left flank. That was the fellow who screened all visitors headed for the second floor, accepting money for the jakes the pleasure girls had enticed into a romp in one of the upstairs cribs.

Daniel made his way down the three steps to the carpeted floor of the drinking and gambling hall. As he started toward the bar, a man coming down the steps behind him accidentally knocked into him, almost sending him sprawling onto an occupied table to his left.

"Oh, hell—sorry!" came the apology. The

318

man glanced at Daniel over his shoulder, gave a deferential pinch to the brim of his brown derby hat, then continued with another man, chatting obliviously, to a recently vacated table off the front of the bar.

Daniel got his feet solidly beneath him, feeling the heat of anger warm his cheeks. He cursed under his breath.

Wolves.

He continued forward, ignoring the predictable stares from the tables he passed.

"Poor bastard," he heard a man mutter beneath the room's low din.

Daniel approached the bar, waved a hand to catch the eye of one of the bartenders, and said, "Where's Hennessey?"

The bald barman, who wore a black silk band around his upper right arm, tipped his head back and jerked his chin to indicate the closed door on the second-floor balcony, near the top of the stairs. The door had a brass plate attached to it. Daniel knew from previous visits that Kreg Hennessey's name was etched into the plate.

Daniel turned to the stairs and cursed. He hated stairs. He hated them even more at the moment because he still hadn't fully recovered from the ride to town from the ranch headquarters.

He considered asking the barman to send someone to fetch Hennessey but nixed the idea. He didn't want anyone doing him any favors.

Besides, he needed to talk to Hennessey in private, behind closed doors.

They had important, private matters to discuss. They'd have to discuss them upstairs.

Dammit!

Daniel headed for the stairs.

When he was ten feet from the bottom of the broad, carpeted staircase with ornately scrolled banisters, a man's voice rose out of the room's general din, pitched with insolence and brash mockery. "Well, well, well—to whom do we owe the honor of a visit from the crippled Stoleberg *boy*—Daniel Stoleberg himself?"

CHAPTER 28

Daniel stopped and turned unsteadily.

Three men sat at a table eight feet away. All three regarded him mockingly with eyes glassy from drink. The man who'd spoken—Sheb Grissom—smiled more brightly, more insolently than the others.

Daniel had fired the puncher from the Tin Cup crew earlier in the year for drunkenness and general disobedience not to mention sloth. He was a ne'er-do-well who occasionally got ranch work when warm bodies were needed for the spring roundup, though he'd rarely remained on any one ranch for long.

Daniel had given the man a chance despite Grissom's reputation, because he'd had cows to gather from the winter pastures and calves to brand. McCrae usually got first pick of the puncher crop because he could afford to pay better. It hadn't taken Daniel long to realize his mistake in hiring Sheb Grissom.

"How ya doin', crip?" Grissom was a wiry, ugly man with close-cropped sandy brown hair and a square, bony face with two bulging brown eyes. He smiled an exaggerated, death's-head smile as he lifted his half-full schooner of beer in mock salute. "Still limpin' around the Tin Cup while the *real* men do the work?"

He dipped his chin and belched loudly.

"Now, Sheb," said the man sitting to his left, slapping his ragged hat across Sheb's shoulder in feigned castigation, "that ain't no way to talk to a cripple! Show some respect, will ya?"

The three men howled.

The rest of the room had quieted down. Daniel looked around the room, through the drifting tobacco smoke. The other diners, drinkers, and gamblers had turned their attention to Daniel and the three men rawhiding him.

None objected. Most stared sober faced, not outwardly enjoying the show but not objecting, either. Enjoying it, most likely, on one level or another, though they tried to hide it.

One of the famous Stolebergs was getting taken down a notch. Never mind that he had only one arm and that his legs were as stiff as fence posts. That he hated himself about as much as any man possibly could. That his own personal travails, both physical and mental, had shriveled his heart down to a lump of black coal.

Wolves.

Daniel turned again to Sheb Grissom and the other two men still howling in laughter, Grissom slapping the table as he bent over his knees.

"Did you ever hear the joke about the fella who

was busier'n a one-armed man in a fistfight?" asked the third man.

They all laughed even louder.

A few of the other men sitting around them chuckled incredulously then glanced at Daniel sheepishly, and looked away.

Daniel stared at the three laughing drunks.

Rage was a wildfire burning inside him.

He stared at each laughing man in turn, at each red face bloated with laughter, tears streaming down stubbled cheeks. Grissom looked at Daniel again. Seeing the object of his derision still standing before him, so calmly enduring the humiliation, Grissom laughed even louder, slapped the table even harder.

Daniel felt his chest rising and falling heavily. His cold, black heart thumped against his breastbone.

The rest of the room was nearly silent. The only sounds were the howling laughter of Grissom and his two just-as-ugly, just-as-worthless partners.

Daniel felt his right hand drop over the handles of the .44 Colt holstered on his right thigh. Delight rippled through him as his hand began to slide the revolver from the holster. It was as though another man were sliding the gun from the holster, but it was Daniel's cold black heart beating with feverish expectation and anticipation of what was going to happen without him even having decided to do it.

As the gun's barrel cleared leather, Grissom glanced up at Daniel again.

The man's drink-bleary and humor-bright eyes found the gun in Daniel's hand near the holster. Grissom stopped laughing. His lower jaw loosened and his eyes widened as he looked up at Daniel's stony face in which burned the eyes of a killer.

The two others, still laughing, glanced at Sheb Grissom. When they saw that Grissom was no longer laughing but gazing quite seriously now at the crip, they turned their own gazes to Daniel. They both stopped laughing when their eyes went to the gun that Daniel now aimed straight out from his right shoulder.

"Hey," said the vermin to Grissom's left. His long, horse-like face hung slack, as though the muscles had melted away beneath the skin. "Hey, now . . ."

When Daniel clicked his Colt's hammer back, the men sitting around Grissom's table lurched from their chairs and scrambled for cover, some dropping to their knees behind other men still sitting at tables. One of the quickly vacated tables was knocked over, glasses and plates clattering onto the floor.

A man cursed and clutched his bruised knee as he dropped down out of sight.

When four tables around the table at which the three vermin sat had all been vacated, and the sudden flurry had dwindled back to silence, Grissom slapped his table angrily and lurched to his feet, jutting an enraged finger at Daniel and shouting, "How dare you aim a gun at me, you low-down dirt—!"

The blast and the bullet cut him off, the blast rocketing loudly around the room while the bullet punched through Grissom's grimy work shirt over his heart. Ricocheting off a rib, the bullet exited Grissom's upper torso from just under his left shoulder blade and plowed into one of the recently vacated tables behind him, shredding a ham sandwich and tossing a shot glass high in the air.

Grissom's only reaction to having just been killed was a little jerk. He stared, wide-eyed, at the man who'd killed him. He looked down at the blood spurting from the hole in his shirt and made a gurgling sound.

The other two vermin at the table looked at Grissom in shock.

As the horse-faced man looked at Daniel and then leaped out of his chair, grabbing the old hogleg on his right hip, Daniel's Colt roared again, painting a round, blue hole in Horse Face's forehead, to the left of a triangular shaped birthmark. The back of Horse Face's head blew across the table the shredded sandwich was on.

Daniel calmly slid his smoking Colt to the left.

The last surviving vermin screamed, *"No!"*

and raised his hands as though they would shield his face from a bullet. As if to prove him wrong, Daniel clicked the Colt's hammer back and dropped it on a third live round in the wheel.

It blew the third vermin's right index finger off before chewing into the nub of the man's left cheek and slamming him back in his chair, which toppled over backward as it and the third dead vermin thundered onto the carpeted floor.

The third vermin shook as though stricken with a seizure, still seated in his chair.

Grissom was still standing on the other side of the table from Daniel. He stared at Daniel as though in wide-eyed fascination. The front of his shirt resembled a bright red bib growing redder by the second.

Grissom opened his mouth as though to speak then fell forward onto the table before him, arms thrown straight out to both sides, cheek pressed against a pile of coins and playing cards.

Daniel lowered the Colt and looked around the room.

The room was so quiet that he could hear his own heart beating only a little faster and heavier than normal. Even the street outside the place was quiet. Two little boys stood with their hands and faces pressed up against the front window, peering in, one about four inches taller than the other one.

A dog wagged its tail beside them.

Most of the men in the room were standing now, staring wide-eyed and open-mouthed at Daniel. The two bartenders stood staring at him from behind the bar, one holding a bottle and a shot glass as though he'd been frozen mid-motion.

Boots thudded on the steps outside of Hennessey's. The door opened and in came the big-gutted town marshal, Watt Russell, flanked by his tall, lanky deputy, Chet Diggs.

"What in God's name . . . ?" Russell said as he moved heavily down the three steps and into the room, his ragged duster flapping about his cumbersome frame.

Flanked closely by Diggs, he pushed through the crowd. When he'd shoved aside the last two men standing between him and Daniel, he stopped suddenly, scowling at Daniel still holding his smoking Colt down against his right leg.

Russell stared at Stoleberg. His eyes dropped to the Colt in Daniel's hand then shifted to the three dead men to Daniel's right now as he faced the front of the room. Russell and Diggs shared a look of unspoken shock, then both men turned to gaze once more at the unlikely killer.

Daniel slid his Colt back into its holster. He felt a smile tug at his mouth corners. An enormous feeling of satisfaction washed over him.

He looked around the room once more, at the faces gawking at him as though he were a . . . a

. . . well as though they'd just found an unlikely wolf in their midst. An especially wild one, though they'd all thought he'd been as docile as a cottontail.

He looked at the two boys and the dog on the other side of the window and then at Russell and Diggs again.

"Fresh meat for the stray dogs," he said.

He turned and started walking toward the stairs again but stopped when he saw Kreg Hennessey standing on the balcony over the room, to the right of the stairs. Hennessey stared down at Daniel without expression.

Daniel continued to the stairs, glancing at the bouncer who now stood by his table to the left of the staircase, his playing cards in his hand. The bouncer stared at Daniel then lowered his chin deferentially, shock lingering in his eyes.

Daniel wanted to smile but did not. He placed his hand on the rail and started climbing. As he did, a sudden roar lifted from the saloon behind him, as though a collective held breath had just been released.

"Someone fetch the galldamned undertaker!" Watt Russell's voice rose above the din.

The staircase was roughly twice as long as the stairs in the main house at the Tin Cup headquarters. But Daniel would be damned if he'd stop for a blow. By the time he finally hoisted his right foot onto the second-floor hall, and then the left one, each one as heavy as a blacksmith's anvil, he was sweating so much that even his hair was damp beneath his Stetson and his shirt was sweat-basted to his back beneath his coat.

Hennessey stood before him, one brow arched. His broad, pitted face with the long, black side whiskers that met over his fat upper lip to form a mustache, was paler than usual. His lips were swollen, bristling with sutures.

Who on earth had belted Kreg Hennessey?

He was a big man, but today he looked gaunt, eyes sunken into his head. His eyes were pink-rimmed as he said, "To what do I owe the pleasure?" His swollen lips made the words come out a little funny, like he had rock candy in his mouth.

Daniel drew a breath, then another, and swallowed. His right knee was shaking. Ignoring it, he said, "We have to talk."

Hennessey glanced over the balcony rail at the room below, where men swarmed around the three dead vermin. The saloon owner pointed over the rail with his right hand. "You owe me for that rug."

"Take it out of the money for the right-of-way."

"I will," Hennessey promised.

He moved through the open door in the balcony's back wall. Daniel followed him into the office and closed the door. As the saloon owner walked in his bow-legged, lumbering fashion to the large desk on the far side of the room, Daniel noticed that he, like the bartender downstairs, wore a black silk band around his right arm.

"What are the arm bands for?" Daniel asked.

Hennessey continued around behind the desk and sat heavily down in the high-backed leather chair. Leaning forward and entwining his thick, beringed hands on the blotter before him, he looked across the room at Daniel but said nothing.

"His son."

Daniel hadn't realized a third man was in the room until he'd heard the voice. He followed it to one of the two high-backed leather chairs angled in front of the desk, facing it. The speaker sat in the chair on Daniel's right. Daniel could see only the very top of the crown of the man's brown hat, and his boots on the floor beneath the chair, one hooked behind the other.

Hennessey blinked once, slowly, as though to corroborate the other man's information.

Daniel walked shakily up to the desk. He stepped between the two chairs and placed his hand on the back of the right one, which was the one the other man in the room was sitting in.

Stanley Cove was an odd-looking, crow-like man in a shabby suit coat over a gold and brown checked vest, and baggy broadcloth trousers.

His high-crowned black Stetson had apparently weathered the abuse of many high-country storms.

He had narrow eyes, long nose, and sharp, upturned chin. Three days' worth of beard stubble shadowed his features.

He wore two pistols on his hips, their walnut grips polished by usage to a high shine.

"Well . . . if it ain't the return of the prodigal son," Cove said, giving a crooked grin.

He had a drink in his left hand. There was a plaster cast around his other hand, extending halfway up his forearm. The arm angled across his chest in a white cotton sling. He, too, wore a black silk band, on his left upper arm, since the right arm was busy with the cast and the sling.

"What happened to your hand, Cove?"

Cove's grin turned to a glare. "What happened to yours?" He glanced at Daniel's empty sleeve.

"Touchy." Daniel looked at Hennessey who stared at him dully, as though his mind were elsewhere. A half-filled glass of what appeared to be whiskey sat near his right elbow. A fat cigar smoldered in an ashtray near the whiskey.

Hennessey stared dully up at Daniel, for whom the shock at hearing of the death of the saloon owner's son made him need to sit down even more than his ascent of the stairs had. He sagged into the chair to the left of Cove and pondered the information.

"Well . . . I'm . . . I'm sorry, Kreg. About Riley, I mean." It was a bald-faced lie, and Hennessey likely knew it. There was no man on earth in more dire need of having his ticket punched than Riley Hennessey. Kreg probably knew that, as well. "How did it happen?"

Hennessey spoke for himself this time. "Same way Stan broke his paw and I got my mouth smashed, two teeth broke. Stockburn."

"Ah."

"Have you seen him?" Hennessey asked.

"I have. He rode into the Tin Cup headquarters with four of your men lying belly down across their saddles."

"Bohannon one of 'em?"

"Yes."

"Damn!" Hennessey pounded the desk with the end of his fist.

"What were Bohannon and the others doing on Tin Cup range?"

Hennessey frowned at him, the heavy brows mantling his eyes forming a large, lumpy ridge. "You know what they were doing. They were moving McCrae beef onto your land. Just like we arranged."

"Yeah . . . about that," Daniel said. "That's got to stop."

"Stop?" both Hennessey and Stan Cove said at the same time, incredulity sharp in their eyes.

Daniel looked at the hand splayed across

his right thigh. It was abnormally large and calloused from having had to perform the work of two hands for the past ten years. He hesitated, struggling to find the words, embarrassment burning his ears. "Uh . . ."

"I know," Cove said with a knowing grin. "It's that pretty little McCrae piece of work."

Hennessey sipped his whiskey, swallowed, and stretched his swollen lips and thick, black mustache with waxed ends back from his large, ivory-colored teeth. "I heard Lori McCrae was back in town. After only a month away." He glanced at Cove, then slid his coldly mocking eyes back to Daniel. "That bit of interesting gossip wouldn't have anything to do with why you've had a sudden change of heart so late in the game, would it?"

Daniel's heart thudded. He looked at his hand again, opening and closing it, then looked across the desk at Hennessey once more. "Look, Kreg . . . I didn't know you were going to kill those men. Those track layers. We never agreed to murder!"

"Oh?" Hennessey said. "How did you think I was going to get them out of there so I could sabotage the rails and the work train? Ask them very politely if they wouldn't mind please leaving while I blew up the rails and the work train?"

Stanley Cove laughed.

Exasperation bit Daniel hard. Now, his heart

was finally beating fast. It was beating hard, anger and frustration burning inside him. He pounded the edge of the desk before him, leaning forward.

"Stockburn's going to find out, Kreg! He's going to sniff it all out! I think it best to err on the side of—"

"That's why I brought in Slim Sherman."

Daniel leaned forward in his chair, the urgency of the situation coming to a head inside him. "Sherman missed the shot!"

"What?" both Hennessey and Cove asked again at the same time.

Daniel said, "Sherman had Stockburn in his sights, and he missed!"

"How do you know?" Cove asked.

Daniel didn't grant Hennessey's lowly underling, a back-shooting Texas killer who fancied himself a gunslinger, the courtesy of a glance.

To Hennessey, he said, "I rode out to the line shack on Blackbird Creek and found him there, nursing a nice gash in his cheek. Stockburn gave him a scar he'll take to his grave if he lives to be a hundred. Which he won't. Stockburn will get him. He almost had him last night, and he would have if that shack hadn't had a back door!"

Daniel sat back in his chair. "I want out, Hennessey. I made a hasty decision in throwing in with you. It's too risky. I didn't agree to cold-blooded murder!"

Hennessey and Cove shared another conspiratorial glance. Cove leaned toward Daniel and rubbed the back of his right hand across Daniel's cheek with mocking gentleness. "Oh, come on, now, Master Stoleberg, I know her skin is fair, an' she does know how to fill out a shirtwaist, but—"

Daniel drew his head away and swatted Cove's hand away with his own. "Get your filthy stinky hands off of me, you common privy rat!"

Instantly, one of Cove's six-guns was in his hand. The killer extended it out over the arm of his chair at Daniel's right temple and clicked the hammer back loudly. Cold anger flickered in the man's small, lake-blue eyes, above his gritted teeth.

Daniel stared at the gun, which Cove held steady as stone. Daniel felt a strange calm wash over him, his heart suddenly slowing.

It was like the way he'd felt just after he'd made the decision to kill the three vermin downstairs. He vaguely wondered if, had his fall into that rattlesnake nest not happened, he wouldn't have made a good professional killer himself. He'd heard to be really good you couldn't fear your own death.

He didn't fear it now. He stared at the maw of Stan Cove's gun barrel, and simply waited for the bullet that would end his misery.

"Stan," Hennessey said. "Young Stoleberg's

in love." Mockery lilted in his voice as he sat back in his chair, leaning a little to one side and canting his head, grinning, and said, "And . . . word has it . . . a child's involved."

Enunciating each word slowly, carefully, he added, "A bastard child . . . born out of wedlock."

Daniel glared at the man.

Hennessey blinked slowly. "Go home, boyo. Go hide under your bed. I called my new men back to town. I was going to give them their pay and their leave. Since Sherman apparently isn't up to the task of sending Stockburn under, they'll more than adequately fill his boots. It might be a little more public than I would have liked, but, what the hell—that useless Russell won't cause any trouble. Maybe public's better, anyway. A good show of force. Should've done it that way from the very beginning!"

The saloon owner puffed his stogie, ruminating darkly. "Stockburn is about to die very hard and very bloody. After they see the great Wolf of the Rails lying dead on Wind River Avenue, the Stewarts will beg a buyer to take the Hell's Jaw Line off their hands for a wink and a handshake! They'll have no choice but to sell to me. They sell to me or they'll get what Stockburn's gonna get!"

He puffed the stogie again with satisfaction.

Cove chuckled.

Deflated, Daniel sank back in his chair.

He'd come here hoping to snuff the fuse before it reached the powder keg. Now he saw it wouldn't be possible.

What kind of crazy, bloody scheme had he fallen prey to?

Only, he hadn't fallen prey to it. The scheme to sabotage the rails and the work train, to run the Stewarts out of business, and to throw in with Kreg Hennessey—with Daniel's ill father's money, no less!—had been his from the very start.

Why hadn't he seen how crazy and diabolical it was? How could he have schemed against his own family?

Why hadn't he realized you didn't go into business with diabolical killers like Kreg Hennessey?

Now, because he had, all was lost. Everything his father and brothers had fought and worked so hard for would soon be gone because of one crazy, hasty decision he'd made two months ago when his heart had felt as broken as the rest of him.

Now he had blood on his hands. In fact, he'd bathed in the stuff. The range would soon erupt in all-out war, and there was nothing he could do to stop it.

"You look like you could use a drink," Hennessey noted, holding up the bottle. "Bracer?"

Daniel climbed heavily from his chair, gritting his teeth. If he hadn't seen Cove still aiming his revolver at his head, he would have drawn his .44 and blown the saloon owner's brains all over the wall behind him.

"Go to hell, Kreg!" he wailed, hearing his voice quavering with exploding emotion. *"Just go to hell!"*

As the cripple made his tormented way to the door, the two wolves howled their mocking laughter behind him.

CHAPTER 29

Forty-five minutes after Stockburn had left Lori at Wrath of Jehovah Lutheran Church along the Big Sandy River, he rode through a bright-yellow aspen copse.

Leaves rained down around him, flashing with blinding brightness in the mid-morning sunshine. The balding, pale tree crowns, a network of cream-colored branches, danced in the breeze against the faultless arch of cerulean blue.

There wasn't a cloud in that vast sky. The air was clean and cold. It smelled like dead leaves and aspen bark.

To each side of Wolf, high canyon walls rose, lumpy with stone and bristling with conifers and deciduous trees whose roots somehow clung to those steep, boulder-strewn slopes though Wolf couldn't believe there was much more than an inch of nourishing soil on those castle-like bastion walls.

When he and Smoke rode out of the copse and into a clearing of needle grass and sage, he reined the gray to a stop. He frowned down at the ground before him.

He nudged the horse ahead, turning his head from one side to the other, inspecting the ground around him. His gaze held on a cow pie large enough to half-bury a tuft of purple mountain sage.

"Whoa, boy."

Stockburn swung down from the saddle. Holding the reins in his left hand, he removed his right-hand glove and poked his finger into the green-brown offal pile. He pulled the finger out, looked at it . . . sniffed it.

"Two, maybe three days old."

He wiped his finger off on the ground, returned the glove to his hand, straightened, and continued to look around. He found more pies roughly the same age as the first one. The hooves of a large number of shod horses and cattle marked the ground. Branches of sage clumps were trampled and torn.

Stockburn walked ahead, leading Smoke, swinging his gaze around, studying the ground closely, spying more and more indentations made by cow hooves. A herd had been moved through here, pushed from Stockburn's left to his right.

Possibly a couple of herds moved at different times, because he found some pies at least a day, maybe two days older than the first ones he'd discovered.

It also appeared that a small group of riders had ridden through here after the cows had been ridden through. The horse sign—hoofprints and apples—was fresh, maybe only a few hours old.

Someone had followed the tracks of the herd and the men who'd herded it east.

Stockburn scratched his chin. "Now, what the hell does *that* mean?"

He continued walking slowly across the path of the recently moved herds. He judged he'd walked maybe fifty yards when he came to the path's far end and could see no more tracks or cow pies.

Stockburn stopped, turned to stare back across the trail, and thumbed his hat brim back up off his forehead. "Hmmm."

He looked to the west, on his right. The canyon wall opened over that way. He could see the narrow gap.

Swinging his gaze to the east, on his left, he saw another gap in the wall over there, on the far side of a narrow stream that ran through a gravelly bed between the ridge wall and the aspen copse.

"So," Wolf said, speaking quietly to himself, his voice pitched with incredulity, "a good-sized herd was pushed through the western gap into the eastern gap. From the direction of the McCrae and toward the direction of the Stoleberg range. Hmm. Might be interesting."

How so?

He didn't know. This time of the year, men moved cows. Maybe that's all these tracks meant—men moving cows as part of the usual autumn gather.

He was on his way to the site of the rail crew

341

massacre, though, which meant he had bigger fish to fry today than worry about men moving cattle through open range.

Maybe things would clarify a little once he'd given the massacre sight a thorough scouring.

Wolf swung up onto Smoke's back and continued his journey along the canyon floor.

Slim Sherman stared through his Sharps sights at the buckskin-clad, black-hatted figure moving through the aspens below his perch on the canyon's east wall.

He slid the Sharps' barrel slowly from left to right, tracking the horseback rider's slow, steady movement through the aspen copse. Soon, in seconds, the man would ride out of the trees and into the open.

Sherman's heart thudded, hiccupping. Sweat had popped out on his forehead a minute ago, and now one of those sweat beads started to dribble down into his right eyebrow.

Damn!

Sherman pulled his head away from the stock of the long rifle and brushed a sleeve of his elk hide coat across his brow. He didn't need sweat getting into his eye. Sweat stung when it hit the eye, and a stinging eye would foul his aim, sure as tootin'.

Slim gave his brow another scrub, nudging his hat back up off his forehead, then snugged his cheek back up against the rifle's walnut stock again. He aimed quickly, gazing through the rear sliding ladder sight and arranging the bead on the end of the barrel on his target, for he had only a few seconds left before his quarry would ride out of the trees and into the open.

He drew his index finger back snug against the fifty-caliber rifle's trigger, keeping the sights lined up on Stockburn's head.

Sherman's heart beat even faster.

No, no, don't do that, he silently told the pesky organ. Damn thing's as nervous as a cat in a room full of rocking chairs!

As Stockburn and the smoky gray horse cleared the last aspens and rode into the clearing, Sherman lowered the Sharps' barrel slightly, and settled the bead through the ladder sight on the man's broad back, just below the wool-lined collar and between the man's shoulder blades.

Sherman held the sights steady, staring at a silver-dollar-sized area on the light tan of the man's buckskin coat. The assassin drew another breath, held it, frustrated at his damnable racing heart, and started to squeeze the trigger.

"Hey, Slim—how's it hangin'?" The girl's voice was like a punch to Sherman's own back, right between his shoulder blades.

The killer jerked with a start, pulled his index finger off the trigger at the last tenth of a second before he would have sent a wild round into the canyon.

He turned and looked up to see Ivy Russell squatting on the lip of the ridge eight feet above his nest. The tomboyishly pretty blonde grinned down at him, blue eyes flashing in the high-country sunlight, straight blond hair tumbling to her shoulders.

Ivy rested her elbows on her well-turned thighs and entwined her gloved fingers, as though she was doing nothing more than squatting by a cook fire, waiting for a pot of mud to boil, not interrupting a paid killer in the discharge of his duties—namely, killing one overly snoopy Wells Fargo railroad detective named Wolf Stockburn!

Sherman glanced into the canyon at Stockburn, then whipped his angry gaze back to Ivy. "Jumpin' Jehoshaphat—what the hell are you doing up there, Ivy? You like to have taken twenty years off my life!"

He felt cold sweat dribbling down the sides of his face.

"I was just passin' by and seen your horse ground-tethered on the ridge, and thought I'd stop and say hi, maybe chew the fat a little's all." Ivy frowned as she gazed back at him, suddenly peevish now herself. "Don't get your drawers in such a bunch, Slim!"

Sherman glanced into the canyon again, where Stockburn was just then dismounting his horse.

Sherman looked at Ivy again and gestured urgently with his left hand. "Get down, fer chrissakes! Get down, Ivy! Get back off the ridge!"

Ivy chuckled. "Well, which do you want me to do, Slim—get down or get back off the ridge?"

"Both!"

Ivy laughed.

Infuriated, Sherman glanced back into the canyon. Stockburn was walking around, leading his horse. Slim couldn't get a clear shot at him now, for the horse was too close, sometimes obscuring his view. The detective was a little too far up canyon now, as well.

Besides, Slim was too damn shaken.

Damn that girl!

He looked up the ridge. Ivy had backed away from the lip and was out of sight from Slim's position. He depressed the Sharps' heavy hammer and rose from his rocky nest in the side of the ridge.

He scrambled up the ridge wall, trying to keep the rocks between him and the canyon. He didn't want Stockburn to see him. He hoped the detective hadn't spied him. Everyone said he had eyes in the back of his gray head. Sherman had to try another shot at him or risk a long dark sleep with only the worms as company.

Hennessey had already paid him half of the five hundred dollars the saloon owner had agreed to cough up for the detective's getting fed "a pill he couldn't digest." If Slim failed and let Stockburn live, he not only wouldn't get paid the second half of the agreed-upon bounty, he'd have to return the money he'd already been paid.

That would be too humiliating, not to mention reputation ruining, to think about. Besides, knowing Hennessey as well as he did, Sherman doubted the saloon owner would let him get out of the territory alive. He'd have him killed if only to set an example to others who might fail him.

No, you didn't fail Kreg Hennessey. At least, you didn't fail him and not get a lonely, unmarked grave out in the wild-and-lonely for your error.

Slim glanced once more into the canyon then quickly hoisted himself and his rifle up onto the ridge's lip. He dropped and rolled several feet away from the ridge before gaining his knees. Ivy sat on her butt on the ground nearby. She sat leaning forward over her bent knees, hands wrapped around the tips of her men's pointed-toed stockman's boots, grinning as though she hadn't had this much fun in a month of Sundays.

Sherman saw her horse grazing with his horse off down the slope to the east, reins hanging loose, both mounts without a care in the whole consarned world.

Slim cuffed his hat off his head and absently fingered the bandage on his right cheek. The fast climb up the ridge and the roll had kicked up the burning pain of the wound. Trying to ignore it, he glared at the girl and said, "You know, it's been a long damn time since I been this mad at a girl as pretty as you, Ivy!"

"Now, Slim, you learned the other night that there is very little *girl* left in Ivy Russell." She shot him a smoldering smile over her boot toes. "You said I was all *woman*—remember?"

Slim's cheeks warmed. "What're you doing here?"

"Like I said, I was just passin'—"

"Oh, hog water—you weren't just riding through the area and *just happened* to see my horse, Ivy. You've been following me when I told you to go back to town. Now will you tell me why? Why are you bedevilin' me this way? I got a job to do, dammit!"

Ivy frowned, sucking in her cheeks. She released her boots and sat back, stretching her nice legs out, crossing her ankles, and resting her weight on the heels of her hands. "I'm bored, Slim. This is boring country for an imaginative girl like myself."

"What you need is a job."

"Slingin' hash in the Cosmopolitan for twenty-five cents a day and tips? No thank you!" Ladder rungs of deep wrinkles stretched across her pretty forehead as she turned her head to one side and narrowed an accusatory eye at her companion. "Or are you suggesting, like Kreg Hennessey has suggested himself a time or two, that I go to work for him? *Upstairs?*"

In spite of his frustration and lingering anger at the girl, Sherman chuckled and let his eyes roam where a gentleman's would not. "You'd be a hell of a money-maker—I'll give you that, Ivy!"

"You cad!" She threw a rock at him. It bounced off his shoulder.

"Ow!" he said, making a face and rubbing his shoulder.

"That didn't hurt and you know it!"

Sherman plucked a grass stem and twirled it between his fingers. He studied Ivy shrewdly. "How well do you know Hennessey, anyway?"

As the girl stared back at him, her expression changed gradually. A faint blush rose in her suntanned cheeks that were as smooth as a peach. "Why should I tell you?"

"I had me a feelin'!"

"You *did?*"

"I seen you in there last week. Or maybe it was the week before last. Anyway, I was leavin' a crib—compliments of Kreg himself—and I seen you slip down the hall toward the rear stairs. It was maybe two in the mornin'. Leastways, I thought it was you. Never was sure. But . . ." Sherman studied her suspiciously. "Just got me a feelin'."

Ivy lifted her chin, haughtily. "A lady don't share her secrets with just anyone, Slim."

"What do you see in him?"

Ivy hiked a shoulder and looked off, her eyes growing softly speculative. "Oh, I don't know. A girl gets bored in this country, Slim. Besides, I'm the curious sort." She looked at Sherman over her shoulder and said with her own shrewd grin, "You'd be surprised the interesting things that go on, and that you hear about, over at Kreg's place."

"Oh, 'Kreg', is it?"

"Sure. Why not?" she asked, lifting her chin again and narrowing her eyes.

"I bet you do keep yourself entertained over there." Slim chewed the weed stem, nodding. "Bet he pays you—don't he? That's why you don't seem to need a real job, got time to ride to hell an' gone. I doubt your old man makes enough to keep his own fat gut padded."

"You got that right. You keep your mouth shut about what you just heard about me. If my pa ever found out . . ." Ivy shook her head. "Pa would go after Hennessey and Kreg would kill him—right then and there like that!"

"I bet he would."

Slim paused, stared off, thinking, then returned his gaze again to Ivy, who was also staring into the distance, looking mildly bored again, as what seemed to be her lot in life. Her blood ran too hot for this country. But, then, maybe it ran too hot for any country.

"Say, there, Miss Ivy—you wouldn't be tryin'

to keep me from killin' Wolf Stockburn, now, would you?"

"Hell, no!" Ivy scrunched up her face in a scowl. "I don't interfere in no one's business. Even blood business." She paused briefly, then added, "I mean, it's too bad in a way, though, isn't it? I mean . . . a man like that . . ."

"A man like what?"

"You know—like Stockburn. Famous rail detective. One who's put so many bad men and even some bad women behind bars. Do you know he even rode Pony Express? Held off a whole party of Injuns single-handed. Not even twenty years old!"

"No, I didn't know that."

"He killed Bill English in Wichita."

"Bill English? Stockburn killed English?"

"Yep."

"Damn. No, I didn't know that, either," Slim lied. He did know it. He just didn't like to reflect on the fact of Stockburn's notoriety. Or on all the men Stockburn had killed. Deep down, Slim thought that maybe that was the reason his heart felt all fluttery every time he had the detective in his Sharps' sights.

"I just mean, ain't it sorta like killin' a rare wild animal? Sorta like killin' a white buffalo or somesuch? Kind of a shame. Especially when he's gettin' it from ambush. I mean, when you get right down to it, it ain't even a fair fight, Slim."

Ivy narrowed an admonishing eye at the back-shooting assassin.

Sherman wasn't offended. An idea had just occurred to him—a sure-fire way to be able to ride back to Wild Horse and collect the second half of that five hundred dollars from Hennessey.

"What're you smilin' at?" Ivy asked, smiling now herself.

"You wanna help?" Slim said.

"Help?"

"Yeah. You wanna help me kill the Wolf of the Rails? The Gray Wolf himself? The *Wolf of Wichita?*"

Ivy frowned skeptically, but her eyes glittered like freshly minted pennies. "How?"

Sherman canted his head toward the canyon. "Ride down there, catch up to Stockburn, keep him distracted while I draw a bead on him."

Ivy gasped with feigned outrage. "So you can *shoot* him?"

Grinning, Slim blinked slowly. "Yeah, that's the idea, Ivy. So I can shoot him. Look at it this way—you'll be the last to see him alive. That might make you sorta famous."

Ivy pondered on that as she studied the ground over the toes of her crossed boots.

She turned to Sherman and grinned adventurously, shrugging her slender left shoulder. She looked like a girl who'd been given a fine pony for her birthday. "Why the heck not?"

CHAPTER 30

Stockburn checked Smoke to a stop and stared ahead at the twisted rails that resembled long, silver snakes ripped out of the earth to lay bent in death on either side of the cinder-paved rail bed.

A hundred yards beyond the twisted rails lay the dynamited work train, the burned-out hulks of the locomotive, tender car, and supply cars looking like scattered dominoes to each side of the graded rail bed. Most had been blasted onto their sides.

Stockburn rode up near the first of the overturned cars, swung down from Smoke's back, and dropped the horse's reins. He loosened the gray's saddle cinch, for Wolf figured on being here awhile, inspecting the sight of the massacre, and he wanted the stallion to be able to forage freely.

It was nearly noon, the sun straight up in the sky.

The sun rained down, dancing on the grass and sage and on the fir and pine boughs to each side of the canyon, to the music of mountain bluebirds and chickadees whose piping was punctuated now and then by the raucous chitters of squirrels or the equally grating calls of irritated crows.

Stockburn poked an Indian Kid into his mouth,

fired up the cheroot, and walked around the burned-out train, smoking absently while he scoured the torched and overturned cars and the ground around them.

He was looking for something. But he wouldn't know what that something was until he found it.

He spent a good half hour inspecting the ruined work train, moving slowly, occasionally kicking a rock or a charred sage clump, dropping to a knee to brush his hand across a hoof print, trying to make out anything particular about the horse's shoe impression in the gravelly soil.

There were plenty of shoe prints and two-week-old horse apples, but nothing to distinguish any of the signs from the signs of a thousand other horses.

Lighting another cheroot, he walked over to the pale canvas tents of the work crew. He'd saved the tents for last, because he knew that it was going to be harder distinguishing anything the dead rail layers had left behind from anything their attackers might have left.

Smoking, pondering, musing, walking slowly around and sometimes over the torn-down canvas flapping like wash on a clothesline, he found plenty of shell casings. Mostly .44s and .45s with a few .38s. The guns of the rail crew had been left behind, some of the rifles and revolvers hidden beneath the fallen, wind-buffeted canvas.

Around what he assumed was the mess tent

were air-tight vegetable tins, beef tins, and a barrel of salted beef that predators had obviously gotten into, for the barrel was overturned and only bits of the beef remained.

Part of a cured ham lay in the shade of a twisted cedar, covered with dirt and pine needles. Bite marks shone in the fist-sized chunk of remaining meat, probably dropped by a couple of snarling coyotes maybe chased away by a puma who found better feeding in the beef barrel.

The tent canvas was liberally stained with blood where the rail crew, awakened in the dark of night, had been gunned down while dressing or feebly, possibly blindly returning fire on the ghostly raiders. Those dead men, now lying on the slight rise fifty yards beyond the camp, hastily erected wooden crosses all the remaining evidence of their previous existence, had left behind clothes and bedrolls and overturned cots.

There were playing cards, pencil stubs, half-written letters in childish cursive, a smashed fiddle, wallets, and even a few greenbacks and coins attesting to the fact that the posse riders who'd ridden up from Wild Horse to bury the fallen had not seen fit to steal from dead men.

There were combs, toothbrushes, lumpy soap cakes, cracked mirrors, a pair of dentures, a single leather boot lying off by itself, the initial AW having been stamped into both mule ears lying slack to the side. The boot's owner had probably gotten double-dee-damned tired of having his consarned boots stolen by other men in the crew, so he'd stamped them to prove they were, by God, his!

Frustrated at not having found anything of obvious investigative interest, Stockburn cursed and gave the boot a kick. The boot and something else flew upward.

The second thing arced away from the boot to land in the sage several feet from where the boot landed atop a sage clump fifteen feet from where Wolf had kicked it.

From where he'd kicked *them*.

He hadn't seen the second object before he'd inadvertently kicked it.

Scowling curiously, Stockburn walked over, dropped to a knee, plucked the object off the ground, and held it up to inspect it.

Only a whiskey flask. Tin with a leather covering. He sniffed the lip. Whiskey, all right.

A flask. Nothing more. He'd seen others out here.

He was about to give it a disgusted toss but stopped the motion and brought the flask close to his face once more. There was something different about the flask.

The hide covering looked expensive. It was made from smooth, polished cowhide with fancy red stitching. The stitching on one side of the flask took the shape of a miniature mountain range.

The stitching on the other side of the flask formed the monogram:

K. HEN'Y.

"Kreg Hennessey," Stockburn muttered.

Between him and the sabotaged work train, Smoke gave a shrill whinny.

Instantly recalling that this was the place the bastard with the large-caliber rifle had tried to blow his head off from long-range, Stockburn dropped the flask and reached across his belly to fill his right hand with the silver-chased, ivory-gripped Peacemaker holstered on his left hip.

Dropping to a knee and extending the .45 half-way out from his right side, he looked around.

Spying no imminent threat, he glanced over his left shoulder. Smoke was gazing toward the east side of the canyon, in the direction of the rise on which the rail crew was buried. Stockburn followed the mount's gaze.

As he did, a rider rode out of the aspens and birch beyond the makeshift cemetery.

At first the rider was a horse and rider-shaped shadow jostling against the lighter shade cast by the trees around it. Then, as horse and rider rode out of the shade of the trees and into the sunlit clearing, Stockburn saw blond hair tumbling over narrow shoulders clad in a checked shirt.

Behind Stockburn, Smoke whickered, still

edgy, skeptical. Smoke was a cautious horse. But, then, after all that Wolf had gotten them both into over the years, why wouldn't he be?

The horse coming toward Stockburn lifted its head and released a greeting whinny. Smoke answered in kind then shook his head, still careful, making the bridle chains clink. The rider leaned forward and gave her horse, a brown and white pinto, an affectionate pat.

Horse and rider rode around the side of the wooden crosses tilting up out of the ground, painted gold by the sunshine at the head of the dozen freshly mounded, rock-crowned graves.

The rider—tall and shapely in her red shirt and tight denims—batted her heels against the pinto's flanks, and the mount lunged into a rocking lope. The rider's oval-shaped face was partly hidden by the shadow of her hat brim, but when she was within a hundred feet of Stockburn, her red lips stretched a smile, showing the white line of her teeth.

Stockburn lowered his Peacemaker and rose, looking around cautiously. Seeing no one else riding toward him, he slid the Colt back into its holster and snapped the keeper thong into place over the hammer.

Ivy Russell leaned back in the saddle, jerking back on the ribbons, and the pinto thundered to a jouncing halt before Stockburn, turning a little to one side.

Wolf squinted against the dust rising from the short grass and sage.

"Fancy seeing you here, Ivy," Stockburn said.

"Hi, Wolf."

"What brings you to these parts?"

The pinto fidgeted, lifting its head sharply. Keeping a tight hold on the reins, Ivy leaned forward and gave the pinto's left wither another pat. "A girl has to get out of town from time to time. Stretch her legs a bit, breathe the fresh air. Miss Martindale agrees."

"Miss Martindale?"

"My mare." Again, Ivy patted the horse's wither. "I named her after my teacher."

Smiling up at the girl on the mare as frisky as she herself was, Wolf planted a disbelieving fist on his hip. "Ivy, are you telling me you went to school?"

"I most certainly did. Learned my letters and everything; even how to cypher to a point. I was a dang good student, Wolf!"

"I can't believe a young lady as restless as you could sit still long enough to be a good student."

"I got all 'A's until . . ."

"Until . . . ?"

"Until Miss Martindale kicked me out. When I was twelve. She said I was a distraction to the boys."

"She said that?" Stockburn exclaimed with fabricated incredulity.

"Can you believe it?" Ivy said, grinning down at him.

Stockburn studied her comely figure. What a torture she had to have been. She was torturing him *now,* just sitting her horse before him, the mountain sunshine sparkling like gold dust in her hair, glittering in her soft blue eyes.

"Yes, I do believe it," Wolf said.

Ivy snorted and looked away, blushing. Turning back to Stockburn, she shook her hair back from her face and said, "What're you doing way out here, Wolf? Investigating?"

"Yes, I am."

Ivy cast her gaze at the ruined rails and sabotaged work train. "Have you found any important clues?"

"I don't know." Stockburn crouched to retrieve the leather-covered flask from the ground. He tossed it up to Ivy, who caught it against her breasts. She looked at it. "A whiskey flask?"

"Look at the initials on the back."

Ivy flipped the flask in her hands, frowned down at it. "Hmm," she said, returning her gaze to Stockburn. "What do you make of that, Mister Rail Detective?"

"I wouldn't think too many folks around would sport those initials."

"I reckon not."

Stockburn reached for the flask. "I reckon I'll be heading back to town to have a little palaver with the man to whom this flask no doubt belongs. See if Hennessey has any idea how it might have gotten out here."

Stockburn stuck a finger in the corner of his mouth and whistled. Smoke put his head down, whinnied, and came running.

"Can I ride along with you, Wolf?" Ivy asked. "I was about to start back that way myself."

"Why not?" Stockburn dropped the flask into a saddlebag pouch, secured the strap with the buckle, then mounted Smoke, and he and Ivy Russell started back south in the direction of Wild Horse.

Ivy leaned forward against her saddle horn as she rode to Wolf's right, between him and the ruined rails on her own right side. "Wolf, you've met Hennessey. You know damn good and well that if you go walkin' into Hennessey's place you may not walk out again."

"He must have hired some muscle to replace those I turned toe down in the restaurant then."

"Oh, he's got plenty of muscle. Don't you worry about that!"

"How much muscle? Say, a dozen or so men?" Killers and rustlers? he did not add. The second part was a building suspicion. Had someone— Kreg Hennessey—sent riders out here to massacre a track-laying crew *and* to rustle cattle?

Why?

What dog did Hennessey have in the fight out here?

Was the McCrae and Stoleberg war about to explode again?

Ivy shook her head as though to shrug off Wolf's question. "He might have given that flask to someone. You know—as a gift."

"To one of the men who just happened to turn out to be one of the killers of the railroad crew?"

Ivy shrugged, sighed. She seemed a little frustrated. "I don't see how you could prove different."

"You're right, I certainly need more to make a case. If there's a case to be made, that is."

Stockburn turned and cocked an eyebrow at the pretty blonde riding beside him. "Young lady, you sure are smart for a gal who got kicked out of school at age twelve for distracting the boys. Are you sure you haven't been reading for the law?"

"The law? Oh, hell—you can have the law. My old man's the law in these parts, and you saw how he stacks up."

"Is he in Hennessey's pocket?"

"Who? Pa? Everyone in Wild Horse is in Hennessey's pocket in one way or another. If they're not, they're Kreg's enemy." Ivy wagged her head. "You sure don't want to be Kreg's enemy."

"Kreg, huh?"

"What?"

"How well do you know Kreg Hennessey, Ivy?"

Stockburn noticed a little color rise in her tanned cheeks, and her eyes were briefly sheepish before she regained control of her expression. "Oh, I don't know."

She lifted her chin proudly, defiantly, and drew her shoulders back so that her shirt drew taut against the twin cones of her bosoms. "Not as well as some, better than others. Why do you ask?"

"That's a fine horse you're riding."

Ivy frowned. "What's that got to do with the price of tea in China?"

"Just a nice-looking horse, that's all. Did your pa buy it for you?"

Her frown deepened. "A *friend* bought it for me."

They were riding through the aspen copse now, sunlight and shade dappling them and the ground around them, their horses' hooves crunching the freshly fallen leaves.

"Is Hennessey your friend, Ivy?" Stockburn knew he was likely treading into shallow water, but suspicion had started nettling him, like a patch of itchy skin in a hard-to-scratch place, when her expression had changed as she'd read the initials on the flask.

She was a grand if earthy coquette, with

sexuality dripping off every inch of her. She didn't have a job, but she rode a fine horse, and she seemed to have a lot of free time on her hands.

What was she *really* doing out here?

Ivy fired an indignant, taut-jawed look at him. "What're you getting at?"

Smoke whickered, tossed his head.

Ivy looked at the smoky-gray stallion, frowning. "What's the matter with him?"

Stockburn looked around, reaching forward to slide the Yellowboy from its scabbard. "That's what I'd like to know."

As the rear stock cleared leather, Stockburn cocked the rifle one-handed.

Smoke whinnied and suddenly reared, lifting his front hooves high

To Wolf's right, Ivy yelled in a shrill, impatient voice, *"For godsakes, would you take the damn shot before—"*

Stockburn had heard the high whine of the bullet slicing through the air just inches in front of Wolf's belly as the horse's hooves clawed skyward.

There was a resolute smacking sound to Wolf's right.

As the stallion dropped back down to all fours, Stockburn saw Ivy's shirt buffet back sharply against her chest. The girl screamed and flew off the pinto's right hip.

Stockburn leaped off Smoke's back and rammed his rifle butt against the stallion's left hip. As Smoke galloped forward, whinnying shrilly and shaking his head angrily, Stockburn pressed the rifle's butt plate against his right shoulder.

He'd already spied the smoke from the ambusher's shot, and seen, too, the ambusher himself perched halfway up a leafless aspen fifty feet into the woods ahead and on Stockburn's left.

The man was just then canting his head against his rifle's stock, taking aim at Stockburn.

Wolf aimed his own rifle quickly and fired a half a blink before his would-be assassin's rifle belched smoke and flames. The killer's bullet moaned wide of Stockburn and thumped into a tree as Wolf sent four more bullets hurling into the aspen.

The rifleman gave a wail and fell back against the aspen's trunk as bark and small branches danced in the air around him. He dropped the rifle and gave another wail as he fell from his perch at a Y between the trunk and a stout branch.

He smacked a branch below his perch, twisted in the air, smacked another branch, twisted again, and smacked yet another branch, grunting with each impact.

He fell the last ten feet straight down to the ground where he struck on his face and belly, and bounced with one more grunt.

CHAPTER 31

Stockburn rose and levered another round into the Yellowboy's action.

He looked at the rifleman lying under the aspen tree he'd been perched in. The man was moaning and breathing heavily, his body lying at an odd angle.

He was too broken up to be an immediate threat, so Stockburn turned and hurried over to where Ivy lay belly up on the forest floor. Her right leg was folded beneath her left one. Her arms lay nearly straight out from her shoulders, gloved fingers curled toward her palms. Her hat lay in the dead leaves several feet away.

Ivy's blue eyes stared up at Stockburn, but she wasn't seeing a thing. The large, bloody hole in her chest had shredded her heart.

"Dammit!"

Stockburn wheeled and walked over to where the shooter lay beneath the aspen. He looked down at the man who lay in a crumpled heap, a bulge in his lower leg showing one obvious break. He was lean and hawk-faced; long, thin brown hair hung down from the horseshoe-shaped bald spot at the top of his head. He was the same man—the bastard with the large-caliber Sharps—whom Stockburn had seen in the line shack the night before.

Blood matted the man's chest; it flowed from his smashed lips as well as from a nasty gash in his right temple. The fall had opened up the long gash arcing up from the man's left cheek to nearly the corner of his left eye, which one of Stockburn's own bullets had likely carved the previous day. The bandage was gone.

The man looked up at Stockburn, his eyes wide and round with shock. His chest rose and fell sharply. The man opened his bloody mouth, winced from the pain likely racking every inch of him, then said very softly, raspily, "Did I kill Ivy?"

"Yes," Stockburn said, fuming.

"Damn," the man said with true regret.

His eyes rolled up, his lead tipped up slightly and to one side, and his chest fell still.

"You bastard!" Wolf rammed his right boot into the man's ribs, making the body rock.

He walked over and dropped to a knee beside Ivy. The poor, dead girl.

Stockburn knew she'd somehow aligned herself with the bastard with the big rifle, but her death still grieved him. She might have been a flaming coquette and got herself mixed up with all kinds of trouble in and around Wild Horse, but he would not, could not believe that she was anything but an innocent, a naïve bystander exploited and corrupted by the evil men around her.

Men like Kreg Hennessey.

She'd been too damned pretty for her own good. Stockburn had barely known her, but he was going to miss her.

He turned to where Smoke stood looking back at him from the far end of the aspen copse. Wolf stuck his finger in the corner of his mouth and whistled. Twenty minutes later, he and Smoke had fetched the rifleman and Ivy's horses, and Stockburn had tied both bodies, wrapped in their own bedrolls, over their saddles.

He stepped into his own saddle and started the trip back toward Wild Horse.

Lori McCrae was also headed back toward town.

In fact, she was galloping into Wild Horse now as long shadows stretched out from the buildings on the west side of the broad main street.

It was almost five o'clock. Supper fires were stoked all over town, and the smoke waved like tattered flags over the rooftops. The shopkeepers were hauling their wares off the boardwalks fronting their shops and into their stores in preparation of closing.

Two dogs—a thick-furred collie and a short-haired mongrel were fighting over a bone in front of Cyrus Milgram's Haberdashery. One had probably swiped the bone from the butcher shop while old man York had been butchering in his rear shed and the other one, in typical dog fashion, wanted it all for himself.

But, then, dogs weren't all that different from men, Lori silently opined in only a vague sort of way. She had more important things on her mind than dogs fighting over bones.

Lori angled her buckskin to the street's right side, opposite the haberdashery and the fighting dogs, to where Watt Russell stood outside his two-story stone and wood-frame jail house/office, staring up the street to the south. The middle-aged town marshal had his thumbs hooked behind the cartridge belt encircling his thick waist, the belt and shells mostly hidden by the man's heavily sagging gut.

"Marshal Russell!" Lori called, halting the buckskin in front of the man.

Russell jerked his head toward the girl with a start. "Miss McCrae!" He looked surprised and puzzled as he studied her, then slowly slid his still-puzzled gaze up the street to the south again.

Turning back to Lori, he said, "I don't . . . I don't under—"

"Understand what?"

"Well . . ." Russell hooked his thumb to the street beyond them.

Lori had no time for the man's thick-headedness. Her father had said that Watt Russell was "soft in his thinker box," and Lori didn't doubt it a bit. She said, "Have you seen Wolf Stockburn, Marshal?"

Russell turned back to her again, his puzzled

expression becoming a look of indignation, color rising in his cheeks. He was most likely remembering how Lori and her father's attorney had compelled Russell to release Stockburn from his jail under threat of dire legal consequences after Stockburn's dustup in the Cosmopolitan with Kreg Hennessey.

"Stockburn? No, can't say as I have. Can't say I want to see that—"

Lori shook her head. "Never mind that. He was supposed to meet me earlier this afternoon at the Lutheran church by the Big Sandy River, and he didn't show. I thought he might have ridden to town. I'm worried something might have happened to him, Marshal. He rode up to inspect the scene of the massacre again."

Lori hadn't ridden up that way herself, because she'd been worried her father's men, maybe even one of her brothers, who were likely engaged in the fall roundup up near where the track layers had been killed, might see her and force her to return home against her will.

She'd known that finding Stockburn here, without his having stopped to pick her up at the church first, was a long shot. But she hadn't been able to sit still. Besides, she didn't want to spend the night alone in that creepy church.

"I got no truck with Wolf Stockburn," Russell grumbled, turning his attention back toward the south. "That man's been nothin' but a thorn in my backside. Maybe you can answer me this question, Miss McCrae."

The marshal shuttled his puzzled look back to Lori. "What's your brother and three hands from the Triangle gonna do with all them guns they're loadin' into their ranch wagon yonder?"

"What?" Lori said, shocked. *"Where?"*

"Over there."

Lori followed Russell's pointing finger toward where a ranch wagon sat in front of Hyde's Gun & Ammo shop, on the street's west side roughly a half a block south of the jailhouse. Sure enough, Lori's oldest brother, Law, was handing a square wooden crate to one of the two Triangle hands standing in the wagon's low-sided box, one hand crouching to receive the crate.

A third hand just then emerged from the shop's open front door, carrying two Winchester rifles in his hands, with a third one clamped beneath an arm. As Law turned to walk into the shop, Lori said in a hushed voice that betrayed her own befuddlement but also a good bit of fear, as well, "I have no idea, Marshal."

"I take it you didn't ride into town with them . . . ?"

"No, I did not," Lori replied to the inane question. Russell had seen her ride into town not more than two minutes ago—alone.

"Well, I reckon I'd better go over and have a talk with 'em, then." Scowling curiously, apprehensively toward the gun shop, Russell stepped down off the boardwalk. Pausing to bend his legs as he hitched up his sagging canvas trousers, he set off up the street at a southwesterly angle.

"Marshal, please don't tell them you've seen me in town!" Lori appealed to the man, keeping her voice down.

She wasn't sure if Russell had heard her. He gave no indication but only ambled in his shamble-footed way toward the gun shop from which Lawton McCrae, clad in his usual cream Stetson with a curled brim, plaid work shirt, and batwing chaps, was emerging carrying two more Winchester repeating rifles.

Lori had grown up around rifles, had even shot them herself from time to time; she could tell these were Winchester repeaters, all right.

Lori quickly neck-reined the buckskin to the north, keeping her head down, not wanting Law to see her. She galloped back the way she'd come until she reached the north end of town.

She swung the buckskin west around an abandoned stable and then turned south along the alley paralleling the main street along the backsides of the main street-facing business buildings.

When she came to the rear of Hyde's Gun & Ammo Shop, she stopped the buckskin, swung down, and dropped the reins. She strode quickly up along the north side of the gun shop, between the gun shop and a barber shop on her left.

As she approached the front of Hyde's, she pressed her right shoulder up against the shop's north wall, crouching, not wanting to be seen from the street. Fortunately, this break between the buildings was filled with the deep-purple shadows of the early autumn dusk, concealing her well.

At least, she hoped it was. She couldn't be too careful. It Law spotted her, he'd drag her home, for sure.

Watt Russell moseyed up to the Triangle wagon.

At least, he tried to mosey. Truth was, he was a might on the tense side.

The Triangle riders, backed by a powerful man—a man much more powerful than Russell had ever been or ever would be, even with a badge pinned to his shirt—made him nervous. There were three powerful men in or around Wild Horse—Norman McCrae, Rufus Stoleberg, and Kreg Hennessey.

All three made him nervous.

Russell cast a look into the wagon and whistled. "Now, that there is quite a load of guns and ammunition!" He gave a nervous chuckle.

The two hands standing in the wagon looked back at him.

"Goin' on a big hunt this fall, are ya?" Russell asked, trying to sound affably conversational.

"You could call it a hunt," Lawton McCrae said as the tall, thirty-five-year-old rancher, with the long, bowed legs of a natural horseman, said as he stepped out of Hyde's Guns & Ammo Shop. He was carrying three or four cartridge bandoliers over his shoulders, all belts sporting glistening new shells.

"You don't say," Russell said, leaning against the wagon and hooking his thumbs behind his own cartridge belt. "What you goin' after? Some of them big elk that been movin' down into the lower meadows? You know, I can hear them of a night when I'm sittin' out on my front porch, having a last smoke and a cup of coffee. Kinda eerie soundin'—that bugling during the rut!"

He chuckled dryly.

"Nope." The customarily stone-faced, taciturn Lawton McCrae handed the four sets of cartridge bandoliers to the two men standing in the wagon.

That's all he said: Nope. Wasn't going to give Russell the respect and decency of any explanation at all. That's how the McCraes were. They were uppity that way. They saw themselves as bigger than the law.

Anger burned in Russell's cheeks as Law McCrae turned to walk back into the shop again, not even looking at the lawman standing at the rear of the wagon.

"Well, doggoneit, Lawton, what in the hell *are* you goin' after, then. Can you tell me that? I *am* the law here in town. And I *am* a deputy county sheriff, to boot. I mean, it ain't like I'm just bein' snoopy!"

McCrae stopped five feet from the shop's front door. He turned back to Russell and said, "What's the matter, old man? Did you run out of spittoons to empty in Hennessey's Saloon?"

The two men in the wagon chuckled. The fourth man laughed from inside the shop behind McCrae.

Russell's heart thumped in the old lawman's ears. McCrae was referencing the widely held belief that Russell was merely here to haul Kreg Hennessey's water. He'd always tried to shrug off the reputation and to keep his chin up in spite of it.

The only problem was the tactic rang a bit hollow, for the belief was not all that far from the truth. Russell had hauled Hennessey's water in the past. More than a few times, in fact. But that was back when he'd been drunk more than sober, and he hadn't been able to resist the temptation of the extra money he'd occasionally found in envelopes slipped under the door of his house.

Now he was working on getting his good reputation back. That's why Law McCrae's words, delivered so evenly and coldly, backed by a cold set of hazel eyes, wounded him so deeply. They made his heart throb and his right knee quiver.

Yeah, he'd helped Hennessey against his enemies. He'd jailed innocent men, and he'd freed guilty men, but he'd never done anything to earn the wrath of the uppity McCraes.

When Russell could not find the words to speak, Law McCrae stepped forward, pointing an accusing finger at the middle-aged lawman and further hardening his straight fine jaws. He narrowed his hazel eyes.

"I'll tell you this, Russell, since you're so concerned. We wouldn't have to do what we're about to do if you'd been doing your job. You always talk about how you're a deputy *county* sheriff. Well, I sure don't see you out in the county all that much. Where were you when Stoleberg long-looped a good hundred and fifty of our beeves and hazed them on to Tin Cup graze?"

"What?" Russell said, finally finding his tongue. "What're you talkin' about? I thought you—both families—done buried the hatchet. Or, leastways called a truce!"

"That is obviously what old Stoleberg wanted us to believe," McCrae said tightly, his voice quavering with barely checked emotion. "But yesterday during the fall gather, my men came across tracks of a large bunch of moved cows. *Our* moved cows. They found those cows in a box canyon on Stoleberg graze.

"Ol' Rufus was obviously holding them there, intending, probably after the moon had waned, to

375

ship those beeves to market as his own—just like he used to do before the so-called truce!"

"So Stoleberg is who you're huntin'?" Russell said in disbelief, his own voice now quavering on the implication of a renewed, all-out land war. He remembered the last one. It had been hard, and it had been bloody.

You might think a land war affected only the two warring factions. But it didn't. Especially not when the two warring factions had such influence over the town that supplied them and that banked their money.

A land war like that pitted other, smaller ranchers and farmers against each other, business-men against businessmen. Passions could burn and spread like wildfire. It could mean the ruin of a whole town, a whole county.

"That's right," McCrae said. "We've had enough. We're kicking that whole damned outfit out with a cold shovel. We're gonna kill every man and we're gonna burn every building to the ground and sift the ashes when we're through. What's theirs will now be ours.

"Stoleberg doesn't have enough men nor guns and ammo to stand against the Triangle. Shouldn't take long. Not long at all. Don't worry, Russell. You go to bed with a bottle and one of Hennessey's whores. I'm sure he'll give you a nice deal on one. We'll let you know when the smoke's cleared."

The cold-eyed McCrae glanced at the men in the wagon. "Dave, Pete—get that wagon ready to roll!"

Russell took a lumbering step forward and said, "Hold on, hold on! How can you be so sure it was Stoleberg who rustled your beef?"

But Lawton McCrae was done talking.

He swung around and walked into the shop, saying, "You got the numbers all tallied up, there, Ray? Come on, get to it. We don't got all night!"

A minute later, the two ranch hands sat down on the wagon's hard wooden seat. One of the two released the brake and swung the horse into the street, turning around and heading north.

"Hy-yahh!"

Law McCrae and the fourth ranch hand followed on sleek ranch horses, the wagon rattling, hooves thudding, the sounds dwindling as the men, guns, and ammo merged with the shadows slanting across the rolling purple prairie beyond the town.

CHAPTER 32

As Watt Russell stood gazing after the departing Triangle men from beneath the crown of his high-crowned black Stetson, Lori McCrae stepped out of the shadows between the gun shop and the barber shop. She glanced worriedly to the north where her brother and the hands and the horses and wagons were jostling dots growing ever smaller.

Russell glanced at her. "You heard?"

Lori nodded. "I don't believe it. The Stolebergs wouldn't rustle our cattle. They have no reason to. They want peace, not war. They just want to get by."

She looked at the big lawman. "Either someone else rustled those cattle and wanted the blame to fall on the Stoleberg family, because they wanted to see a land war, or my brother is lying about those cows. My family has another reason to be crossways with the Stolebergs, Marshal. It has to do with me."

"I know."

"What?" Lori looked at the big man with surprise. The man's unexpected response had been like a slap to her face.

Russell returned her gaze and shrugged a heavy shoulder. "I hate to say it, Miss McCrae, but

378

most folks know. Word got out right after the boy was born. Folks don't talk about it over much, on account of them bein' afraid of your family and the Stolebergs, as well. But we all know. Don't worry. I don't hold it against you."

A strange tenderness entered the marshal's voice. "I know . . . I know how . . . *things* . . . can happen. You can't control a pretty, restless girl anymore than you can tame the wind." He sighed, looked off, wagged his head, then turned to Lori again. "But the reason your brother came to town for guns and ammo ain't about you. Leastways, it ain't only about you."

Lori frowned. "How do you know?"

"I just know, that's all. Somethin' else sparked that fire."

Russell's brow furled as the thuds of an approaching horse sounded. Both he and Lori turned to gaze north again.

The lawman said, "Now, who's that?"

Lori squinted her eyes as she tried to clarify the rider moving toward town along the trail her brother had just rode out on. The approaching rider, wearing a black hat and a buckskin coat, was trailing two horses.

"Wolf," Lori whispered, hope rising in her.

Stockburn's gut tightened when he recognized the beefy gent standing beside Lori as Watt Russell. He was relieved to see Lori, for when he

379

hadn't found her at the church near the Big Sandy River, he'd thought maybe her family had taken her kicking and screaming back to the Triangle.

He wasn't as enthused about seeing Watt Russell, however. He had bad news for the man.

Stockburn reined up, staring toward Lori and the marshal. Knowing there was no use in prolonging the inevitable, he gigged Smoke forward, trailing the other two mounts by their bridle reins. The westward-tumbling sun brushed the prairie before him, between him and town, with soft copper hues.

The shadows of Lori and Watt Russell angled on the ground beside them, to the east, growing longer and longer as Stockburn and his dark cargo approached.

"Wolf," Lori said, gazing up at him with concern as she walked up to meet him. "When you didn't meet me at the church?"

"I know," Stockburn said. "I got delayed."

He stared at Russell. The lawman seemed to have had a premonition about what . . . or who . . . Stockburn was carrying belly down across one of the horses behind him. Or maybe the big lawman had seen the blond hair hanging down toward the ground from the blanket roll it had tumbled out of during the ride.

The man stood gazing at the brown-and-white pinto and the girl lying belly down over the saddle. His face was stony but his eyes were wide. His feet didn't move. They might have been mired to the ground.

Lori stepped back and looked at both horses. When she saw the bodies, she raised a hand to her mouth, muffling a gasp.

"I'm sorry, Russell," Wolf said.

The Wild Horse lawman shifted his gaze from the pinto to Stockburn, his eyes wrinkling at the corners, deep lines carving the ruddy skin of his broad forehead. "That's her, ain't it?"

"I'm afraid it is, yes."

A shopkeeper who had been washing his front windows behind Russell and Lori had stopped to gaze silently toward the two horses carrying the bodies. More men on the boardwalks of other shops, or crossing the street on foot, turned to stare toward Stockburn, Lori, and Watt Russell, as well.

With what seemed an effort, the old marshal pulled his feet free of the invisible bog they'd been mired in. He ambled slowly forward. His face grew pale, the skin hanging slack, as he approached the pinto's left side.

He stared down at Ivy's blanket-wrapped body, at the long hair hanging straight down to the ground so that its very tips brushed the dirt of Wind River Avenue. Russell drew a deep breath, then with another brief struggle managed to drop to one knee.

He reached out with his right hand, grabbed

a handful of the blond hair, and ran his fingers through it.

He gave a strangled sob and shook his head.

Suddenly looking ten years older than he'd looked the other day, in his office, Russell turned to Stockburn and said, "Who?"

Stockburn jerked his chin to the chestnut gelding standing off Smoke's right flank, hanging its head as though in a nod to the solemnity of the occasion. "Him."

Russell grunted as he lifted his heavy bulk to his feet. He walked around behind Ivy's horse and came up between the two horses. He crouched and parted the fold in the blanket covering the bastard with the large-caliber Sharps, stared down at the man's face, then turned to Stockburn.

He looked as though he'd just eaten something sour.

"Slim Sherman. Sharp-shooting regulator. I seen him in town." Russell shook his head distastefully then looked at Stockburn again. His eyes glistened. "Why'd he shoot Ivy?"

"The bullet was intended for me," Wolf said, his stony features belying the sickness he felt inside. "Do you know who hired him?"

Russell nodded slowly, keeping his angry, bereaved gaze on Stockburn. "Yep."

Wolf reached back and pulled the flask out of his saddlebag pouch. He handed it down to

Russell, who looked at it, then looked back up at Stockburn.

"Is it the man who that flask belongs to?"

"Yep."

Stockburn reached down and plucked the flask out of the marshal's hands. "That's all I need, then."

He dropped the reins to both packhorses and started to boot Smoke forward but stopped when Russell held up a hand and said, "Wait."

Russell stepped forward, looking up at Wolf. "A dozen riders rode into town last night. They're all over at Hennessey's place."

"A dozen, eh?"

"Around that."

Stockburn thought about that, nodded. "So, he called his jackals in."

"I suspect he'll sic them on you."

"I don't doubt you're right."

Lori walked up to the other side of Smoke from Russell, gazing worriedly up at the rail detective. "Wolf, if you go over there alone, you'll be carried out."

He smiled, remembering that Ivy had warned him in similar words.

"Ah, hell, I'm not stupid." Stockburn gave the girl a reassuring smile and tossed the flask in the air and caught it. "I just aim to have a powwow with the man." He glanced at Russell. "Keep her with you."

Russell drew a deep breath and nodded.

Stockburn booted Smoke on up the street.

Faces turned as he passed the now-closed shops. Small clumps of cowboys and drummers standing outside saloons and the Cosmopolitan Restaurant turned toward him, skeptically. They muttered darkly among themselves.

Wolf put Smoke up to one of the several hitchracks fronting Hennessey's Wind River Saloon & Gambling Parlor and swung down from the leather. He tied the horse to the rack and slid his rifle from its saddle sheath.

He cocked the Yellowboy one-handed, off-cocked the hammer, and rested the rifle on his shoulder. He paused to dig a three-penny Indian Kid cheroot from a pocket inside his coat. He stuck the cheroot in his mouth and scratched a match to life on the hitchrack.

He lit the cigar.

Through the smoke billowing from his lips, he saw three men in shabby business suits standing at the base of the three steps rising to the saloon's front door. They were small, prim men in well-trimmed beards and mustaches. Attorneys or accountants, maybe. They each held a frothy beer mug.

They'd turned to study the tall, gray-haired, gray-mustached man in the buckskin coat and black slouch hat, the Yellowboy resting on his shoulder.

"Evenin'," Stockburn said, blowing out another long smoke plume.

The men scowled at him. They shared dubious looks. One looked at Stockburn again, looked at the rifle on the big man's shoulder, looked at the Peacemaker that had been exposed when Stockburn had unbuttoned his coat and pulled the left flap back behind the ivory-gripped revolver.

The prim man flushed and said, "I, uh . . . I reckon I'd better get on home."

He turned, started to walk away with his beer, then, remembering the beer, turned back to the other two men. He took a big drink from his glass then shoved the glass at one of the others, who accepted it incredulously.

The now-beerless man ran the back of his hand across his bearded face, glanced at Stockburn once more, then hurried off down the boardwalk to the south.

The other two men looked at Stockburn again. They looked at each other, flushed, then set their own beer glasses and the extra glass down on the boardwalk at the base of the saloon. They hurried off in separate directions, one twirling a walking stick, both casting skeptical glances back over their shoulders at the big rail detective behind them.

Stockburn stepped up onto the boardwalk. He took one more drag off the Indian Kid then dropped it and mashed it out with the heel of his boot. He mounted the saloon's front steps and went on inside through the heavy oak door.

He stood looking around the smoky sunken saloon hall.

The place was hopping. There were three bartenders, clad in white silk shirts and red silk waistcoats, scurrying around behind the horse-shoe-shaped bar. All of the gambling layouts looked like small anthills.

There were a good fifteen or so men bellied up to the bar, turned toward each other, talking. Another twenty or so sat at tables, drinking, playing cards, conversing, or flirting with the several painted ladies making the rounds.

The smell of tobacco smoke, beer, liquor, man sweat, and cheap perfume wafted against Stockburn still standing at the door.

He didn't see Hennessey so he walked down the steps to the drinking hall floor and wended his way through the tables to the bar. As he did, he noticed quite a few faces turn toward him, hard eyes staring. He'd already picked most of Hennessey's killers out of the crowd here in the drinking and gambling hall. They hadn't been hard to spot.

They might have gotten shaves and haircuts and maybe even baths since they'd hit town last night, and they might have had a good romp or two upstairs on the second floor. But they still had the gimlet-eyed look of soulless killers.

They all wore well-used and just-as-well-cared-for hoglegs on their hips or thonged down low on their thighs. Two, in some cases three apiece.

They were not similarly attired. But they had the same hard, quick eyes and bony faces and panther-like movements of practiced killers. Of men who could ride into a camp where hard-working men were dead asleep and kill those hard-working men without warning and with a savagery unknown to even the most savage of wild animals.

Wolf waved to catch the attention of one of the beefy bartenders and called, "Where's Hennessey?"

The barman scowled at him.

The men near Stockburn and the barman fell silent and turned toward Wolf.

"Who wants to know?" asked the barman. He had closed-cropped brown hair and a shaggy beard.

"Where's Hennessey?" Stockburn asked again, putting some steel in his voice.

More conversations stopped.

The silence stretched away from Stockburn like ripples from where a rock had been tossed into a lake.

Suddenly, the saloon was only half as loud as it had been when Stockburn had first walked into it. It grew quickly quieter as more men nudged each other to silence.

More and more faces turned toward him, eyes flat with menace. One of those pairs of eyes belonged to an amber-eyed man standing five feet away from Stockburn, against the bar on Wolf's right.

Stockburn recognized him as the hired killer Tom Cole from the Montana Territory. He was tall and wiry, with a flat face and a nose like an eagle's beak. He was recently shaved, and his close-cropped brown hair glistened with barber's pomade that smelled like mint.

He was turned toward Stockburn, his wool coat pulled back, one long-fingered hand—an oddly feminine-looking hand—draped over the grips of the .44 holstered high on his left hip. He blinked owlishly and studied Stockburn with his amber owl's eyes. The man was like a raptor or a snake; he didn't so much think as react to his instincts, and his instincts right now were telling him to do the job he'd been brought here to do.

Kill Wolf Stockburn.

A rumbling voice cut through the room's sudden silence. "Up here, detective!"

CHAPTER 33

Stockburn kept his eyes on the weirdly flat, soulless eyes of Tom Cole.

Cole glanced up and beyond Stockburn. The killer removed his hand from the grips of his .44, let his wool coat drop down over the holster.

Stockburn glanced over his right shoulder. Kreg Hennessey stood on the balcony overlooking the saloon, in front of his open office door. The tall man with the Burnside beard and badly swollen lips held a drink in one hand, a cigar in the other hand.

His eyes bored into Stockburn's, and without expression he beckoned with his hand holding the burning cigar. He turned and walked back into his office, leaving the door open.

Stockburn looked around. Everyone in the room—at least, everyone Wolf could see from this side of the bar—was turned toward him.

Stockburn glanced at Tom Cole again. Cole picked up his shot glass and raised it in dark salute to the rail detective, his face and eyes as flat and as expressionless as before.

Stockburn swung around, shouldered the Yellowboy again, and crossed the room to the stairs. He climbed the broad staircase, occasionally glancing over his shoulder into the room behind him. All eyes were still on him.

At least, most were. Several men—likely townsmen with a keen and sudden sense of their own mortalities—were moving quietly toward the door.

Stockburn gained the top of the stairs. Approaching the open door, he stopped, briefly pondered the Yellowboy on his shoulder, then lowered the rifle to the floor, leaning it against the wall, left of Hennessey's open office door.

He strode inside, reaching into his left coat pocket.

"Hold on!" The admonition had come from his left, where Stanley Cove sat in a deep leather chair near a liquor cabinet, his broken wrist in a white sling across his chest. Cove had his left hand on the revolver resting on the right arm of his chair. He was looking warningly at the hand Stockburn had shoved into his coat pocket.

"Don't soil your drawers, Stanley." Wolf pulled the flask out of his pocket and showed it to the broken-limbed toughnut.

Cove flared a nostril.

Kreg Hennessey sat behind his desk, straight ahead of Stockburn. There was a third man in the room, sitting in a short brocade-upholstered sofa to Wolf's right. Russell's former deputy, the stocky, square-headed, thick-necked Sonny sat on one end of the sofa, in what appeared a second-hand three-piece suit that was barely containing his lumpy body. Sonny held a sawed-off, double-barreled shotgun across his thick thighs.

He had a smug smile on his doughy face.

"How's your head, Stockburn?" Sonny asked.

"How's your head, Sonny?"

Sonny smiled more brightly. "Just fine."

"You're moving up in the world. A real upstart." Wolf flashed a crooked smile at the moon-faced lad. "I'm gonna kill you. You know that—don't you?"

Sonny scowled and flushed as his indignant eyes flicked toward Hennessey slumped down in his chair behind the desk so large that he nearly resembled a child behind it. Stockburn tossed the flask over the desk.

Hennessey jerked both hands up and caught the flask just before it would have struck his tender lips.

"What the hell . . . ?" Hennessey glowered at Stockburn.

"Recognize it?"

Flushed with anger, Hennessey inspected the flask. "Well, I'll be damned!" he said, looking over his desk in wide-eyed surprise. "Where did you find it?"

"At the scene of the massacre."

Hennessey let out a large breath of air and slumped back in his chair again, arms draped over the chair arms. He rolled his head from side to side, chuckling whimsically. "I've looked all over for that damn thing!"

"Must've lost it in all the commotion. You know—horses galloping, guns popping, innocent men screaming as you and your hired killers triggered bullets into them as they leaped from their cots."

"You can imagine!" Hennessey looked down at the flask in his right hand, chuckled again, then leaned forward to set it on his desk. "Thanks for retrieving it. I hope you didn't come for a finder's fee."

"Why'd you do it?"

Hennessey shrugged. "Business opportunity."

"Not making enough money here in town?"

Again, Hennessey shrugged. "You can never make too much money, Stockburn. When I was offered the opportunity to establish my own line . . . across Stoleberg land . . . for a pittance compared to that which the Stewarts paid Norman McCrae . . . well, hell, not taking such an offer and further diversifying my business interests would have been like leaving money on a table. I'm not a man who can leave money on any table."

"Did Daniel Stoleberg make you the offer?"

"Sure."

"Why?"

"You'd have to ask him. I don't ordinarily discuss personal matters with my business associates. That said"—he tipped his head back to gaze at the ceiling with an air of vague speculation—"I *think* it might have something to do with one young lady named McCrae, who turned her back on young Stoleberg in his hour of need. *Hours* of need, I should say, pity the poor, one-armed cripple. To be promised such a bride and then having her family turn her against you. And, then, having the fruit of such a promising union reminding you every day of what you'd lost . . ."

"The boy."

"Is it a boy? I wasn't aware of the sex."

Still standing in the middle of the large office, between Stanley Cove on his left and Sonny on his right, Stockburn said, "I still don't understand. Why the rail line, for chrissakes?"

"Like I said, he and I never discussed it. Our relationship is purely business. If I were to continue to speculate, however, and to reflect on the wisps of gossip flying here and there around town, I would say that he was so fed up with both families that he wanted to ruin them both. Let the war that had been brewing for years finally erupt and take them all down. Fitting punishment for what they'd done to him—one side taking the girl away, his own father insisting on raising the child to replace the one McCrae had murdered so many years ago."

Hennessey stared with satisfaction across the

desk at Stockburn, sipped his drink, and set it back down on his desk.

Slowly, softly, he continued: "Take them all down except *him*. When the smoke cleared, he could leave that damnable ranch where he'd known such heartache, and move to town, where he and I would oversee the spur line, which, of course, would run through Tin Cup graze. That's where it should have run in the first place. Less rugged terrain and a more direct route to Hell's Jaw Pass. The only reason it did not was because Norman McCrae had more sway with the Stewarts."

"Sweetening the pot for you was the fact that moving the rail line gave you the opportunity to exact revenge on McCrae for several years ago backing the opera house you tried to pass the ordinance against. Because you wanted the largest, most lucrative business in Wild Horse, and you chafed at the idea of competition—fair or otherwise."

"Ah, revenge," Hennessey said, smiling his death's head smile, slumped back in the chair, head canted to one side. His eyes were still red from grief. His smashed lips resembled ground beef. "Surprising how that age-old notion propelled so much of this, isn't it?"

The smile faded suddenly, the saloon owner's face becoming a mask of animal hatred. "Thank you for making my own matter of revenge so sweet and easy, Stockburn!"

He placed both hands on his chair arms, leaned forward across his desk, and shouted, "Kill him!"

Stockburn palmed both Colts, clicking the hammers back at the same time. He extended the right-hand one toward Sonny, who was just then leaping from his seat and angling the double-barreled shotgun toward Stockburn.

Wolf shot him twice in the chest, punching the fat kid back into the sofa, triggering both barrels of the shotgun into the ceiling.

In the periphery of his vision, Wolf saw Stanley Cove leaping from his chair, raising his revolver in his left hand. Thank God he wasn't a lefty or Stockburn would have been sporting a third eye.

Instead, the bullet that would have cored him raked across his left cheek as he turned to face Stanley, who screamed shrilly when he saw his mistake—and Stockburn's bigger, silver-chased Peacemaker bearing down on him like the jaws of hell opening, spitting smoke and fire.

The Peacemaker roared, filling the room with its thunder.

Stanley Cove sat back down sporting that third eye he'd intended for Wolf—a third eye in the dead-center of his forehead. Cove lifted his chin, squeezing his eyes closed, then slid straight down the chair till he was sitting on the floor. He'd left most of his brains in the chair.

A gun popped to Stockburn's right. It was a thin report, like that from a small-caliber pistol.

Sure enough, when Stockburn swung back to face the desk, he saw Kreg Hennessey extending a pearl-gripped, over-and-under Derringer from over his desk. Wolf glanced down to see blood oozing from his own upper left arm, through the hole in the sleeve of his buckskin coat.

"Did you like that, Stockburn?" Hennessey snarled through his toothy grin. "Here, have one more!"

Stockburn threw himself back into a chair as Hennessey triggered another round. The bullet warmed the air at the end of Wolf's nose as he flew backward in the chair, both him and the chair flipping backward onto the floor. Wolf grimaced against the burning pain in his upper left arm, rolled onto his shoulder, then climbed to a knee.

Hennessey had just opened a desk drawer and was hauling a Merwin & Hulbert Army Model revolver up with his right hand, gritting his teeth as he swung the gun toward Stockburn.

Wolf snapped up both Colts and blew Hennssey, screaming, straight back in his big chair. Wolf fired a third time, but he wasn't sure the third shot hit home because by then Hennessey and his chair were out of sight below the desk.

Stockburn snapped a wary look at the open door. None of the gunmen from downstairs were rushing in at him.

Well, that was nice. Couldn't let his guard

down, though. He might have taken out a few snakes, but he was still firmly mired in their lair.

He heaved himself to his feet with a grunt. He holstered one Peacemaker, glanced at Sonny sitting on the sofa, head canted to one side, and then at Stanley Cove, slumped on the floor in front of the chair that wore most of the contents of his head.

"Nasty business," Wolf wheezed, clutching his left arm with his right hand, ambling out the door and into the hall.

He reached down and picked up the Yellowboy. He couldn't help noting how quiet it was in the drinking hall below the balcony.

Damned quiet.

Too damned quiet.

Hmm.

Stockburn took the Yellowboy in both hands and walked slowly over to the head of the stairs. He turned to gaze down the broad-carpeted stairs into the saloon hall below.

The crowd had thinned considerably.

In fact, Stockburn hastily counted around, say, a dozen men standing around the big hall, spread out around it, staring toward him, their guns still in their holsters but their eyes grave and menacing.

Only the killers remained. The townsmen had retreated to the safety of hearth and home.

Stockburn didn't blame them. He wouldn't mind heading that way himself about now.

Stockburn sighed. Suppressing the pain in his left arm, ignoring the cool wetness of his own blood dribbling down his arm inside his coat sleeve, he started walking slowly down the stairs. He shifted the Yellowboy to his left hand and held up the right one, palm out.

He manufactured an amiable smile as he regarded the dozen men before him. They regarded the Wells Fargo detective like he was the only jackrabbit at a coyote convention.

That's how Wolf was beginning to feel, too.

He stopped halfway down the stairs, broadened his smile and said, "The fun's over, fellas. The boss is dead. Time to all go home now, get a good night's sleep. Maybe ponder on your wicked deeds, think about making amends . . ."

He couldn't corral them all himself, but he didn't intend for them to get away scot free. Not after the savage murders they'd committed at the behest of Kreg Hennessey. But, without help, he'd done about all he could do here. For now.

Now, it was time to call in the U.S. Marshals. He and the marshals would hunt these men down one by one and make damn good and sure they stood trial for the crimes they'd committed. Stockburn recognized a few of the faces before him from wanted circulars. The others wouldn't be too hard to run down—not after the others started going to jail.

It didn't take jailed men long to get right chatty.

"The boss is dead, fellas," Stockburn repeated, the smile on his face getting tighter by the second.

The killers stood gawking at him like coyotes around a campfire, inwardly slathering over the rabbit meat sizzling on a spit.

They wouldn't want to do it here, would they?

Right here in the open, for all the world to know what they'd done?

Whom they'd killed . . . ?

On the other hand, why not? What was Watt Russell going to do about it? They'd kill Stockburn, mount up, and ride the hell out of Wyoming, maybe head for Texas or Old Mexico and wait for their trails to cool.

That's what they were thinking, all right. Sure enough.

CHAPTER 34

A large cold worm flipped in the railroad detective's belly.

Instantly, he turned the fear to fury. He had to. A frightened man didn't shoot nearly as straight as a mad one.

Time to get mad. Real mad. *Right now!*

One of the killers before him slapped leather. Then another . . . another . . . and another . . .

Stockburn dropped to a knee, shouldered the Winchester, and clicked the hammer back.

Guns flashed and thundered before him.

The Yellowboy leaped and roared in his hands.

He took two devils out right away, throwing them over tables while blood plumed from their wounds. But the bullets buzzing around Wolf as the others scrambled for cover, cursing and shouting and flinging lead from their hoglegs, were getting closer by the heartbeat.

Stockburn had a vague notion that he had about three, maybe four more seconds left on this side of the sod, though because he was so damned busy slinging lead, he had no time to either worry about his imminent death or reflect on his life.

It was better this way.

He'd always known he'd go out in a hail of hot lead. He'd hoped it would be later as opposed to sooner, but this way was a hell of a lot better than wheeling himself around some pious Christian charity home in a push chair, soiling himself, having his Indian Kids and tangleleg confiscated by the Sisters of Sobriety, and believing he was Julius Caesar.

He'd just gut-shot one of the dogs firing up at him from over an overturned table near the base of the stairs when he saw in the upper periphery of his vision the saloon's front door open beyond the eleven or so remaining crouching and firing killers.

Two men scurried through the door and dropped to their knees atop the steps rising from the drinking hall floor. Both were wielding rifles.

Great! As if Stockburn didn't have his hands full enough without two more of Hennessey's loyal stalwarts joining the party to add their own lead to the storm!

But . . .

Wait.

The two men atop the steps on the far end of the room began firing at the killers. Not at Stockburn.

Huh?

One of them, the bigger man whom a brief glimpse told Wolf was Watt Russell, gave a wild whoop, and shouted, "Die, you low-down dirty dogs!" He added above the rocketing blasts of the Winchester snugged up taut against his shoulder—"Die, you cussed vermin! *Die!*"

Three of the killers went down almost instantly, yelping and hollering in shock and misery.

As Russell and Stockburn's second guardian angel hammered away at the screaming, scurrying, dying killers, Stockburn emptied his Winchester into the bloody, smoke-hazed crowd below him, then rose from his knee, filled his fists with both Peacemakers, and continued flinging lead where he spied movement through the fog.

The killers had been caught in a deadly whipsaw. As soon as Watt Russell and the second gent had joined the hoe-down, the killers, while not outnumbered, had been badly out-positioned. Their opponents had the high ground; the killers had also been flanked.

Stockburn fired another round into the smoke haze, then pulled his smoking Peacemakers down. The only thing moving down there now was powder smoke.

On the other end of the room, orange stabbed from the maw of Russell's revolver, angled down toward the floor before him and maybe halfway between the marshal and the bar. The shot evoked a clipped scream and a dull thud.

"There's another one," Russell's partner said, and fired at the floor toward something Stockburn couldn't see. The target was on the far side of the bar.

A man grunted. A dull thump followed.

"The rat was tryin' to crawl to its hole!" Russell's partner exclaimed.

Then Wolf recognized the voice as well as the silhouetted figure there in the smoke haze beside the thick-bodied Russell.

Paul Reynolds—ramrod for the Hell's Jaw track-laying crew.

Reynolds lifted his head and pointed his arm toward Stockburn or maybe a little above, shouting, "Stockburn—behind you!"

Wolf wheeled as a gun roared at the top of the stairs.

The bullet punched into the carpeted step inches from Stockburn's left boot.

Wolf emptied both Peacemakers—one shot from the right one, two from the left one—into the tall, lumpy silhouette looming over him at the top of the stairs. The man jerked back then stumbled forward. He folded over himself, like a jackknife closing, and tumbled heavily, loudly down the stairs.

Stockburn stepped to one side as the man came to a stop on the steps beside him, feet up, head down, the body slanted sideways. The ugly face of Kreg Hennessey stared up at Stockburn with its dead open eyes and its swollen lips bristling with stitches ensconced in the Burnside. Two of Wolf's last shots had punched through his right cheek and his thick, wrinkled neck, respectively.

"That the end of 'em?" Reynolds called. He and Russell stood side by side atop the steps by the door, looking toward Wolf.

"That should do it." Stockburn crouched to pick up his hat. A bullet had blown it off his head. Make that two bullets. Lifting the hat from the floor, he poked two fingers through the holes, then chuckled at his good luck.

He'd missed saddling a golden cloud by the width of a cat's whisker.

He'd had help, though, as well.

He stuffed the bullet-riddled topper on his head, walked down the stairs, and crossed the room to the front. The wafting powder smoke, fetid as rotten eggs, burned his eyes. He stepped over bullet-torn bodies, around overturned tables and chairs.

Russell and Reynolds dropped down the front steps and met Stockburn a few feet out from their base.

"Thanks, fellas," Wolf said, a little puzzled by the help but grateful just the same.

Russell gazed through the smoke toward the stairs. His craggy features were grim, despondent. "The bastard as good as killed Ivy. He hired Slim Sherman. Him an' Daniel Stoleberg. They was in it all together, Stockburn. These men drove McCrae's cattle onto Stoleberg graze to cause a land war. A big, final showdown between the two outfits."

He wagged his head shamefully. "And I was

part of it because I did nothin' to stop it. Didn't tell you about it. Didn't do a damn thing but sit in my office with my thumb up my ass!"

He ripped the town marshal's badge from his coat and handed it to Wolf. "Here you go. You can throw that down the nearest privy. I'm not worth the nickel's worth of tin it was stamped from."

He swung around, tramped up the stairs, and went out through the open door.

Reynolds gazed after the grief-stricken marshal.

"Where'd you come from?" Stockburn asked him.

"I was in here havin' a drink when you walked in. When you headed upstairs, I went over to the Territorial to retrieve my rifle. I had a feelin' you were gonna need a hand or two. I was on my way back over here when I ran into Russell wielding his own Winchester."

"He has more sand than I gave him credit for."

"He does at that."

"I have to apologize, Reynolds," Stockburn said.

"Oh? Why?"

"When you told me you avoided the massacre because you were in town meeting with the Stewarts, yours was the first name I scribbled onto my list of suspects."

The ramrod grinned. "You wouldn't have been doin' your job if you hadn't, Stockburn."

"You saved my bacon tonight. Call me Wolf."

"All right." Reynolds shook the detective's

extended hand. "Wolf it is. I'm gonna go over and tell the Stewarts they can continue with the rail line now. They'll be happy to hear that. They're hiring a new crew and are itchin' to get the line finished by the time the snow flies."

The Hell's Jaw foreman winked and went out.

Stockburn turned to take one more look around the smoky room. The three bartenders were once again standing around behind the bar, behind which they must have taken cover when the lead had started to fly. One moved to the curve in the horseshoe and bent forward to stare down over the bar at the two dead men lying entangled near the brass rail running along the bar's base, like lovers embracing in sleep.

The barman turned to Stockburn, who said, "Time to find other work, gentlemen."

They looked at each other.

Stockburn walked out through the saloon's open door.

He stopped when he saw Lori standing before him, looking up at him, her eyes awash with mixed emotions.

"You're wounded," Lori said.

Lamplight from the saloon's windows shone in the blood on his upper left arm.

"I'm all right."

"I heard what Russell said." The girl looked down at her small hands entwined before her. "Daniel—him and Hennessey."

"I'm sorry."

Lori looked up at Wolf. Lamplight glistened in her tear-filled eyes. "I broke his heart. But I didn't mean to."

"I know." Stockburn stepped forward and gathered her up in his arms, drawing her close against him, hugging her. "It's not your fault."

She sobbed, quivering.

Finally, she lifted her head to gaze at him gravely. "Wolf, my brother Law was in town with three other Triangle men just before you came. They loaded a wagon with guns and ammo. They're going to confront the Tin Cup. They think it was the Stolebergs who rustled the Triangle cattle when it was only Hennessey and Daniel."

Stockburn winced. "Damn. I met them as I was riding in. Was wondering what they had in that wagon." He glanced at the saloon behind him. "Hennessey's still wreaking havoc after he's dead." He looked at Lori. "I'll ride out there first thing in the morning. I'll try to defuse the situation."

"I'll ride with you."

"Oh, no. You stay in town. I saw one young lady killed today. I won't watch another die tomorrow."

Lori pulled her mouth corners down, nodded.

"In the meantime," she said, "let's get you over to the hotel. I'll tend that wound for you."

"Did you get a room?" Wolf asked as he and Lori started for the Territorial.

Lori nodded, smiled crookedly up at him. She had one arm snaked around his waist. "I put it in your name."

Stockburn gave a droll chuckle. "That's going to get around Wild Horse in no time!"

"Why not?" she said with a weary sigh. "Everything else about me has."

Stockburn woke with a start.

He wasn't sure what had awakened him, but he hadn't slept well. All night, the gun blasts from inside the Wind River Saloon & Gambling Hall had echoed inside his head. Also, his left arm throbbed so that any position he lay in wasn't comfortable. He hadn't slept for more than a few minutes at a time.

Or he hadn't thought so, anyway. Maybe he had. It appeared later than he'd thought. He'd left the curtains partway open over the window on his left; he thought he could see some cream in the sky beyond the dark roof top on the opposite side of the street. His inner timepiece that had awakened him, he realized now.

He sat up. Beside him, Lori groaned.

She lay mostly concealed by the bed covers, which were drawn up to her chin. Her chestnut hair spilled across the white pillow beneath her head. She lay facing away from Stockburn, her body loosely curled beneath the covers.

Lori moved her head a little, groaned again.

"Keep sleeping," Wolf whispered. "Early yet."

He'd slept fully dressed atop the sheet and quilt, covered by only a spare blanket. He sat up, tossing the blanket aside, wincing at the throbbing pain in his arm. It was only a flesh wound caused by a .22-caliber bullet, but he felt like a rabid rat was trapped in his arm, trying to chew its way out.

"Whiskey," he grumbled, sitting up and reaching for the whiskey bottle on his bedside table.

He popped the cork, took a hearty pull of the panther juice. Then another.

One more for the road.

He got a fire going in the coal stove in the room's corner to beat away the autumn chill for Lori when she rose.

He stepped into his boots, shrugged into his coat, set his hat on his head, grabbed the Yellowboy from where it leaned against the wall by the door, and quietly left the room.

He had a quick breakfast with two cups of black coffee laced with whiskey at the Cosmopolitan, then headed to the livery barn for his horse. Fifteen minutes later, he was on the trail to the Stolebergs' Tin Cup ranch, hoping to arrive before all hell broke loose.

He didn't make it.

CHAPTER 35

Stockburn heard the menacing rattle of gunfire as he closed within a mile of the Tin Cup headquarters, on the southern end of the Wind River Mountains' southeastern flank.

He'd been trotting Smoke through the long, dry valley that dropped from the pass farther west, giving the horse a breather after a long gallop. Now as the shooting grew louder and more desperate and angrier, he booted the mount into a hard run.

He rode hell-for-leather, the Tin Cup headquarters growing from a dime-size gray splotch on the short-grass prairie ahead and below, until Wolf could make out the house and individual buildings and corrals.

Smoke puffed up from a dry ravine cut into the prairie a hundred yards out front of the headquarters. The ravine ran in a gradual curve across Stockburn's trail. More smoke puffed around the headquarters yard as the Stoleberg riders returned fire on the McCrae men hunkered down in the shallow ravine.

"Come on, Smoke—hurry!" Stockburn yelled, whipping the horse's right hip with his rein ends.

He knew the horse was already running at full speed, but he couldn't restrain himself.

He wanted to reach the Tin Cup headquarters before the mid-morning skirmish exploded into a months'—or even years'—long range war spreading like a wildfire throughout the southern Wind Rivers.

When he was a couple hundred yards from the ravine in which the Triangle riders were forted up, shooting toward the house—at least, Stockburn assumed the Triangle riders were in the ravine; he wasn't yet close enough to see them clearly—he checked Smoke down to a full stop.

He reached back into one of his saddlebag pouches and pulled out a white underwear top. It had been white at one time, that was. Now it was sort of off-white. Stockburn didn't always shop for new clothes when he needed to.

Still, the washworn shirt, discolored by all the lye soap it had been washed with, would have to serve as a truce flag. Quickly, he tied the flag to the end of his Winchester's barrel then booted Smoke into another ground-devouring gallop.

As he drew within a hundred yards of the ravine, he began waving the rifle and truce flag from side to side, hoping like hell all players in the skirmish playing out before him would respect his makeshift guidon.

"Hold your fire!" he bellowed into the wind, waving the flag broadly. "Hold your fire! Hold your fire! Hold your damn fire!"

As he approached the ravine, several Triangle men turned toward him, some of them swinging their rifles toward him, their faces anxious and skeptical beneath their hat brims.

"Hold your fire!" Wolf shouted again.

"Stockburn?"

The question had come from Lawton McCrae.

The eldest McCrae sibling was hunkered down behind a rock at the lip of the ravine. A dozen or more other McCrae hands, including the younger brother, Hyram McCrae, were lined out along the east bank of the shallow ravine bristling with sage and small cedars.

The men glowered back at the buckskin-coated rider just now slowing his horse behind them.

"What're you doing out here, Stockburn?" Law McCrae said, face flushed with anger. "This is Triangle business!"

Fortunately, the Tin Cup hands and whoever had been shooting from the house, were respecting Stockburn's flag, which he continued to wave, holding the rifle high above his head. "Hold your fire!" he yelled to the house, then rode on across the ravine, between the two McCrae brothers.

"Where the hell are you going, Stockburn?" Law bellowed.

Stockburn galloped into the Tin Cup yard, still waving his flag. "Put your guns down!" he shouted. "Put your guns down! This is a manufactured war." He stopped Smoke roughly halfway between the ravine and the Stoleberg house and curveted the mount.

He turned back to the ravine and yelled, "The Stolebergs did not rustle your beef, McCrae. At least, not all of them. Only one of them arranged for it to happen!"

"What?" yelled both McCrae brothers at the same time.

"You heard me!"

Stockburn looked around the Stoleberg yard. Men had posted themselves behind the hitch-and-rail corral that ringed the yard. One had taken a bullet to his lower leg, Wolf saw. Other hands, hard-eyed with anger over the unprovoked attack, glared out over rifle barrels extended around the corners of outbuildings.

Three were hunkered down behind a ranch supply wagon they'd overturned in the middle of the yard, off the big, rambling house's north end. Several more, including two of the three Stoleberg brothers, Carlton and Reed—had taken positions on the house's broad front porch, down on their knees behind roof support posts.

Reed appeared to have taken a graze across his left cheek. Blood dribbled down from the cut toward his jawline.

"Daniel Stoleberg!" Stockburn yelled, looking around, not seeing the one-armed, thirty-year-old son of Rufus Stoleberg. "Daniel, are you here?"

They all looked around, glancing at each other

in silent consultation, then cast their gazes around the yard.

"I haven't seen him yet today," said the big, raw-boned Carlton Stoleberg. "In fact, he wasn't at supper last night."

Behind him, the glass of a house window had been shot out. Carlton's wife, Grace, stood behind the shot-out window, holding the little boy, Buster, rocking him gently, trying to comfort the frightened, crying child.

One of the men hunkered down behind the hitch-and-rail corral yelled, "He crawled into a bottle an' slept in the barn last ni—"

"Here!" a voice called from behind the cabin.

Stockburn followed the call to a log barn near the long, L-shaped bunkhouse flanking the house and the windmill at the yard's rear. The small barn door left of the large double stock doors opened and a lean, bent figured tripped out of the building.

Holding a bottle in his hand, down low by his side, Daniel Stoleberg shuffled toward the front yard. He looked like hell. He wore no hat, and his long, thick brown hair hung down over his eyes. His shirttails were untucked. Suspenders flopped down his sides.

He came forward, his heavy feet scuffed the ground, kicking dust up around his knees.

"Here!" he wailed. "The prodigal son spent the night in the barn!"

He came slowly around the house's north end, stumbling toward Stockburn. His face was a mask of high emotion behind his flopping hair. He laughed, sobbed, laughed again.

He stopped six feet away from the rail detective, tossed his head to shake the hair back from his face, choked back a sob, took a drink from the bottle, and glared up at Stockburn. "What is the meaning of this, big man? How dare you interfere in the affairs of better men than you! This war has been brewing for years. Hell, for centuries! It's time to blow up the whole damn range! Kill everybody, sift the ashes, and start anew—from scratch!"

"Daniel!" Carlton Stoleberg moved off the porch and into the yard, regarding his younger brother skeptically.

"The only problem is," Daniel said, still gazing up at Stockburn, slurring his words, "I can't regrow my arm. I can't uncripple my legs. I can never be a whole man again . . . no . . . not anymore than I can go back in time and *not* fall into that nest of vipers!"

"Daniel!" a girl's voice called from the west, muffled with distance. "Daniel!" came the cry again, louder this time as Lori McCrae galloped toward the ranch atop her buckskin.

"Lori!" Lawton McCrae said, rising from his position behind the rock and regarding his sister with red-faced exasperation.

Ignoring her brother, Lori galloped the buckskin across the ravine and entered the yard at a full run, drawing back on the reins when she was ten feet from Stockburn, her loose hair bouncing high off her shoulders.

She glanced at Wolf. Of course, she'd followed him out from town. He'd had a feeling she would.

She leaped down from the buckskin's back and turned to face her lover, Daniel Stoleberg. He stood regarding her as though she were a ghost from the distant past. Maybe a lover he'd loved during a journey to another land a long, long time ago.

He'd never expected to see her again.

He held the whiskey bottle down low by his side. His face was that of a ruined, embittered man who'd lost everything, even his soul.

He sobbed now, scrunching up his face, hanging his head in shame. "I didn't know he was going to kill those men." He looked at Lori, then at Stockburn, tears dribbling down his pale cheeks. "I didn't know he was going to commit murder. I thought he . . . we . . . were just going to sabotage the rails, the train . . ."

He swung clumsily around to face Carlton and Reed Stoleberg. Both brothers—taller, more rugged than Daniel—had moved tentatively out from the house to stand fifteen feet away. "I betrayed you, Carlton. Reed, I betrayed you. I got no excuse. All I can say is I deeply regret it."

He hung his head again, sobbing, his hair hiding his face.

Daniel dropped to his knees in the hard-packed yard, his chin to his chest, and cried. He dropped the bottle, sagged forward until he pressed his forehead to the earth, and cried.

Lori hurried over to him, dropped to a knee beside him. "Daniel!"

"I'm sorry, Lori." He shook his head. "I thought you were gone."

"Well, I wasn't. And I'm not."

Lori lowered her head nearly to the ground, beside Daniel's. She stretched her arm around his back. Holding her mouth very close to his right ear, she said, "I'll never leave you again, Daniel. I promise."

Daniel straightened. He turned to Lori, his face swollen with tears. "You won't?"

"Never. I'll never leave you and Buster again."

She turned to where her two brothers Lawton and Hyram had walked up out of the ravine to stand nearby. Each held his rifle low in his right hand, looking perplexed, deeply befuddled. A couple of their men had walked up, as well, and flanked the two McCrae brothers.

Lori stared at Lawton McCrae as though awaiting an answer to an unspoken question. Lawton turned to Hyram. Hyram smiled. Lawton did not smile, but he turned back to Lori, and nodded, averting his gaze.

"What's this?" yet another voice said. "What's this all about?"

Stockburn lifted his gaze to see Rufus Stoleberg walk out from the base of the porch steps, heading toward Stockburn and the other men and the young woman with them.

Atop the porch steps, Grace held little Buster, rocking him gently. The boy had settled down now in the aftermath of the shooting and was looking around in wide-eyed fascination, pointing his wet finger.

"What's this?" Stoleberg said again, glancing at Stockburn and then at the McCrae men. Unexpectedly, a broad smile creased his craggy features. "Everybody here already? It's early yet. But since it's Sandy's birthday, let's get the hoe-down started early!"

The McCrae riders glanced at each other dubiously.

Stoleberg walked in his old horseman's bandy-legged fashion up to his youngest son, and crouched over him, placing a hand on his shoulder. "Come on inside, Sandy. Come on, son. Your mother's gonna get you all gussied up for the dance. Don't you remember, boy? It's your birthday! Folks is coming from all around to sing and dance and eat cake and drink lemonade! We butchered a beef and everything!"

The addlepated oldster looked at the McCraes and beckoned broadly with his short, thick arm.

"It's a little early yet but come in anyways, neighbors! I'll tell the cook to get the steer on the spit! The sooner the better and the more the merrier!"

He laughed, danced a little jig in a short, tight circle, waving both arms, then sauntered on back to the house, clapping his hands and hop-skipping like a schoolboy on the way to see his girl.

Lawton and Hyram McCrae gazed after him, jaws slack, eyes wide in shock at the old man's condition. Apparently, they'd had no idea about Rufus Stoleberg's mental deterioration.

Lori pulled away from Daniel. "You heard your father," she said quietly, gently. "Let's go inside. Let's go inside and see our son and make plans for raising him up proper—you and me."

She turned to look up at Stockburn. "It's all right, isn't it?"

Stockburn thought it over, quickly deciding not to put Daniel Stoleberg in any of his reports to the Wells Fargo office in Kansas City. It was true that Daniel had collaborated with Hennessey in the massacre of the rail-laying crew, but the young man, crippled and grief-stricken, pining for the woman he loved, hadn't been in his right mind.

Wolf had believed him when he'd said he hadn't known Hennessey would kill the rail crew. Daniel Stoleberg was not a murderer. He was just a very mixed-up young man, one with a dark side, and for good reason.

Stockburn himself knew a little about dark sides.

Maybe, just maybe, Daniel would make amends and redeem himself by marrying a good woman and raising his son to grow up fine, strong, and good.

Lori smiled. She helped Daniel to his feet, and they shuffled off to the house, arm in arm.

That left Stockburn, the two McCrae brothers and the two Stoleberg brothers regarding each other doubtfully, maybe a little sheepishly. Maybe the old man, even as addlepated as he was, had shone how friendly things could have been over all these long years had the two families been good neighbors instead of blood enemies.

"What do you fellas think?" Stockburn asked, glancing from one faction to the other. "Time to bury the hatchet forevermore?"

They all looked at each other.

Lawton McCrae glanced at his brother.

Hyram hiked a shoulder. "We got our beef back. No harm done, Law."

Lawton thumbed his hat brim up off his forehead as he stepped up to Carlton Stoleberg, pulled off his glove, and extended his bare hand. "I reckon—since we're gonna be kin an' all."

Stockburn smiled.

He reined Smoke around and booted him into a trot. He'd take his time, resting the stout but tired horse often, maybe arrive back in Wild Horse in time for a late lunch.

| Books are produced in the United States using U.S.-based materials | Books are printed using a revolutionary new process called THINKtech™ that lowers energy usage by 70% and increases overall quality | Books are durable and flexible because of Smyth-sewing | Paper is sourced using environmentally responsible foresting methods and the paper is acid-free |

Center Point Large Print
600 Brooks Road / PO Box 1
Thorndike, ME 04986-0001 USA

(207) 568-3717

US & Canada:
1 800 929-9108
www.centerpointlargeprint.com